Look what people are saying about D.B. Reynolds's *Vampires in America* . . .

"Terrific writing, strong characters and world building, excellent storylines all help make Vampires in America a must read. Aden is one of the best so far." A TOP BOOK OF THE YEAR!
—*On Top Down Under Book Reviews*

"In one of the most compelling vampire books I've read in a while, Reynolds blends an excellent mix of paranormal elements, suspense and combustible attraction."
—*RT Book Reviews on LUCAS*

"Reynolds takes us on a roller coaster of emotions and delivers reading satisfaction. She can write rings around so many of today's authors. She develops her characters to the point where we live in their skin."
—*La Deetda Reads on DUNCAN*

"Remarkably fresh and stunningly beautiful! Sophia is as enchanting as she is dangerous!"
—*FreshFiction.com*

"Move over Raphael, there's a new lord in town."
—*Bitten by Paranormal Romance on JABRIL*

D.B. Reynolds's
Vampires in America
from ImaJinn Books

Raphael

Jabril

Rajmund

Sophia

Duncan

Lucas

Aden

Vincent

The Cyn and Raphael Novellas

Betrayed

Hunted

Unforgiven

Vincent

by

D.B. Reynolds

IMAJINN

ImaJinn Books

Annie's Book Stop
anniesplainville.com
508-695-2396 MA 02762

This is a work of fiction. Names, characters, places and incidents are either the products of the author's imagination or are used fictitiously. Any resemblance to actual persons (living or dead), events or locations is entirely coincidental.

IMAJINN

ImaJinn Books
PO BOX 300921
Memphis, TN 38130
Print ISBN: 978-1-61194-555-3

ImaJinn Books is an Imprint of BelleBooks, Inc.

Copyright © 2014 by D.B. Reynolds

Printed and bound in the United States of America.

All rights reserved. No part of this book may be reproduced in any form or by any electronic or mechanical means, including information storage and retrieval systems, without permission in writing from the publisher, except by a reviewer, who may quote brief passages in a review.

ImaJinn Books was founded by Linda Kichline.

We at ImaJinn Books enjoy hearing from readers. Visit our websites
ImaJinnBooks.com
BelleBooks.com
BellBridgeBooks.com

10 9 8 7 6 5 4 3 2 1

Cover design: Debra Dixon
Interior design: Hank Smith
Photo/Art credits:
Man (manipulated) © gekaskr | Fotolia.com
Background (manipulated) © Dary423 | Dreamstime.com
Background (manipulated) © Fromac | Dreamstime.com
Tattoo © warvox.com

:Lvcb:01:

Dedication

For the next generation . . .
Heather, Vanessa and Michael
Jason and Jessica
James and Blake

Prologue

Tucson, Arizona

LANA ARNOLD SPUN the dial on her home safe and reached inside. She was heading out on a new job and needed a backup weapon and cash. Her next job would take her to Mexico, and cash was king down there. And the gun was simple common sense.

She had her usual Sig, and, of course, she was never without a few knives hidden about her person, but more firepower was always better. That same principle meant she should be taking one of her bounty hunter dad's guys along for the ride, but this was *her* job, no one else's. She was a bounty hunter, too, and the contract hadn't come to her dad's agency, but to her personally. Besides, this was the kind of job she hoped to do more of. It was a job for a private investigator, not a bounty hunter. Not that she didn't enjoy working for her dad; she just didn't see herself chasing criminals for the rest of her life. So when the request had come in from the attorneys representing Cynthia Leighton and Raphael, she'd jumped on it.

At first glance, it seemed to be a simple missing person's case. But she suspected there was nothing simple about it. First of all, Raphael happened to be a vampire—a very powerful vampire if rumors were true—and he wanted a message delivered to some old guy named Xuan Ignacio, who'd been hiding in Mexico forever. Second was the money. The fee they were offering was significant and would put a nice bump in the fund she'd set up toward opening her own investigation firm someday. Apart from a desire not to be chasing skips at forty, she wanted to forge her own path, to be someone other than Sean Arnold's daughter.

She also figured the job must be important to Raphael, and if she did well, maybe they'd send more business her way. Of course, it was entirely possible that the high fee was only intended to compensate for the danger she might be walking into. But Lana trusted that Leighton would have warned her about any specific threats up-front, so that probably wasn't an issue.

Apart from the money, though, there was a twist to the case that pretty much eliminated the idea that this was a *simple* job. And that was the letter from Raphael to a vampire named Vincent Kuxim, asking him to assist Lana in locating this Xuan Ignacio. Lana had Googled Kuxim, hoping to find out why Raphael would want him involved, but she'd come up with nothing. All she knew was what Leighton's attorneys had told her on the phone prior to sending the documents. They assured her that, while Raphael's note to Kuxim might appear to be a request, it was phrased in a way that all but guaranteed Kuxim would agree to help her. Lana wrote this off to vampire politics, since the request seemed perfectly ordinary to her, and no one seemed inclined to educate her any further on the subject. The lawyer had made it very clear, however, that Raphael wanted Vincent Kuxim with her when she found her quarry.

Lana wasn't sure how she felt about that. She supposed that, ultimately, it would all depend on who Vincent Kuxim was. The only details the attorneys offered were that he was a vampire—no surprise there—and that he controlled the city of Hermosillo in Mexico. What no one had come out and said—but what she'd happily bet money on—was that Xuan Ignacio was a vampire, too. Supposedly, he'd been hiding out in Mexico a long time, and Lana was guessing "a long time" meant centuries rather than decades.

She tucked her backup weapon—a 9mm Glock—into her backpack and put the cash in an outside zippered pocket. On a whim, she grabbed a couple of flashbang grenades from the box in her safe, slammed the safe door, and spun the dial to secure it. She stood and got ready to leave, activating the alarm on her security system, then made sure the door was locked behind her. Within minutes, she was on her way to Hermosillo, Mexico.

She only hoped Vincent Kuxim was in town when she arrived. And that he was inclined to do Raphael a favor.

Chapter One

Hermosillo, Sonora, Mexico

VINCENT WALKED out onto the balcony and stretched to his full height, heedless of the fact that he was completely naked. His house was on the very edge of a private compound, and his balcony looked out on nothing but silent desert. Although the balcony could have been in the middle of a busy city, and he still wouldn't have cared about showing a little skin. Or even a lot.

He was in Hermosillo, in a private compound that was one of Enrique's many properties in Mexico. Although the vampire lord hadn't been here in years and probably didn't even remember that he owned it. The Mexican lord's personal preference was to stay in his villa in Mexico City, while *Vincent's* preference was to hang out in whichever residence kept him as far away from Enrique as possible. Hermosillo was nice, and so was the estate on the water in Los Cabos, mainly because both were places where Enrique rarely ventured.

As little as forty years ago, Enrique had still been touring his territory on a regular basis, but these days, if any traveling was required, he usually sent Vincent. The one exception to that rule was anything involving the other North American vampire lords. Historically, that had meant Enrique had attended the once-a-year meeting of the North American Vampire Council.

But lately, the continent had been roiling, with old lords dying, or being killed, left and right. In the last couple of years, four of the territories had seen new lords ascend, and two of those ascensions had required special meetings of the Council. The other two new lords had been kind enough to time their takeovers to coincide with the annual meeting dates. A new lord's ascension didn't require the Council's approval—power was the only thing that mattered among vampires. If a vampire could take and hold a territory, it was his. But it was customary for the Council to *welcome* their new colleagues . . . which was a polite way of saying the Council wanted to look the new guy over and decide if they could work with him. If not, his tenure would be very short. Because, while an individual vampire lord might be powerful, he wouldn't stand a chance against the full Council. Unless that vampire was Raphael. No one really knew what Raphael was capable of, and thus far, no one had been foolish enough to try and figure it out.

Vincent drew in a deep breath of the bone-dry air. It was fresh and clean tonight. Some nights, if the wind was blowing the wrong way, he'd pick up the oil and metal stench from all the new industries popping up in Hermosillo. He knew it brought a lot of jobs to the locals and couldn't begrudge them that, but he'd liked it better when Enrique had first set up shop here a century ago.

And just thinking *that* made him feel like a grumpy old man bemoaning the good old days of his youth. It was bad enough that he *was* an old man, even if he'd never look it. But he didn't need to think like one, either.

His cell phone rang from inside—it was his lieutenant, Michael, checking in as the night began. Strictly speaking, Vincent wasn't supposed to have a lieutenant since he was actually Lord Enrique's lieutenant himself. Especially since he'd made Michael a vampire without gaining Enrique's permission ahead of time. His lord and master hadn't been pleased with him about that, but Vincent hadn't particularly cared. If he'd waited for Enrique to give him the go-ahead, he'd never have a vampire child of his own making. The old man held onto his prerogatives like a spoiled toddler with his toys or a greedy miser with his money.

When confronted with the done deal of Michael's existence, however, Enrique hadn't had the guts to order the new vampire's execution, even though it would have been within his rights. He'd probably been reluctant to challenge Vincent, suspecting he wouldn't obey the order. And he'd have been right. Vincent would have told him to go fuck himself, and that could have gotten ugly.

Vincent wasn't Enrique's lieutenant out of love or respect. He'd clawed his way to the top the old-fashioned way, by killing everyone who stood in his path. He was the strongest fucking vampire in the old man's stable and had been for well over a hundred years. He fulfilled his duty to Enrique, who was both his Sire and his lord. He was loyal and, when it suited him, obedient. He pretty much ignored everything else by staying away and avoiding confrontation, while Enrique pretended he still ruled the territory with absolute power.

Vincent picked up the cell phone on his way to the walk-in closet. "Yo, Michael. What's up?"

"Good evening, Sire," Michael said dutifully. When necessary, the two of them could be as formal as ancient Vampire protocol required. But they were friends more than anything else, each the one person the other could rely on without question in the dog-eat-dog world of Enrique's rule.

"Yeah, yeah," Vincent replied. "Any blowback yet from that mess in Acuña?" Vincent didn't know all the details, but a group of European vamps had made a play against Lord Raphael just two weeks ago. It had all gone down in Acuña, which was a small city just this side of the U.S. border, thus placing their little *tête-à-tête* neatly inside Mexico.

Reports had it that Raphael had wiped the floor with the visiting vamps. That wasn't exactly a surprise to Vincent, but what *was* surprising was the fact that the meeting had taken place *inside* Enrique's territory. Vincent had no proof that Enrique had played a role in that particular clusterfuck, but he had strong suspicions. There was no way in hell that a group of vamps powerful enough to think about going up against Raphael could have crossed into Enrique's territory without him knowing about it.

And Vincent also knew that Enrique suspected Raphael's hand in all of the recent territorial changes in North America, and that Enrique didn't like it. He thought Raphael was trying to take over the continent, and that Mexico would be the next domino to fall.

Vincent predictably disagreed with his Sire on the subject. Not even Enrique could deny that the European vamps had their eyes on North America, which made it a smart move for the Council members to form alliances with each other. But Enrique saw no reason why he should risk himself and his vamps defending anyone else's territory. Vincent sided with Raphael in believing they would all be stronger if they stood together.

"You mean other than the strange piles of dust in some old church?" Michael asked in response to Vincent's question about the confrontation in Acuña.

"Yeah, other than that," Vincent replied dryly.

"I've had reports . . ." Michael hesitated, which made Vincent's attention sharpen.

"Michael?"

"I need to double-check the details. I should have some answers for you by the time you get to the office."

Vincent frowned. He suspected Michael had all the information he needed, but didn't want to discuss it on the phone. Enrique's spies were always listening, and cell phone signals were way too easy to intercept. He glanced at the digital clock by his bedside. It was nearly eight. Spring was upon them, which meant the days were slowly getting longer. It wasn't the best time of year for vampires.

"All right. I'll see you in the office then," he told Michael.

"Yeah, about that. You have an appointment tonight."

Vincent trolled through the files in his brain, but came up with nothing. "No, I don't."

"Yeah, you do, *jefe*. Some bounty hunter. He comes with a referral from Raphael himself."

Vincent frowned. What the fuck was Raphael up to? First a battle on Enrique's territory and now this?

"A bounty hunter with a referral from Raphael? Why?" he asked.

"Don't know. The guy called from the road today, spoke to Lou in the front office. Lou made the appointment and left a message for me."

"What time's the appointment?"

"Ten."

"Well, fuck. There goes my evening. I gotta get dressed. See you in thirty," he said and hung up. But he couldn't help wondering what it meant that Raphael was referring people directly to Vincent instead of going through Enrique. Especially since Vincent didn't think he'd exchanged ten words with the powerful vampire lord in the entire time he'd known him.

He started pulling clothes out of the closet for the evening. A pair of jeans—black since he had a business appointment—and a long-sleeved T-shirt, also black. Sitting on a bench inside the walk-in closet, he pulled on socks and his favorite cowboy boots, ditto on the black. It wasn't that he was giving in to the stereotype of how people thought a vampire dressed—all in black—but clothes just didn't matter to him. Going with one color made it easy. Besides, he wore blue jeans as often as he did black. That was enough variety for him.

He glanced in the mirror before heading out, doing a quick fingercomb through his longish black hair and a more detailed check of his beard and mustache, which was his one true vanity. He had his hair cut once a month, but his beard he trimmed every night. He knew he was considered handsome, and God knew he used his looks when it came to attracting women—because if there was one thing on this earth that he loved, it was a soft, willing woman—but other than the beard, he didn't worry overmuch about his appearance. He showered, he shaved, and he kept in shape because it was a matter of survival. And that was it.

There were more important uses for his time and energy, including, it seemed, doing a favor for Raphael. He didn't know if he should be wary or exhilarated by that development.

The compound where Vincent and the other Hermosillo vamps lived was a square that covered the equivalent of two city blocks. Vincent's office was in a building on the opposite side of the property from where he lived. It sat outside the main perimeter wall and was the only structure, other than the adjacent night club, with a public entrance. Since nothing of value was kept there, apart from a few pieces of office equipment, its only real security was video surveillance of both the parking lot and the lobby entrance. However, it was still locked down at sunrise, along with the rest of the compound. If a human wanted to pay a visit, they came after sunset, or not at all.

Lou—whose name was actually Louisa—was Vincent's human secretary. She arrived around noon and worked in a small office inside the main compound until Vincent rose for the night. Then she took up her position at the reception desk outside his office.

As usual, there was a lot of activity in the area as Vincent made his way through the gardens to his office building. Hermosillo had a substantial vampire population attracted by the more than 700,000 humans who lived there. And, since vampires tended to live in groups, many of them lived right here in this sprawling compound. Vincent could hear voices from elsewhere in the compound as he walked, but he didn't see anyone. This part of the estate was heavily landscaped, as if to deny the encroaching desert outside the walls. It was thick with palms and other tropical plants, fragrant with the scent of their flowers. It took an army of gardeners to maintain the landscaping, and a water well that had been dug solely for that purpose. It wasn't very ecologically sound, but Vincent enjoyed the results too much to protest.

He nodded at the two vamps guarding the exit gate as he passed through the perimeter wall and into the public part of the compound. No palms graced the concrete walks here. The grounds were well maintained, but, in keeping with the desert environment, they were landscaped with low-lying cacti and stone. Twenty strides took Vincent to the building that was his office. It was an unassuming structure, with nothing to indicate that it was occupied by one of the most powerful vampires in the territory. He took the three stairs to the heavy, iron-banded back door, entered the appropriate code on a locking keypad, and pushed inside, immediately feeling the temperature drop several degrees. Even in summer, the building's thick stone walls blocked the burning Sonoran desert temps. Vincent's boots clomped loudly on the tiled floor and he could hear voices coming from his office. But none belonged to his visitor, though. Not yet.

He entered his private office from the rear, walking past his desk and out a second door to the small lobby where Michael and Lou were waiting for him.

"Good evening, Louisa," he crooned, smiling when his greeting elicited a blush and a duck of her head, even though she'd been working for him for more than ten years, and was old enough to be his mother, if one judged solely by appearances, that was.

"Good evening, Vincent," she responded briskly. It had taken him years to get her to call him by his first name. "You have an appointment," she informed him.

"So I understand. Ten o'clock?"

"Yes, sir. Your other messages are on your desk."

"Got it. Michael, join me. Louisa, *mi amor*, hold my calls, would you?"

She blushed again at the endearment, but nodded sharply and said, "Yes, sir."

Vincent grinned, then threw a come along gesture at Michael to follow as he ducked back into his office. He strolled over and sat behind his desk, a beautiful monstrosity of black walnut, waiting until the door was closed before giving his lieutenant a questioning look.

Michael didn't waste any time. "I'm getting a lot of reports, both human and vampire, that just over a week ago, a pair of vamps were spotted driving hellbent from the North, stopping only long enough to sleep and drain a few unwilling donors on their way to Mexico City."

Vincent had made Michael a vampire for a variety of reasons, but he'd proven to be an inspired choice. As a vampire, his power was second only to Vincent's, and as a lieutenant, he was a positive genius at cultivating sources and gathering data. He'd embraced the information age with a vengeance and knew everything there was to know about computer networks and, frankly, how to pry into places that tried to keep him out.

"Driving," Vincent repeated, thinking about this latest development. "Any positive IDs?"

"Two females, that's all we know for sure. For the record, however, I've got another source who claims that one of the vampires at the showdown in Acuña was Raphael's sister."

Vincent's eyes widened in surprise. "The sister no one's seen in months? What's her name . . . Alexandra? Everyone thought she was dead."

"That was my understanding, too. But what if she's not? And if she was in Acuña, simple odds say that she was probably one of the females who made a beeline for Mexico City and Enrique right after."

Vincent swore softly. "What is that bastard up to?" he muttered.

Michael nodded. "I'm trying to verify the sister's ID, or at least find someone who knows if she's alive or dead. But you know Raphael's people. They're loyal to a fault, and damn if his network security isn't impossible to break through. I can't get word one from anyone who'd know about the sister's status. The guy who claims she was in Acuña is a cop whose wife overheard a conversation outside the hotel where the European vamps were staying. She also claims the vamp calling herself Alexandra was *with* the Europeans."

"Alexandra arrived with the Europeans? How'd that come about?"

"Don't know, but I *do* know that she didn't cross into Mexico with Raphael. And she didn't return to the U.S. with him either. I have video from the border crossing in both directions. There were only five people traveling with Raphael, and the only woman was his mate."

Vincent thought about what that might mean and realized he didn't have a fucking clue. "Are the two females who raced to Mexico City still there?"

Michael shook his head. "Doubtful. A private plane departed Benito Juarez airport with a flight plan for Paris. There was one passenger, a female who arrived via limo from Enrique's HQ. My guess is that passenger was one of our travelers."

"What about the other one?"

"Unknown."

"Shit. I don't want to go to Mexico City."

"Have you ever seen the sister? Does anyone know what she looks like?"

"I saw her across the room at a party once after a council meeting in Malibu."

"Is the sister like a female version of Raphael?"

"That would make her one very big woman, Mikey." Vincent snorted. "No, Alexandra's a tiny thing, especially by today's standards. No more than five feet tall without shoes. She's got black hair, like he does, but that's all I could make out. I don't think I'd recognize her on the street, but I might be able to pick her out from a photo. I'm guessing you have a shot of the female vamp who caught that flight?"

Michael thumbed through his cell phone and held it out. "It's grainy because of the distance."

Vincent took the phone and frowned down at the image. It had obviously taxed someone's zoom lens to the max, but . . . "That's not the sister," he said. "Hair color can be changed, but the body isn't right. This woman's too big. And the look's all wrong. It's not Alexandra."

"So Raphael's sister is either dead or in Mexico City. What the fuck, *jefe*?"

"I wish I knew." Vincent pinched his nose between his thumb and forefinger, wondering if he should call Enrique and ask what was going on. On one hand, if there was a plot afoot that involved Raphael's sister, Enrique should be told. On the other, if Enrique was *part* of the plot . . . well, fuck. There was nothing in the lieutenant's manual that said Vincent had to follow his lord as far as suicide.

"Is there someone in the South we can tap for information?" he asked Michael. "If Raphael was in Texas, Anthony or one of his people must have known about it."

Vincent's working relationships with vampires in the South were far better and more extensive than those in Raphael's territory in the far west. This was because the southern territory shared a huge border with Mexico, with a lot of traffic back and forth, both legal and not-so-legal. Vampires didn't involve themselves in human affairs, but that didn't mean they were immune to the violence and social disruption that sometimes occurred. The U.S./Mexico border had been very uneasy of late; uneasy enough that Vincent and his counterparts in the South had consulted with each other often.

"I'll reach out," Michael said. "In the meantime—" He broke off when a scream sounded on the far side of the compound, from the direction of the public nightclub, which was also a blood house. Almost on top of the scream, all three phones started ringing—Vincent's cell, Michael's cell, and the office phone. Vincent was still holding Michael's phone, so he hit *Answer*.

"We got trouble, Mike," a male voice said. "We need Vincent—"

"You got him," Vincent snapped as he and Michael headed out of the office at a run. "Be there in two."

The nightclub was down the block from Vincent's office, and it was designed to be the very opposite of subtle. Music pounded from inside, so loud that not even the best soundproofing could contain it. The heavy bass sounded like the heartbeat of some slumbering leviathan lying within the building. Four nights a week—Thursday through Sunday—a long line of humans showed up ready and eager to be blood donors, and sexual partners. The two went together. It was evolution's way of making sure vampires got what they needed to survive. They were the perfect predator.

The line started at the bouncer's station at the front door and trailed well past the twenty feet of velvet rope to wind around the side of the building to the parking lot. If the vampires had wanted, they probably could have generated the same crowds every night of the week, but those living in the compound needed a break from the teeming humanity in the city all around them. Or, at least, Vincent did. He liked humans well enough. They sustained him in more ways than one. But they were noisy and always seemed to want something from him, which was odd when you considered that he was the one feeding from *them*.

He'd made it clear when he took over the Hermosillo compound that the club would be closed three nights a week, and no one had objected. At least not within his hearing.

When he and Michael raced up to the entrance, he noticed that the club was crowded as usual. What wasn't usual were the screams emanating from inside and the humans trying to shove their way out through the single open door. Or for that matter, the roars of angry vampires coming from inside.

Fuck. This wasn't good on so many fronts. *Good thing I wore black jeans tonight*, Vincent thought. They didn't show the blood as well.

"My lord!" the bouncer shouted when he caught sight of Vincent. He was struggling to maintain some sort of order among the fleeing humans, trying to keep them from trampling each other as they fled the club. "What can I do?"

"Stay on the door," Vincent growled. "And get rid of them," he added, pointing at the line of club goers still waiting their turn to get in. They were craning their necks and gawking at the screaming and frenzied humanity rushing out of the club, yet none of them appeared ready to surrender their place in the queue. If anything, they seemed more excited than ever at the prospect of getting inside.

"The club is shut down for the night," Vincent ordered, then spun around as the humans closest to the door overheard and groaned a loud protest. Almost as one, they backed away from his cold stare, their eyes wide, their little, mortal hearts going pitty pat with fear. Except for one pretty little blonde whose wide eyes were filled with an entirely different emotion. Vincent wanted to roll his own eyes in disgust. Humans. Some of them had no sense of survival at all. It was amazing the species had flourished as well as it had.

But he didn't have time for a lesson in survival, or even a horny blonde.

He yanked open the second of the double doors, shattering the bolt holding it closed. A few humans immediately tried to use the new wider escape route, but after getting a fang-baring snarl from him, they shied away, clearly deciding that he was a greater threat than whatever they were running from.

Vincent strode into the club and stopped. The thumping bass of the music was so deep, it made his teeth ache. His vampire-enhanced vision could see well enough despite the intentionally dim lighting. Shadows were cultivated in here to give the illusion of privacy. Sex was pretty much always the result when a vamp took blood from the vein, and in the sexual rush triggered by the vamp's bite, no one worried overmuch about where they were or who might be watching. Unbridled sex, whether in the corners or right out on the dance floor, was pretty much the norm.

But that's not what was happening out there right now. Five big vampires dominated the center of the dance floor, their fangs bare and gleaming, their shoulders hunched and fingers curled in a blatant display of aggression from all sides. Three human females were huddled against the bar, trapped there by the angry vamps in front of them. One of the females was bleeding profusely from a neck bite that someone hadn't bothered to seal off properly. Or more likely, given the mood of the five vamps, the biter had been interrupted before he could finish.

There were other vampires still in the club, too. They were gathered in the shadows around the dance floor, some protecting clumps of humans, others positioned to block the door, smart enough to know that they couldn't let the combatants spill outside. It was one thing for a crowd of panicked humans to fill the street; it was another thing entirely for a bloody vampire battle to do so.

Vincent saw all of this with a glance and took a split second to consider his options. He was powerful enough to shut down all five combatants without lifting a finger. He could be subtle and simply drop them unconscious. Or if he wanted to be showy, a blast of power would reduce them to so much meat writhing on the floor. On the other hand, it had been a very long time since he'd been allowed to indulge his less civilized side.

"This one's mine, Mikey," he muttered, feeling a grin of anticipation split his face. He loved a good brawl.

"Ah fuck, *jefe*. You get all the fun."

Vincent stormed in, his fingers sinking into the shoulder of the first vampire he encountered. The vamp was too deep in his own rage to realize who had grabbed him and spun with an enraged snarl. But Vincent was waiting for him. With an uppercut to the jaw, the vamp flew through the air before collapsing like a broken puppet against the far wall. At the same time, the guy's allies realized there was a new player on the field and roared their displeasure. Howling a joyous battle cry of his own, Vincent waded in, his fists pounding, blood flying. He grabbed one vampire by the throat, his fingers digging in so deeply that blood spilled out of the vamp's mouth and ran down his neck before his eyes abruptly focused on Vincent in recognition.

"Mercy, my lord," he choked out, and Vincent tossed him aside. He had no interest in killing anyone tonight.

A massive blow slammed into his back, hard enough that he staggered a half step. With a furious yowl, he shifted his weight to one foot and spun, kicking out with the opposing foot, recognizing his assailant as the first vamp he'd grabbed, even as he sent him sailing across the floor to crash into the bar.

The smell of spilled liquor rose up in an overwhelming cloud as the three women who'd been huddled nearby shrieked and scurried for cover, clutching each other beneath a rainfall of shattering glass. The vampire himself was so berserk with battle lust by then that he jumped to his feet almost immediately and charged back into the fray as Vincent was grabbed from behind by a third vamp. A powerful arm circled his throat, crushing his esophagus and pulling his head back hard just as the charging vamp shoulder-butted him in the gut, nearly snapping his spine in two.

"Son of a bitch," Vincent swore. It was one thing to enjoy a good brawl, it was another to be crushed between a couple of brainless behemoths. He reached for his power and slammed it into the gut-butting berserker, sending him sliding across the floor to smash into the bar once again. But this time, the guy stayed there, slumped in a puddle of liquor and glass, his chin on his chest, hands lying limply by his sides.

Reaching behind him with both hands, Vincent grabbed the fucker who was trying to grind his neck into dust. The vamp shrieked in pain as Vincent's fingers dug into muscle and bone. He bent his knees and flipped the vamp over his head and onto the floor where he stomped the breath out of the idiot's chest, then kicked him across the dance floor to join his buddy in the wreckage of the bar.

"You're paying for that fucking bar," he roared at the two of them, then turned on the two remaining combatants with a wild howl. They took in the copper gleam of his eyes and the blood of their compatriots dripping from his curled fingers. Recognition sank in, dousing their battle rage like a bucket of ice water, and they dropped to their knees.

"My lord," one of them muttered. "We didn't know it was you."

Vincent raked his gaze over the crowd of vampires still lingering in the shadows. "Get those humans out of here," he commanded. They leapt to obey as Michael crossed the floor to hustle away the three women near the bar, who'd apparently been at the center of the dispute. Within moments, the doors were closed, with only vampires remaining in the nearly-silent club. Even the music had been turned off.

Vincent felt a warmth drip over his chin and realized that somewhere along the way, he'd gotten a split lip. "Son of a bitch," he swore and grabbed the bottom of his T-shirt, pulling it up to wipe away the blood as he turned to glare at the offending vampires, all of whom were now on their knees and more or less conscious.

"Do I have to tell you how fucking stupid this was?" Vincent demanded. "All that pussy just waiting to be had, lining up at the fucking door, and you idiots come to blows over a piece of ass?"

"She's mine," one of them mumbled. "He had no right."

Vincent stared at the talkative vamp. "Are you mated?" he asked quietly.

The vamp's mouth tightened briefly. "No, my lord."

"So when you say *mine*, you mean . . . what, exactly?"

"I was dancing with—"

"Silence," Vincent snapped. If the vamp said another word, he was going to kill the fucker and save evolution the need to do it for him.

"The five of you will pay for all damages. I'd ban you altogether, but you'd probably end up draining people on street corners and cause me an even bigger fucking headache than you already have. So, I'll give you this warning. One more incident like this—one, gentlemen—and it will be your last. I'll kill you myself."

He glared around the room, catching the eye of all five of the kneeling vamps, including the two still groaning in the wreckage of the bar. "You assholes got that?"

"Yes, my lord," they muttered more or less in unison.

Vincent's cell phone chimed from his pocket. He ignored it long enough to offer the vampires one last quelling look, then pulled it out and looked at the screen. It was a text from Louisa, telling him that Raphael's bounty hunter had arrived. Great. Just fucking great.

He searched the club until he found the manager in the crowd. "Take care of this. I want to open on schedule Thursday night. If you need muscle, these assholes will do."

At least the fuckers had decided to break up his club on a Sunday. They still wouldn't be able to repair all of the damage before Thursday, but they could at least rig something functional and replace the broken glassware and spilled liquor.

The manager was smart enough not to bring up any of those details, however, seeming to understand that Vincent wasn't in the mood for practical discussion. His only response was a snapped, "Yes, my lord," and a nod of the head.

Vincent nodded in turn, then, motioning for Michael to follow, he strode back into the night. He even managed to conceal his grin until the two of them were well away from the scene.

LANA SLID HER Yukon into the parking lot of a neat, Southwestern-styled office building. It was fairly new, no more than five years old by her guess, with the usual Pueblo-style accents added strictly for effect. She didn't have a lot of experience with vampires, only what she'd gained through her business association with Cynthia Leighton, but she'd noticed that they were deadly serious about a couple of things. One was their personal security. They had top of the line security systems, and while their houses or office buildings might be designed to blend in with their surroundings, they were usually far sturdier than the norm. The other thing she'd been made aware of was their preference to remain apart from humans. They did business with them, they drank their blood, for sure, but they always lived apart, even if it was only a house with a bigger-than-average yard down the block. They didn't live in apartment buildings and they didn't have human friends. Some of them had husbands and wives—mates, they called them—but the human mate went to live with the vamp, not vice versa. And that suited Lana just fine. More power to them and may they live long and prosper. But she was happy to remain apart.

She opened the door of her Yukon and climbed out, her attention immediately drawn off to the right where she could see the lights and crowd surrounding a busy nightclub. Except that on this particular night, the crowd seemed to have gotten out of control. People were pushing their way *out* rather than in, and she could hear the muted sounds of an altercation coming from inside the club.

Whatever was going on in there wasn't her business, though, so she shrugged, leaned into her SUV, and grabbed the backpack she used in lieu of a purse. Slipping it over one shoulder, she closed her door and locked it before walking around to climb the three stairs to an unassuming office door. There were no gold-engraved signs, no fancy embellishments, just an ordinary wrought-iron railing and three concrete stairs leading to a slightly deeper top level, where a small, plastic, engraved sign invited visitors to announce themselves. She looked around and found a basic speaker set-up. She pushed the button and heard a faint buzzer from inside.

"Yes?" a woman's pleasant voice inquired.

"Arnold Recoveries for Vincent Kuxim." She tried to pronounce the last name correctly. She'd been intrigued by the unusual name and looked it up, discovering that it was Mayan in origin, with the x pronounced as "sh," like Kushim. She remembered from a college history class that the Mayan civilization had pretty well collapsed over a thousand years ago, so she thought it must be a family name passed down through the generations. Although, she supposed, anything was possible with a vampire.

A new buzzer sounded, louder and harsher this time, and the door opened a couple of inches. Lana took that as an invitation to go in, so she pushed the door open the rest of the way and stepped into the office.

The evenings were cool this time of year, but it was even colder inside the office. She was glad she'd worn her long-sleeved T-shirt and short, black combat jacket.

An attractive middle-aged woman whose appearance matched the pleasant voice over the intercom was sitting at a desk. Her eyes went wide when Lana walked in and she tipped her head a little, as if trying to see if anyone was behind her.

"Is it just you then?" the woman asked.

Lana gave a puzzled frown, pretending not to understand. When she'd called to make this appointment, she hadn't corrected the secretary's assumption that the Arnold who'd be showing up would be her father. The people she encountered in her line of business weren't always the most law-abiding types, and she preferred not to advertise the fact that a woman was about to show up all alone.

"Just me," she confirmed. "I have a ten o'clock appointment?"

"Yes, you do," the woman agreed, a smile playing over her lips. "What was your name again, dear?"

"Lana Arnold, Arnold Recoveries."

The woman's smile grew. "Well, Ms. Arnold, Lord Vincent was called away for a moment, but he'll be right back. I've already texted him to let him know you're here. Can I get you anything while you wait? Something cold to drink? Or maybe a coffee?"

"No, thank you." The last thing Lana wanted after driving a caffeine-fueled 250 miles, nearly nonstop, to get here on time was more coffee. For that matter, she didn't feel like sitting down either. But it would be rude to pace in front of the woman's desk, so she wandered over to the farthest chair, sat down, and pulled out her phone. She and all the guys in her dad's office worked often enough in Mexico that they each had a separate cell phone for when they were in-country. The farther one got from the U.S., the more necessary it became. Lana's habit was to switch over as soon as she crossed the border, which was why she was able to sit in Kuxim's waiting room and get some business done.

She was scrolling through her e-mail, deleting most of it, when the outer door opened and something like an electrical current ran through the room, making the small hairs on the back of her neck stand up. She looked up to see a dangerous-looking male standing there. Dangerous not only because of his size—which was considerable, a couple of inches over six feet and most of that muscle—but because of the blood staining his fingers and still dripping from a split lip down his chin and into a neatly trimmed beard. He appeared to be in his late twenties and had a mustache to go with the beard, wavy black hair, and brown eyes with pretty flecks of color that she supposed would be called hazel, but they seemed more copper to her. And right now, those pretty eyes were giving the receptionist an irritated look which he almost immediately transferred to Lana.

"*¿Dónde está tu jefe, cariño?*" he asked her in Spanish, which translated to *Where's your boss, sweetheart?*

Lana pocketed her phone, then stood and gave him a dry look. "I don't have a boss, darling," she said in deliberate English. "What I *do* have is an appointment with Vincent Kuxim. Is that you?"

He stared at her with no expression for a long moment, then his eyes lit up and his lips curled into a sexy-as-hell smile. "Call me Vincent. But I gotta say, you don't look like a bounty hunter."

"You have a lot of experience with bounty hunters?" she asked, knowing she should be more polite, because she needed this guy's help. But she couldn't stop herself.

His smile widened into a grin. "More than I'd like. Come on into the office." He moved out of the doorway, and she saw there was another man behind him, also a vampire, she assumed. He was just as big as Vincent, but the polar opposite in looks—blond with green eyes, his hair cut brutally short, his face clean-shaven, very all-American handsome. He gave her a brief once-over, then gestured for her to go ahead of him after Vincent. She would have preferred having both of them ahead of her, but she wasn't about to admit that, so she nodded and followed Vincent into the office.

"My lieutenant, Michael," Vincent said, indicating the other vampire. "Have a seat." He gestured at two heavy chairs sitting in front of a huge wooden desk that was obviously an antique. Its design was in keeping with the Southwestern theme of the building, but it wasn't a new piece. It was heavy and old, the wood stained with age, and it was beautiful.

"Forgive my appearance," Vincent said, swiping at his chin with the hem of his black T-shirt and baring a smooth expanse of golden skin and gorgeous muscle in the process.

Lana kept her face expressionless, but she didn't think for one minute that the belly peepshow had been unintentional. She dealt with Latin males all the time. She knew the type. He was extraordinarily handsome and he knew it. He wanted people to think his longish hair was accidental, the result of skipping a haircut or two. But he probably spent an hour in front of the mirror getting it just right, not to mention the time he spent on the beard and mustache. He reached to open a drawer and she caught a glint of gold through the silky, black strands of his hair. He had an earring in his left ear, a simple gold ring, but thicker, like a cuff worn low.

Michael reappeared from somewhere off to the right—probably a bathroom, because he handed Vincent a wet towel. Vincent used it to clean the blood from his hands, then swiped it over his face and tossed it back. A few moments later, he yanked off his bloodied T-shirt and dumped it in the trash. Despite her best intentions, Lana's throat went dry. His body was perfect—sculpted muscle defined broad shoulders and strong arms, his chest was deep, and his abdomen ridged above a pair of low-slung jeans. As if that wasn't enough, an intricate tattoo covered his left bicep, something colorful and pre-Hispanic, she thought. Mayan maybe, considering his name. She couldn't tell for sure and didn't want to stare long enough to figure it out. A guy who looked like that didn't need the ego boost. Thankfully, he pulled a clean shirt on over his head and tugged it down, covering himself before she did something she'd regret. Like drool.

Ugh. Had she been thinking she knew his type? She did, and she avoided them like the plague. They were far too much in love with themselves to play nicely with anyone else.

She waved a hand at his obvious dishevelment. "I can come back if—"

"No, no," Vincent interrupted, settling back into the chair in his new, clean T-shirt. "There was a minor altercation at the club. And we heal fast." He grinned at her, inviting her to share the joke.

She simply gazed back at him.

"Well," he continued, sounding like he wanted to harrumph at her for ignoring his stellar humor. "How can I help you, Ms. Arnold?"

"Call me Lana," she told him, figuring if he was to be called Vincent, then she should return the favor. "My client wants a message delivered. I was told you could possibly assist in locating the recipient of that message."

"Who's your client?"

She didn't answer his question directly, only said, "As I mentioned to your receptionist when I called earlier, it was Raphael who suggested I contact you."

"Raphael," Vincent repeated, staring at her as though he could read the truth of her words written on the inside of her skull if he only stared hard enough.

"I have a letter for you," she said blandly, reaching for her backpack and pulling out the leather portfolio which held her notes on the case. "Would you like to see it?"

Vincent blinked. He clearly hadn't expected that.

"I would, thank you," he said, holding out a hand. She noticed his knuckles were torn and still seeping blood. Obviously, the fight had been a fairly brutal one. Which probably explained the fleeing crowds and the noise she'd heard coming from inside the club when she arrived.

Vincent took the letter from her, clearly not bothered by the state of his hands. He scanned the note from Raphael with the same laser intent that he'd used to study her moments before. Then he turned it over to Michael, who'd taken up a position standing behind his left shoulder.

"Okay, so let's say I'm inclined to do Raphael a favor," Vincent said. "Who's the missing person?"

"Xuan Ignacio," she said, watching for his reaction.

He frowned. "Xuan Ignacio? He's a folk tale. The oldest vampire in Mexico, and blah, blah, blah. I don't think he's even real."

"Raphael thinks he is."

"So Raphael's your client?"

"Raphael knows I'm looking for Xuan Ignacio," she hedged, still not willing to reveal any more than necessary. "And, as you see, he suggested you could help."

Vincent obviously noticed her careful language and scowled at her. She imagined he wasn't used to being stymied like this. She knew from her conversations with Leighton that vampire social and/or political structure was fairly rigid, with power concentrated at the top. A vampire like Vincent, who ran a city the size of Hermosillo, would have a lot of power, at least in his own domain.

"All right," he conceded. "So where do we start looking?"

It was Lana's turn to scowl. "I thought *you'd* know," she said, biting back her impatience.

"Hey, you came to me. I don't claim any special knowledge."

Lana pursed her lips in disgust. This was a fool's errand. Vincent might be the prettiest male she'd ever seen, but he clearly wasn't the sharpest. Or maybe he just didn't want to help her and was playing dumb, being a pain in the ass to get out of the obligation without offending Raphael. And that was a major inconvenience for her. She'd rather have no help than drag a hulking vampire around with her like a reluctant teenager, but Raphael wanted this guy on the job. Damn. She considered her options. Vincent Kuxim might be a vampire, but he was also a guy. An alpha male guy. And Lana had a lot of experience with those. Hadn't she all but grown up in her dad's office surrounded by bounty hunters? You didn't get much more alpha than that. So, she knew that the best way to get their cooperation was to pretend you didn't need it. That was the one thing their giant egos couldn't handle.

She closed her portfolio with a snap, slipped it into her backpack, and stood. "Thank you for your time," she said politely. "If I have any questions I think you can answer," she said, not able to resist adding an ounce of snark, "I'll give you call."

She made it all the way to the closed office door before she heard Vincent's chair slide back on the tile floor. "Wait," he said or, rather, *ordered,* that one word being laced with a touch of annoyance.

Unfortunately for him, Lana didn't take orders from anyone, except her dad on occasion, and certainly not from temperamental vampires who bloodied their knuckles fighting. She ignored him and reached for the doorknob.

"I said *wait*." There was a hell of a lot more than annoyance this time. And when Lana went to twist the door handle, it wouldn't budge.

A ripple of unease tickled her gut. She tried another discreet, and ineffective, twist, then spun around with a glare.

"OPEN THE DOOR, Mr. Kuxim," Lana Arnold demanded, and her dark eyes flashed with anger.

It was the first real emotion Vincent had seen from her, and it both intrigued and relieved him. She'd been so controlled from the moment he'd walked into the office. She hadn't responded to his charm at all, and, frankly, Vincent was used to women being swayed by him. Old, young, single, married—it didn't matter. His entire life, even before he became a vampire, woman had always responded to him the way his assistant Louisa did. They blushed, they stammered, they pursued him left and right, but they always went along with what he wanted. Except for this one. If he hadn't caught a brief reaction from her when he'd taken off his shirt—and that, no more than an involuntary widening of her eyes and a single jump of her heartbeat before she became the Ice Queen again—he'd have suspected Lana the Bounty Hunter favored women. He took a few seconds to indulge in the time-honored male fantasy of picturing the woman in front of him in the arms of another woman. Nice.

But then he was back in the present with a very pissed-off Lana Arnold. Anger looked good on her. It made her much more attractive, more human. She wasn't his usual type—too tall, too lean, and sure as hell too opinionated. He favored short, plump women whose goal in life was to make him happy. But Lana Arnold was a good-looking woman. Her height gave her a certain elegance, and her leanness was all sleek, taut muscle encased in a black T-shirt and combat-style pants. It was inherently masculine clothing, but the shirt clung to her chest, and the pants hugged her narrow hips and a firm ass. Not an ounce of fat, he'd bet. She had gorgeous bone structure with high cheekbones and a slender jaw, a sexy mouth with a full lower lip, and long black hair braided down her back. Her lashes were black, too, framing eyes that were an unusual pale brown.

Eyes that were glaring daggers at him from across the room. He noticed the fingers of her left hand going bone white as they tightened on the strap of her backpack, while her right hand, which *had* been holding the doorknob . . . Uh oh. Time to stop gazing at the bounty hunter before her fingers found the knife sheathed inside the thigh pocket of her nicely-fitting combats. He'd been so busy admiring the way they hugged her hips and ass that he'd ignored the perils. Talk about being blinded by sexual attraction.

Even if he wasn't actually attracted to her.

"Sit down, Lana," he said gently, putting all of his persuasive skills into it, and maybe cheating with a touch of vampiric push.

Her glare redoubled its ferocity. "Don't you dare try to force me against my will."

It was Vincent's eyes that went wide this time. She shouldn't have been aware of what he was doing. Either he'd gotten rusty—which he hadn't—or Lana Arnold was unusual indeed.

He raised his hands in surrender. "I apologize. It was automatic."

"Don't do it again."

He gestured at the chair she'd vacated. "I won't. Sit down . . . please."

She gave him a long, distrustful look, then moved her hand from where it had been creeping toward her weapon and crossed slowly back to the chair. She sat without ever taking her eyes off of him.

Vincent sank slowly into his big chair, watching her as one would an unpredictable and wild animal. He didn't know about the wild part—although, let's face it, she was a female bounty hunter, so not exactly timid—but she was *absolutely* unpredictable. He'd never met a human who was immune to the persuasive power of his vampire blood. It was the one ability that every vampire possessed to some degree, because it was a major part of what made them successful predators.

"I don't know where to find Xuan Ignacio," he told her carefully. "But," he added, holding up a hand to forestall her objection, "that doesn't mean I can't find out. There are vampires older than I am, including several in this city."

She tilted her head curiously. "I got the impression from my client that you were the master, or whatever you call it, of Hermosillo."

"I am Lord Enrique's lieutenant," he corrected evenly. "As such, I spend much of my time in various cities on his behalf. Although Hermosillo happens to be my favorite," he confided with a wink that was meant to be engaging.

She didn't react other than to pull out her portfolio and a pen to make a note of some sort. Cursed woman.

She looked up from her notes. "If there are older vampires than you in this city, then why are you in charge?" she asked.

"Age does not equal power for a vampire," he told her. "There are some who are born, or reborn, to power, and some who will never attain real power, no matter how long they live."

She made a little moue with her mouth, as if intrigued by this tidbit of vampire lore. "All right," she said. "So where do we start then?"

Vincent didn't know what to think about her quick assumption that they'd be working together. His plan had been to question a few of the older vamps and give her a call. She was watching him carefully, though, and there was just a hint of challenge there, as if daring him to prove he was up to the task of solving her puzzle. Fine, then. Two could play that game. He knew he could survive in her world; he'd been doing it for over 150 years. Let's see if she could survive in his.

"I'll need to make a few phone calls," he told her. "Give me an hour."

She nodded once, then put her things away again, and stood. "Thank you. I'll be back then."

Vincent stood with her. "You're free to wait here," he said quickly. "Louisa could arrange some refreshments. Dinner if you're hungry."

She studied him for a moment, giving away nothing. "Thank you, but no. I have arrangements of my own to make." She walked over to the door and didn't even hesitate in reaching for the handle. It opened easily, of course. He'd already decided to take a different approach with Lana Arnold.

She opened the door and looked at him over her shoulder. He thought he saw the tiniest bit of amusement in her pale eyes. "I'll be back in one hour," she told him, then walked out of his office.

He followed the tap of her footsteps across the tiled lobby, heard the door open and close, and then the sound of a vehicle starting up and driving away.

"So what do you think?" he asked Michael, who was now sitting in the chair next to the one the bounty hunter had occupied moments before.

"At least you knew this Xuan Ignacio existed—even if only in fairy tales. I've never even heard of him."

"That's because you're still a toddler with fangs."

Michael snorted. "And you're an old man . . . *my* old man as it turns out. Weird. Okay, so I'll ask the same question our lovely bounty hunter did. Where do we start?"

"You think she's lovely?" Vincent asked, more curious than anything else.

"Hell, yeah. Can't fake those cheekbones or those bee-stung lips. Not that she needs to fake anything with a body like that. Athletic. I like it."

"You like anything with a pussy, my friend. But hands off this one."

Michael's eyebrows shot up in surprise. "She doesn't seem your type at all, *jefe*."

"She doesn't, does she?" Vincent said thoughtfully. "Maybe it's time for a change."

Chapter Two

LANA WAITED UNTIL she was in her SUV and back on the highway before letting out the breath she felt like she'd been holding for an hour. Vincent Kuxim might be a powerful vampire, but as a man, he was positively nuclear. She'd never bought in to the whole pheromones and instant attraction bullshit, not when it came to people, anyway. But, damn, that man oozed sexuality. He was a walking, talking hazard to the female population.

It had taken every ounce of the control she'd developed over years of working with her father's testosterone-laden bounty hunters to keep her feelings hidden. She should have been immune to men like Vincent by now, especially ones with that Latin charm of his. She lived in Arizona and encountered Hispanic males on a daily basis in her work. And plenty of her skip traces took her across the border into Mexico, too.

But she suspected Vincent's appeal had more to do with being a vampire than his Hispanic ancestry. Or maybe his vampire talents had simply built on the Latin charm that was already there. He'd told her age didn't equal power, but maybe power equaled charisma. He'd certainly used that power on her when she'd tried to leave the office. Or at least he'd attempted to. And he'd been surprised as hell when it didn't work. For that matter, she'd been surprised, too. She'd felt something like a tug on her brain and had instinctively fought against it. But until she'd caught him staring at her like she was a two-headed calf, she hadn't considered what that pull might be or where it had come from.

Leighton had warned her when they'd first started working together that vampires had some weird talents and quirks, and, in truth, Lana had encountered too many to list. She'd reached the point where she simply wrote off anything weird that happened around vampires as just one more oddity. But she'd never encountered anything like that mind tug before. Of course, she'd never met a vampire as powerful as Vincent before, either. Maybe whatever it was inside her brain that had resisted his attempts to influence her was so strong that it had brushed off other, weaker vamps without her even being aware of it.

If that was true, it seemed like a good thing. She'd have to think about it, but not until after this job was done. She had to work with Vincent to find Xuan Ignacio for Raphael. She could worry later about weird vampire powers and what it all meant.

But now, she had an hour to kill, and her first priority was checking into a hotel. She was accustomed to running on caffeine and going without sleep, but since she had the time—and since she'd spent hours in her car getting here—she was going to grab a shower and change clothes. She'd made reservations at the San Sebastian hotel. It was nicer than most and reasonably priced, as well as secure enough for a woman traveling alone. That didn't mean she wouldn't keep a knife or two at hand when she went to sleep, but odds were she wouldn't have to use them.

As soon as she got to her room, she locked the door and started to strip. On her way to the shower, she freed the heavy braid, combing her fingers over her scalp and letting her hair hang loose. It was a heavenly sensation, better even than taking off her bra, which she did a moment later. The bra was a black athletic style. It was on the tight side, but her breasts were no more than average—nicely shaped, but a B cup on a good day. Her hair, on the other hand, was thick and long and heavy, and gathering all that weight into a tight braid was a constant pull on her scalp. Wearing it down wasn't an option when she was working, however, no matter what the movies showed. She could have cut it short—in fact, she probably should have—but it was her one concession to femininity. Besides, she loved it.

The shower was hot, the water pressure weak, but she'd come to expect that in even the best hotels in these days of water conservation. The great thing was, she could stand there for as long as it took to soap and rinse her body, and then wash and condition her hair. When she emerged, the pale mocha skin she'd inherited from her Irish father and Mexican mother had a rosy tint and she felt a million times better.

Unfortunately, the warm massage of the water had also reminded her that she'd slept only a couple of hours before hitting the road, so she popped the top on a can of Coke from the cooler she kept in the car. It wasn't coffee, but it would do until she could mainline the real thing.

Wrapping herself in one towel and her hair in another, she pulled down the bedspread and tossed it in a corner. She'd read somewhere that hotel bedspreads were havens for all sorts of unpleasant things, and that they were rarely washed. Her job required that she spend a fair amount of time in hotel rooms, so she'd taken it to heart.

Propping all of the pillows against the headboard, she sat on the bed and opened her laptop computer. The hotel offered wireless Internet, so she logged on and went first thing to a website where one could pull up a sunrise/sunset table for just about anywhere in the world. She located the one for Hermosillo, downloaded it, then e-mailed it to herself so she'd have it on her cell phone as well.

Switching back to the human world, she logged into her office voicemail and discovered several messages, including one from her dad. She'd called from the road and left a message on his home number, not wanting him to worry, but not wanting to argue with him about taking one of the guys along either. His message ordered her to check in daily, something she didn't intend to do. And the rest of the messages convinced her that her dad wasn't waiting for her to call either. There were . . . she counted . . . eleven messages from Dave Harrington, one of her father's hunters, probably his number one hunter if she was honest. Dave was a big, handsome guy, with wild blond hair, and he was very good at his job. He was also very good friends with his boss, aka Lana's dad. In fact, they were such good friends that the two of them had decided Dave should be Sean Arnold's heir apparent, with Lana his princess, the one he'd marry and thus solidify his role as successor. As if.

Lana had actually given in and dated Dave during her first year in college, mostly to please her dad. Dave had turned out to be sweet and attentive and full of plans for their future together. And she'd been nineteen and naïve enough to believe him.

Until she'd discovered that the prince was just another dog who fucked a different woman in every town before coming home to his clueless princess.

Lana had been a tomboy most of her life, so she hadn't done much dating in high school. Dave had been her first really serious relationship. They'd gone out for a year and a half, and it had hurt Lana more than she wanted to admit to discover he'd been cheating on her the whole time. She'd had enough pride to make a clean break, but, predictably, Dave hadn't understood the problem. Apparently, the woman-in-every-town routine was common among the guys in her dad's office, including her dad himself. They were just men, after all, and away from home a lot. They had needs. What else were they to do?

But that was seven years ago. Lana had long since moved on and never looked back, while Dave still persisted in introducing her as his fiancée. It was embarrassing to her, but she still had to work with Dave Harrington, so she skimmed through his messages, just in case one of them said something important. Unfortunately, they were all variants on the same theme. Predictably, her dad, the traitor, had told Dave what she was doing. Dave had therefore appointed himself her partner for the venture and was demanding that she stay *right where she was* until he could join her. Unfortunately—or fortunately from her point of view—he didn't know exactly where she *was*, and so she was instructed to contact him immediately with the details.

Lana rolled her eyes and deleted all of the messages unanswered. Dave Harrington was a good hunter and would probably make a horrible husband for some woman someday. But it wouldn't be her. He was ten years older than she was, and about a hundred years out of date. He still thought women should clean the house, cook dinner, and have babies. And not worry when her husband strayed, as long as he came home on time.

Lana, on the other hand, had discovered that she had no desire to clean a fucking house, she couldn't cook, and if her dad and Dave wanted grandbabies, they'd better find another incubator, because that was *not* Lana's idea of heaven. And when it came to her lovers, she had no desire to share.

She dashed off a quick e-mail to her dad. No details, because he'd just pass them onto Dave, but she let him know she was okay and that the investigation was proceeding smoothly. Dave would find her eventually. Finding people was their profession, after all, and she wasn't making any serious effort to avoid detection. Pinging her cell phone would be the fastest way. She'd paid cash for the hotel, but he could still track her e-mail back to the local network. She figured she had a day to get out of Hermosillo and on the trail of Xuan Ignacio before Dave showed up. She hoped Vincent was prepared to move fast. Otherwise, she'd leave him behind.

She considered what his reaction might be when she told him that, and she smiled.

An hour later, she was out in front of Vincent's office for the second time that night. She'd changed clothes, but they were pretty much the same as what she'd had on before—a black long-sleeved T-shirt, black combat-style pants and jacket, and lace-up black boots. She had her favorite Sig holstered in its usual place, the shoulder harness hidden by her jacket, and her usual three knives concealed on her person—one in a custom sheath in her right boot, a second in her thigh pocket, and a small but deadly three and a half inch blade in her side pocket. Her hair was back in its tidy braid, still wet underneath, because the crappy hotel hairdryer hadn't had enough power to dry it completely in the time she'd had to get ready.

But the air in Hermosillo was warm. It would take care of her wet hair soon enough, and the cool dampness felt good against her freshly moisturized skin.

As she grabbed her backpack and locked up, she noticed that the nightclub was now completely shut down. No lights, no music, no people crowded around the entrance. She could see light leaking from the closed door and shuttered windows, as if someone was inside, but there was no partying. Maybe they were cleaning up whatever mess had been created earlier—a mess she had no doubt Vincent and his bloodied knuckles had contributed to.

The door to Vincent's office clicked open before she got to the top step, proof that someone was paying attention.

"Welcome back, Ms. Arnold," the same receptionist said with a quick smile. "Go on in. Lord Vincent is expecting you."

Lana kept her surprise from showing. She'd expected him to keep her waiting, simply because he could. Maybe it wouldn't be so terrible working with him after all. Except for that rampant sexuality of his, of course. She'd have to be on guard against that. And maybe switch to cold showers until this job was over with.

VINCENT ROSE TO his feet when Lana Arnold entered his office and caught her quickly hidden look of surprise. But he'd been raised to stand when a lady entered the room, even when the lady was dressed like a soldier and wearing a gun. Hell, maybe especially then. Her long, dark hair was back in its confinement, although she'd washed it while she was gone. He could smell the shampoo and sense the lingering trace of moisture.

He'd set Michael the task of working the phone list, trying to find a vampire in Hermosillo who'd actually known Xuan Ignacio. In the meantime, Vincent had gone on an Internet search seeking the dirt on Lana Arnold. Unfortunately, or maybe fortunately, there wasn't much dirt to be found. She'd graduated from University of Arizona with a degree in biology—that had been a surprise—and was now employed by her father, Sean Arnold, in his reasonably successful fugitive recovery, aka bounty hunter, business. Sean employed three hunters full-time, including Lana, and subcontracted several more on a case by case basis. Most of their work was for skip traces, but they did other tasks as well, like tracking down the scions of rich families who'd gone astray and bringing them home to Mummy and Daddy. This current job of Lana's, delivering a message to a long-lost vampire, wasn't their usual fare, and he figured it was a one-time deal.

Lana herself lived alone and had never been married. That particular detail pleased him, although why it should was still a mystery to him. She was an attractive woman. Fine. She was also a difficult one. Not so fine, at all.

Lana dropped her backpack on the chair in front of his desk, then leaned across and offered a handshake. Vincent took her hand automatically, although instead of shaking it, he raised it to his mouth and touched his lips to the back, lingering a bit to savor what was very soft skin for a bounty hunter. Her muscles tightened perceptibly, and he released her hand before she could pull it away. But he'd been watching her reaction, and he'd caught the vaguely disappointed look on her face, the raised eyebrow that said he was being predictable and boring. Vincent hated to be predictable and boring.

"Did you have any success?" she asked, dropping her hand to her side with a fidgety motion as if she was fighting the urge to rub it against her pants leg to remove the taint of his kiss.

Vincent's eyes narrowed, but he'd be damned if she'd out-cool him. "My lieutenant, Michael, spoke to two of the older vampires in town," he replied smoothly. "They've agreed to meet with us."

"Can we meet tonight?"

Vincent didn't answer her question. "You seem eager for the hunt, Lana. Is there some urgency that I'm unaware of?" he asked, instead.

"No," she said quickly. "I mean not exactly. But we do like to make our client happy."

"Especially the ones who aren't headed to jail, hmm?" he said, only half-joking.

"Our *client* is never the one going back to jail," she informed him, obviously not even half-amused.

"Of course," he murmured, then gave her a wink, simply to test the bounds of her reserve. She had to break eventually. "Well, you're in luck," he told her, "because as it turns out, both vampires are available to meet us tonight." He didn't add that he hadn't *asked* them for a meeting at all. This wasn't a fucking democracy. If he wanted to talk to a vampire, they made themselves available or they suffered the consequences.

"Will they be coming here or—"

"They're on their way. Unless you object, we'll all meet in the conference room and have a nice chat."

"That works."

"No pictures," Vincent clarified immediately. "No video, no recording of any kind."

"Of course not," she agreed. "I'll just take notes if that's okay."

"And you'll share, of course."

She tilted her head, giving him a curious little smile. "Distrustful much?"

"We've got good reason to be distrustful when it comes to humans, Lana," he told her seriously, leaving out the fact that he was even more distrustful of his fellow vampires.

She blushed in embarrassment—on behalf of her fellow humans?—and it was a sight to see. A rosy wash of color heated her lovely golden brown skin, the first crack in her armor. Vincent enjoyed the moment, then gestured toward the door.

"The conference room is across the hall. How's your Spanish?"

"Not fluent, but more than conversational."

Vincent nodded. "If you don't understand something, let me know. Don't ask them directly, ask me. These are old vampires, and you're both human and female. They're very traditional, and from a time when women didn't run things."

"They don't run things now either," she murmured and gave a little smile when he laughed. Another chink in the armor? Maybe.

"Well, they don't run everything, anyway," he conceded, letting laughter color his words. "But it will be easier tonight if we do this particular thing my way."

"That's why I'm here. You're the expert," she said.

LANA WAITED FOR Vincent's response.

"Yes, I am," he said smoothly. No real surprise there, despite his earlier reluctance. She was willing to bet he could be smooth as silk when he wanted to be, right up to the moment he seduced a woman off her feet. He directed her out of his office and across the hall, resting his hand on her lower back under the guise of guiding her to the conference room. It was an innocent touch, polite even. But he was a little too close for innocence. She could feel the heat of his body, smell his clean, masculine scent, and the polite touch suddenly seemed shockingly intimate. She stiffened, but managed to avoid pulling away. She needed Vincent's cooperation to complete this job for Raphael, and insulting him by jumping at the slightest touch was hardly the way to gain that cooperation. And his ego didn't need to know that he affected her that strongly.

She entered the conference room to find Michael and two other vampires waiting for them. They were sitting at a heavy wooden conference table, another stunning antique that looked like it had once been a dining room table in some rich Mexican landowner's hacienda. The leather chairs scattered around the table, on the other hand, were the height of modern comfort.

Lana sank into one of the comfy chairs gratefully. Her body was beginning to get cranky in its demand for sleep, with each old injury starting to make itself known, from the arm she'd broken at the age of ten to the damaged muscles in her back from wrestling with a 250-pound fugitive last year. She swallowed a sigh of relief as she settled into the chair and studied the two vampires sitting on the other side of the table. Vincent had said they were old, but as with all vampires, their true age wasn't clear. Both appeared to be in their twenties, one slightly older than the other, and they were both short and dark, with stick-straight hair and black distrustful eyes.

Vincent didn't bother with introductions. He strode into the room behind her, sat in one of the chairs and began speaking in rapid and somewhat archaic Spanish, snapping out what sounded very much like an order.

Lana translated in her head and knew she didn't get every word, but the thrust of it was, *You will tell this woman what you know of Xuan Ignacio.* Definitely an order.

The two older vampires nodded, their faces giving away very little. But Lana would have sworn she saw a flash of fear in their eyes before they turned their attention to her. They seemed to be waiting for her to ask a question. She gave Vincent a glance. He was the one who'd told her not to speak to them directly, after all.

"*¿Dónde vive?*" he began. "Where does he live?"

"Pénjamo," the slightly older-looking one said in accented English. "On El Cero San Miguel. It has always been so."

"*El Diablo*," the younger one agreed, nodding.

Lana frowned. The devil? What the hell did that mean?

"Fairy tales for stupid children," Vincent dismissed almost angrily. "Have you met him?" he asked, directing his question at the older vampire.

"Once," he said. "He appeared as a man, but not like you or I. He is pale like a ghost, with white hair and eyes that are blind but see everything."

Vincent made an impatient gesture. "Where was this?"

"I spoke truth, my lord. I never had words with him, and I saw him only once. On El Cero San Miguel. That's where you'll find him."

Vincent swung his chair slightly to give Lana a skeptical look. "Any questions?"

"More than one," she admitted.

"Let me rephrase," he said. "Any questions our visitors can answer?"

Lana frowned. "I don't want to insult anyone—" she said, stopping when Vincent shifted his attention to Michael and gave a jerk of his head toward the door. Before Lana had fully registered his intent, Michael and the two older vamps had vacated the room, closing the door behind them.

"I wasn't finished," she snapped, irritated that he hadn't given her a chance to question the older vamps. Why'd he bother to ask her if he was going to be such a jerk about it?

"Yes, you were," he said, raising her ire all over again with his dismissive attitude. "Look, whenever a question starts with *I don't want to insult anyone*, someone is about to be insulted. For all their centuries of living—or maybe because of them—those two remain unsophisticated and very traditional at heart. You're both a woman and a *gringa*. If they took something you said amiss—and it wouldn't take much—they'd clam up and refuse to help you any further. And they'd only be *that* polite because I was in the room with you. Besides, they believe every word they said." He shook his head in disbelief. "It's difficult to understand such persistent superstition."

Lana was somewhat mollified by his explanation, but couldn't help retorting, "*You* seem to understand them just fine."

Vincent smiled, clearly choosing to ignore the sly insult in her words. "I know what they were talking about. I know *where* they're talking about."

Lana sighed, fingers itching for her computer so she could Google this El Cero San Miguel for herself. Unfortunately, all she had was Vincent. She preferred Google, but Raphael's clear intent had been for Vincent to be with her when she finally handed the message to Xuan Ignacio. Her original plan had been to find Xuan herself and bring him and Vincent together for the big finish, but she was beginning to think the whole thing would go more smoothly if she had a local guide along on the journey. And the most logical person for that was Vincent. She could kill two birds with one stone. If she didn't kill Vincent first.

"So you think they're reliable?" she asked him.

"They're telling the truth as they know it. Celio, in particular, the more talkative of the two, is very reliable. If he says he saw Xuan Ignacio in the flesh, then he did."

"What's this El Cero San Miguel he talked about?"

"It's in Pénjamo, a city in Guanajuato, at the foot of the mountains. El Cero San Miguel is essentially a big hill that's reputed to be haunted. It's something of a tourist destination for those interested in such things."

"That's what the other one meant when he called Xuan Ignacio the devil. He thinks Xuan's the devil who haunts this hill."

"I told you," Vincent said with a careless shrug, "they're superstitious."

"All right, well how do I—? Damn it, I need my computer. Can we return to the modern age now?"

Vincent laughed, then stood and held out his hand. "Come on, we'll go back to my office."

Lana ignored his hand. She didn't need help standing, for God's sake. She crossed back to his office, feeling his presence behind her again. She was much too aware of him, and he was much too intent on making her feel that way. If they were going to travel around Mexico together, she'd have to figure out a way to deal with that.

Going directly to her laptop, she pulled up a map of Mexico, zeroing in on Pénjamo. Fuck. It was a good thousand miles from Hermosillo. A long drive. Especially with Vincent sitting right next to her.

"That's a long drive," she observed out loud, testing the waters.

"Especially for a woman alone," Vincent commented.

"I could fly."

"*We* could," he said agreeably.

She looked up to find him giving her a knowing grin.

"Raphael wants me along when you find Xuan Ignacio. Deny it all you want, but I know Raphael's your client, and you told me you like your clients happy. So, it looks like we're going to Pénjamo, *querida*. But I'd rather drive." He winked at her.

Lana gritted her teeth. With every minute she spent in Vincent's company, her attraction to him seemed to grow. He was like one of those oozing fungi in a monster movie that started out small, but eventually ate you up whole.

"You're probably pretty busy here," she objected. She might need his help, but she didn't have to admit it too easily. His ego was big enough. "I'd understand if you couldn't leave right away. I thought I'd locate Ignacio first, then—"

"Being the boss does have it benefits, and I'd hate to disappoint the big guy."

He wasn't going to make this easy for her. What a shock. All right, then, she'd suck it up. "You up for road trip?" she asked.

Vincent's grin widened. "Why, Lana, I thought you'd never ask."

Chapter Three

"I DON'T LIKE YOU going off like this, *jefe*," Michael said the next night as he followed Vincent down to the private garage below his residence, where their personal vehicles were parked. In Vincent's case, he had two. The first was a Venom Black, 2014 Viper TA, but that wouldn't do for a trip across the Mexican desert. So he headed for the second vehicle, which was also black, but much more substantial. It was a Suburban SUV, with black-tinted and bulletproof windows all around, and a body that was armored right down to and including the undercarriage. Vincent was a powerful vampire, but even the strongest of them could be taken down by enough bullets. A wooden stake might be the traditional method of execution, but anything that tore a vamp's heart apart worked just as well.

"You're just jealous that you're not coming with me," Vincent told his lieutenant as he pulled open the back hatch and threw his duffel into the cargo space.

"Fucking A," Michael agreed. "Why is that anyway? Who's going to watch your back?"

"Lana appears to be quite capable."

"*Lana* would just as soon stick a stake in you."

Vincent slammed the hatch shut and turned with a grin. "You think so? I think she's quite taken with me."

"You're delusional."

"So you don't think I'm irresistible?"

Michael snorted. "Seriously, *jefe*, why do I have to stay here?"

Vincent stopped and faced him directly. "Because I don't want it to be obvious that I'm gone. This is for Raphael. Do you understand what that means? I'm doing a favor for a rival vampire lord. And if that's not enough of a reason to keep this mission on the down low, there's also Enrique's role in whatever went down in Acuña. It can't be a coincidence that Raphael's request shows up two weeks after someone tries to kill him with Enrique's help. And who the hell is Xuan Ignacio that Raphael wants him so bad?"

"*Fuck me*," Michael swore. "You need someone at your back."

"What I need is for you to put pressure on your sources, find out what happened to Raphael's sister. Is she dead? I need to know."

"I'll let you know as soon as I find something, but, Sire—" He waited until his use of the honorific drew Vincent's focused attention. "—do not go to Mexico City without me. No joke."

Vincent nodded. They both knew that there could only be one reason he'd go to Mexico City—to challenge Enrique for the territory. The confrontation was inevitable and had been for a long time. The two vampires had been dancing around it, neither sufficiently motivated to upset the status quo. It was only a matter of lighting the right match. And if Enrique found out Vincent was running all over Mexico at Raphael's request, it might just be the spark that lit the fire.

"No worries on that front, Mikey. If I get anywhere near Mexico City, you'll definitely be there. I'll need you with me."

Michael nodded, still unhappy. "What if something happens here, like at the club the other night? What do I tell the others?"

"You could have handled the club without me," Vincent said offhandedly and strode around to the driver's side of the SUV. "As long as you're here, the others will assume I am, too. But if anyone gets too curious, give me a call, and I'll handle it. I'm taking the sat phone as well as my cell."

He slipped into the driver's seat. "Don't look so sad, Mikey. I'll bring you a present."

Michael raised his hands in a double *fuck you* salute.

Vincent laughed as he closed his door and turned the key, then lowered the window and waved as he drove out of the garage.

LANA LEFT THE hotel without checking out. She was registered for one more night and could have saved money by checking out early, but decided against it. In her business, it never hurt to leave people wondering exactly where you were. By paying for the extra night with an automatic checkout, no one would know she'd already departed for parts unknown. At least not right away. She'd put out the "Do Not Disturb" sign for extra insurance, but that wouldn't fool a determined investigator like her dad or Dave Harrington. She didn't think they'd gotten this far yet, but she preferred to assume the worst. It was the best way to be prepared when the shit finally hit the fan, and it always did eventually.

She went down the back stairs, avoiding the lobby. Her Yukon was parked at the very end of the parking lot. She unlocked it, stashed her duffel in the back, and was standing in the open hatchway scrolling through her contact list for Vincent's number, when a black Suburban rolled up behind her and stopped.

Tossing the phone aside, she pulled out her Sig and turned in a single movement. The black-tinted window closest to her slid down to reveal Vincent behind the wheel, grinning like an idiot. A particularly handsome idiot, but one nonetheless.

"You gonna shoot me before we even get started?"

She gave him a cool look. "Don't tempt me," she said, re-holstering the Sig. "I thought I was picking *you* up."

"I don't believe we discussed it," he said cheerfully. "But since I'm already here, climb in."

"I think we should take my vehicle. It's less conspicuous."

"Where we're going, conspicuous is good. It makes you less of a target."

"That doesn't make any sense."

"It does in Mexico, *querida*. Mine's bulletproof. How about yours?"

Lana scowled, but she had to concede that one to him. "Fine," she agreed. "But we'll switch off driving."

Vincent snorted dismissively. "I don't think so."

"We've got a thousand miles to travel. You drive at night, I'll drive during the day. We'll get there faster."

"We'll travel at night and stop to sleep during the day like civilized people."

"Civilized people sleep at night. And what if there's no place to stay when the sun comes up?"

"There will be."

"How do you know?"

"Because I programmed the damn route, and *I'm* driving," Vincent growled, finally losing his cool.

Lana gave him a smug look, permitting herself a tiny smile of satisfaction. "Fine," she said carelessly, as if the whole issue had never mattered. "Unlock the back."

"It's unlocked," he snapped.

She didn't say anything, but her smile widened as she turned and grabbed her duffel, then walked over and threw it into the Suburban's cargo space. Going back to her Yukon, she gathered the rest of her gear—the backpack with her laptop, portfolio, and identification papers, plus her cooler which she'd filled with ice and Coke from the vending machine, along with some travel food. She frowned, thinking that the vampire probably wouldn't be sharing her candy bars and chips, then wondered exactly what he *would* be eating. Not her, that's for sure.

She dumped everything in Vincent's back seat, then climbed into the passenger side of the Suburban, sinking down into a seat that was far more luxurious than the one in her Yukon. Maybe it was a good thing that they were taking Vincent's SUV, after all. Although she didn't think it said much for their future working relationship that they couldn't even get out of the parking lot without an argument.

"I'm not sure this is going to work," she said as Vincent made a tire-screeching turn south onto Route 15, which would take them almost all the way to their destination

"What's that?" he asked absently, cutting around and in front of the other cars, as if they were on the Daytona speedway instead of a public highway.

"You and me, working together. We don't seem to get along."

He swiveled his head to give her a long look, and his gold earring flashed in the lights from the dash. "We'll get along fine, *querida*. You'll see."

Lana rolled her eyes at the endearment, but didn't say anything. She was determined to get this job done, which meant she was stuck with him for the next several days. But she was a professional. She could swallow a little bit of irritation if it meant finding this ghost vampire of Raphael's, doing the job, and getting back home.

It didn't hit her until about a hundred miles later that she'd be doing a lot more than sitting next to Vincent in his big SUV. She'd be sharing a hotel with him, too.

Fuck.

Chapter Four

LANA REACHED FOR her bottle of water, snatching her hand back when she brushed against Vincent's arm that was resting on the center console. You'd think a huge SUV like the Suburban would have plenty of room for everyone, but Vincent was so damn *big,* and his shoulders so wide. It was no wonder that he was constantly draping himself over the console and shoving into her space. She slanted a look his way and saw one side of his mouth curled up in a smug grin. He'd noticed her reaction to their touch, of course. He noticed everything. She was beginning to question her original strategy for dealing with him. She'd thought cool and professional was the way to go, but her indifference only seemed to goad him into doing things to irk her.

Things like . . . that! He'd just picked up her water bottle and brought it to his mouth, taking a mouthful as she stared in disbelief. Did he expect her to drink out of that now? She didn't even share water bottles with people she knew.

"So, Lana," he said, putting the bottle back in the cupholder without looking at her. "How'd you become a bounty hunter? It's not exactly a career choice most little girls dream of, is it?"

Lana stared at him until he glanced over at her, his eyebrows raised in question.

"We're going to converse now?" she asked coolly.

Vincent smiled slightly, his gaze once again focused on the strip of highway ahead of them. "Sure," he said. "Why not? We've got hundreds of miles to kill."

Lana studied him a moment longer, then said, "Okay. A question for a question. I answer one, then you answer one."

He shrugged. "Fine by me."

"My father's a bounty hunter," she said, answering his question. "How did you become a vampire?"

"Oh, no," Vincent said, letting out a dismissive laugh. "That's not how the game's played. I already know your father's a bounty hunter. I want to know why *you* became a hunter like your dad. What does your mother think?"

"That's two questions, but okay. I pretty much grew up in my dad's office. My mom had a job, so the office manager was my babysitter, and the guys who worked for him considered themselves my uncles. Some of them still do."

"Your mother didn't work for your father, like you do?"

"No, she was in sales. She still is, but now she's mostly busy being a wife to someone else. My parents divorced when I was eleven years old. They shared custody until I was twelve, when my mom married her lover and moved to California. They couldn't agree on custody at that point, so they made me choose."

"That's fucked."

"Yes, it was. I was *twelve*. At the time, I told myself it was because they both wanted me so badly. But now, I think it was because neither one of them cared either way." Lana realized she was sounding more than a little bitter and moved on. "Anyway, the choice came down to what mattered the most to *me*. And twelve-year-old girls are pretty shallow. All I knew was that if I went with my mom, I'd have to change schools and make all new friends. And I wasn't that good at making friends in the first place. So I picked my dad."

"Do you love your father?"

"Of course," Lana said, but it sounded weak even to her own ears. Vincent was silent for a moment, and she hoped he hadn't noticed.

"Do you get along?"

"I became a bounty hunter, didn't I? I work for the man."

"That's not what I asked."

"What *are* you asking? You're not my therapist, Vincent."

"Fair enough. What about your mother?"

"We get along okay. We've never had much in common."

"Why'd you have trouble making friends?"

"Too much of a tomboy, I guess. I was the son my dad always wanted."

"Who was your best friend? Girls always have those, right?"

Lana smiled, remembering. "Gretchen Foster. She lived in the apartment building behind my dad's office. We sort of bonded in our mutual misery."

"She was a tomboy like you?"

"Oh, no. Gretchen was beautiful."

"You're beautiful."

Lana blinked in surprise at that simple statement. He said it so matter-of-factly, not like a come-on, but as if he really meant it. She was silent long enough that he glanced over at her.

"You are," he said quietly, seeming puzzled by her response.

"Yeah, well," she mumbled, then finally said, "I definitely wasn't then, but Gretchen was. And teenage girls can be mean. All the guys loved Gretchen. She never went out with any of them, but they hung around her anyway, and the other girls hated it. They started a rumor that Gretchen was easy, and that's why all the guys liked her. That she'd put out for any guy who wanted it."

"But she wasn't."

"The very opposite. I don't think Gretchen had so much as a date until junior year in high school. Her parents were very strict. She went to school and came home right after."

"So how'd the two of you get together?"

"Like I said, her parents were strict. They expected good grades, and Gretchen had a problem with math. I was kind of a whiz at it, so we traded. She solved my problem and I solved hers."

"I don't understand."

"She read all the fashion magazines, knew all about makeup and clothes and stuff. I didn't have a mom, and my dad didn't exactly keep *Vogue* lying around the office. So, Gretchen taught me girl stuff, how to dress, do my hair, my makeup. And I tutored her in math."

"What'd your dad think about his *son* learning girl stuff?"

She laughed. "Yeah, once I sprouted breasts, he did a complete one-eighty. He decided he didn't want me around the office as much. I think he worried about his guys getting ideas." She almost added, *At least until he picked out my husband for me.* Thank God, she didn't. Vincent would have been all over *that* one.

"Where's Gretchen now?" he asked.

"We went to college together, and she met a guy. They got married after graduation and have two kids. They live in New York."

"Happy ending."

"Yeah, it was." Lana lapsed into silence, then frowned. "And that was way more than one question. You owe me."

Vincent laughed with such joy that Lana forgot to breathe for a moment. Vincent scowling or smirking was gorgeous. But Vincent laughing? That went so far beyond gorgeous she didn't have a word for it.

"I guess I do," he agreed, seeming unaware of her fascination. "Ask away."

Lana swallowed, giving her overreacting hormones a chance to cool down. Maybe she needed to get laid more often if a simple laugh could do that to her. How long had it been since she'd had sex? She frowned. So long she couldn't remember exactly. She'd have to remedy that when she got home. But right now, she had to deal with the vampire next to her, and he was waiting for her to ask a question.

"Okay," she said. "I still want to know how you became a vampire. And . . ." And what? She had to say something before he noticed she was babbling. "And, I get a second question too, so how old are you?"

"Those are pretty personal questions for a vampire, Lana," he said, with no trace of his prior humor.

"So was asking me about my parents' divorce," she countered quietly.

He nodded. "You're right. All right, then, settle back, *querida*, and I'll tell you a tale of two brothers.

Texas, 1876

"PLEASE BE CAREFUL, *mijo*. And take care of your brother."

Vincent buckled the last strap on his saddle roll and turned to his diminutive mother. "Mama." He hugged her carefully, like the delicate doll she resembled. Even with two giant sons and more than twenty-five years of living in sin with his father, she was still the most beautiful woman on the ranch. That might be a son's love talking, but he saw the light in his father's eyes, too, every time he looked at her. She'd been a poor girl from Guatemala, a maid in his grandparents' big house, when she'd caught his father's eye. Those same grandparents now refused to acknowledge Vincent or his younger brother because they were bastards. Born of love, but out of wedlock. His father was the only son and scion of his wealthy family's cattle empire, but they'd sworn they'd disown him if he married so far beneath his station.

They'd gotten their way, but so had Vincent's father. He hadn't married his Guatemalan lover, the mother of his sons. But he'd never married anyone else either. Vincent and his brother, John, had grown up on the ranch. Not in the big house, of course. Their parentage went unacknowledged, even though everyone on the ranch knew about it. Maybe their horses were a little better bred, their tack a shade more finely made, but as soon as they were old enough, they'd worked from sunup to sundown just like any of the other ranch hands.

And today, the two brothers were off on their first cattle drive, heading for Abilene and the giant livestock markets there. Normally, they'd have gone on a cattle drive a long time ago, but their darling mother had objected, saying it was too dangerous, and their father could deny her nothing. So, year after year, her sons had remained behind.

John hadn't minded so much. He was content on the ranch, apprenticed to the cattle doctor, which was why he wasn't here enduring their mother's tears as her sons went off to Abilene. John was on the other side of the ranch helping the doctor load supplies. Vincent, on the other hand, wasn't content to live his entire life in one place. He wanted to see the world beyond the ranch, to visit the big city of Abilene, to see the wide plains of Kansas and beyond. Anywhere and everywhere that wasn't the ranch where he'd grown up.

"We'll be careful, Mama," he assured her, kissing her forehead. "We always are."

"*Sí*, I know. I will wait for you."

"Take care of Papa."

"Pfft." His mother made a dismissive gesture, but Vincent saw the love in her eyes, too.

The drive boss shouted the order to mount up, and Vincent sucked in a relieved breath

"I have to go, Mama. We'll be careful, and we'll see you before the Nativity."

"Oy, such a long time, *mi hijo,*" she whispered fervently and hugged him tightly. She was strong for such a tiny woman.

Vincent extricated himself with another kiss on her forehead. She'd keep him here all day if he didn't break it up now. He swung up onto his horse and, with a jaunty salute, bid farewell to his beautiful mother, not knowing it was the last time he'd ever see her.

"CAN'T WE JUST go home?" John asked months later, throwing a stick at Vincent from his seat on the other side of their small fire. "Wasn't Abilene enough?"

The cattle drive was over, and it had been nowhere near as exciting as Vincent had hoped. Their big adventure had been nothing but months of dirty, hard work, long days in the saddle, and bad food. On the other hand, he and his brother were now free to make their way back home at their own pace, and Vincent was determined to make the most of it.

"One Mexican cantina, little brother, a few miles out of our way. That's all I ask. This might be our only chance."

"The cattle go to market every year, Vicentillo."

"But who knows if we'll be allowed to go? If our grandfather dies, Papa will own the ranch, and he'll never send us again. Mama won't let him."

"*If* Grandfather dies," John snorted. "That old man is too mean to die."

"Even the devil gets his due, Juanito."

"Very well, one cantina, but you—" He broke off suddenly, spinning to stare into the darkness. "Who's there?" he called, raising his voice as he scrambled for the gun belt he'd set aside earlier.

Vincent stood at the same time, his Smith and Wesson already in his hand as the bandits rushed their small camp—filthy, hard-looking men who came in shooting, muzzles flashing in the darkness. Vincent watched in horror as the first bullets tore into his brother's chest. John flew through the air, driven by the force of their impact. Vincent's finger jerked on the trigger, his weapon exploding with heat, but it was too late. A searing pain tore into his gut, and he found himself slammed backward onto the hard dirt of the Texas plain. He twisted, searching for John, reaching for the brother he was supposed to take care of, the brother he'd promised to bring home to their mother for Nativity.

Jagged pain sliced into his chest. And suddenly, he knew that neither one of them would ever see home again.

Chapter Five

Mexico, present day

"THAT'S HORRIBLE," Lana said, staring at the vampire sitting next to her. He'd recited his story with no emotion, as if it had all happened to someone else. He didn't say anything, but stared straight ahead, his gaze seeming to be riveted on the narrow white strip that was all they could see of the road in their headlights. They were on a particularly barren part of the highway, so he was traveling well above the speed limit. But he handled the big SUV as easily as he might have something low and sweet and built for speed, one hand on the steering wheel, the other draped over the center console, fingers tapping a rhythm to music only he could hear.

Lana could understand his need for emotional distance from such painful events. And she kept forgetting that, although he looked like a man in his mid-twenties, he was much, much older than that. Maybe what to her was a terrible tragedy, because she was just hearing about it, was for him a distant memory. She might even have believed that, if he wasn't trying so hard to pretend it didn't matter.

"I'm not that familiar with guns from back then, but if they shot you in the chest, why didn't you die?"

He glanced over at her then, but only to scoff. "What? You don't think vampires are dead? Isn't that what all of you humans believe about us?"

Lana forgave him for being a rude jackass, given the terrible events he'd just relived for her.

"I don't know about humans in general, but *I* know you're not dead," she told him. She didn't say anything else, because while she knew they definitely didn't rise from the dead the way some popular fiction had it, she had no idea what *did* happen to make them vampires. The only person who might have been able to fill her in was Cynthia Leighton, and while Leighton had passed on quite a few helpful tidbits of information over the course of their business together, the two of them were exactly that—business associates rather than friends. They exchanged details and results, not gossip.

That was partly why she'd agreed to exchange information with Vincent. He'd been curious about her—although Lana couldn't imagine why, other than to fuel what was, no doubt, his need to charm every woman he came into contact with. But since her history was quite ordinary, she'd been willing to trade the humdrum facts of her life for the far more intriguing details of his.

Vincent had gone quiet now, though. He didn't seem inclined to play their game any longer, even though he hadn't answered her first and most important question yet—how he'd become a vampire. Obviously, he hadn't died the night he was shot, but just as obviously, it had somehow led to his becoming a vampire. She didn't think he'd have shared something so personal otherwise. And what about his younger brother? Had John died? Or had he become a vampire, too?

She was dying to ask, but didn't have the heart for it. For all that Vincent was acting cool and unaffected, no one could recount their own near-death experience and not feel *something*.

"Story time's over for tonight," he said finally. "The sun will be up soon. We have to think about stopping."

Lana checked the in-dash nav system. They'd made good time, although they'd been forced to slow down for the more-populated areas. Vincent was determined to keep a low profile for reasons he hadn't shared with her, so he didn't want to risk getting pulled over for something as trivial as speeding. They could probably get away with nothing more than a fine, but even that would create an official record that a determined person could use to track their whereabouts.

They were also slowed by all that bulletproofing which made the Suburban an excellent choice for crossing dangerous territory, but also made the vehicle a lot heavier. It drank fuel like a motherfucker, and since there were stretches where they couldn't be sure of a gasoline station, they sometimes had to stop even before the tank was empty, just to be sure it didn't happen at the wrong time.

And let's not forget that at each place they stopped, Vincent had to charm every female in sight. Old, young . . . hell, if there was a baby girl around, he'd probably have charmed her, too. And none of the women seemed to care that Vincent was traveling with Lana. For all they knew, she could be his girlfriend, even his wife. It didn't matter. The worst one had been the teenager at the first place they'd stopped. She'd taken one look at Lana, scoped her up and down, and completely dismissed her. As if the girl *knew* that Vincent would happily replace Lana with some dopey teenage gas station cashier.

Not that Lana wanted him for herself. Hell, no. It was just the principle of the thing.

She narrowed her gaze on Vincent, then rolled her eyes in disgust, as much with herself as with him. What did she care how many women he flirted with? She pulled out her cell phone and punched up their location. Her energy would be better spent finding a place to stop before morning.

"What about Guamúchil?" she asked, zooming in on the map. "We can stop there. It's a good-sized city, and we shouldn't have any—"

"We'll be stopping before that," Vincent interrupted. "A small town about fifty miles northeast."

"I don't see—"

"It won't be on the map. The town's too small."

"Then how do you—"

"I've been there before. There's a cantina. She has a couple of rooms and the place should be empty this time of year."

She. Of course there would be a *she.* It seemed that men, or maybe she should say *males*, were the same everywhere. At least the kind of males she seemed doomed to meet. They were risk-takers, thrill-seekers, high testosterone, adrenaline junkies who drew women like flies and seemed incapable of settling for just one. She reminded herself that she didn't give a damn how many women Vincent charmed, seduced, or fucked.

"Did you program it into the nav?"

He glanced at her, perhaps sensing something of her mood, but his only verbal reply was a terse, "Yep."

Almost twenty miles later, the nav system dinged a warning. Vincent immediately slowed, coming to a near stop in order to make a sharp left turn onto a road that Lana wasn't sure she'd have noticed even in daylight. It wasn't paved. She could see, and feel, that much. The Suburban took to the new surface with relative ease, but then, Vincent was barely doing thirty miles an hour. She could hear rocks pinging off the undercarriage, but there were no potholes and the tires weren't slipping as much as she'd have expected if they'd gone truly off-road.

Vincent suddenly turned off the headlights, but kept going as if nothing had changed. Lana couldn't make out a damn thing.

"What are you doing?" she asked, straining to see ahead.

"I can see better without them out here."

Lana shifted her gaze back and forth between Vincent and the pitch black road. "You can?"

A tiny smile lightened his expression for the first time since he'd interrupted his own story. "I can. Don't worry, Lana. I'll take good care of you."

"I'll take care of myself, thank you. You just drive."

His smile grew. "Whatever you say."

"What about this cantina?"

"What about it? It's fairly popular with the locals, mostly because of the music. There's a classical guitarist there. One of the finest in the world."

"What's his name?"

Vincent shook his head. "You won't have heard of him."

"How do you know?" she demanded, feeling insulted. She happened to like classical guitar.

"It's not you, *querida*. No one's heard of him unless they've been to this place. He doesn't record, he doesn't travel. He simply plays his guitar."

Lana gave him a curious look. There were layers to Vincent Kuxim. Layers wrapped up in a very pretty package. She blinked and brought herself back to reality. Pretty or not, he was a vampire and a player. And she wanted no part of either.

Chapter Six

"*VICENTILLO, MI corazón! Tanto tiempo sin vernos!*"

Lana stood in the doorway of the small, crowded cantina and watched as the woman greeted Vincent like a long-lost friend. Or a lover. She called him her *heart*, although she did add that she hadn't seen him in a long time. So maybe they were old lovers, still friends. *Fuck buddies, maybe*, Lana thought nastily and didn't know why she cared.

The woman had been beautiful in her youth. You could see it in the smooth, golden glow of her skin, the flash of her dark brown eyes, the soft curve of her jaw. She was lovely still, but age and life were reflected in her face now, too. That life had been a good one, though, if her broad smile was any indication. She was the very picture of a woman who'd found a life she wanted and lived it to its fullest.

Lana wondered at the stab of envy cutting into her chest. She had a good life, didn't she? She was doing what she wanted, something she loved. Sure, she couldn't see herself chasing down bad guys when she was forty . . . or fifty, like Vincent's latest admirer. But for now, she was exactly where she wanted to be. Wasn't she?

Vincent certainly seemed as happy to see the woman as she was to see him. He had a big smile on his face—not the snarky grin he usually favored Lana with, but a genuine smile filled with warmth and something more than simple affection. Had they been lovers? Their close embrace certainly spoke of a long and intimate familiarity.

"*Marisol, te me haces más bella cada vez que to miro,*" Vincent said, gazing down at her. *You're more beautiful every time I see you.*

The woman, Marisol, brushed away the compliment the way beautiful women did when they thought the sentiment was true, but were pretending modesty. She and Vincent kissed cheeks and then went in for a full-on lip lock. Okay, maybe that was an exaggeration. Their mouths touched, but Lana didn't think there was any tongue involved. Once the kissing was done with, they hugged again, then exchanged a few soft words. Marisol patted Vincent's chest and started toward Lana, moving with purpose. Lana drew back before she realized that Marisol wasn't aiming for her, but for a small desk in a shallow alcove on the wall to her left.

Vincent followed and the two of them continued their conversation, speaking Spanish so rapidly that Lana had to strain to catch what they were saying. Even then, she couldn't be sure she was translating every word correctly, but the general context was clear.

"Rodrigo showed up again, and you know I can't say *no* to him," Marisol was saying over her shoulder to Vincent as she bent over the desk.

"Rodrigo? Shouldn't he be in *your* bed?"

"Vincent! What kind of question is that?" she exclaimed, turning to gaze up at him, one hand to her chest in a gesture as scandalized as it was fake. "Besides, you know I like younger men," she added with a lascivious wink that confirmed Lana's earlier suspicions.

"More than one, as I recall," Vincent teased back, which had Marisol fanning her face.

"Well," she said, clearly still flustered by the memory Vincent had invoked, "it means I have only the one room, but it's yours if—"

"That's fine," he assured her, even though Lana found the words anything but reassuring. One room? "Lana's my bodyguard," Vincent continued. "She'll stay with me."

Lana's stare bored holes in his back as she contemplated all the ways she could kill him without moving a foot from where she stood, but he remained blissfully unaware. So much for vampire telepathy. Either that, or he was ignoring her.

Marisol handed Vincent a key, then stretched up to kiss him, her hand lingering along his jaw. "You know where it is, my darling. Will I see you tomorrow night?"

"Of course, do you think I would leave without hearing Chencho play?"

"Sweet boy." She patted his cheek, then hurried back to her guests, but not without giving Lana a thorough head to toe scan on her way past.

"Come on," Vincent said, turning toward Lana and tilting his head to the outside door. "We have time to clean up and get you something to eat before sunrise."

Lana couldn't help noticing that his voice was all-business, completely lacking the warmth he'd shown to Marisol.

"I'm your bodyguard?"

"I thought you'd prefer that to lover."

She scowled at him. "Look, if you'd like to stay here with—"

"Lana."

She looked up to meet his gold-flecked eyes.

"I'm tired," he told her. "I may be a vampire, but I don't enjoy sitting in a car for hours at a time any more than you do. I want a shower, and then I'm going to sleep."

"Sleep as in . . ."

"Yes," he said, looking somewhat bemused at her inability to come right out and say he'd be doing his vampire thing. "*Sleep as in.* Now, can we go to the room?"

She turned to follow him out the door. "I can't share a room with you."

"Why not?" he asked, leading the way down a narrow path between the cantina and another low building.

"I barely know you."

He shrugged. "Your virtue is safe with me. I'll be dead to the world."

Lana frowned. "I told you, I know vampires aren't dead."

He turned around to face her. "It's a saying, Lana," he informed her dryly, then took a curving path to the left, which ended at a small cottage with two separate entrances. They were on opposite ends of the building and each was marked by a short walk and a wooden door painted a bright color. Vincent's door appeared to be blue, although in the dim light, she wouldn't have sworn on it. Both doors were framed by crawling vines that Lana thought to be jasmine, given their lovely, light scent. Although, with her knowledge of flowers, they could have been almost anything else and she wouldn't have known the difference.

Vincent unlocked the door, then pushed it open and walked inside without turning on a light. Lana paused in the doorway to let her eyes adjust, then crossed to a small table and turned on a lamp.

"Sorry," he said from across the room where he was already stripping off his jacket. "I forget sometimes."

"Forget what?"

"That humans can't see in the dark."

"You can?"

He nodded absently. "Quite well. Do you mind if I take the first shower?"

Lana blinked at this reminder that she was sharing a room with Vincent. Vincent of the broad shoulders and washboard abs. She sighed. She was definitely earning her paycheck on this one.

"Sure, go ahead."

He grabbed the hem of his long-sleeved T-shirt and pulled it over his head. She swallowed a second sigh. She'd forgotten the tattoo. Broad shoulders, washboard abs, and a tattoo. Good thing he was ugly. Fuck.

"I need to get something from the SUV," she said, knowing it was lame even as she said it. "Will you be okay here?"

"Quite safe," he assured her and began popping the buttons on his 501s.

Lana caught a glimpse of flat belly and chiseled obliques and yanked the door open. "I'll be right back," she said. Then she quickly made her escape.

VINCENT GRINNED as the door closed behind Lana. He'd needed some privacy and figured if he started undressing, she'd run for it. Nice to know he hadn't lost his touch completely, though he'd begun to wonder. She did seem impervious to his charm, but maybe not his body. Hmmm.

Marisol clearly didn't think he'd lost his touch, or anything else. If he'd even hinted, she'd have dumped the young man in her bed and spent the night with him instead. But he wasn't here for that. Besides, he was determined to win Lana over. She was resisting him for now, but he did love a challenge. And he didn't like to be ignored.

He heard her footsteps fade down the walkway and pulled out his satellite phone. Michael hadn't called all day, which he took as a good sign. But he wanted to be sure. He entered the number from memory. He didn't program numbers into this phone, since the fact that he was carrying it meant he was traveling, often in unfamiliar territory. And that usually meant there was the potential for danger. Best not to hand out information to one's enemies.

Michael answered on the second ring. "Good evening, Sire."

"Strictly speaking, it's morning, Mikey."

"Yes, but there's generally nothing good about morning, so . . ."

"Point taken. Anything I need to know?"

"No one's noticed you're gone, if that's what you're asking."

"I don't know whether to be hurt or relieved."

"Be relieved. The club's shut down for repairs, so activity is on the slow side. And there have been no calls from Enrique."

"Speaking of . . . any news on Raphael's sister?"

"Possibly. I have one report that says she's dead. I'm trying to confirm it, but my source says she was questioned, determined to be useless, and then executed on the spot."

"Cold. Was it Enrique?"

"On that my source is unsure. It was done in Mexico City, in Enrique's headquarters, but indications are that he was not the executioner."

"Interesting. Of course, her very presence in his HQ is evidence that Enrique plotted against Raphael."

"Yeah. Tell me something, *jefe*. Alexandra was double bound to Raphael. They were human siblings by birth, plus he was her master for a couple of centuries, right?"

"Something like that."

"So, even if he wasn't her master anymore, wouldn't he know if she was dead? I mean, Raphael is hella powerful. Wouldn't he feel her death anyway?"

Vincent considered Michael's question. There was no bond stronger than that of a vampire and his Sire—or so he'd been told. He'd never felt particularly attached to Enrique, that's for sure. His loyalty to the old man was based solely on practicality and personal ambition. On the other hand, he was Michael's Sire and they were tight. He'd die to defend his child, and he was pretty sure Michael felt just as strongly about him.

But Raphael had been Alexandra's master, not her Sire. The story was that they'd been turned during the same attack, but by different Sires. He'd heard that it had been a couple of centuries before Raphael had rescued Alexandra from unknown but awful circumstances. He'd then killed her Sire and had been her master ever since. And while that bond might not have the same strength as that of a Sire, two hundred years was a hell of a long time. And as Michael said, they had the sibling bond going for them, too.

"You may be right," he said thoughtfully. "In fact, I bet you are. So, if Alexandra's dead, then Raphael already knows it. So what's his next step? He hires Lana Arnold to deliver a message to a vampire no one's seen in more than a hundred years. At least no one reliable. And not just that, but he writes *me* a letter, asking for help, and making it clear he'd prefer that I be there when she finds said vampire. Those events have *got* to be related."

"My thoughts, exactly. So what're you going to do?"

Vincent blew out a long breath. "If a powerhouse like Raphael thinks that I need to meet Xuan Ignacio, then I'm going to find the fucker and figure out why. I'll keep the sat phone live, if you need me."

"And remember your promise."

Vincent frowned, but didn't say anything.

"No Mexico City without me," Michael reminded him.

"Not a chance, Mikey."

"Stay safe, *jefe*."

"Talk to you tomorrow."

Vincent disconnected, then stripped off the rest of his clothes and walked naked to the shower. He hadn't been lying to Lana. The Suburban was a comfortable ride, but spending that many hours sitting on his ass was exhausting. And his trip down memory lane with Lana hadn't been a thrill either. He'd liked hearing her story, but then for some reason, he'd volunteered his own, even though he hadn't thought about that final trip with his brother in a long time.

He turned on the water in the shower and waited until it ran hot. Marisol's cabins were fairly primitive, with one exception. She had excellent water pressure and wasn't afraid to use it. He stepped under the spray and let the pounding heat wash away the long night.

THE SHOWER WAS still running when Lana ventured back to the cottage. She cursed under her breath. What was he doing in there? She'd intentionally taken her time, strolling around the grounds, lingering outside the cantina, listening to the sounds of revelry inside. There'd been music, but it hadn't been the classical guitar player that Vincent had talked about. Either he'd played earlier in the night, which seemed likely, or he wasn't here yet. She'd heard Vincent say something about staying long enough tomorrow night to hear *Chencho* play. That must be the guitarist.

But now she'd seen everything there was to see without venturing out into the desert. And Vincent was still in the shower, leaving his discarded clothes scattered all over the floor on the other side of the bed.

The bed. One bed.

She looked around, trying to figure out where she could sleep. Obviously, Vincent would take the bed, because typical male, he had no shame. He would have stripped naked right in front of her if she hadn't left. He clearly expected her to share the bed with him. In fact, he'd no doubt take pleasure in knowing that it made her uncomfortable. Granted, it was a very big bed, with plenty of room for two people to sleep well apart. Marisol didn't stint on her cottages. Colorful rugs had been scattered over tiled floors, and heavy drapes covered the lone window, so there'd be no problem with sunlight. The king-sized bed took up much of the room, but there was a tiny round table and two chairs by the window, and small, square bedside tables on either side of the bed that were just big enough to hold some personal items along with the compact lamp that stood on each of them.

Lana rounded to the far side of the bed and turned on the second lamp. There was enough room between the bed and the round dining table for her to sleep on the floor. It wasn't the most comfortable sleeping arrangement, but she'd had worse. She eyed the bed's fluffy down comforter. That'd help with the hard tile floor. She wondered if vampires needed comforters when they slept.

"We can both sleep on the bed."

Lana squelched the urge to jump at the unexpected sound of Vincent's voice. She hadn't even heard the shower turn off. Some bounty hunter she was.

She turned . . . and immediately lowered her gaze to avoid seeing Vincent in a towel and nothing else. "I don't think that's appropriate," she said, pretending to study the floor. "I can—"

"Lana."

He didn't say anything else until she finally looked up and met his eyes. And only his eyes!

"Once I'm asleep, I don't move, *querida*. You'll be perfectly safe."

"I'm not worried about safety," she protested. "It just doesn't seem—"

"I thought I was the nineteenth century person here. What happened to women's lib and all that?"

"Fine. I'll sleep on the damn bed. Happy now?"

He grinned at her. "I am. Are you hungry?"

Her gaze dropped briefly downward before snapping back to his face. "Yes," she said almost defiantly. And for the first time since she'd met him, Vincent seemed somewhat taken aback by her one word response. Not rattled, but definitely off his game . . . for all of a few seconds.

But then his grin widened slowly and his eyes went lazy. "You can eat anything you want, *querida*," he murmured, his voice a deep, sexy purr.

Lana's breath caught in her lungs. Vincent Kuxim was too sexy by half and she was crazy to be alone with him in this tiny room with its big bed. She managed to give him a cool look, raising a single, skeptical eyebrow.

"Dinner," she told him dryly. "Is Marisol still serving food?"

Vincent winked at her, not at all put off by her indifferent response. "She'll have something ready for us by now. She likes to feed me."

"Will she mind—?"

"You're my bodyguard. You have to eat. Are you going to shower?"

Lana felt gritty and sweaty, as if she'd walked those 300 plus miles through the desert instead of traveling in air-conditioned comfort. But she was *not* going to get undressed with a half-naked Vincent in the room.

"I'll shower later," she told him. "I'll wash my face and hands before we go over, but I can wait until you're finished."

"I'm done with the bathroom. Why don't you go ahead, and I'll be dressed by the time you're finished."

Lana nodded. That sounded like the perfect arrangement. She took off her jacket and draped it on the back of a chair, then unzipped her duffel and retrieved the smaller case that held her toiletries. Stepping over the pile of Vincent's clothes, she started for the bathroom before realizing that Vincent, still half-naked, was blocking the bathroom doorway. Not wanting to seem like a fainting virgin, she was prepared to scoot past him when he suddenly stepped out of her way.

She still had to get too close to him, close enough that she could smell the clean scent of his skin, could feel the heat rolling off his big, shower-warmed body. Was it the shower, she wondered. Or was he simply as warm as a regular human man would be? Weren't vampires supposed to be cold? She was tempted to ask him, but remembered abruptly that he was standing there in a towel. Deciding that now was definitely not the time for a vampire tutorial, she kept her eyes elsewhere until she was safely inside, then pushed the door closed and finally let out the breath she'd been holding.

Setting her toiletry case on the sink, she grabbed a clean hand towel and wiped down the mirror so she could see the damage the day had done. She nearly groaned out loud. No wonder that teenager had dismissed her. She looked awful. Her eyes had dark circles and she was sweaty and disheveled, with flyaway strands of her hair tangled around her face and falling out of her once-neat braid. That explained Marisol's doubtful look, too. She seemed like the kind of woman who always looked her best, even if just stepping out for a gallon of milk. One look at Lana, and she'd probably decided that, bodyguard or not, Lana wasn't worthy of her precious Vincent.

Lana smiled at her own reflection, vain enough to feel a spark of smug satisfaction that she and Vincent were sleeping together, at least as far as Marisol knew.

She straightened and turned on the hot water at the sink. If they were going to have dinner with Marisol, then she'd have to make some effort, for her own pride if nothing else. She might not scream sensuality the way the other woman did, but she wasn't *that* bad either. Vincent had said she was beautiful, although she didn't believe him. She'd make an effort tonight, though. Not for Marisol, and not for Vincent. But for herself. And for Gretchen.

The room was empty when she emerged from the bathroom, and her first thought was that if she'd known Vincent was going to leave, she'd have taken a damn shower and felt a hell of a lot better. Too late now. She'd washed her face and arms, brushed her teeth and put on deodorant. That, plus a clean shirt and Levis, instead of her combats, would have to do. She'd also freed her heavy hair from its long braid and brushed it out. She was still re-braiding it when she opened the outside door and found Vincent sitting in perfect stillness on a slatted wooden chair to one side of the walkway.

It was a beautiful night, a fact that she'd missed while zooming across the desert in the blacked-out Suburban. The moon was at three-quarters and waxing, its silver light painting the desert in hues of black and gray. This far out from the city lights, the sky was perfectly clear, and there were plenty of stars to be seen. It was the kind of night that tempted one to find someplace to lie back and simply stare up at the universe. She shivered slightly, the air cool after the warmth of the room. It wasn't cold enough to break out the puffy coats, but there was enough of a chill in the air that she was grateful for the tank top she'd pulled on under her long-sleeved T-shirt and combat jacket.

Vincent looked over when she approached him, her braid over her shoulder as she finished tying it off with a completely unsexy coated rubber band.

"Do you ever wear your hair down?" he asked, his deep voice an unexpected caress of velvet in the moonlight.

Lana felt an odd tug in her chest at the question, implying as it did an awareness of her as a woman, not simply a bounty hunter.

"Not when I'm working," she told him, careful to keep her voice casual. "It gets in the way."

Vincent studied her for a moment, long enough that she began to feel uncomfortable and had to fight the urge to twist the long braid in her hands.

"Are you ever not working, Lana?"

"Of course. When I'm home and stuff."

"And stuff," he repeated with a slight smile. He waited a moment, then said, "Well, even working women need food. Are you ready?"

"Yep. Do you have the key?"

He stood, then pulled the key out of his pocket and handed it to her. It was still warm from his body, and she was tempted yet again to ask him about vampire body temperatures. But something about the night didn't invite intimate questions like that. Or maybe the opposite was true—the night was already far too intimate and she didn't want to go there.

She walked back to lock the door, then returned and held the key out to him.

"You keep it," he said. "In a little over an hour, you and that door will be the only things standing between me and sudden death. I'd rather you have the key."

Lana blinked in surprise as she digested what he was saying. She'd known all along that he would *sleep* during the daylight hours, but now that the time was upon them, it frightened her a little. She really *would* be his only line of defense.

"Don't worry, *querida*," he said, tugging at the braid that still lay across her breast. "I've stayed with Marisol many times over the years. We're among friends."

"How long's it been?" she asked suddenly.

"How long's what been?"

"Since you've stayed here," she said, then felt her face heat as she rushed to explain. "I only mean that things have changed in Mexico over the last few years. Places that were once safe might not be anymore."

"You're right. But Marisol is well connected and, frankly, so am I. The forces behind the recent violence, what your government calls TCOs—"

"TransNational Criminal Organizations," Lana provided, her brain already conjuring up conspiracies between vampires and the cartels who controlled most of Mexico.

"Yes, exactly. They enjoy what you might call a detente with the vampire community. They don't touch what's ours—people or businesses—and we don't rip the beating hearts from their chests."

Lana frowned. "You're kidding, right?"

"Not a bit," he assured her.

"So, you do business with the *narcos*?"

"Not me personally, and none of my people either. But I can't account for everyone else. That's Enrique's job."

Lana found that barely reassuring. But since she wasn't here to go into business with Enrique or even Vincent, she let it go. Once this job was over, she'd go back to Arizona and probably never see Vincent again. That should have made her happy, but it didn't. And since she didn't want to examine *why* it didn't, she let that go, too.

"If we only have an hour until sunrise," she said, changing the subject, "we should get going."

"By all means." He gestured down the curving walkway, then fell into step beside her. As they came around the low building separating them from the main cantina, the mellow sound of guitar music began to drift around them.

"Is that the guitarist you talked about?" she asked in surprise. "Is he still playing?"

"His name's Chencho, and that is his music, but it's a recording."

"How can you tell?"

"For one thing, he never plays this late. For another, the sound is too cold. That's a CD. An LP would sound better."

"LP. You mean an actual vinyl record? They were all scratchy and stuff. Digital sound is cleaner, it's supposed to be nearly perfect."

"It is, and some people prefer that. But art is human expression, and if there's one thing I've learned, it's that humans are far from perfect."

"But vampires are?"

"Are what? Perfect? Hell, no. Perfection is boring, Lana. Perfection is death."

"You know, you never answered my second question," she said thoughtfully, struck by his philosophical musings on the human condition.

"Which one's that?" he asked, even though she was certain he remembered.

"How old are you?"

"I'll save that for the next leg of our journey together," he told her, stepping up and opening the cantina door with a grand gesture.

"That's not until tomorrow night," she reminded him.

"I'm aware, *querida*. Let's have dinner."

Lana was already walking through the open door when his words registered. "Are you eating, too?" she asked in surprise.

"*Vicentillo, mi amor!*" Marisol appeared like magic from the next room, a hand held out in greeting, which Vincent promptly grasped and brought up to his lips for a lingering kiss.

As he straightened, he looked right at Lana and said, "Dinner is served."

Chapter Seven

LANA CRACKED OPEN the bathroom door after her shower. Cool air rushed in as she peeked at the bed where Vincent lay sound asleep. Or whatever. What did you call a vampire's daytime sleep? Did he dream? Maybe she'd use one of her questions tonight to ask him that. But right now, she was mostly concerned with ascertaining that he was, in fact, truly out of it and that he wasn't going to witness her naked walk into their shared room.

She'd considered taking her clothes with her into the bathroom, but one, they'd get wet from the shower's steam, and two, the idea had seemed a little too maiden-auntish, even for her.

The room was dark, with only one lamp burning on her side of the bed. The drapes were pulled tight over the windows in the bedroom, but the narrow window high up on the bathroom wall wasn't covered, and sunlight escaped the cracked-open door to cast a narrow ray over the end of the bed.

Lana stared at it for a long moment, then gasped in horror and slammed the door shut. Leaning against the closed door, she tried to picture the bed with Vincent in it. Had he been completely covered? Had the light fallen on him directly? Surely, he would have grunted in pain or something, wouldn't he?

Damn.

Standing on the closed toilet seat, she did her best to cover the window. It was a single pane, opening downward from the top. She opened it enough to jam a towel in there, then cranked it shut so that most of the light was blocked.

She opened the door again, her gaze riveted to the foot of the bed where the narrow strip had appeared before. There was a little light from the top of the window, but it didn't touch the bed. Good. She wrapped the towel more securely around her chest and stepped into the room, closing the door behind her. A glance at Vincent told her he wasn't moving. He was lying on his stomach, fast asleep, his face turned away from her, both arms tucked under a pillow and the covers down around his waist.

"Don't look," she whispered to herself, deliberately turning her gaze away. "Don't look, don't look," she repeated, then caught a flash of color on smooth golden skin and turned to stare. Damn, but he was pretty. All broad back and sleek muscles. The color she'd seen was the tattoo she'd caught sight of earlier on his left bicep. She wanted to get closer to check out the detail, but didn't want to ogle. Actually, she *did* want to ogle, she just didn't want to get caught. He was completely naked under those covers. He'd stripped down to nothing right in front of her, with absolutely no sense of modesty, and fallen into bed only moments after they'd returned from the cantina early this morning.

She'd half-expected the place would be empty when they'd gone over for dinner, but the party had been going as wild as if it had been midnight instead of nearly sunrise. At first, Lana thought Vincent had called ahead and thus the big party. But Marisol's surprise on seeing him had seemed genuine, so maybe they partied like that every night around here. It made her wonder what they did with the rest of their time. Then she decided she didn't want to know. This area was home to one of the major drug cartels, and Vincent had said Marisol was well connected. Maybe that's what she was well connected *to*.

But whatever the reason for the late night revelry, it had certainly suited Vincent's needs nicely. Every woman in the place had made her way over to their table during the course of the meal—Lana's meal, that was. Vincent didn't eat. But he did manage to greet every single female in the room as if they were each the last woman on earth—flattering, kissing, stroking. And he'd disappeared more than once, ostensibly to dance, but there wasn't enough of a crowd to get lost in. It had been obvious to Lana that Vincent and his partners had done more than dance, and they'd done it somewhere other than the dance floor. The only exception to Vincent's sensual charm offensive had been a young girl who didn't look much older than sixteen. He'd been sweet to her, had kissed her hand in a courtly gesture, and then sent her on her way with a smile.

Lana had thought Marisol might be jealous of all the attention Vincent was getting from the others. But she'd seemed perversely delighted, gazing proudly at Vincent every time he came back from one of his little excursions, as though he'd been paying her a compliment by sucking down on her customers and friends. Lana didn't know exactly what their relationship was. She only knew that every time Vincent disappeared with another dark-haired lovely, she'd felt like an idiot, sitting there watching them walk away. But then, she was only a bodyguard, right?

Standing there wrapped in nothing but a towel, she relived her earlier embarrassment and scowled down at Vincent's sleeping form. Suddenly, it was easier to tear her gaze away from his naked perfection. She strode over to her side of the bed, where her duffel sat in the dim yellow light of the single lamp, and got fully dressed even though her only immediate plans were for sleep. Or so she hoped. She didn't know if she'd be able to sleep with Vincent next to her in the bed, even if she was fully dressed. But she had to try, because her eyes were gritty and her muscles ached with exhaustion.

She pulled on fresh underwear—including a bra, because there was no way she was going braless around the walking seduction that was Vincent—and then donned her usual traveling outfit of Levis and a long-sleeved T-shirt. She put on socks, but left her boots off, and compromised by leaving the pants unbuttoned, although she did zip them halfway. And she left her hair down. She hated to sleep with it braided. It gave her a headache and there was little worse than starting the day with an aching head.

Tucking her dirty clothes into the laundry bag she always packed, she turned back to the bed and contemplated their sleeping arrangements. Vincent was right. It was a very big bed. But he was a very big guy, and a bed hog to boot. He'd started out on one side of the bed, but he'd stretched out so that he now took up well more than his half. And he sure as hell was not the stereotypical image of a vampire at rest, either. He was supposed to be lying on his back, board stiff, with his hands crossed over his chest. Instead he was sprawled on his stomach as if he didn't have a care, the sheet barely covering his hips, his tattoo glinting gold in the yellow lamplight.

Suddenly curious about the mysterious tattoo, she glanced all around, as if expecting to find someone watching, then tiptoed around the bed and crouched down to study it more closely. She cursed, realizing there wasn't enough light. Moving forward slightly, she examined Vincent's face for signs of awareness. Finding none, she stretched over him and turned on the light on his side of the bed, then went back to her study of the tattoo. It was a four-pointed star in shades of gold and brown with the face of the Mayan Sun god grimacing in the middle of a beaded circle and a green stylized band on either side. Lana didn't have any tattoos, but all of her dad's hunters did, and she had a good idea of how much talent went into creating something as beautiful as this. She reached out to trace her finger over the image, then pulled back guiltily.

It was bad enough that she was ogling him in his sleep. It didn't seem fair to touch him, too. Although, knowing Vincent even as little as she did, she doubted he'd mind. She stood and turned off the lamp, then returned determinedly to her side of the bed. Vincent Kuxim was the very image of male beauty and too sexy by half. Hell, too sexy altogether if his effect on the female population of the cantina was anything to judge by.

And lucky her, she got to sleep in the same bed with him. Fuck, fuck-ity, fuck.

Grabbing the spare blanket—there was no way she was getting under the covers with him while he was naked—she lay down gingerly, careful to stick to the very edge of the bed. She snagged the single pillow he'd left for her, then straightened the blanket and closed her eyes.

The last thing she remembered was thinking she was never going to fall asleep.

VINCENT WOKE WHILE the sun's last rays still glowed above the horizon and was immediately aware that someone was in the room with him. Not only in the room, but in his bed. And she was sound asleep.

Sensing no threat, he remained still for a long moment nonetheless as he considered this unusual circumstance. Vincent frequently shared his bed with the women he fed from. The act of taking blood was intensely sexual and, since male vampires were blessed with the kind of stamina and recuperative powers that kept their partners happy, an encounter typically resulted in a great deal of mutual pleasure. He didn't know about female vamps. He'd never had sex with one and had never thought to ask.

But even though he might share his bed for the *night*, he never, as in *never ever*, shared his bed through the day. He'd never trusted any of his human partners that far. Michael knew this, which was why he'd been so surprised that Vincent had decided to travel alone with Lana Arnold. Generally, Vincent traveled with a security team that included daytime guards. And he always slept alone.

In this case, however, Vincent's desire for secrecy, and Raphael's tacit endorsement, had made him take a chance on Lana. Especially since he'd sensed no duplicity in her, and, as a powerful vampire, he'd definitely have known. Most humans were imperfect liars. They experienced a physical response to the stress of lying, and a vampire with even modest power could detect these responses. This wasn't true of sociopaths, but Lana Arnold wasn't a sociopath. One didn't live over 150 years among humans without being able to detect the predators among them, especially when one was an accomplished predator himself.

And those thoughts brought him back to the woman lying next to him, sound asleep.

With a slow smile, he shifted oh so carefully, understanding intuitively that if Lana woke, she'd be out of the bed in a flash. She probably hadn't intended to sleep at all, much less to get so close to him that he could feel the heat of her body along the entire length of his right side.

Pushing up off his stomach and onto his left side, he propped himself up on one elbow and studied her in the darkened room. It was cold and she was covered by only a thin blanket, which was probably why she'd unconsciously moved so close to him, drawn to his warmth. Vampires didn't run as warm as humans, but they weren't as cold as some fiction would have them, either. The sensible thing would have been for her to climb under the comforter with him, but she was still pretending she wasn't attracted to him. Did she realize how much she gave away by choosing *not* to sleep under the covers with him?

He scooted carefully closer. Lana was lying on her side facing away from him, and she was fully clothed. He rolled his eyes, but wasn't really surprised. He *was* surprised, and delighted, to discover that she'd left her hair free from the confines of its perpetual braid. As he'd suspected, it was beautiful—a wavy flow of black silk covering her shoulders and back. Unable to stop himself, he lifted a lock of it and rubbed it between his fingers, finding it every bit as soft and sensuous as it looked. He imagined all that hair sliding over his body as she licked her way down over his belly, as she took him in her mouth . . . and his cock went instantly hard. His thoughts took off, anticipating all the ways he could take her, all the places he could taste her.

He froze as she sighed in her sleep, waiting to see if she'd wake. Twirling the lock of hair around his finger, he lay there, undecided as to whether he wanted her to wake up or not. When her breathing smoothed back into sleep, he smiled and pushed the comforter away from himself, so that the only thing separating them was the sheet. And then he slowly curved his body around hers until his still-hard cock was pressed up against the firm swell of her ass. When she still didn't stir, he went even further, draping his arm around her waist, releasing the full weight of it slowly until his fingers rested on the bare skin of her taut stomach in the gap between her T-shirt and her unzipped jeans. Lowering his head, he buried his face in the warm silk of her hair and inhaled deeply, taking in her scent. Delicious. Clean, sweet, female.

Minute changes in Lana's muscles warned him an instant before she woke with a controlled jerk. She lay still, awake and aware, trying to pretend she wasn't. Vincent wiped the smile off his face and closed his eyes, feigning sleep himself, slitting his eyes open just enough to watch through his lashes as she slowly turned her head to check him out. Her body relaxed upon seeing that he was still asleep, and she began to move slowly, inch by inch, trying to extricate herself from his embrace without waking him. Or, so she thought.

Vincent had to fight to keep the grin off his face, but eventually Lana managed to scoot free of him, continuing until she'd rolled right off the bed and onto her feet. She stood there studying his half-naked and, to her eyes, sleeping body, complete with the erection that she couldn't see under the sheet, but had undoubtedly *felt* against her ass. In fact, she stood there staring long enough that Vincent felt his cock beginning to harden even further, hard enough that he could feel it pushing against the covering fabric. Lana must have seen it, too, because she gave a guilty jolt and jerked her gaze up to his face to be sure he was still asleep. Seeing that he was—or so she thought—she blew out a breath, then hurried around the bed and out of sight.

Vincent didn't move until he heard the bathroom door close and the water start running in the sink. Then he rolled onto his back and stretched luxuriously, while fisting his aching cock. He intended to have Lana Arnold before this was over. Listening to her shuffle around the bathroom, he called back the thought of having all that silky hair flowing over his body, her warm, wet mouth closing over his cock, her teeth scraping gently as she sucked harder and harder . . . He came with a swallowed groan only seconds before the bathroom door opened and Lana peeked out.

"Good evening, Lana," he said pleasantly, jumping out of bed and heading for the bathroom without any pretense at covering himself.

She managed to control most of her startled reaction and was careful to avoid brushing up against him as he strode past her into the bathroom. But Vincent smiled in satisfaction. She was a tough one, but she wanted him all right.

He took a quick shower, just enough to wash himself off, but he shaved properly, carefully trimming around his beard and mustache. He brushed his teeth and fingercombed his hair, then rattled the doorknob noisily to warn her.

"I'm coming out, Lana," he called, not bothering to conceal his laughter.

But when he opened the door, she'd already left. The curtains were pulled back, the bed was pulled up, and her duffel was gone. Good thing he had the keys, or she'd probably be on her way to Pénjamo by now. He frowned, then quickly patted the pockets of his jeans to verify that she hadn't lifted the keys while he'd slept. But no, they were there. He breathed a sigh of relief and began pulling on his clothes, planning for the night ahead.

He'd fed well before retiring this morning, so there was no need to top off before leaving, although the selection in the cantina had been delicious, more than he could have hoped. Marisol had regretfully told him that her lover was new and she didn't want to stray, but she also understood Vincent's needs and was not a jealous woman—at least, not where he was concerned. She'd made sure there were plenty of women for him in the cantina, most of them available as sexual partners, too, if that had been his preference. But he hadn't even considered taking any of them up on it. It would have been in poor taste to have sex with one woman when traveling with another, even if he and Lana weren't lovers . . . yet. Though he had every intention of making her his lover before the trip was over.

He stomped his feet into his boots and laced them up, then pulled on his jacket, threw the last of his things into his duffel, and with a final look around, left the cottage. Lana was just coming out of the cantina when he walked by on his way to the parking lot.

"Good evening, Lana. Did you get some dinner?" he asked.

She nodded. "More breakfast than dinner, but yeah. It was good. This is a weird schedule you keep, vampire."

"Not like I have a choice," he said, with a shrug. "Let me put this in the SUV and say good-bye to Marisol, then we can get out of here."

"My duffel's already sitting by the SUV," she told him, appearing slightly irritated. "I didn't have the keys to put it inside."

He could have offered them to her, but he still wasn't convinced she wouldn't leave him in the dust. So instead, he said, "I'll take care of it and come back."

She nodded. "Marisol's inside. I think she's waiting for you."

Her words were innocuous enough, but the attitude was much more telling. She was very curious about his relationship with Marisol. Maybe he'd tell her about it later if she was nice to him.

The thought made him grin. She caught his smile and narrowed her eyes in growing annoyance. Which only made him grin harder.

"I'll wait in the SUV," she told him. "If that's all right with you."

"Do you promise not to drive away and leave me?"

Lana rolled her eyes and tsked loudly. "Of course not."

"So you *will* leave me?"

"No!" she snapped. "I promise not to leave you, okay?"

"Good enough. Then, here—" He held out his duffel and the keys. "You can take my duffel, and I'll go say good-bye to Marisol. We can leave sooner that way."

"Oh, joy."

Vincent laughed and barely managed to stop himself from patting her on the ass as he walked past her and into the cantina.

LANA STARED OUT her window as they zoomed down the dark highway once more, but she wasn't looking at the scenery. She was studying Vincent's profile as it was reflected in her window. And she was remembering the masculine beauty of his naked body, his fully aroused naked body, if she wasn't mistaken. It was possible that he hadn't been *fully* aroused, since he'd been asleep. But he'd been more than erect enough to remind her that it had been too long since she'd had a lover, erect enough to make her wonder what it would be like to have sex with a vampire. They were said to be terrific lovers. Maybe it was all those years of practice. She couldn't imagine the biting part was much fun, although none of the women Vincent had disappeared with last night had seemed to mind. And Marisol was clearly a fan.

"I could have slept in the SUV if you'd needed privacy, you know," she said, admitting to herself that she was probing.

Vincent shot her a puzzled frown. "Why would I need you to do that?"

"I know that when you feed, it involves sex. If you'd wanted the room to yourself, I'd have understood."

"I don't sleep with the women I feed from."

Lana snorted in polite disbelief. "Right. That's why you sleep naked." Damn. That was the wrong thing to say.

Vincent grinned. "Were you ogling me, Ms. Arnold?"

"I didn't need to ogle with you prancing around the way you do."

"I don't prance."

"The hell you don't."

"Well, regardless, I don't sleep with my partners. Ever."

She frowned. "Why not?"

"It's a matter of security. You saw what it's like. I'm totally out of it. In fact, you could have made me your plaything while I slept, and I'd never have known."

"In your dreams, vampire."

"Hmm, maybe. You did admit you were ogling."

"I admitted no such thing. Besides, if you're so vulnerable, why would you allow me in the room with you?"

Vincent shrugged. "Because Raphael trusts you."

"Raphael doesn't even know me. The job came from Cynthia Leighton."

"Trust me, *querida*, Leighton and Raphael are one and the same. You're here because Raphael wants you here."

"He's not a god, you know."

"No, not a god. But he is one scary vampire."

Lana studied him in the glow of the dash lights, then turned away to stare at the darkness outside the front window. She wasn't sure she liked the idea of being manipulated by anyone like that, especially not an über powerful vampire whose abilities she couldn't hope to comprehend.

"You owe me an answer," she said, abruptly tired of contemplating things she didn't understand.

"An answer to what?" he asked absently.

She turned to face him. "I asked how and when you became a vampire and you promised you'd finish the story tonight."

He slanted his gaze in her direction, holding it long enough that she grew a little nervous. They were going close to 100 miles an hour. Granted, they seemed to be the only vehicle on the road, but still.

"All right," he said abruptly and faced forward once more. "Where did we leave off?"

"You and your brother had just been attacked. You'd been shot."

Something an awful lot like sadness swept over Vincent's expression and he sighed. "That was the beginning . . . and the end."

Chapter Eight

Texas, 1876

VINCENT WOKE TO overwhelming pain. Every length of muscle, every inch of bone in his body ached, and his blood was like fire.

"The pain will fade," a man's voice said.

Vincent tried to respond, tried to turn his head to see the speaker, to jump up and defend himself, but his muscles wouldn't cooperate. He lay nearly flat on his back, his head propped up against what felt like rocks. There was a fire burning, though he had no clue if it was the same one he and his brother had been sitting at when they'd been ambushed.

Memory of the attack gave a new urgency to his fears. John had been shot, too. Where was he?

Vincent finally managed to twist his head around, nearly blinded by the brightly burning flames, straining to see into the darkness beyond. But he was unable to find whoever had spoken.

"Where's my brother?" he asked, shocked at the rough sound of his own voice.

"He was gravely injured," the stranger responded.

Vincent's heart clenched and he struggled uselessly. "Is he dead?" he croaked.

"He's recovering, as you are, although not so rapidly."

"Who are you? Come around where I can see you."

A dark-haired man stepped into view. He was short of stature, but trim and fit, older than Vincent by ten or more years. And he appeared to be a man of means, his clothes better than most, his face pale and almost delicate-looking, his hair and beard clean and neatly cut.

"Who are you?" Vincent asked again.

"I am the one who saved your life. So tell me, how did you come to these unfortunate circumstances?"

"We were on our way home from Abilene when those men attacked us."

"Abilene," the stranger repeated. "That's a cattle town."

Vincent started to nod, then froze when the movement set his head to pounding. He swallowed the nausea and said, "We work on a ranch in Texas."

"Do you know the men who attacked you? Or why they wanted you dead?"

"No. I imagine they were common thieves, after our horses and money."

"Possibly. Sleep now. We will have much to discuss when you wake."

Vincent started to protest that he wasn't a child to be coddled into sleep, but before he could utter a single word, his eyelids grew heavy and blackness descended.

The next time he woke, the pain was gone. More than gone. He felt better than he had since starting the cattle drive weeks before. How long had he been asleep?

He sat up and stared around. It was nighttime again, and the fire was still burning. It might have been the same campsite or not. One looked pretty much looked like the other. His gear was piled to the left, John's next to it, but . . . he didn't see his brother.

"Good evening, Vincent."

He twisted around, watching as the same dark-haired man strolled into the firelight. He strained to remember, but didn't recall giving the man his name.

"Are you feeling better?" the man asked.

Vincent studied him before answering. Who was this man? Some Good Samaritan who came upon the two brothers and decided to help? That was unusual enough that Vincent was wary of the stranger. He didn't look like a priest or a brother whose job it was to help the unfortunate. On the other hand, he couldn't deny that the man had helped him, had gone so far as to remain nearby while Vincent regained his senses.

"I am better. Thank you. May I have your name?"

"I am Enrique Fernandez del Solar."

"And how do you know my name, Mr. del Solar?"

"I know a great many things, some of which you will learn over time."

Vincent jumped to his feet, abruptly aware that he *could do so*. He didn't simply feel better, he was completely healed. How long had he been out? He rubbed a hand over his chest, shoving aside the bloody remains of his shirt, and found nothing but the shiny, pale skin of a fading scar. It was as if he'd been shot months ago, rather than . . . He abruptly recalled getting shot, the piercing pain when the bullet hit his chest. Hell, he should be dead, not wondering how he'd healed so quickly. He shouldn't have healed at all!

Fear seized him, not for himself, but for John. He searched the campsite, staring into the darkness beyond the fire, discovering that he was able to see far more than he should have.

"Where's my brother?" he demanded. "What have you done to us?"

"Ah. As to what I've done to you, I've changed you forever. Made you better."

Vincent spun around and strode across the campsite to face down Enrique. "What does that mean?" he growled.

"I've made you Vampire," Enrique said, seeming unperturbed by Vincent's threatening demeanor, even though Vincent was both taller and more muscular than he was.

"Vampire?" Vincent scoffed. "Are you mad? Vampires only exist in stories made up to scare misbehaving children."

Enrique smiled placidly. "We're quite real, boy. And you're one of us now."

"I don't believe you."

"No? Try this."

Without warning, Enrique slashed out with a knife, faster than Vincent could follow, faster than he would have thought possible, slicing deeply into Vincent's bicep through his shirtsleeve. It bled instantly and profusely, soaking through the torn fabric, but then it simply . . . stopped. Muscle and skin were shifting beneath his disbelieving eyes, knitting themselves together with a searing heat that was not altogether unpleasant. He ripped the shreds of cloth away and rubbed a hand over the nearly-healed wound. It was sore, but no more than that.

Vincent swallowed hard, his heart pounding as he raised his eyes to stare at Enrique . . . at the *vampire*. Just thinking such a word made him feel foolish, but it also frightened him like nothing ever had before. He'd been made into a monster, an unnatural creature who killed other humans and drank their blood to survive.

"Oh, don't be foolish," Enrique chided him, as if reading his thoughts. "You don't need to kill the humans you feed from. In fact, I will teach you the ways to make it quite pleasurable. For both of you."

"Both of us? You mean my brother? Where is he?"

"Ah. I'm afraid . . . the transference is a taxing thing. Very hard on a body. And your brother was grievously wounded."

"Where is he?" Vincent asked again as a sick knowledge rolled through his gut.

"He didn't make it, Vincent. I'm sorry. He's dead."

Vincent didn't say anything. He couldn't. He spun away and walked into the darkness beyond the campfire. He needed to be alone with his grief, and his guilt. His brother was dead and it was his fault. He'd been the one who insisted they join the cattle drive. John hadn't wanted to go, but he hadn't want Vincent to go alone. And now he was dead. He'd never go back and become an animal doctor for their father. And their mother . . . *¡Dios mio!* Their mother! How could he tell his mother that her youngest son was dead? She would die of grief. And she would never forgive him.

He groaned out loud, his legs giving way beneath him as he collapsed on the cold desert ground. Tears spilled in a flood down his cheeks and he buried his face in his arms. Better to die than to face his parents with this terrible loss, with his failure. The grief built up in him until he thought it would tear open his chest, until the pressure was so great that he threw his head back and howled.

"I am sorry, Vincent," Enrique said from behind him.

Vincent leapt to his feet, spinning to face the stranger, the man who claimed not to be a man at all. "Let me die," he demanded. "I want to die with my brother."

The man gave him a pitying look. "Don't be foolish, boy. You're grieving now, but you'll soon see this for the gift it is."

"I didn't ask for your gift," he hissed back at him.

"It was the only way to save your life."

"You should have let me die with my brother."

Enrique tsked impatiently. "Enough of this foolishness. You'll thank me someday, but for now, you must simply survive. And that means finding a place to rest before daylight. Come."

"Where's my brother's body? I want to bury him."

"It's gone. I did try to save him, you know," he added waspishly. "You should thank me."

Vincent only glared at him distrustfully.

Enrique sighed. "When a vampire dies, he turns to dust. Your brother was already Vampire when he died. There's nothing to bury."

Vincent groaned again. Could this get any worse? What would happen to his brother's soul? Would God understand that it had not been John's choice to be made unholy?

"Come," Enrique snapped again. "Sunrise is almost upon us."

"Sunrise?" Vincent repeated numbly, feeling as though he was in a dream, a nightmare.

"Your first lesson, boy. You want to be dust like your brother? Then stay here and wait for the sun to rise. If you want to live, then come with me."

Not bothering with whether Vincent followed him or not, Enrique walked back to the campfire and began adjusting the saddle on a brown horse that Vincent had never seen before. It was standing placidly next to his own black gelding, but John's chestnut was nowhere to be seen.

"My brother's horse," he said distractedly, still having trouble thinking straight.

"The bandits took it. Yours ran, but I managed to round it up for you. I'm leaving now. You can follow or not."

Vincent watched in a daze as Enrique mounted his horse and rode away into the night. He could hear the clopping of the animal's hooves, the chiming of the buckles as clearly as if he stood only feet away. He thought about what the vampire had told him, that the clean light of the sun would burn him to dust if he lingered. And he tried to find the energy to care.

Did he want to die? Or did he want to live?

He stared at the campfire, like the one he'd so recently shared with his brother, John. How they'd laughed about the cattle drive and imagined their futures. A future the bandits had stolen from them. Enrique hadn't done that. He'd made a choice for them that he had no right to make, but he hadn't caused any of this. No, that blame belonged to the men who'd attacked them in the first place.

And in that moment, Vincent decided. He'd live long enough to avenge his brother's death. At least that long. And then he'd decide what came after.

Mexico, present day

"And did you?" Lana asked somberly. "Did you ever find the men who attacked you?"

"They were already dead. Enrique had come upon them as they ran from our campsite and killed them all."

"But he said—"

"Yeah. He said they stole John's horse and let me assume they escaped. He wanted me alive for his own reasons, so he said whatever he thought would work."

"He's your boss?"

"In a manner of speaking. He's the Lord of Mexico. Different thing altogether."

"Do you like him?"

"Hate the fucker, to be honest. But he's the guy in charge, so I try to get along."

Lana let out a sharp laugh. "You don't seem like a guy who gets along."

Vincent turned and gave her a crooked grin which amped his already high levels of gorgeousness to somewhere in the stratosphere.

"Are you saying I'm not a team player, Lana?"

She shrugged one shoulder. "No, I'm saying you don't strike me as the kind of guy who'll kiss ass to climb the corporate ladder."

Vincent's grin disappeared and his face went hard, his eyes cold. "You don't know much about vampires if you think I got where I am by kissing ass. I climbed the corporate ladder by killing anyone who stood in my way."

"Hey," Lana objected, pretending her blood hadn't frozen in her veins when he looked at her like that. "I said you didn't seem like the type, remember? Relax, tough guy."

The tension in the cab ratcheted down a few turns, and she felt her blood begin to flow again.

"Touchy subject," he muttered.

"Obviously." Deciding a change of subject was in order, Lana said, "So what does your trip planner have in store for us tonight? Where are we stopping?"

"Somewhere around Durango. I haven't done much business in that area, so we'll have to check it out."

"No Marisol waiting to greet you tonight?"

"I'm afraid not. But Durango's a big town. I'd rather not go into the town itself, but there are bound to be smaller communities within a few miles. Just enough for a motel, and a cantina or two."

He gave her a grin that said he knew what she was thinking. But since she was thinking it would be nice to have a room to herself tonight, she figured if he really *did* know her thoughts, he wouldn't be grinning like that. Whatever their motel accommodations, though, she doubted he'd be lonely. As long as the town was big enough, there'd be plenty of women waiting to welcome him to their blood supply . . . and their beds. Not that she cared either way. If he wanted to be a man slut, that was his business, not hers.

"You want me to find a place and call ahead?" she asked.

"Call if you want, but it's not necessary this time of year."

Lana shrugged. Fine with her. She'd rather set eyes on a motel before committing anyway.

They rode in silence for a while, Vincent's attitude noticeably cooler than it had been. She'd obviously offended him with the kiss-ass remark, and maybe she'd done that on purpose. She'd needed to gain some emotional distance after hearing the story about his brother dying. She didn't want to feel sympathy for Vincent, didn't want to feel anything other than a businesslike . . . courtesy. Yeah, that's what it was. Two people doing business together, who would go their separate ways in the end.

"Does Enrique live in Hermosillo, too?" she asked, and immediately wondered why the hell she'd said anything. What happened to the idea of courteous silence?

"Enrique lives wherever he wants. He has places all over Mexico."

"Including Hermosillo?" she asked, pushing the subject now, because it was so obvious that he didn't *want* her to.

Vincent glanced at her briefly, then said, "He hasn't been to Hermosillo in a very long time, which is why I live there."

"So where *does* Enrique live?"

"Why do you want to know?"

"Just curious. Why? You think I'm going to attack Enrique and take him down?" She laughed, then had an idea. "Wait, if I *did* kill him, would that make me your boss? Didn't you say that's how one advances up the ranks among vampires?"

Vincent didn't pretend to hide his disdain for that idea. "Yeah, right.

You'd last all of three minutes before a real vampire removed you from office."

"Spoilsport."

He snorted dismissively. "You learn to deal with reality very quickly when you're a vampire."

Lana thought about that, thought about a young Vincent waking up to find his world torn apart.

"Did it hurt when you became a vampire?" she asked him quietly.

"I don't remember much of the actual process. It hurt like hell when I woke up the first time, though."

"What about the first time you . . . you know, drank blood. Was that weird?"

Vincent shot her a suspicious look. "What's with the fifty questions? You writing a tell-all or something?"

"Just making conversation. You don't have to talk about it if you don't want to."

"Good. I think it's my turn anyway. You owe me some answers."

She waved her hand in a dismissive gesture. "Ask away."

"When did you lose your virginity?"

Lana gasped loudly and turned to stare at him in disbelief, which only made him laugh. "I'm not telling you that," she said.

"Okay, how about this?" he said, still laughing. "Do you have a boyfriend?"

Lana considered whether to answer or not. If she admitted she didn't, would he try to seduce her? Not because he was attracted to her necessarily, but simply because that was what he *did*. On the other hand, if she lied and told him she had a boyfriend, he might consider it a challenge. She sighed, wishing she'd never agreed to this stupid question and answer game in the first place. She'd have been better off with a book.

"No boyfriend," she said at last.

"Never?"

"I didn't say that," she snapped. "I've had a few. They didn't last."

"Hmm."

"What hmmm?"

"I was just thinking it must be hard to be in a relationship when you travel so much of the time."

"Uh-huh."

"Anyone serious?"

"Only one."

"Who was he?"

"Someone who turned out to be a player, like all the rest of you."

"You have a very low opinion of the male half of the species, *querida*."

She didn't say anything to that, because it was true. They rode in silence a while longer, until he asked, "How do you know Raphael?"

"I don't. I told you, I deal with Cyn. You probably know she does some investigative work. Sometimes she needs someone checked out in my neck of the woods, and she calls me. It's faster, plus I get the impression that Raphael likes her to stay close to home."

"That's an understatement. Vampires are possessive as a matter of course. But when you consider the extra aggression and territorial instincts a vampire lord has, I'm surprised she's not kept in a basement. A very nice basement, but a basement nonetheless."

"She doesn't strike me as a woman who'd put up with that."

"I think you're right. I've never met her, only seen her across the room. Her rep is pretty serious, though."

"I'd like to meet her in person someday. We've only spoken on the phone."

"Which bring us back to the task at hand. Why does Raphael want us to find Xuan Ignacio?"

"You know everything I do. Did you ask Enrique if he knew Xuan?"

"Not a chance. You know that territorial instinct I was talking about? Well, let's just say Enrique would not be thrilled to discover his lieutenant is on an errand for Raphael."

"You're Enrique's lieutenant? I didn't know that. That's high up the ladder, isn't it?"

"Only Enrique is higher."

"So if you think Enrique's an asshole, do the other vampires think you are, too?"

His grin finally returned as he said, "I sure as hell hope not."

"Michael seems to like you."

"Michael is mine. He's pretty much hard-wired to like me."

"Yours? You mean you made him a vampire?"

"I did. He's my only child."

"So he *has* to like you? But you said Enrique was your Sire and you hate him."

"Guess I'm a better Sire than Enrique," he said distractedly, his attention on a mileage indicator to the right side of the road. "I think we're nearly there. Check the GPS."

"Yes, sir," she said, snapping a salute.

"Please."

Lana smiled as she pulled up the immediate data on the GPS. "Ten miles," she said. "Nearly there. You want to stop on the outskirts or go on in?"

"We'll do a drive through and decide."

Thirty minutes later, Vincent was holding a flimsy door open so Lana could walk into their room for the night.

"Don't tell me," she said, staring at the ugly comforter on the lone king-sized bed. "They only had one room available."

"Not exactly," Vincent said, pushing his way past her to dump his duffel on a dresser that looked as if it might collapse under the weight. "But they didn't have any adjoining rooms, and you're supposed to be my bodyguard."

"We're partners, Vincent. *Temporary* partners. The bodyguard thing was just a story you made up for Marisol, so she wouldn't think you'd lost your magic touch with women."

"Ouch! So, you don't care if some bandit who's jealous because his girlfriend talked to me in the cantina sneaks into my room while I'm helpless and stabs me in the heart?"

"Maybe you should just avoid speaking to any strange women," she suggested sweetly.

"But the only woman I know in this town is you. Are you offering?"

She scowled at him. "Fine, I'll watch you sleep."

He gave her a devastating smile. He might think she was immune to his charms—in fact, she really hoped he thought that—but when he smiled like that? Her stomach fluttered, her mouth went dry and parts south shivered with desire. She managed to keep all of that out of her expression, however.

She balled up the comforter and threw it in a corner, then dropped her own duffel on the bed. "Can we get something to eat now?"

"Sure thing. That place between here and the gas station looked like it was getting ready to go all night long."

"I'm surprised there's anyplace open this late."

"Vampires aren't the only creatures who do their best work at night, *querida*. Especially in Mexico."

The bar Vincent had noticed was only a block away from the motel, but they drove anyway. In Lana's experience, it was always better to have your own wheels close at hand. The parking lot was mostly filled with aging American sedans. Their SUV stood out like the proverbial sore thumb.

"Do you have good security on this thing?" she asked as they climbed out and headed across the lot.

"Pretty damn good. The windows are close to unbreakable, the locks are solely electronic and there are three separate alarms. The final one shuts down the engine until the proper code is entered."

She nodded and repeated, "Pretty damn good."

"I take my security seriously. That's why I need a personal bodyguard."

"That's getting old, Vincent."

"Aren't we all?"

"Not you, apparently."

They rounded the building just as a band started playing something that sounded like a cross between American country and Mexican traditional. Lana was sure the style of music had a name, but she didn't know what it was. She didn't usually travel this deep into Mexico. Skips on the run from the U.S. justice system tended to stick close to either the border or the Pacific coast where there were more people, and where English was spoken almost as frequently as Spanish.

She and Vincent passed the first of two big, open windows fronting the bar. There was no glass in the openings, just shutters that had been thrown back and locked in place. From inside came the sounds of people having a good time and imbibing a lot of liquor, but the rest of the street seemed to be deserted. It made her uncomfortable. If Vincent was right and there was the kind of business being conducted in this town that worked better in the dead of night, then this bar was likely to contain a whole lot of people she'd rather not meet. She reminded herself that despite his blatant charms and playboy ways, Vincent was probably the most deadly person in the bar. But still . . .

She frowned and did an automatic pat-down, checking her weapons and gear.

"My phone," she muttered.

Vincent was staring into the crowd through the window, and she grabbed his arm to get his attention.

"I left my phone in the—" Her words faded away when she saw the look in his eyes. It was a look she'd never seen on his face before, the look of a predator sizing up his prey.

"Um, you go on inside," she told him, letting go of his arm and smoothing the long sleeve of his T-shirt carefully. "Give me the keys, and I'll join you."

He pulled the keys out of his pocket automatically and held them out, but then he hesitated, turning his eyes to meet hers in a long stare as if weighing her loyalty.

"I'm getting my phone," she said impatiently. "I'm not going anywhere."

He grinned, but it lacked his usual charm. And the look in his eyes told her his thoughts were already far away. The hungry predator had once again overtaken the calculating vampire. He dropped the keys into her hand without a word and walked through the door of the cantina.

Lana let out a breath. Clutching the keys in her left hand, she spun on her heel and headed back toward the parking lot. It took only a minute to open the locks and grab her phone. She noted in passing that the SUV didn't beep in response to the remote command, but stayed completely silent. Interesting. She'd just locked the vehicle back up and was about to return to the cantina when a second SUV turned into the parking lot in a hurry, tires spinning and kicking up gravel.

Stepping instinctively back into the shadows, she let the bulk of the

Suburban conceal her as she observed the new arrivals. They were remarkable not only because of their tire-skidding arrival, but because their SUV was much nicer than every other vehicle in the lot, with the exception of the one she and Vincent were driving. That alone made them suspect. But when the doors opened and four burly men stepped out, Lana knew she didn't want to get in their way. These guys weren't here to party. They weren't laughing. Hell, they were barely talking to each other.

She wished suddenly that she'd insisted Vincent walk back to the SUV with her. Because whatever these thugs had planned, it couldn't possibly be good. Under other circumstances, she'd have climbed into her SUV and driven away.

But Vincent was in that bar. And powerful vampire or not, they were partners.

Lana checked her weapons once more. She had the three knives she always carried, plus the Sig 9mm in a shoulder rig under her jacket with a spare magazine in her jacket pocket. She considered going back to the SUV for more ammo—she'd stashed two more mags in the glove compartment—but decided that if it came down to a shootout between her and those four men, not to mention any allies they had in the bar, more ammo wouldn't make much difference. She still only had one gun with her, since her Glock was in her duffel back at the motel. She hadn't anticipated needing it for what should have been a quick trip to the local cantina.

She waited until the new arrivals were out of sight. Then, telling herself she was going to walk into the bar, grab Vincent, and get the hell out of there, she started across the parking lot.

The crowd was just as noisy as it had been a few minutes earlier. Trying to be subtle, she slipped through the open door and found a space along the wall to the far side of one of the windows where there wasn't much light. Despite her brown skin and black hair, she knew she stood out as an American. Her height worked against her, as did her clothing, but it was more than that. It was an attitude that would take more than a change of clothes to conceal. So she stuck to the shadows and searched the crowd for Vincent. As big as he was, he should have stuck out almost as much as she did, but she'd discovered early on that people saw whatever Vincent wanted them to see.

She found him at last, on the edge of the dance floor. He was surrounded by locals, mostly women, currently charming a local girl who was flirting shamelessly and probably thought she was in control. Little did she know . . .

Vincent bent down to whisper something in the girl's ear, and Lana thought for sure they were headed for a dark corner. But suddenly, another woman appeared out of the crowd. She was older than the girl Vincent was talking to, her body and movements speaking of a confidence and maturity that was years removed from the child she was about to supplant. She was also stunningly attractive, with a voluptuous body that drew the eye of every man she rubbed up against on her way through the crowd.

Vincent sure as hell noticed her, and so did his original victim . . . er, donor. The older woman walked over to them and whispered in the girl's ear, running a hand up and down her arm in a gesture that could have been perceived as soothing. But something about the whole thing rubbed Lana the wrong way. Especially when the girl shot a look past Vincent, and Lana saw the same four men who'd skidded into the parking lot. *Bad men*, she thought again. And it looked like they had their eyes on Vincent.

Lana got a sick feeling in her stomach. She'd just pushed away from the wall, intent on dragging Vincent out of there bodily if she had to, when the beautiful woman pulled him out onto the dance floor. Vincent laughed and rested his hands on her voluptuous hips as her arms went around his neck. The music slowed and they began dancing, the woman not even trying to be subtle as she rubbed her breasts against Vincent's chest, as her hands caressed his shoulders, his neck . . .

Lana's gaze sharpened as she saw the danger. Vincent seemed to catch it at the same moment, but they were both too late.

The woman flipped two small knives into her hands and sliced both sides of Vincent's neck in a single coordinated move. Vincent's eyes were copper flames as he roared his outrage and shoved her away, the movement only serving to dig the knives deeper as she flew backward. Propelled by his power as much as his fury, the woman flew across the suddenly empty dance floor and crashed into the stage, toppling equipment as the band ran for it. Bar customers were screaming, pushing their way toward the door, some jumping through the open windows in a bid to escape the carnage.

Vincent fell to his knees, his hands slapped over either side of his neck in a fruitless effort to staunch the bleeding. Lana started forward and his eyes suddenly lifted to meet hers with an intent stare. He gave a minute shake of his head and she jerked to a stop. She frowned and he stared harder. He was trying to tell her something. But what? The four men pushed away from the bar and headed toward Vincent. He was soaked in his own blood, kneeling in a pool of it on the dance floor.

Inside, Lana was screaming. Instinct was telling her to rush over and help him, to drag him out of there if she had to. But reason—and Vincent—were telling her something else.

His blood had already begun to slow by the time the four men reached him, becoming a sticky, sluggish trickle instead of a nightmarish gush of red. As improbable as it seemed, not even this was enough to kill him. And the four men apparently knew it. They'd clearly wanted him weakened, not dead.

They grabbed Vincent and dragged him toward the door, scanning the crowd as they crossed the now deserted dance floor. Lana shrank behind a group of three couples, bending her knees to blend in better. She didn't know if the bad men were looking for her, or if they even knew about her. But if they saw her, they'd know she didn't belong. And if they grabbed her, she'd have no chance of getting to Vincent before they carried out their plans for him, and it wouldn't be good.

Lana hung back until they'd been gone a while, listening to the chatter around her, trying to discover whatever she could about who the men were and, more importantly, where they were taking Vincent. She caught hints of a compound outside of town, of a very dangerous man whom no one named, but everyone talked about. No surprise there. This was *narco* territory. What she didn't understand was why they'd taken Vincent. He'd told her the vampires had a détente with the cartels of Mexico, so why grab him?

She listened to the rapid conversations going on all around her, but none of these people knew anything about Vincent's situation, nor did they care. With the threat gone, they were ready to resume their partying. People who'd fled to the streets began to filter back inside. Someone had poured what looked like kitty litter on the dance floor, to soak up Vincent's blood, and an older woman was now industriously sweeping and scrubbing it away, while the band recovered their equipment and resumed playing. Even the bartenders were pouring, the crowd thick around the bar as people replaced spilled drinks. Meanwhile, the woman who'd attacked Vincent had staggered to her feet and was making her wobbly way out through the front door.

Lana followed the woman's halting movements. She couldn't handle four bad guys, but one conniving bitch? That she could do. She slipped along the wall and trailed the woman outside. Vincent had done some damage when he'd thrown her across the room, but none of the bad guys had cared enough even to check her out, much less see her home safely.

Lana watched her stumble and fall to her knees on the sidewalk, then cling to the wall as she struggled to rise. Picking up her pace, Lana touched the woman's arm.

"Are you okay?" she asked in Spanish. "Can I help you?"

The woman looked up, saw who was asking, and forced a laugh before replying in heavily accented English. "Are you with the pretty one? The vampire?"

"Is that the man you tried to kill?" Lana asked, pretending not to understand.

"Only the power of God can kill one like that."

"Why do those men want him dead?"

"They don't." The woman leaned heavily against the wall, panting for breath as she looked up to meet Lana's eyes. "You should go home, forget about him. He is evil."

"I can't," Lana admitted. "I'm sworn to protect him."

"Then you are a fool," the woman whispered.

"Where did they take him?"

She laughed again, coughing with the effort it took. "You will die if you go there."

Lana shrugged. "We all die eventually."

"Do you have a car?" the woman whispered.

"Yes."

"Take me to my home, and I will tell you what you want to know."

Lana considered the woman's offer. Obviously, she couldn't be trusted. But there was no question that the men had deserted her, and, besides, Lana wasn't that easy to get rid of.

"Fine," Lana said. "But try anything, and I'll kill you."

The woman gave a small cynical laugh, as if she didn't credit the threat, but then she met Lana's cool stare and her laughter died. She nodded grimly. "I only want my bed. I hurt very much."

"Good," Lana muttered, helping the woman to her feet. "I hope whatever they paid you was worth it."

Once they were in the SUV, the woman—Lana considered asking her name, but discovered she didn't care—directed her to a small stand-alone house about two miles from the bar. It was generally neat and tidy, with flowers in boxes beneath the front window sills and in clay pots along the walkway. It was probably pretty in the sunlight, if one gave a fuck. Which Lana didn't.

She parked in the short driveway, grabbed the keys and headed around the front of the SUV. Lana opened the passenger door and the woman groaned as she tried to get out. Taking her arm, Lana eased her down to the running board and then the ground. They made their slow way over to the front door which the woman opened with a set of keys she produced from a pocket in her skirt.

Once inside, she slumped exhaustedly into an overstuffed chair. "Can you get me some water?" she asked in a voice that was mostly a whisper.

"I'm not here to nurse you," Lana said coldly. "I said I'd get you home. You're home. Now tell me where they took him."

"Water," the woman rasped. "Please. So I can tell you."

Lana was growing angrier and more impatient by the minute. She was tempted to get the water and throw it in the devious woman's face, but that wouldn't get her out of here any sooner. So, she opened the refrigerator, grabbed one of several bottles of water, and handed it over.

"Okay. Talk."

"My name is Fidelia Reyes."

Lana only stared. She didn't give a fuck what the bitch's name was. And if she thought Lana was stupid enough to hand over her own name, she was crazy as well as devious.

"You are a fool," Reyes muttered.

"And you're a dead woman if you don't start talking."

Reyes shrugged, then gasped at the movement and hugged herself with both arms. "Your vampire hurt me badly."

"You're lucky he didn't kill you. Talk. Who sent you after him?"

"La Maña, the *narcos*."

"How did they know he'd be here? We just arrived in town, and no one knew we were coming this way."

"The other one recognized him and told the *patrón* who he was, that he was a powerful one."

"What other one? Who're you talking about?"

"The other vampire."

"Another vampire lives here? And he works for these *narcos*?"

Reyes nodded. "*Sí*, yes. But he does not work for them. They own him."

Lana frowned. She'd never heard of a vampire being owned by humans. That didn't mean it never happened, but wouldn't Vincent have known if there was another vampire around? He was Enrique's lieutenant, which, according to him, meant he knew almost as much as the vampire lord himself did. And Hermosillo was his home. Surely, he'd have heard about something like this happening practically in his own backyard? Something was definitely not right here.

"You said they don't want him dead. What do they want him for?"

"He has power. He'll be their slave, like the other one, but better."

Lana stared. The local cartel guys thought they could make Vincent their slave? This was not going to end well.

"So, where do I find him?"

"Go home, *señorita*. Forget about him."

Lana laughed dismissively. "Not gonna happen. Now, tell me where they are."

Reyes sighed and shook her head in an obvious comment on Lana's sanity. "They have a compound, a hacienda, outside of town. Not far. Go south. There is a big rock that looks like a giant hit it with a hammer. And there is a road. But the hacienda has a wall all around it and many guards."

"Have you been there?"

"Many times, but I will not—"

"I don't want your company." She cut Reyes off, anticipating her protest. "I want to know where in the compound they're likely to keep him, what building?"

"They will do with him like the other one. It is a small building, a shack, in the courtyard where there is no shade, only sunlight. It has many windows with shutters that can open and close. If the vampire is good, they close all of the shutters. If he is bad, they open and he suffers the daylight."

"They burn him?"

"It is God's punishment for his evil."

Lana rolled her eyes. "What about at night? They can't control him at night."

"They do as I did tonight. They bleed him during the day and feed him only a little."

Lana thought she was going to be sick. This is what they had planned for Vincent? She pounded her fist into the wall, trying to think. She was only one person. She couldn't take on an entire compound of cartel thugs. They'd happily gut her and leave her to rot. And that was if they didn't rape her to death first. But she couldn't abandon Vincent either. She considered calling Michael for reinforcements, but by the time he got down here, it might be too late.

"Is there a time when the guards aren't paying attention? I don't know, like a shift change or something?"

The woman tried to laugh, but sucked in a pained breath instead. "This is not a *maquila* to have bells and clocks. Forget him. Go home."

"I can't. He's . . . a friend."

"You are a fool," she said again.

Lana opened her mouth to say, *thanks for nothing*, but Reyes wasn't finished.

"If you are set on dying with him, you must act now, today. There is a big delivery and many of the *sicarios*, the soldiers, are gone."

"When do they come back?"

Reyes shrugged. "Maybe some very late tonight, many others tomorrow. They do not tell me such details."

"All right. What else can you tell me?"

Reyes gave her a weary look, and Lana thought she'd reached the end of her cooperation, but then she said, "During siesta, there is only one guard on the shack and very few in the yard."

"Where is this shack?"

"In the courtyard. It is easy to see. There is nothing but dirt—no gardens, no trees."

Lana shook her head, then spun on her heel and headed for the front door.

"Go home, *gringa*. You cannot save him. He is the devil's creature."

Lana paused with her fingers gripping the doorknob, her jaw clenched. She told herself it wouldn't do any good to go off on Reyes, that her energy was better spent planning Vincent's rescue. But then, from behind her, she heard the glug of the water bottle as Reyes took a drink, heard the woman exhale deeply, the sound of a person relaxing after a hard day's work.

Forcing the words out around the anger squeezing her throat, Lana turned back toward the woman. "We'll be back. And if I were you, I wouldn't be here. He'll kill you. And I won't stop him."

Chapter Nine

LANA'S FIRST STOP was the motel where she and Vincent had checked in before going to the cantina. There was no telling where this other vampire—the one Reyes claimed was enslaved by the local *narco* boss—had seen and recognized Vincent. It might have been at the gas station when they'd first pulled into town, or at the motel, or, hell, just driving by. But with no way to know for sure, she didn't want to leave their things at the motel. Especially since she didn't know what the day's rescue would bring. If Vincent was weak or injured, he might need a safe place to hole up for a few hours. It would have been better if she could track and find Vincent tonight, when he, theoretically at least, could help in his own rescue. *Theoretically* because he hadn't been looking too healthy when they dragged him out of the cantina. And if Fidelia Reyes had been telling the truth, they sure as hell wouldn't be giving him any blood to help him heal, either. Lana couldn't help wondering if the *narcos* knew just whom they had on their hands. Yeah, the informer vamp had told his bosses that Vincent was powerful, but did they know he was probably equal in power to Enrique himself?

Lana sighed, thinking all that power might not do him any good if they kept him starved for blood, or burning in the sunshine. She rubbed her chest, trying to ease an actual ache in her heart at the thought of Vincent being tortured like that.

When she arrived at the motel, she parked in the lot of the *bodega* next door, pulling around back where there was little traffic at this hour. Vincent's SUV was too noticeable, although she'd probably be glad of all that bulletproofing when she broke him out of his prison. Reyes had said the siesta slowdown later today would be her best chance, but obviously, Lana wasn't going to take that at face value. The sky was just beginning to lighten, but she still had an hour before daylight. She'd drive out there as soon as she picked up their things, park some distance away, then trek in and scope the place out herself before deciding on a plan.

Walking down the alley, she approached the motel from the back, sidling along the building's outside wall until she could see the motel parking lot and the street in front of it. Standing in the morning shadows, she stood perfectly still for a few minutes, her eyes peeled for anything out of the ordinary. Years of hunting bad guys who didn't want to be found had made her pretty damn good at spotting when things or people seemed out of place. But she didn't see anything like that. Maybe the vampire snitch hadn't told them about her. Or maybe he hadn't realized Vincent was traveling with anyone.

Once in their room, she grabbed the few things they'd unpacked and shoved them back into the duffels. She left the lights on, hoping that if anyone came looking for her, they might at least be slowed down by the possibility that she was still there. Then, slinging both bags over her shoulders, she headed out the way she'd come, being sure to hang the *No Molestar* tag on the door first.

Back at the SUV, she threw both duffels into the back and, following Reyes's directions, drove south out of town. It wasn't long before she saw the rock formation where she was supposed to turn, saw the bright lights still burning against the sunrise and the high wall of the compound in the distance. She didn't turn, but continued driving until she could no longer see the compound, figuring if she couldn't see them, they couldn't see her either. Then, taking advantage of the SUV's reinforced undercarriage and four-wheel drive, she turned off the road completely and headed into the desert abutting the compound. She drove until she found a cluster of huge rocks huddled beneath a short rise, then did a 180º turn and backed into the cover of the rocks so that she was hidden from the road, but could still make a quick getaway when she and Vincent returned.

Switching off the engine, she listened to the ping of metal as it cooled, and leaned back, realizing abruptly that the seat was too far back. She was tall, but the seat was adjusted for Vincent's height and in all the rush and stress of the last hour, she hadn't bothered to change the settings. Tears pricked her eyes for the first time since they'd taken Vincent. She knew it was partly exhaustion, but she couldn't turn off her brain, couldn't stop seeing Reyes slice Vincent's throat, the blood pouring in a red flood over his chest as his eyes met hers across the room. She sucked in a deep breath and fought the tears back. That was the one thing that kept her going, the look in Vincent's eyes when they met hers, the certainty that she would remain free, that she'd find him and break him out.

Turning off the interior lights, she climbed out from behind the wheel and hunkered down on the side of the SUV away from the road. It was much colder outside, the morning sun still too weak to provide warmth, but she needed to use her iPad and didn't want random flashes to give her away. Fortunately, there was cell coverage out here in the middle of the desert, probably thanks to the very bad guys whose compound she was plotting to invade.

She opened her iPad and pulled up Google maps, quickly locating the town, then expanding outward until she spotted the *narcos'* compound. She smiled, thinking that while the drug lords were powerful, they weren't more powerful than Google. Nor did they have the kind of pull that could get their compound blurred out of the map image. She had a very nice bird's eye view of the forecourt, which was nothing but dirt, just like that bitch Reyes had said.

The compound itself consisted of several buildings, including more than a few which were detached from the main hacienda, but it was obvious which one was the shack where Reyes had assumed they'd keep Vincent. Lana studied the layout and had a single thought. *Not good.* She'd have to go over the wall, cross a good thirty feet of wide open ground, disable the guard—only one, if Reyes could be trusted, which she'd already proved she couldn't be—break into the shack, and somehow get a weakened Vincent out of there.

And there her plans stuttered to a halt. She couldn't break him out of there in daylight! Fuck. Vincent would be dead weight and he was far too heavy for her to carry over a damn wall. But even if she *could* somehow manage to carry him, the sunlight would kill him.

Damn, damn, damn.

She closed her eyes and tried to think, but she was just so fucking tired. Her brain wasn't working the way it usually did. So she tried another tack, breaking the operation down to its essential parts. First, she needed to get in there. She frowned down at the iPad and tried to zoom in on the shack itself, wanting details. What was the building made of? Was there a lock on the door? And, if so, could she deal with it? But the resolution wasn't good enough and the angle wasn't right anyway. She could see something that looked like the shutters Reyes had talked about, though, which only confirmed what she already knew, that she had the right building.

And then she thought about the other guy, the vampire who'd snitched to his cartel boss about Vincent. Was he in there with Vincent? She sure hoped not. But if he was . . . she'd simply have to stake him. After all, he'd betrayed Vincent. She didn't owe him anything.

But they've tortured him, a little voice reminded her. *They've kept him a slave.* Was he responsible for his actions under those conditions? Was he even capable of defying his masters?

She dropped the iPad on top of the case at her side, then pulled her knees up to her chest, and buried her face in her arms. This was all too much. She wasn't some kind of special ops super hero—she was a bounty hunter. Yeah, sure, she was a fair shot, and she was a wiz with a knife. But she didn't know much about planning a tactical assault. She couldn't shoot her way out of a crowd without getting a scratch, or leap over even a small building in a single bound.

She rested her head back against the warm metal of the SUV and sighed. No, she was no superhero, but somehow, she would figure out a way to rescue Vincent. Because she knew if the tables were turned, he'd do the same for her.

"Okay," she said out loud, then continued the conversation in her head, remembering that she was in hiding. First, she tallied up the things she had going for her.

One, they wouldn't expect her, because they didn't know about her. She had to believe that. If they'd known, they would have taken her in the club or tracked her down afterward.

Two, she had this cool SUV for an escape vehicle, all bulletproof and slick, and fully gassed up to boot.

Three, she had weapons. Her Sig 9mm as well as the Glock and plenty of extra ammo and, of course, her knives. They wouldn't hold up against an army, but a guard or two, she could handle. And then there was Vincent. Given the way he'd managed to throw Reyes across the bar, even after being sliced and diced, she figured he was their best weapon. But it might be worth checking his duffel to see if he had anything else stashed—

Lana blinked in sudden realization. *Vincent* was their best weapon. She stared at the hillside in front of her, at the million and one details revealed in the pink light of a new day. Okay, so she had to break *in* during the daylight, but what if she didn't break *out* until after dark? If she could get into the shack with no one seeing her, she could be there when Vincent woke up and they could break out together. Of course, he'd probably need . . . Fuck. He was going to need blood, and somehow, she didn't think the nice drug traffickers would have left a bag of blood on a doily-covered tray for his dinner.

She was going to have to be his dinner. Damn. Vincent was going to laugh his ass off about this. He'd be lucky if she didn't stake him in his sleep when this was all over with.

But first, she had to rescue him.

LANA CHECKED Google maps again, wanting to verify her position relative to the compound. She wasn't too worried about the hike in. She was an experienced hiker, in good shape, and her combat boots were worn in and good for walking long distances. But if she and Vincent were racing for their lives on the way out, it would be better if they didn't have to run a mile or more across the open desert to get to their escape vehicle.

The terrain wasn't completely flat in this part of Mexico. The Sierra Madre mountain range ran parallel to the coast between the ocean and the interior, and the men who were holding Vincent had built their compound so that it was tucked right up against the foothills of those mountains. It probably gave the back courtyard of the hacienda some shade in the afternoon, and having the bulk of the hills at their back likely provided the crooks with a false sense of security. Lana looked at those hills and saw a convenient place from which to spy on the compound. But most of the people who lived around here were probably either too afraid to do any spying, or worked for the cartel and so not inclined to do so.

She studied the map until she was confident she knew where her vehicle was relative to the compound, and had mapped out a trail that would take her there. She knew it was rough—Google's view of this remote location didn't include the kind of ground obstacles that could screw up a hiker—but it would at least keep her going in the right direction. Satisfied she'd done everything she could to prepare, she climbed into the backseat and stretched out. She didn't really expect to sleep, but figured she could at least close her eyes and find her inner Zen for a few hours. Not that there was much chance of that. She was eager to get started, impatient to get her first real look at the compound, since she couldn't fully plan until she saw what she was dealing with. She set her phone alarm for two hours and closed her eyes.

Twenty minutes later, she was still awake. Apparently, it didn't matter how tired she was. Her brain had refused to shut down. So rather than drive herself crazy counting sheep, she'd given up. Standing in front of the open cargo hatch, she exchanged her Levis for her black combat-style pants, needing the extra pockets for supplies, and replaced her long-sleeved T-shirt with one that was sleeveless. It was going to get hot before the morning was over, and while she couldn't do without the jacket, the shirt at least would be cooler. A small bottle of water went into one of her jacket pockets. It was the bare minimum she'd need, but anything more and she'd need a separate backpack. One of the spare mags for her Sig went into the pouch on her harness, the others into the deep pocket on her thigh. Her compact first-aid kit, fairly complete for all its size, went into her other thigh pocket, along with a small Maglite. Her Sig was holstered on the harness, with a silencer zipped into the inside pocket of her jacket. She considered taking the Glock, but decided against it. She only had so many pockets and, besides, she was aiming for stealth not firepower. *That* meant knives, and she had plenty of those. The nine-inch stiletto went into her boot, a six-inch fixed-blade in a sheath on her thigh, and the three-and-a-half inch push button in her pocket. But while she hadn't exactly come on this trip prepared for combat operations, she was a bounty hunter. Half of her job description was surveillance, and she *was* prepared for that.

Unzipping one of the inner compartments of her duffel, she shoved her hand deep into the pocket, mouthing a silent *aha* when her fingers touched her binoculars. They were compact, but amazingly powerful, very handy when sitting outside an apartment waiting for her fugitive to show. She went to grab them, but her fingers closed in on something else, too.

Something she only vaguely recognized because she'd bought it a few months ago on a whim, in Mexico, as a matter of fact. But she'd never used it. It was a morphine-filled auto-injector, similar to an EpiPen in form, but with the entirely opposite effect. At the time she'd bought it, Lana had been coming off a retrieval where the skip had been big and mean and not at all happy to discover he was not only being brought in, but by a woman. She'd had a partner for that job, but as often as not, she worked alone. The episode had made her consider what might have happened if she'd been alone and the big guy had decided to fight back. So when she'd seen the morphine auto-injector only a few days later, she hadn't thought twice. She'd picked up three of them and shoved one in her duffel. The other two were still sitting in her refrigerator back home. But this one was going to come in very handy indeed.

It took her the better part of four hours to climb the hill and make her way down the other side and around to a position where she could see into the compound. She moved slowly, careful to avoid standing out against the hill, thankful for the sun which was rising behind the hill and casting her into shadow. When she found a good position, she settled down to watch. Surveillance work was both tedious and exhausting. Sitting in one place, staring at the same thing for hours, might seem easy, but the boredom got to you after a while, eating into your concentration, making your body stiffen up as muscles demanded movement.

There was a lot of activity in the compound, despite Fidelia Reyes's insistence that most of the guards were gone. Lana identified the shack easily enough, although, since it was constructed of concrete block, she wouldn't have called it that. To her a shack was something rickety and made of wood.

But the single armed guard was right where he was supposed to be, sitting on a chair only a few feet from the "shack's" only door. A patio-style umbrella in a metal stand gave him a circle of protection from the sun, but angled the way it was, it would cut into his line of sight, too. She wondered why they had a guard at all, since the vampires weren't going anywhere during the day. But then, she assumed it was force of habit. If there was a prisoner, there must be a guard, even if that prisoner was a vampire and thus completely immobilized by sunshine.

Either that or the guard was designed to keep possible allies, like Lana, out, rather than keep the vampires in.

In any event, at least that much of Reyes's intel was accurate. Lana used her binocs to zoom in on the details of the shack, including those damn shutters. As far as she could see, the slats were all closed down tight, so Vincent's captors hadn't decided to torture him yet. Maybe they hoped to persuade him to their way of thinking. Or maybe they really didn't understand the difference between their current vampire slave and a vampire powerful enough to be second-in-command of an entire territory. She had a feeling they were going to find out before this was over.

Satisfied that the shutters were no threat, she focused on the door, or, more importantly, its lock. Among the many illicit skills she'd been taught by her father's hunters over the years was lock picking. The guys had treated her like a clever pet, or, more charitably, a mascot, teaching her all sorts of tricks. Most locks were easy enough for a reasonably smart child to get through, but she was better than that. Way better. Her dad thought her skill at lock picking came from the fact that she was a woman, that her fingers were more delicate, and also more sensitive. She didn't know whether that was true, but she did know she could open a lock faster than any of the guys in her dad's office.

The trick in this case would be getting inside the shack without anyone realizing she had done so. If it was a padlock, she was out of luck. It might be easy to get through, but it would be impossible to make the lock appear engaged from inside the shack. She scooted several feet to her left, trying to get a better angle on the locking mechanism. She was still moving, in a bent-over half-crouch when there was a sudden flurry of activity down below. Dropping where she stood, she watched as three SUVs appeared from around one of the out-buildings and pulled up to the entrance of the main building. The wrought-iron gate clanged open and two children came rushing out of the house, followed at a more sedate pace by a couple who were obviously dressed for church. The woman's skirt fell a modest two inches below her knee, and she wore a lacy cardigan that covered her bare arms, while a black lace mantilla covered half of her long, dark hair. The man wore a pale suit with a tie, and the children, both boys, wore miniature versions of the same thing.

Lana frowned, trying to remember what day of the week it was. Traveling all night and sleeping all day confused her calendar, but she'd arrived at Vincent's office on Sunday, which made this . . . Wednesday. Maybe the day was a religious holiday. Mexico was mostly Catholic, but despite both of her parents being nominally of the same faith, Lana hadn't been raised with any religion.

Whatever was happening down below, however, was good for her. The man about to go off with his family was obviously someone important, maybe even the big boss, because he was taking a whole bunch of guards with him. Two went in the SUV that the family climbed into, and another six piled into the remaining vehicles. The guard manning the shack had risen to his feet as soon as the family had appeared, and he stayed that way, standing stiff and straight as if at attention, until the SUVs had exited the compound and sped down the dirt road, leaving a plume of dust behind them. Almost immediately, the guard slumped back into his chair, looking more bored than ever.

Lana's heart sped up as she contemplated what the boss's departure meant for her. This could be her best chance to get inside the shack. With the big man gone, everyone would relax, especially the guy guarding the shack, who hadn't appeared that alert to begin with. He had to know there was no chance of anyone trying to escape. But even more importantly, there were now eight fewer armed guards in the compound.

She switched her focus to the surrounding wall. It was at least ten feet tall and was constructed with the same kind of blocks used to build the shack. Except that the shack walls had been left bare, while the perimeter wall had been painted a suitably pleasing shade of pale yellow. There were plenty of foot and handholds between the blocks, if one knew how to make use of them. But while Lana was a passable climber, scaling the wall wasn't her first choice. She started looking for a shortcut, something that would give her a step up onto the wall, so she wouldn't have to climb the whole thing. It didn't look good. The best she could hope for was a pile of mossy rocks that never saw the sun. They would be slippery as hell, but they were close enough to the wall at one point that she could use them as a starting point. Unfortunately, she'd still have to climb the rest of the way.

She sighed, staring down the hill and pursing her lips in irritation. Damn Vincent. Why couldn't he have been an asshole, someone she could leave behind without a thought? She began repacking her gear, securing it for a quick descent, followed by a damn wall climb. She was so fucked. She was probably going to end up the prisoner of a Mexican drug cartel. If she was lucky, they'd ransom her back to her father. If not . . . well, she didn't want to think about that. Not when she was about to launch what was probably the riskiest venture of her entire life.

Damn Vincent.

LANA'S CLIMB DOWN to the edge of the compound was unexpectedly easy. She moved slowly, checking every foothold, because she couldn't afford to let something as avoidable as a twisted ankle ruin everything. But between the uneven terrain, the morning shadows, and the rough scrub growing between the rocks, there was enough cover that she was never in danger of being tracked unless someone was specifically watching her location. But it didn't seem as if anyone was. There were guards, but their focus was clearly on the main gate and the open desert and road beyond it.

In no time at all, Lana found herself balancing on the very slick and uneven surface of the rocks she'd identified from above. They were even shorter than she'd hoped, giving her maybe two feet of a start on the ten foot wall. Stretching her arms straight up, she could touch the flat top of the wall, but just barely. She'd need to climb at least another two feet in order to lever herself up and over, and once there, she'd have to move quickly. The guards might not be paying much attention, but they were far more likely to notice her sitting on top of the wall than they had been when she was creeping down the hillside.

Zipping her various pockets closed, she flexed her fingers and started up. Her first effort was unsuccessful, succeeding only in sending her slamming back down to crack her knee painfully on the slick rocks. She hunched down, rubbing her knee and telling herself she could do this. That she had to because Vincent was in there and as unlikely as it seemed, he needed her. She stretched her leg out, putting her foot on the ground and bending the knee experimentally. It hurt like hell, and the feeling of tightness told her it was probably swelling, but it still worked. So she stood, balanced herself on the rocks, and tried again.

She dug her fingers into the cracks, her boots sliding over the smooth, painted surface. Eventually, she managed to throw one forearm over the top. It wasn't enough to pull herself over, but she hung on, muscles straining as she used the little bit of leverage she had to lessen the weight on her legs. Finally, with a maneuver that was both awkward and painful, she got both arms over the top of the wall, and there she hung for several minutes, waiting to be discovered, listening for the shouts and gunfire that would end her life.

But the outcry didn't come. She'd worried that there might be guards she hadn't spotted, someone taking a break among the heavy greenery of the garden or sitting behind one of the chimneys on the roof. When no one reacted, she swallowed a grunt of effort and dragged the top half of her body all the way over, quickly forcing her legs to follow, and then half-fell, half-dropped down to the dusty ground where she froze. No one sounded an alarm, but she remained still for several minutes, checking out her surroundings. There was an iron gate to her right, and she could see the gardens on the back of the house through its weathered bars. To her left was a windowless building that she thought was a garage. The SUVs she'd seen earlier had come from this direction, and it matched the mental map she'd made of the place after studying the image on her iPad. It was pure, good fortune, but she'd stumbled on an excellent spot. The forecourt where she needed to go was just around the corner, with the shack about thirty feet beyond that. She could hug the shadows between the garage and the main house until she reached the courtyard, then use the landscaping close to the house itself for several more yards as she came up behind the lone guard.

Working as silently as possible, she rearranged her gear, unzipping the pockets holding her backup mag and morphine, and checking everything else to be sure it was secure. She drew her 9mm, retrieved the silencer from her pocket, and threaded it on. She didn't plan on shooting anyone, but if it came to that, she didn't want to alert the entire compound.

With the Sig in one hand, she stood and began making her way along the garage wall to the forecourt. Once she got there, a quick peek showed it was as quiet as it had been ever since the SUVs took off. The guard was slumped in his chair, his submachine gun resting on an ample belly, a hat pulled low over his brow. If Lana were an optimist, she might have thought he was asleep. If she could have counted on that, she'd have skipped the skulking around, walked directly up behind him, and slapped him with the morphine auto-injector. But she wasn't much on optimism. It was too much like wishful thinking, and that could get a hunter killed.

So, she stuck to her original plan, sneaking along the wall of the main house, ducking beneath windows with their decorative iron bars, slipping behind bushes, stepping over cacti, until she was nerve-rackingly close to the guard. He was sitting roughly fifteen feet to her left and no more than six feet ahead of her.

This was it. She pulled the auto-injector out of her pocket, holding it in her left hand as she removed the plastic cap with her teeth, feeling a ridiculous twinge of guilt when she let the cap fall to the ground. With the 9mm in her right hand and the auto-injector in her left, she steeled herself and stepped away from the house. There was no time for doubt, no room for hesitation. Feeling like there was a target on her forehead the whole time, she strode directly up behind the guard and shoved the auto-injector against his bare neck. He made a funny, whistling kind of a grunt, jerked once as if trying to straighten from his slouch, and then slumped forward.

Lana had considered what would happen once the guard woke from his drugged sleep. Would he remember someone hitting him from behind? Or would he simply assume he'd fallen asleep and be grateful that no one had noticed? She had no idea how long the effects of the morphine would last. But either way, she'd be trapped inside the shack with Vincent by then, and it would be far too late to change her plan. Hopefully, if the guard did raise an alarm, no one would think or even *want* to look inside the vampires' prison.

All of these thoughts raced through her head as she hurried over to the shack and crouched down to get her first good look at the lock. Except that there wasn't one. She wasted a full minute staring in disbelief, then scanned every inch of the door, looking for traps. When she didn't find any, she realized it made sense. There was no need for a lock during the day because the vamps were asleep, and at night, even an ordinary vampire would be strong enough to rip the door off its hinges, so a lock would be useless. Add to that Fidelia Reyes's claim that the *narcos* kept their pet vamp weak and well-trained, and he'd probably been so conditioned to obedience that he'd never considered trying to escape.

Vincent, on the other hand, was an entirely different category of vampire, as his captors were about to discover.

She opened the door slowly, worried about letting sunlight inside, but as it turned out, it didn't matter. Vincent was at the far end of the shack—

far being a relative term—lying beneath the largest of the shuttered windows. His height made him too long to stretch out completely, so he was resting on his side, rolled into an uncomfortable-looking fetal position. The other vampire was literally huddled in a corner, sitting with his legs bent and tucked against his chest, his arms wrapped tightly around his knees and his head resting on his arms. It looked even more uncomfortable than Vincent's fetal curl.

Lana pulled the door quietly closed. It was hot and dusty inside the small building. Not an ounce of fresh air circulated and the floor was nothing but bare dirt. She couldn't believe the other vamp had lived this way for who knew how many years. Lana knelt next to Vincent, her heart pounding, her lungs straining for air in the intense heat, sweat already beginning to soak her shirt beneath the jacket.

He was wearing the same bloody clothes he'd had on last night, and his hair was matted and sweaty. She brushed the heavy strands off his forehead and froze, thinking there was blood in his hair, but then realized his sweat itself was slightly pink. One of the side effects of consuming nothing but blood, apparently. He was breathing slowly, but easily, and considering the severity of his injuries last night, he looked damned good. She'd seen what the Reyes woman had done to him, seen the blood gushing out of his veins in a river of red. The wounds were still there on his neck, but they were healing already. If he'd fed properly, they might have been gone completely by now. She stroked her fingers gently over the dark pink scar tissue, then pulled her hand back, feeling abruptly uncomfortable. She and Vincent were friends, not lovers. She didn't have the right to touch him like that.

Judging the distance to the door, she repositioned him slightly, so that his legs had more room. If anyone opened the door, she could always move him. But then, if anyone opened the door, they'd *both* be in a world of hurt.

Taking off her jacket, she removed the various pieces of gear from the pockets, setting them on the ground where she could get to them in a hurry. The jacket itself she folded and placed under Vincent's head. He might not be aware of what was going on, but she couldn't bear the sight of him lying in the dirt.

She touched him one more time—resting her hand on his chest, feeling the slow steady beat of his heart—then positioned herself between Vincent and the door and leaned back against the concrete wall with a sigh. Now that she was in here, she had hours with nothing to do but wait. She'd never planned on sneaking in this early. It was supposed to have been during the afternoon siesta, not right after breakfast. But the boss's excursion into town had been an opportunity she couldn't pass up. She looked around and saw nothing but dirt and block walls. And this was what the other vampire came "home" to every morning. Lana eyed him curiously. It was difficult to judge, with him curled into the corner like that, but he definitely seemed smaller than Vincent. Of course, Vincent was bigger than most men, vampire or not, so it probably wasn't a fair comparison. This other vamp looked like he was about her height and weight, which made him slender for a man. And he looked young. Vampires all looked young, for the most part, but since their appearance reflected the age at which they were turned, there were definite variations. This guy didn't look any older than eighteen or twenty.

And then there was the fact that he was huddled into a corner like a scared mouse instead of a vampire who could snap a man's spine with ease. That alone told her more than she wanted to know about his life and how he was treated. She didn't *want* to feel sorry for him. After all, he'd set up Vincent to be captured and enslaved by the same people who tormented *him* daily. But the very fact that he had been tortured, even if only by his imprisonment in this box, made her question his guilt. Had he ever known anything else? Were vampires like ducks? Did they imprint on whatever parent figure found them first? And if that person was someone who would lock you in a dirty prison every day, did that shape who you became?

She wondered if any calculation of the other vamp's guilt was going to matter to Vincent. He didn't strike her as a forgiving kind of guy. Her warning to Fidelia Reyes hadn't been said in jest. She had no doubt that Vincent would go after the woman just as soon as he'd dealt with his current captors, which would be in . . . she checked the time on her sports watch and nearly groaned out loud. She still had at least six hours to go before the sun went down. Six hours of sitting on a dirt floor in the stifling heat after a night of no sleep with nothing to do. She didn't fool herself into believing she wouldn't doze off. Maybe if it hadn't been so hot, she could have managed. But between the heat, the boredom, and the lack of sleep . . . she had to assume logically that her eyes would close eventually.

Knowing this, she kept the 9mm with its silencer in her right hand. If someone opened the door unexpectedly, she wanted a quick, quiet reaction. She didn't want to raise the entire compound because the sleeping guard outside woke up and got a bug up his ass to check the prisoners.

And then, as prepared as she figured she could be, she settled back against the wall next to Vincent and waited for sunset.

Chapter Ten

VINCENT WOKE WITH the perfect, instant memory of where he was and what had happened. He remained still, his eyes closed, breathing slowly. There were others nearby and he needed to know who they were before he gave himself away. It took only seconds to identify... Lana? What the fuck was she doing here? He'd warned her off as best as he could last night and had thought she'd acknowledged the warning. He'd seen her fade back into the crowd. Had they caught her anyway?

But even knowing it was Lana sitting closest to him, he didn't move. There was another vampire here, someone he didn't know. There was no reason he should personally be acquainted with every vampire in Mexico, although as Enrique's lieutenant, he knew more than most. But this one... he drew the other vampire's scent into his nostrils. Vincent didn't know his physical age, but as a vampire, he was young, turned no more than a few years ago. And since he was locked in this crappy prison, he probably wasn't all that powerful either.

Granted, Vincent was in the same crappy prison, and he was certainly powerful enough. But he'd been taken by trickery. And, besides, this prison wasn't going to hold him for much longer.

He also knew that the other vamp hadn't been taken by violence the way Vincent had, not recently anyway. The only strong scent of blood—other than Lana's enticing and readily available supply—was the blood soaking Vincent's clothes, and that was easily identifiable as his own.

So who was this guy? Enrique hadn't created any new vampires that Vincent knew of, and he had spies close to Enrique who reported to him on just that sort of activity. So, was there a master in Enrique's territory who was siring new vampires without the Mexican lord's permission? And, if so, why would that master go to such lengths to take Vincent? The woman's sneak attack in the bar—the soon-to-be-dead woman—would only work once, and anyone strong enough to be a master vampire would know that he couldn't hold Vincent. Whoever had orchestrated the assault last night had wanted him taken alive. If they'd wanted him dead, they could have shot him, to much greater effect.

But Vincent was very much alive, and he had to wonder what the mastermind behind his capture was hoping to accomplish. Even weakened, Vincent was still a match for almost anyone in Mexico. Excepting Enrique, of course, although at full strength, Vincent was a match even for him. That parity in strength was part of why Vincent and Enrique didn't get along. The Mexican lord wanted a powerful lieutenant, but not one who could best him in a challenge.

But Enrique wasn't behind last night's attack. If he'd wanted Vincent out of the picture, he'd have killed him directly—or at least tried. There was nothing about this situation that made sense. But of all those senseless things, the only one that truly worried him was the fact that Lana was imprisoned next to him.

He opened his eyes. What a dump. Block walls and a dirt floor. He glanced around, moving only his eyes. Shutters with nothing behind them but the last gasp of daylight. The sun was already below the horizon or Vincent wouldn't be awake. The little bit of light left was simply the gleam of sunlight over the curve of the earth. For most vampires, even that remnant of sunlight would have kept them asleep, but the more powerful vampires, like Vincent, could rise as soon as the sun itself dipped below the horizon. He still couldn't walk into that light, but it didn't keep him down either.

Those shutters, on the other hand, told a different story. They were designed to torture vampires. He'd seen something like it once, but it was so long ago that he couldn't bring the memory into focus. He would have, with a little concentration, but there were more important things to worry about right now.

Lana was sitting between him and the door, her head against the wall, her eyes closed, but with gun in hand. Her arms were bare and he realized he was lying on her jacket. He smiled. She was guarding him and she'd given him her jacket as a pillow. She cared. He'd known he would win her over eventually. Although he could think of a hundred better ways to do it.

The other vampire was squeezed into the opposite corner as if to make himself as small a target as possible, and Vincent experienced a surge of raw anger at the way the vamp had been treated.

"Vincent?" Lana's whisper was so soft he barely heard it. But he shifted his gaze to her, then reached up and squeezed her arm in a careful warning. She slid down from her sitting position until they were lying face to face, their mouths close enough to kiss. She cupped his jaw carefully, her thumb moving back and forth over his beard. "Are you okay?" she asked.

Vincent fought against the urge to rub against her hand like a cat. "I'm getting there," he told her. "Tell me what happened."

"That bitch—"

"I know that part, *querida*. What happened after?"

"I faded into the crowd like you wanted me to—"

Her words sounded more like a question and he nodded to indicate she'd done the right thing.

"—but as I was walking back to the SUV, I spotted the woman who cut you practically crawling down the street. You tossed her across the room after she attacked you."

"I remember that, too. I should have killed her."

"There's time for that later. Anyway, I gave her a ride home in exchange for some intel on who sent her to attack you. She all but admitted that the cartel owns this whole town."

"It's nearly dark, Lana," he said urgently, wanting her to speed up.

"Right, sorry. Anyway, she told me where they were holding you and what they wanted. That guy over there—" She pointed at the other vampire who was still sleeping soundly, which only reaffirmed his youth. "—is a vampire, but you probably knew that. He's been with them pretty much from day one. He thinks he belongs to them, like a slave. And that's how they treat him. They keep him in this—"

"I figured that out. What do they want with *me*?"

"He knew who you were," she said, indicating the other vamp with a jerk of her head. "He must have seen us when we first pulled into town or something. He knew you were powerful, and he told them about you. They think they can make you their slave the same way they have him. But with you, they'll have a lot more power at their command."

Vincent stared at her, blinking his eyes against the dust, speechless for once. The local cartel bosses—probably a regional HQ of the larger cartel organization—thought, based on their experience with the newbie over there, that they could enslave Vincent?

"So much for détente between the cartels and the vamps," Lana murmured. And she had a point. This shouldn't have happened. Something was seriously wrong here.

Vincent started to sit up, but was forced to lie back down when his head spun dizzily. This was not good. He was weaker than he'd expected. He'd lost blood before, but never so much, so fast. A weaker vamp would have been down for days, might very well have died. If the woman had cut arteries instead of veins, Vincent would be dead, too. There was only so much the Vampire symbiote could do to keep its host alive and well in the face of that kind of trauma.

"Vincent?" Lana had started to sit up with him and now leaned over, her fingers once again soft and warm against his face. "You okay?"

"Still getting there. I lost more blood than I thought."

She gazed down at him, her forehead creased with worry, biting her full lower lip in a way that made his dick hard. Or at least as hard as it could get when he was short a few pints of blood.

"Do you need blood?" she whispered hesitantly.

Vincent wanted to grin, but he knew how much it had cost her to make the offer. He gripped her wrist gently. "I hate to ask, Lana—"

"You're not asking. I'm volunteering," she told him. "I didn't break into this hole just so we could both die here."

"Then, if you wouldn't mind . . ." he said softly.

"You know . . . this wouldn't be happening if you didn't feel the need to seduce *every* woman who comes within five feet of you," she muttered as she slid down next to him again.

"Jealous?" he teased, knowing she was nervous and covering it with irritation.

She gave a ladylike snort of dismissal. "As if." She tugged at the neck of her T-shirt and said, "How do we—"

Vincent could have told her that her wrist would do just as well as her neck . . . but he wasn't that good of a man. He'd wanted a taste of Lana Arnold from the moment he'd met her. She wasn't that wrong about him seducing every woman he met, but that wasn't why he'd wanted to taste *her*. He was willing to admit that part of it was precisely because she'd been so completely immune to his charm. The thrill of the chase and all that. He *was* a predator, after all. But it was more than just the drive to hunt. She was like this self-contained little universe, traveling through life all alone, letting no one truly touch her. She cared about people, like her father and mother, and the men she'd called uncles. But she kept herself apart. It was about responsibility, more about duty than love.

He wanted to know what it was like to be loved by such a woman, wanted to be the flame that finally warmed her heart.

And besides, she had a killer body and all that silky hair.

He rolled up on one elbow, cupped her hip in one hand and gave a tug, pulling her beneath him. Her eyes widened in surprise and maybe a touch of fear.

"Don't be afraid, *querida,* I would never hurt you."

"I'm not afraid. Just do it."

Vincent smiled. Not the most romantic offer he'd ever received, but certainly among the most inviting. He brushed a few loose tendrils of hair away from her neck, lamenting the necessity that had her hair bound into its usual braid. The next time he took her vein, her hair would be spread around her like a silken sheet.

"Vincent?" she whispered, and there was the tiniest tremor in her voice.

"Lana?"

"Is something wrong?"

"Nothing at all." He touched his mouth to her neck and nibbled on the delicate flesh. For such a tough woman, she had very soft skin. His tongue slipped between his teeth for a longer lick. Her skin was salty with sweat, slightly gritty from the dirty floor. It was the most delicious thing he'd ever tasted. He rolled his gaze up and met Lana's confused eyes. Her cheeks were flushed—it was hot, she was embarrassed, but it was more than that. Her heart was racing and her breathing had grown shallow. She was excited by his touch, by the prospect of his bite. And the faint scent of her arousal was even more intoxicating than that of the blood rushing beneath his lips.

He held her gaze for a long moment. Forget the dirty floor, the overwhelming heat of their little prison. In that moment, his world collapsed to him and Lana. She made a soft sound, bending one knee so that his leg fell between both of hers. Vincent groaned, nearly swamped by a wave of hunger, and not only for blood. He wanted to fuck her until she screamed, to lap up the cream of her arousal, and then sink his fangs into her thigh as she bucked beneath him.

He reined in his lust with brutal force. He would have Lana Arnold in every way he wanted. But this was not the place. For now, he would settle for a taste of her sweet blood. If such a thing could be called settling. He lowered his head to her neck, his fangs piercing her skin and sliding into the velvet softness of her vein. A gasp escaped her lips as the euphoric in his saliva hit her bloodstream, followed by a quiet moan as she shivered in his embrace, her bent knee closing over his thigh to hold him close as she flexed against the erection that was straining painfully against his jeans.

Vincent growled soft and low, his fangs still deep in her vein, the dark nectar of her blood rolling down his throat, just as delicious as he'd known it would be.

Lana bit back a cry, her fingers digging into his shoulders as she writhed in the throes of the orgasm brought on by his bite. Vincent lifted his head, licking the two tiny wounds automatically, totally captivated by the sight before him. It took every ounce of willpower he possessed to stop himself from taking her right there. She would have let him. Hell, in her current state, she'd probably have begged him to fuck her and to hell with the dirt floor or the crazy cartel guards right outside the door. To hell with the strange vampire in the corner . . .

Vincent shifted his gaze abruptly and found the other vampire staring not at Vincent, but at Lana. Vincent acted faster than he'd thought possible, jumping up to crouch protectively between Lana and the stranger, growling a soft warning even as he sent a narrow spear of power that forced the other vampire to look at him and not Lana.

The younger vampire's frightened eyes met Vincent's for a brief instant before he lowered them in submission. The vamp was terrified. Hell, living like this, he probably spent most of his waking hours terrified, but he had a particularly good reason to be worried about Vincent. Because this little bastard was the one who'd betrayed Vincent to the local cartel boys, the one who'd set his attempted capture and enslavement in motion. And, yeah, Vincent thought in terms of *attempted* because, although they didn't know it yet, his captors' plan was about to blow up in their faces in a very spectacular fashion.

"What's your name, boy?" he demanded, still blocking the vamp's view of Lana whose orgasm was fading and slowly being replaced by intense embarrassment.

"Jerry Moreno, sir," the vamp mumbled, still not meeting Vincent's gaze.

Vincent tilted his head curiously and on impulse switched to English. "Who's your master?"

"Alessio Olivares Camarillo is my master, sir," Moreno responded in perfect, unaccented American English, which told Vincent where he'd come from, but little else.

Vincent frowned. "I don't know any vampire by that name and certainly no master. Not in Mexico. Is he in the U.S.?"

Jerry Moreno looked up finally and gave Vincent a puzzled look. "*Señor* Camarillo is not a vampire," he said, surprise obvious in his voice.

"Then he's not your master," Vincent dismissed. "I didn't ask whom you worked for, I asked who your master was."

Moreno appeared visibly distraught. "Forgive me, sir. I want to answer your question, but I don't understand."

"Who created you?" Vincent demanded impatiently. "Who made you Vampire?"

"I don't know. No one ever told me."

Vincent stared. He'd never encountered anything like this. The only way a vampire wouldn't know his own Sire was if . . .

"How old are you?"

"I was twenty years old when I woke up as a vampire. That was two years ago, so . . . I guess I'm twenty-two."

"What happened before that? You're American, right? Why were you in Mexico?"

"Yes, sir, my family's in Oregon. I was in the Army. We'd just come back from our second tour in Afghanistan and a bunch of us came down to Mexico on leave. And that's all I remember."

"You don't remember meeting anyone? Getting injured, maybe dying?"

Moreno looked shocked. "No, sir!"

"And have you been here with Camarillo the whole time?"

"Yes, sir. *Señor* Camarillo was the first face I saw when I woke as a vampire. He told me I belonged to him, that he was my master, and he gave me my first blood."

"Not your first blood," Vincent muttered to himself. Some master vamp had taken this kid to the edge of death, fed him his blood, made him a vampire, then essentially bound him to the human drug lord. Had he been the one who killed him? Or had he found him already dying? Either way, he'd turned the boy without his consent.

Vincent caught the boy sneaking a glance at Lana and snapped a whip of power at him. "If you want to survive the next ten minutes, boy, don't look at her," he snarled. "Look at me."

The stark fear in the kid's gaze made Vincent feel guilty, but not so guilty that he was going to let the bastard gawk at Lana.

"You okay, *querida?*" he asked over his shoulder, hearing her sit up behind him and begin to gather her weapons.

"Fine," she mumbled, sounding embarrassed. "Don't hurt the kid."

"He's not a kid. He's a fucking vampire who helped a bunch of fucking humans capture me. Or try to."

"Try to?" she repeated, and he was gratified to hear the snap back in her voice. "Seems like they succeeded."

"You don't believe that," he said confidently. "You wouldn't be here if you believed that."

"Well, don't hurt the kid anyway. They've hurt him enough."

Vincent shot a glance over his shoulder at her. "How do you know?"

"The same way you do, tough guy. Look at the way they treat him, keeping him in this crappy prison, making him sweat all day in the sunshine. And you know they're not feeding him properly, or it would never work."

"He doesn't have much power," Vincent informed her, more than a little pissed that she was defending the vampire who could have gotten him killed.

"But you do," she reminded him unnecessarily. "If they could do this to *you*, imagine what they've done to him."

She had a point. It still pissed him off, but she had a point. He managed not to roll his eyes, but he wanted to.

"Fine," he said, turning back to the other vampire. "Jerry, shake my hand."

"Sir?"

"Shake my damn hand, boy. I want to know who made you."

Moreno frowned, but he held out a trembling hand. Vincent grabbed it tightly, then looked up and caught the kid's gaze. "Let's take a trip down memory lane, Jerry."

Jerry's eyes went wide and Vincent fell into his memories. This was his talent. Every powerful vampire had one, just like every vampire made had some telepathic skill. But the truly powerful vampires were always distinguished by something more, a talent that was unique to them. And Vincent's talent was the ability to delve into a person's memories—whether human or vampire, it didn't seem to matter. The very first time it happened, he'd thought he was the one being captured, that it was the other vampire with the power. But he'd quickly realized that he was in control, that he was literally reliving the vamp's life with him, seeing details that even the vampire himself couldn't have recalled if he'd been asked.

Vincent didn't know where a vampire's abilities came from. Magic, some vampires insisted. Science, others scoffed, the untapped reservoir of the human brain brought forth by the Vampire symbiote. Since the symbiote itself was pretty much a mystery, Vincent figured anything was possible. He tended to go with science though. He didn't really have much belief in magic.

But wherever his talent came from, it had proved itself to be very useful. It had screwed with his head at first as he struggled to separate his own memories from those he tapped into. But he worked that out over time, utilizing some of those brain parts the science types insisted went untapped. He thought of it as building muscles he'd never had to use before, the same way one would exercise and develop muscles to deal with an injury—building new muscles to support the injured ones.

He'd also discovered a darker side to his talent, a useful but cruel application of his unique skill. It was something that he'd called upon more than once in his climb up the ladder of power to become Enrique's lieutenant. Yes, he could gently guide a person into seeing things in their own memories that they'd forgotten. But the dark correlation of that was the ability to *force* a person to see things they'd rather not, to trap them in an endless loop of horror and loss until they went mad, sinking into catatonia, becoming little better than a vegetable, until they died of starvation or worse. Although the "worse," in Vincent's opinion, was being kept alive by someone who thought they were doing you a favor, while you lived a tormented existence inside your own mind.

But he had no such plans for young Jerry Moreno. Not yet anyway. Moreno's fate would depend on what Vincent found.

Setting aside thoughts of Moreno's guilt or innocence, Vincent settled into the young vampire's head. He saw the most recent memories first. Saw the kid at the same gas station where Vincent and Lana had stopped on the way into town, wanting to be ready to take off the next night. Moreno had just happened to be walking out of the convenience store as Vincent stood there watching the numbers turn on the gas pump. Lana had been sitting in the SUV, which was why Moreno hadn't noticed her.

Vincent frowned as he realized what he was seeing. Moreno hadn't simply recognized Vincent as a powerful vampire, he'd actually recognized *Vincent* personally. How was it possible that Moreno knew Vincent, when Vincent didn't know anything about Moreno?

The answer had to lie somewhere deeper in the young vampire's past, and so that's where Vincent went. He dug beyond the recent memories, skimming through the boring, if somewhat violent, routine of Moreno's life as an enforcer for the cartel, speeding all the way back to the last memory

Jerry Moreno had as a human, the final moments of his life before someone made him Vampire. And there, Vincent found what he'd begun to suspect, but hadn't wanted to believe. Because the master vampire who'd ambushed Jerry Moreno on a dark street in Cancun, who'd bled him dry and turned him without so much as a conversation, was none other than Enrique himself.

Enrique was Lord of Mexico. He could make as many new vamps as he wanted. Vincent wasn't even surprised that Enrique had killed Moreno solely for that purpose. Vincent wouldn't have done it, but it wasn't that uncommon, especially among the older vampires. But the outrage was what Enrique had done next, something Vincent had never heard of happening before. Alessio Camarillo had been there with Enrique when Moreno woke to his first night as a vampire. The very first words Enrique had spoken to his new child, words imbued with the power he had as Moreno's Sire, had been an order for the young vampire to obey and protect Camarillo. He'd told him the Mexican drug lord was his master. And that was that. Camarillo had taken Moreno to his compound, and there he'd lived ever since. Treated like a dog, tortured when he did wrong, rewarded with a miniscule ration of blood when he did well. He was never given the blood he needed, never enough to permit him to think for himself, because that might lead him to question his existence.

And God-damned Enrique had known about it the whole time.

Vincent slipped slowly out of Jerry Moreno's memories, step by step, exquisitely careful not to cause any injury or pain. The kid had suffered enough. He didn't need Vincent mucking up his brain.

Vincent came back to himself between one eye blink and the next. Back to the stifling concrete hole that was Jerry Moreno's prison. But not for long.

"Lana?" he said without turning.

"I'm here. What's the plan?"

"You brought a weapon?"

"Of course. I've got my Sig with extra mags. And my knives."

Vincent grinned over his shoulder. "Knives? Plural?"

She met his gaze evenly and shrugged.

"You have a plan for getting out of here?" he asked her.

"You're the big bad vampire. I figured I'd leave that up to you."

"Smart woman," he said. "Here's what we're going to do. We'll blow open that door—"

"It's not locked," Lana told him dryly.

"It's never locked," Moreno volunteered, speaking for the first time since Vincent had gone down memory lane with him. "When I wake, I go to the kitchen to be fed. And then I report to *Señor* Camarillo and do whatever he tells me."

"Not tonight, kid," Vincent growled. "Can I borrow a knife, Lana?"

She blinked in surprise, but offered it willingly enough, handing him the three-and-a-half inch automatic Spyderco with a push button release. It was small, but truly deadly in the right hands.

Vincent took the blade and, without even hesitating, made a vertical slit in his left forearm, starting at his wrist and cutting at least four inches. He then faced Jerry Moreno directly.

"On your knees, boy," he said, putting enough power into his command that the kid immediately rolled up off the ground and crashed to his knees. Vincent held out his bleeding arm and said, "Now drink."

Moreno tilted toward the bloody feast, his nostrils flaring, his fangs bared. But he didn't drink right away. It was a testament to the strength of Enrique's hold over him that instead, he raised his eyes to Vincent with a questioning look.

"Sir?" he managed to say.

"You're a vampire, boy. It's time you learned what that means. Drink and be mine, and we'll get the fuck out of this place."

The naked longing in the kid's gaze was enough to break even a heart as jaded as Vincent's.

"Drink, Jerry," he said gently. "I promise I'll take care of you."

A single pink tear rolled down the young vamp's cheek as he lowered his mouth to Vincent's wrist and finally began to suck down the bounty of blood being offered. Vincent was a damn powerful vampire. His blood was richer than anything Moreno would have experienced since his first and last taste of Enrique's blood when he'd been turned. His sucking was tentative at first, but the longer he worked at it, the harder he sucked, until by the end he was smacking his lips and practically moaning with pleasure against Vincent's arm.

Vincent smiled at his obvious enjoyment, but they had other concerns tonight. It wouldn't do Moreno any good to be freed of Enrique and Camarillo's enslavement unless Vincent and Lana managed to get him out of the compound and keep him far enough away that they couldn't get him back. Which meant Vincent needed to retain all the strength that Lana's delectable blood had given him.

He touched Moreno's cheek lightly and the vamp instantly lifted his head to gaze up at Vincent with utter devotion.

"Jerry Moreno," Vincent said formally. "Do you come to me of your own free will and desire?"

"I do, sir," Moreno whispered fervently.

"And is this what you truly desire?"

"Oh, yes, sir."

"Then be mine," Vincent said, omitting the "drink and be mine" part, because the kid had already drunk his fill. Or at least as much of his fill as

Vincent could spare under the circumstances. It would take several more feedings—from someone other than Vincent, maybe a pretty young human from the bar back home—before Moreno was at full strength.

The young vampire fell back to sit on his heels, looking as dazed by everything that had happened as by the unaccustomed richness of the blood he'd drunk. Meanwhile, Vincent gazed down at his ruined wrist in dismay. It would heal quickly enough, but he'd prefer to wrap it—

"Here," Lana said from behind him. "Let me clean that off. I have some bandages. Not much. I couldn't bring a whole first-aid kit along, but . . ." She produced a compact, red nylon bag which unzipped to reveal a few sealed packets of antiseptic wipes, a couple of gauze pads, and a flattened bandage wrap, along with several Band-Aids of various sizes.

"I don't think the Band-Aids are going to do much good on that," she murmured, opening one of the wipes and beginning to wash away the blood.

"I'll be healed by tomorrow," Vincent told her.

"But tonight, you'll drip blood all over, so let me wrap it."

"Yes, ma'am."

She huffed out a disgusted breath, but she was smiling, and Vincent knew that, at some point in the last twelve hours or so, he'd won her over. Her bite-fueled orgasm notwithstanding, she wasn't ready to jump into bed with him yet, but she liked him. She felt a loyalty to him. After all, she'd risked her life to get in here and save him, hadn't she? But, as he watched her clean and bandage his arm, he had a feeling it was his kindness toward Moreno, and his obvious anger at the way Enrique had used and abused him, that had won her over. Lana might not let anyone get too close, but she cared about right and wrong. And Vincent had shown her that he did, too. He'd gotten over the first hurdle with her, but now he had to get past that last barrier. The one that didn't let her care too deeply, because life had shown her that to care was to be disappointed.

Vincent would show her differently. It was only a matter of time.

But speaking of time, theirs was rapidly running out. Camarillo would be sending someone soon to find out where his pet vampire was, and why he didn't show up at the kitchen on schedule.

Vincent waited until Lana had finished wrapping his arm, then took her hand. "I'm good, *querida,* but I can't take on an army by myself. So we're going to make a run for it. You know a quiet way out of here?"

Lana nodded. "The SUV is less than a half mile away, parked behind a hill just east of here. I came over it this morning. But if you can get us out the gate, it will shorten the distance we have to run."

"We make directly for the gate then. I can—"

"Also," she added, interrupting him. "Fidelia Reyes—the woman who cut you—told me that most of Camarillo's guards are gone. There's a big drug shipment or something. They'll be back tonight, but they might not have arrived yet. I didn't hear anything today that sounded like a bunch of guards coming back, no big noise of vehicles arriving." She frowned, then admitted, "Although I did fall asleep for a few hours."

"If there'd been something, it probably would have woken you, so let's hope for the best. We'll go for the gate. Jerry and I can move a lot faster than you, *querida*. So, you'll let me carry you."

"I will *not!*"

"Lana," he said patiently. "I won't leave you, and if we travel at your human pace, we'll all die. Do you understand?"

Her mouth tightened and she gave him a rebellious stare, but then jerked her head in a nod. "Fine."

Vincent grinned. "I'll be careful, and I won't tell anyone."

"Asshole," she muttered. "You want a weapon?"

"No. You keep those. Just try not to shoot me or Jerry, okay?"

She gave him a one shoulder shrug coupled with a twist of her luscious lips that was a very clear *maybe*.

Vincent winked at her, then turned to Moreno. "You ready, Jerry? You understand the plan?"

"Yes, sir," he responded with far more energy than he'd possessed earlier. "I know the layout and the guard dispositions. There will be two men at the gate, and others patrolling the compound. Lana's right in saying most of the guards are gone, but others will be here. I can run fast, sir."

Vincent nodded his approval. "I know you can. I'll take care of Lana. You just keep up. Anyone takes us on, we take them out. Can you do that?"

"Yes, sir. But if I may suggest, sir?"

"What?"

"A stealthy departure would be best. The cartel owns this town and everyone is armed. Only one guard will be waiting outside this building for me, and I know him. He knows I'm harmless, and he'll probably assume you are, too. He won't expect a woman, but—"

"I can take care of any guards we meet. They won't think anything I don't want them to," Vincent said confidently.

"If they won't expect a woman to be with you, who am I going to be in this little scenario?" Lana asked.

Vincent slung an arm around her waist and pulled her across the dirt floor, bringing her close enough to kiss, if she'd let him. The look on her face told him that was a good way to get bitten, so he simply grinned and said, "You're dinner, what else?"

Lana rolled her eyes. "Don't forget the gun."

Vincent laughed and tightened his hold for a moment before releasing her and standing upright for the first time. Or as upright as he could in the tight enclosure. "Everyone ready?" he asked, all joking set aside.

Vincent

He glanced at Jerry who stood next to him and said, "Yes, sir."

Lana had just finished tucking the first-aid kit back into her pocket. She rolled to her feet, the 9mm gripped in her right hand and held down against her leg, so that it was readily available but not advertised, and gave Vincent a tight nod.

"Let's do this," he said, and pushed open the unlocked door.

Chapter Eleven

JERRY MORENO walked out first, since he was the person everyone expected to see. Lana couldn't help noticing the confidence that cloaked him like a second skin ever since Vincent had fed him. This wasn't the vampire who'd been cowering in the corner less than an hour ago. Standing in the shadowed doorway, Lana kept waiting for the guard to notice the difference in his prisoner, to comment on it, but he never did. Or maybe he was so accustomed to Jerry showing up at sunset that he didn't even look.

He *did* notice when Vincent emerged behind Moreno, however. How could he not? Vincent was a *presence*, at least three inches over six feet and powerfully built. But there was much more to him than just his physical size. There was so much energy crackling around him that Lana expected the bushes to rattle and small objects to move out of his path when he walked. And there was something weird going on with his eyes, too. She'd noticed the copper flecks before, noticed that the light caught them sometimes and they seemed to glow. She'd dismissed it as a simple trick of light, but now she realized it was more than that. With his eyes glowing copper-penny bright, Vincent aimed his smile at the guard and, just like that, it was all over. The guard's mouth went slack, his eyes glazed over, and he stared up at Vincent as if he was the messiah come back to earth.

"*¿Cómo te llamas?*" Vincent asked the guard. Lana understood that easily enough, but she had to concentrate to decipher the rest of their conversation, which was spoken in rapid Spanish.

"*José, jefe. Me llamo José.*"

"Is the big gate the only way out of here, José?"

"No, no, *jefe*, there is a small gate that the gardeners use sometimes, and another that no one is supposed to know about. It is secret and for *Señor* Camarillo's use only. For when he—" José stopped and looked away as if embarrassed by what he had to say.

"He what, José?" Vincent all but purred.

"*Mi patron* is a man, *jefe*."

"Ah," Vincent said, sharing a manly chuckle which only made Lana scowl, because she had a pretty good idea what they were talking about, even while understanding that Vincent was playing the guard for information.

"And is *Señor* Camarillo entertaining this evening? Or should I say *being entertained?*" Vincent's chuckle became a full, deep laugh which was now shared by all three males. Nice. Camarillo was married with children, but he fucked other women on the side. So many that he had a secret door for them to come and go from the compound. What an ass.

"No, no," José assured him. "This morning was *Señor* Camarillo's saint's day."

"But he will still sleep in his private room, won't he?" Vincent asked confidently.

"Oh, *si, jefe*. Always. *Mi patron* has enemies and he would not endanger his family."

"Of course not."

Lana wondered if Vincent was actually buying the *endanger his family* defense. She rolled her eyes in disgust and didn't know why Vincent was wasting time with this useless line of inquiry. She didn't care where Camarillo slept. She just wanted to get over the wall and out of town before he realized his pet vampire was gone.

"Do you know where the *señor* is now, José?"

"*Si*. He sleeps still from siesta, but he will wake soon for the night."

"Excellent. Take me there."

Lana gave Vincent a sharp look. What the fuck?

"Vincent—" she started to protest, but suddenly, he was right there in front of her, looming over her with his much greater height and strength, copper-penny eyes burning bright and pinning her beneath his angry glare. But if he'd thought to intimidate her, he was out of luck. She'd been around big men all her life. She wasn't afraid of them.

She gave him a defiant glare. "We don't have time for this. We need to get gone. You agreed."

"That was before I discovered the asshole was sleeping right around the fucking corner. And there is *always* time for this," he snarled. "No one, and I mean . . . *No. One*. Gets to slice into my neck, throw me into a hot box filled with dirt, and think to bend me to his will. No one, Lana. Lessons must be taught. If you're concerned, you can leave and I'll—"

"Fuck you," she said, going up on her toes to get right in his face. "I didn't break into this place and spend the entire day in a *hot box filled with dirt* just so I could leave you behind."

Vincent's snarl turned into a grin as his arm looped around her waist, holding her in her tiptoe position, smashing her body flush against his. A rash of conflicting sensations chased themselves over her skin and jangled her nerves as her body remembered what it had been like to be crushed under the heavy weight of him, to feel the hard length of his arousal pressing into her thigh. Half of her wanted to stand up and cheer at the feel of Vincent's hard strength holding her in place, while the other half was screaming a warning for her to get away fast.

"This won't take long, *querida*," he murmured. "You and Jerry can—"

"No," she reiterated forcefully. "Where you go, I go. So, let's get this over with."

Before she could stop him, he kissed her fast and hard, then released her, making sure she was steady on her feet before he removed his arm and faced the guard again.

"Let's go, José."

Lana expected José to offer at least a token protest, but she'd clearly underestimated Vincent's control. The guard gave her a knowing wink—and what the hell was that about?—and then marched off across the yard, heading toward the garage, following much the same path that Lana had taken to get to Vincent's prison.

Jerry Moreno followed along readily, not shooting so much as a questioning glance Vincent's way, as if this had been the plan all along. Gone was the idea of making a quick and quiet exit. Suddenly, it was all about vengeance and everyone seemed to understand that. Even Lana. She'd never admit as much to Vincent, but he was right. Camarillo had thought he could capture and enslave Vincent the way he had Jerry. But this time, he'd thought to do it on his own, to cut Enrique out of the equation. It was a power play not only against Vincent, but against Enrique, and Enrique was the face of vampires in Mexico.

Lana might not live power politics the way the vamps did, but she understood the concept well enough. If Vincent left without punishing Camarillo, the human would only try it again with another vampire. Maybe he'd learn from his mistake and take someone weaker next time, someone who couldn't fight back. And that was unacceptable to a man like Vincent. She didn't know him well, but she knew that much. He had that alpha male need to protect those who were weaker than he was. She'd heard the anguish in his voice when he'd recounted the story of his younger brother's death—and Vincent's inability to save him. She even saw it in the way he treated the women in his life. Women might not be inherently weaker, but to a man like Vincent, they would always invoke the urge to protect.

So Lana followed after José and the two vampires, feeling like the tail end of a parade. She had no idea what Vincent planned for Camarillo, and that thought made her hurry until she was walking next to him.

"There might be guards," she said quietly and started to hand him her Sig. "You can take—"

"Keep it," he said, touching her arm. "I won't need a gun."

"But—"

"Watch and learn, *querida*."

Lana frowned, but figured he knew what he was doing. José took them all the way around the garage, past the spot where Lana had come over the wall, through the iron gate she'd noticed and into the gardens in the back of the house. The rich scent of good soil and fragrant flowers greeted her, the cool evening air moist with water from the irrigation system she could still hear running. They followed a path of stone pavers for about fifteen feet, then veered off onto a short, straight path made of something like compressed sand. It led to an ordinary wooden door that looked like it would open to a gardener's storage closet, if not for the sophisticated lock and heavy-duty hinges. There were no windows in the door or the wall to either side of it.

José stopped a couple of feet away and pointed at the door. "This is it, *jefe*," he said helpfully. "Shall I knock for—?"

"No need," Vincent assured him, and Lana wondered how the hell he thought he was going to get through what looked to her like a high security deadbolt. But then he raised one hand palm out and shoved it forward, as if to push open the door . . . and blew it completely off its heavily-reinforced hinges.

Lana stared. She'd heard about vampire powers, but had thought they were limited to things like telepathy and persuasion. This was something else entirely. As if hearing her thoughts, Vincent looked over his shoulder and gave her a wink, then disappeared into the dark room beyond.

Moreno hesitated on the threshold, but for only a second before following Vincent inside. Not to be left behind, Lana hurried forward, careful to avoid silhouetting herself against the door. Ducking inside, she immediately put her back to the wall and waited for her eyes to adjust as a dim light clicked on.

The first thing she saw was Camarillo sitting up in bed, his hand dropping away from the bedside lamp. His mouth was stretched wide in an angry snarl, but as she watched, his eyes glazed over with terror as he belatedly recognized who the intruder was.

"Do you know who I am?" Vincent asked, his voice a drawling purr of danger.

Camarillo nodded wordlessly, his mouth hanging open. Lana didn't know if he was too frightened to speak or if Vincent had done something to silence him.

"And yet you thought to enslave me," Vincent remarked, as if trying to figure out why Camarillo would even consider such a thing. "Just as you enslaved Moreno here," he added, his glittering gaze going hard and unyielding. He took a step closer to the bed and stopped, hands on his hips, head tilted, studying the terrified man. "What shall I do with you, *Señor* Camarillo?"

Camarillo swallowed hard, then licked his lips and found his voice enough to gasp, "Mercy."

Vincent's smile chilled Lana to her soul.

"Vincent," she whispered.

His expression blanked as he turned to look at her over his shoulder. "You should wait outside," he told her.

"He has children," she said, her voice catching slightly.

"So did all of the men and women that he's killed."

"So this is revenge for them?"

His mouth lifted in a half smile. "No. This is revenge for *me*. It's protection for *my* children, the vampires I'm responsible for, men and women like Moreno here who deserve better than to be made into killers on behalf of a fucking drug dealer."

"But it was a *vampire* who did this. Enrique is the one who enslaved Jerry."

"I'll deal with Enrique in due time. But tonight, here and now, I'm making a point. You do not enslave my people, and you sure as fucking hell do not think to enslave *me*—" There was such rage in that one word that he had to pause before finishing his thought. "—without suffering the consequences. There is a price and I'm going to collect. If you can't handle that, then you should wait outside."

Lana stared. He stood there so tall and strong, his power filling the room, rattling papers on the small desk, making the gauze drapes on the big four-posted bed flutter as if in a breeze. Gone was the teasing Vincent, the vampire who flirted and seduced every woman he met. This was the vampire who ruled second only to Enrique, who had the ability to take over a man's mind in an instant, to knock a heavy door off its hinges.

And, for the first time, she wondered what he was capable of. Was he cruel? A killer? If she stayed in this room, she was going to find out. Maybe not all of it, not everything, but she knew Camarillo was going to die, and it wasn't going to be because Vincent put a pillow over his face either.

"Damn it," she muttered to herself, but Vincent heard. One eyebrow went up in a mocking question mark. She nodded sharply, then worked the slide on her 9mm and took up a position near the door.

"I'm staying," she said defiantly.

Vincent tilted his head in acknowledgment, and she wanted to believe there was a hint of respect in there, too. He shifted his attention back to Camarillo who was whimpering unashamedly, his eyes wide with terror at whatever he was seeing in the vampire's face.

"Pay attention, Moreno," Vincent said without looking at his newest vampire protégé, who was glaring his hatred at the man who'd been his proclaimed master only a few hours earlier.

Vincent raised a negligent hand and the bedcovers were ripped from Camarillo's clutching fingers, so that he knelt half-naked, wearing nothing but a pair of drawstring pajama bottoms. His eyes were rolling white with fear, and sweat glistened on his skin, stinking up the room so that even Lana could smell it with her ordinary human senses. He clasped his hands in front of him in a posture of prayer and started mumbling almost non-stop in rapid Spanish. Lana caught only a word or two. He was begging for his life, but whether he was praying to Vincent or to God, she didn't know.

Vincent lifted his hand and curled his outstretched fingers toward his palm in a gesture that was the picture of grace . . . until Camarillo shrieked in torment, his hands clutching his chest, fingers digging into his skin so feverishly that his nails tore into his skin, leaving ragged furrows that trailed blood down onto his belly and thighs.

Lana stared, her lungs squeezed in horror. She'd seen plenty of violence in her life, she'd seen men shot and even been shot herself, but this . . . she'd never seen a man rip at himself like that.

Lana jolted as Camarillo's mouth opened wide, and a horrific keening noise filled the room. It was inhuman, nothing but raw animal agony. And she thought surely this must be Vincent's revenge, to leave the man crazed with pain, a drooling idiot with no thought but to suffer . . . Or maybe not. She pressed herself against the wall at her back as Vincent took that final step toward the bed, until he was right on top of Camarillo, the copper glow of his stare reflecting off the white of the drug boss's eyes, turning them into yellowed marbles of terror. Vincent ran a tender hand along Camarillo's sweaty jaw, trailed a long finger over the swell of the man's jugular . . . and then his hand tightened into a claw and he ripped the man's throat out.

He did it casually, without apparent effort. He simply closed his fingers over Camarillo's throat, squeezed until his fingers met around the bony column of the drug lord's esophagus, and then yanked.

Camarillo choked, a ghastly sound, as his brain begged for oxygen, as his face turned red and then blue, until finally the only thing holding him up was Vincent's grip on his ravaged throat.

Vincent opened his hand. Camarillo collapsed onto the bed in a boneless heap, blood staining the pristine sheets beneath him.

Vincent eyed his bloodied hand in distaste, and Lana waited, half-expecting him to lick the blood away, but he didn't. Instead he used the discarded bedcover to wipe the blood off, then stepped back from the bed and spoke to Jerry Moreno.

"Did you understand what I did?" he asked.

Moreno nodded. "Yes, sir."

"And why?"

"Definitely, sir."

Vincent nodded. "You'll come with us for now. When we reach Pénjamo, I'll have Michael, my lieutenant, fly down and take you back to my headquarters in Hermosillo."

"You will not be returning with us?" Moreno asked.

Vincent shook his head. "Lana and I have business to finish first."

"And what about the others?"

Vincent frowned. "What others?"

"The others like me, the other vampires Enrique indentured to drug lords."

Vincent stared and Lana got that feeling again, as if someone was scraping a live wire just above her skin. Vincent's fury became a living thing, swelling outward in the contained space until it became a tornado whipping around the room, pounding the heavy furniture and knocking a thick silver-framed mirror off the wall. It fell to the bare tile and shattered, sending glittering shards flying everywhere.

Lana gripped the door frame and waited to die, certain that Vincent had finally lost it. But he had better control than that. He sucked in a breath and the storm died. But she could see the effort it took. His muscles were bunched and tight, veins standing out on his bare forearms.

"Where will I find them?" Vincent asked Moreno, his voice tight with repressed anger.

"They are scattered throughout Mexico, but the nearest is Salvio Olivarez. His master lives not far from Pénjamo, just north of the city."

"Vincent," Lana dared to interrupt. "We have to get out of here."

He turned a cold gaze on her, but his eyes warmed almost immediately. "Don't worry, Lana. I can kill them all if it comes to that."

Lana wasn't reassured. "I'd rather it not come to that," she explained gently, because he was clearly so far gone as to be fucking clueless. "Our escape will be ever so much easier if we leave discreetly."

"Or if we leave no witnesses," he countered.

"Vincent," she warned impatiently.

He sighed and asked, "Is José still waiting out there?"

Lana stepped into the doorway and found Vincent's loyal follower still standing guard.

"He is," she confirmed.

"All right. Forget the front gate. We're going back the way you came, over the hill instead of around it. Moreno, you'll tell me everything you know on the drive to Pénjamo."

"Yes, sir."

Vincent cast a final loathing glance at the dead Camarillo, then strode across the room, catching Lana's arm as he went past. "Let's go, good girl."

Lana scowled. She wasn't being *good,* she was being smart. It was only luck, or maybe more of Vincent's magic, that no one had come to investigate Camarillo's screaming. But luck could only carry them so far. They had to get over that wall and on the road before anyone was aware that Camarillo was dead, and that his vampire prisoners were gone.

She kept pace with Vincent as he followed José deeper into the lush green of the garden. It was a beautiful place, full of growing, living things. It seemed wrong that it should exist in the backyard of a man who left nothing but death and destruction in his wake.

José led them to a section of wall that was covered in a thick, creeping vine. Creeping *and* creepy. The trailing plant had dark green, waxy leaves and was heavy with weird hanging pods. With nothing but moonlight to see it by, it looked like an alien thing just waiting to strangle the unwary. Lana eyed it distrustfully, but José turned his head to smile broadly at Vincent and point at the wall. "This is it, *jefe*."

Lana's heart sank, convinced that José had lost it, but Vincent stepped right up to the wall and pushed aside the heavy vine to reveal an electronic keypad.

She moved up close to him. "How'd you know that was there?" she asked absently, studying the keypad and wondering what the birthdates of Camarillo's children were. People tended to be rather predictable in their selection of passwords.

"The device emits a very high frequency noise—probably a short that should have been fixed."

"I don't suppose that high frequency is beeping out the passcode," she muttered snarkily.

Predictably, Vincent was only entertained by her sarcasm. He grinned down at her, then turned his attention to José, who was standing by patiently, awaiting his next command.

"*¿Sabes la contraseña, José?*" Lana asked, beating Vincent to it. Unfortunately, the guard's affections seemed to be reserved for Vincent, because he only gave her a puzzled look before transferring his attention back to the vampire.

"*¿Sabes la contraseña, mi amigo?*" Vincent asked. *Do you know the password, my friend?*

José brightened immediately, standing taller and thrusting his chest out. "*Si, jefe. Es cero nueve uno dos cero seis.*" *Yes, jefe. It's zero, nine, one, two, zero, six.*

Vincent nudged Lana with an elbow, tapped in the key code, then stood back with a satisfied expression as the wall shifted beneath the vines, revealing a crack in the shape of a gate. It was so cleverly constructed and concealed that, even knowing it was there, Lana had to look closely to see the line of its opening. Vincent pulled it wider, then turned to José.

"This is where we part company, my friend," he said, speaking English with almost fond regret. "Sleep now."

Lana started to frown, then drew back when José collapsed where he stood, crumpling down as if every bone in his body had disappeared.

"Is he—"

"Asleep," Vincent assured her. "And he won't remember any of this when he wakes. Come on, you're the one who wanted a quiet exit. Now's the time."

Lana didn't need to be told twice. She hurried through the gate, stopping several yards out to pull out her cell phone and determine exactly where they were. She had the SUV's GPS location programmed in, so it was only a matter of . . . Yep. There they were.

Jerry and Vincent both emerged quickly, with Jerry coming over to stand next to her, while Vincent pulled the gate back into position until it once again blended seamlessly into the surrounding wall.

"We're a little over a quarter mile from the SUV, as the crow flies," Lana told him. "Unfortunately, we can't fly . . ." Her words trailed off and she studied Vincent. "You *can't*, can you?"

"Of course not," he said, appearing offended by the question. As if she hadn't just seen him whammy a man with nothing but his voice and blow through a bolted door with a flick of his fingers. Not to mention the whole ripping out the throat part, but she supposed any strong man, with an equally strong stomach, could have done *that*.

"Just asking," she said mildly, secretly pleased to have finally irked him. "Okay, so with this terrain, our walk is probably closer to a mile, and at night like this, it will be fairly rough going."

"Darkness isn't a problem for Jerry and me. Neither is the terrain. How about you?" he asked, eyeing her up and down.

"I've survived a hell of a lot worse," she told him flatly, hoping he understood that the *hell of a lot worse* part included the company, namely him.

Vincent's half grin told her he understood perfectly and rather enjoyed it. "Let's get going then. You set the pace, Lana."

Lana tucked her cell phone into a jacket pocket. She didn't need the map to tell her which way to go. She hadn't been exaggerating when she'd told Vincent she'd hiked worse. Give her a direction and she would get there, come hell or high water. Flexing her fingers, she started up through the rocky hillside.

Hours later, Lana was in a sort of Zen state as she focused on putting one foot in front of the other and not breaking an ankle in the process. She'd had to resort to using the small Maglite to see by. She was careful with the beam, shielding it with her fingers and keeping it aimed downward to avoid screwing with the two vampires' night vision, not to mention the danger of spotlighting their position for any pursuers. But it had been that or breaking an ankle for sure, so she'd chosen the flashlight. They were on the downward leg of their hike, nearly to the flat of the desert floor, and she was beginning to suspect that Vincent's taking up the rear position on the first part of their climb had less to do with letting her set the pace and more with putting himself between her and any pursuit. Because as soon as they'd crested the hill and started downward, he'd switched positions, leaving Jerry as a rearguard while he led the way, his attitude one of constant readiness.

Thus far, it appeared that their escape had either gone unnoticed, or that Camarillo's men were reluctant to chase down a vampire who could pull a man's throat out. But even without anyone to fight, the idea that Vincent wanted to protect her made her want to like him. Or, rather, like him even more, since the *like him* ship had sailed long ago.

Danger, Will Robinson, she reminded herself. It was bad enough that he was big and sexy and gorgeous and . . . had she mentioned sexy? For him to be a good guy on top of all that seemed like piling it on . . .

"Heavy thoughts, *querida?*" Vincent's deep voice was right in her ear, and she jerked in surprise. He'd been walking several feet in front and she hadn't noticed him dropping back. Which only reinforced what a danger he was to her.

She shot him an annoyed look. "Just thinking about getting out of this town and never coming back."

"There is one more thing we have to—"

"Vincent," she said warningly.

"Lana," he responded, mimicking her tone precisely. "The woman in the cantina."

"What about her?"

"She has to die. You must see that."

"I told you she helped me. She told me where they were holding you. I wouldn't have found you in time without her."

"You also said she only helped you to save her own ass. The bitch sliced my neck and bled me nearly dry, Lana."

"I told her to leave town," Lana said in a rush. "That you'd kill her if she stayed." She met Vincent's scowl with a shrug and added, "So there's no point—"

"But you know where she lives, yes?"

Lana sighed. "Yes."

"We'll see if she took your advice. If not, too bad for her. If so, I'll leave a message guaranteed to give her sleepless nights for the rest of her life."

"We need to put some miles—"

He stepped into her path and stopped, forcing her to do the same.

"Remember what I told you about Camarillo? Why he had to die?" he asked, staring down at her.

She studied him silently, then said, "To protect other vampires, so no one else would try the same thing."

"Exactly. And that goes double for that bitch, because she did it in front of witnesses."

She eyed him a moment longer. "I understand," she admitted, although not without qualms. Because even though she'd warned Fidelia Reyes about what would happen to her if Vincent found her, she hadn't really believed her own words until she'd seen what he did to Camarillo.

Vincent's expression softened the tiniest bit, as if he understood her conundrum and sympathized. Not that it would change his mind at all, she was sure. He nodded, then turned and resumed his lead position, moving down the even hillside with a grace that Lana couldn't hope to duplicate. She thought briefly that it might not be so bad being a vampire sometimes. Then she caught herself.

Not so bad? She must be delirious.

They descended the last few yards, rocks crumbling underfoot with every step until they finally hit the flat desert floor. Lana sighed with relief, hurrying forward until she could see the tail end of the SUV sticking out from between the rocks where she'd parked it.

Vincent grabbed her hand when she would have run for it. "Wait," he cautioned. "Jerry, you and I will go first."

"Yes, sir."

Lana wanted to protest. Sure, she'd been pleased that Vincent *wanted* to protect her, but that didn't mean she *needed* it. She did a dangerous job and worked alone most of the time. Unfortunately, arguing with Vincent would only waste time, so she lagged back, but only by a little bit, as they covered the final fifty yards and the SUV came fully into view.

There were no bad guys waiting for them.

She pulled the remote from her pocket, hit the button and the doors unlocked almost silently. Lana strode over, opened the driver's side and folded herself onto the seat without even taking time to unload the contents of her pockets. That could wait until they were safely away.

She'd just started the engine when Vincent loomed in the open driver's door. He didn't say anything, just stared at her expectantly.

Lana shot him a sideways glance, her focus on programming the nav system for a quick exit. "What?" she asked absently.

"I'm driving."

Lana threw him a dismissive look. "I don't think so. You were nearly dead just a few hours ago. I'll drive. Besides, you don't know where we're going."

"Isn't that a navigation system you're programming there?"

"I'm programming our trip *out of town*, not to Reyes's house. So there."

Vincent, damn him, grinned. "So there?" he repeated.

She leaned and grabbed the door handle, looking up at him with an aggravated glare. "It may have escaped your notice, oh powerful one, but we're running for our lives. Now, move."

He stepped out of the way, but not before taking advantage of her compromised position to deposit a quick, hard kiss on her mouth. Lana blinked in surprise, and her heart double-timed a few beats. *Danger, Will*—Oh, what the fuck. That wasn't working. She shouldn't be attracted to him at all. He was arrogant and bossy and a killer to boot. She didn't fall for killers, she slapped cuffs on them and brought them back to stand trial.

So, why did she find Vincent so damn irresistible?

No, not irresistible. She could resist him. She *would* resist him. One more day and they'd hit Pénjamo. They'd find this Xuan Ignacio fellow, deliver Raphael's message, and that would be it. Vincent would go back to his life and Lana would go back to hers, their paths never to cross again.

So why the hell did that make him harder to resist, instead of less? The image flashed in her mind of Vincent as he'd leaned over her in that hot box of a prison, his eyes glowing a coppery gold, fangs slowly descending as he'd lowered his mouth to her neck. She could still feel the press of his hard body against hers, and she shivered in remembered pleasure of the most intense orgasm of her life. If he could do that with a single bite, imagine what he could do if he was actually making love to her. Her eyes drifted closed . . . and then flashed open as she intentionally called to mind the image of Vincent as he'd ripped Camarillo's throat out, dripping blood and fangs bared. But even that didn't work. Camarillo had been a monster, a purveyor of death and misery, one who no doubt had killed more than his share of innocents on his way up the ladder of success.

The passenger door opened and Vincent slid onto the seat, filling up the vehicle with his bulk, his sheer presence. Lana felt a blush heat her cheeks. She turned away quickly and busied herself with adjusting the mirrors, then putting the SUV in gear.

"Are you sure you want to—"

He didn't even let her finish.

"I'm sure," he interrupted, correctly assuming she'd been about to question if he really wanted to take the time to go by Reyes's place.

"Fine," she snapped. "It's your funeral. You ready back there, Jerry?" she asked, eyeing the other vampire in her rearview mirror.

"Yes."

A man of few words. She liked that. She paused to scan the horizon carefully, looking for dust clouds or any indication that Camarillo's troops were on the move. Seeing nothing, she pressed on the gas pedal and retraced her path, heading for the road that would take them into town.

It was only a few minutes later that they entered Reyes's neighborhood. It was darker than it had been the last time she'd been here, the middle of the night instead of nearly dawn. And there were no streetlights in this part of town. The only illumination came from whatever leaked out from inside the small and scattered houses, the pale flickering of a TV screen from those with satellite dishes on the roof.

Lana avoided the short driveway at Reyes's house, choosing instead to park on the street in case a quick getaway became necessary. Vincent was out of the car before she'd even turned off the ignition.

When she finally hurried around the front of the SUV to stand next to him, he was eyeing the house unhappily.

"Problem?" she asked.

"No one's in there."

Lana scanned the front of the small house. The windows were dark, but a porch light was on. She remembered it still being on the other morning, too, and figured it was probably on a timer. Reyes lived alone. Maybe she didn't like coming home to a dark house after a long night of trying to kill vampires. The bitch.

"Maybe she's dead," Lana commented and found she didn't care either way. "She was in pretty bad shape when I left here."

"Let me rephrase," Vincent said dryly. "No one alive *or* dead is in there."

"We can smell dead bodies," Jerry supplied helpfully, having climbed out of the backseat to stand next to them.

"Huh," Lana said, wondering where her life had taken such a wrong turn that this knowledge didn't even faze her. "She probably took my advice and left town."

Vincent shot her an unfriendly glance. Apparently he was still holding a grudge about that.

"We should go," Lana said, jiggling the keys in her hand.

"Not yet," Vincent said in a dark voice as he studied the empty house.

"But there's no one here, and we can't hang around waiting. It's only a matter of time—"

A deep rumbling noise cut her off. She felt the first shiver of movement beneath her feet and glanced around nervously. Lana had lived through an earthquake once, during a visit to her mother in California. Everyone out there had assured her that, since it was only 3.9 on the Richter scale, it barely qualified as an event. But she remembered that deep rumble of sound and the awful sensation of feeling the earth moving beneath her feet.

"Earthquake," she breathed. She grabbed for Vincent's arm, but froze at the sight of him staring intently at the house, eyes half-lidded, lips pulled back in a snarl that exposed his gleaming fangs.

"Vincent?" she whispered, then spun, scanning the neighborhood, ready to confront whatever threat they faced and finding nothing, only to jerk back around in shock as Reyes's small house shivered on its foundation and the air grew thick with dust. The shivering became a vicious shaking. Cracks spread like a spider's web along the exterior walls, and the sound of breaking wood and shattering glass told the story of what was happening inside. The porch light burst with a sharp pop and Lana covered her eyes to protect them from any tiny pieces of glass flying incredible distances through the sudden darkness. Reaching into her pocket, she grabbed the mini Maglite and switched it on just in time to see Reyes's wooden front door split down the middle as broken tiles showered from the rooftop.

Seconds later, the exterior walls buckled completely and the structure gave way, until, with a final crash of cracking stucco and splintering wood, the entire house folded in on itself.

Silence settled over the night. A cloud of dust and dirt drifted slowly over the remaining pile of debris. No one but the neighborhood dogs seemed troubled by what had happened—no doors opened, no people emerged to exclaim over the abrupt implosion of their neighbor's home.

Lana frowned, turning a full circle to study the undisturbed neighborhood.

"What did you do?" she asked Vincent softly, her eyes still on the quiet houses. She felt more than saw him look down at her.

"I left her and this entire town a warning," he said, and there was such arrogance in his usually friendly voice that she twisted to stare at him.

"Are they still alive?" she breathed.

Vincent frowned. "Is who still alive? There was no one in the house. I told you that."

"I mean the rest of these people, her neighbors."

He gave her a disbelieving look. "What the fuck, Lana? Of course, they are."

"Then why—" She swallowed on a dry throat. "Why didn't anybody—"

"Because I contained the sound. Because you're so all fired up to make a discreet getaway. Jesus, you think I killed all those people? What kind of monster do you think I am?"

Lana studied the destroyed house and realized that for all the noise it had made, it *hadn't* been as loud as it should have been. Maybe it was only because she'd been watching it happen that it had *seemed* so much louder.

She looked up at Vincent in dismay. "I'm sorry, I didn't—"

But he was already turning away. "Yeah, whatever. Let's get out of here. I've had more than enough of this town. Give me the keys." He held out his hand in impatient demand.

"Vincent, I'm sorry," she repeated, handing over his keys.

"Fine." He took them from her and headed around the SUV. "Jerry," he snapped. "In the SUV."

"Yes, sir."

Jerry climbed into the back and Lana slid quickly into the passenger seat, worried that Vincent might just be angry enough to leave without her. He jammed the SUV into gear and took off, tires spitting gravel as she pulled her seatbelt down and clicked it into place. She cut a few sideways glances at Vincent, but he ignored her. It wasn't until he'd taken them back to the main highway and turned south toward Pénjamo once again that he spoke at all, and then it was only to call Michael, using the in-dash speakerphone.

"Good evening, Sire," she heard Michael say.

"Michael, have the jet prepped for tomorrow night. I need you in Pénjamo."

"Yes, my lord. Should I bring—?"

"Some muscle, I'll leave the specifics up to you, and a daylight crew. We have some business locally, but after that you'll be taking a pair of baby—" He glanced in the mirror at Jerry and changed what he'd been about to say. "—young vamps back to Hermosillo. Enrique's doing things he shouldn't. No surprise there, but this is low even for him. I'll provide details when I see you."

"Right. Shall I call when we arrive?"

"That'd be good. Anything else to report?"

"*Nada, jefe.* Club repairs are proceeding nicely."

"Good. See you tomorrow night."

"Tomorrow night, my lord."

Vincent disconnected without another word. In fact, he didn't say or do anything other than stare straight ahead for the next 250 or so miles when they had to stop for gas. Lana had been just waiting for this chance, ever since the first hour passed in silence, figuring she'd swap with Jerry and let him sit next to the sphinx while she napped in the backseat. When they finally pulled into the gas station, she popped out of the vehicle almost before it stopped rolling. Normally, she'd have volunteered to pump or pay, but Vincent, being an old-school chauvinist—and by old school, she met *literally*, since he was closing in on his second century—had made it clear to her early on that such things were man's work. And that was fine by her, especially when *the man* was in a pissy mood.

She made straight for the restroom, changing her mind once she saw, and smelled, it. Years of long-distance traveling had taught her how to hold it when she had to, and this qualified. She headed back to the SUV, then thought about picking up a few snacks for the rest of the trip. She was hungry, and they were only about halfway to Pénjamo. She couldn't see Vincent stopping at a restaurant, not for her, and not tonight, so she found herself standing in the snack aisle, studying an uninspiring selection of candy and chips. She sighed, then turned away and left the store empty-handed. This wasn't her night.

Jerry was pumping gas when she got back to the Suburban. She looked around and found Vincent some distance away in an empty field next to the station, talking on his cell phone. Probably conferring with Michael about "sooper sekrit" vampire shit. Whatever.

She walked over and leaned against the SUV next to where Jerry was holding the gas nozzle. This was an older station with mechanical pumps and no vapor recovery, and the strong smell of gasoline, combined with her empty stomach, made her feel slightly queasy. She moved upwind which helped a little.

"Hey, Jerry," she said. "If it's okay with you, I'll sit in the back for this next leg. I'm going to stretch out—"

"No."

Lana spun around at the sound of Vincent's deep voice. "Excuse me?"

"Jerry will sit in the back."

"Yes, sir," Jerry said immediately. Lana clenched her jaw angrily. Nothing she had to say would ever convince Jerry to go against Vincent. She didn't know if it was a vampire thing in general, a hangover of his days as a slave, or maybe of the military before that. She did know it was frustrating as hell.

"What does it matter?" she demanded . . . of Vincent, not Jerry, because what was the point?

"It matters," he said flatly, then changed subjects as if the matter was decided. "We could make Pénjamo tonight, but we're not going to. I don't want to roll into an unknown situation with dawn about to break. We'll stop well short of the town and head in tomorrow night."

Lana stared at him wordlessly. She could argue. But again, what was the point? Vincent at his most charming could be reasoned with. This Vincent? The master of the universe, my-word-is-law Vincent? Not a chance.

She spun on her heel and climbed into the front passenger seat, but as they pulled away from the station, she decided she wasn't going to roll over and die just to make Vincent's life easier.

"I think we should go all the way to Pénjamo, or at least at close as we can before sunrise. That way you can get an early start tomorrow night."

"And that's why *I'm* driving," Vincent said. "We're stopping before Pénjamo."

"Listen, asshole," she said, suddenly furious. "I may not be driving, but don't forget who sleeps all day long and who doesn't. I can be gone ten minutes after the sun rises, and where will you be then, huh? In some dinky Mexican town with no car, that's where."

"Fine, princess. You pick a city to stop in. But I don't care what you say, I'm not driving into whatever the fuck's going on in Pénjamo with the sun riding my back."

"Fine," Lana muttered and bent to her cell phone.

They drove several more miles in silence, and then he surprised her by saying, "You play dirty, *querida*. It makes me kinda hot."

Lana gave a very unladylike snort. "Anything with a vagina and a heartbeat makes you hot."

"I can't help it if women find me irresistible."

"Not all women," she snapped, but cut a sideways glance at him. It

121

seemed as if whatever bug had been up his ass had worked its way out again. Maybe he'd gotten good news during his secret phone call, or maybe he was just a moody son of a bitch. Either way, she didn't feel like playing nice, so she kept her eyes on her cell phone and didn't say anything, just reached up to the nav system and programmed in the directions to a motel about ninety miles north of Pénjamo that had vacant rooms.

Vincent shifted his gaze to watch the nav display, but his only response when the map came up was a wordless grunt. Lana closed her eyes and leaned against the door, pretending to sleep. Vincent let out an amused chuckle and she remembered, too late, that he could tell she was faking it. But by then she was committed to the pretense and so kept her eyes closed until she finally dozed off.

She woke when the SUV rolled to a stop, her eyes opening just as Vincent turned the engine off and opened his door.

"I hope they have rooms," he said dryly, and headed toward the office.

Lana sat up in concern, worried that she'd made a mistake, that, despite her cell phone search, the lone motel in the small town *didn't* have rooms and now they'd have to race to find a safe place for Vincent and Jerry before dawn. But then she stepped out of the SUV and got a good look at the motel, and recognized Vincent's comment for what it was—a snarky observation about the *quality* of the accommodations, rather than the quantity.

The motel looked like it had been built at least fifty years ago, if not more. The paint was peeling and the railings along the stairs to the second floor were held together by rust. She studied the building with a frown, wondering if it was better to be on the second floor when a building collapsed—so you'd at least fall on top of the rubble—or on the ground floor, so you wouldn't have quite so far to fall.

The SUV door opened behind her and Jerry climbed out, moving so quietly that, if not for the sound of the door, she wouldn't have known he was there.

"You misjudge him, you know," he said without preface.

She glanced at the usually non-talkative vampire. "I don't judge him at all," she said, knowing they were discussing Vincent.

Jerry's expression didn't change. "I've spent the last two years in a place where my life depended on accurately guessing what the humans around me were thinking, anticipating their wants and needs before even *they* knew what they were. I know people, Lana. Vincent could have killed every one of Camarillo's men, but he chose not to."

"He killed Camarillo. And besides, the only reason he didn't kill the others was because we were in a hurry."

Jerry smiled as if she was being foolish. "He could have littered that compound with bodies, left it a ghost town, and strolled out the front gate.

Instead, he didn't even kill José."

"José was harmless," she insisted, ignoring the soft voice of doubt that was whispering in the back of her brain.

He shook his head. "I've seen José quite cheerfully cut the hands off a man for stealing drugs. Vincent is an honorable man, Lana."

"How can you know that?" she demanded, clinging to her argument. "You just met him, and besides, you call him master. How is that any different than what Camarillo was to you?"

His smile became almost pitying. "It's true that Vincent is my master, but I am not his slave. Yes, I owe him my loyalty, but it is freely given. And in return, I am his to protect. Surely you can see the difference? In time, I will fight for him, not because he demands it, but because he is someone I will willingly follow, someone I am honored to protect." He turned and met her eyes directly. "He will rule this territory someday, and I will stand proudly in the ranks of his warriors."

"How do you know all of this?"

He shrugged. "He's told me some things, but mostly . . . I just know."

Vincent emerged from the office at that point, flipping a key fob between his fingers.

"Good news, kids," he announced. "They have rooms!"

Lana rolled her eyes. He might be Lord of Mexico someday, but right now, he was just a big pain in her ass.

"Upstairs or downstairs?" she asked, still worried about the whole collapsed building scenario.

"Upstairs. I'd rather ride the rubble down than be trapped beneath it."

She gave him a sharp look. He'd told her he couldn't read her thoughts. Did that mean they thought alike? Crap. That was even scarier than thinking he could read her mind.

Following Jerry around to the back of the SUV, she pulled her duffel out and the three of them formed a little parade up a set of stairs that was every bit as rickety as they looked. They proceeded down the mezzanine until Vincent stopped at one of the few doors with a working light over it. He inserted the key with a twist and stepped into the dark room, then went directly to the bedside lamp and clicked it on, obviously for her benefit

"Oh, look, we have cable," Vincent said snidely. He was giving her a look from across the room, one eyebrow arched upward as if commenting on the shabby state of the motel that *she'd* sent them to.

Lana avoided his gaze, though privately she agreed. "Interesting design," she commented, taking in the faded, but once colorful, bedspread, studying the lone, oddly-placed window high up on the back wall and thinking they'd have to cover it somehow.

"The walls are fairly thick, and the absence of windows probably keeps the room cooler," Jerry offered as explanation.

Lana nodded absently. Her attention was riveted on the single bed. Dead to the world or not, surely Vincent didn't expect all three of them to—

"You'll sleep in there, Jerry," Vincent said, again seeming to sense her thoughts. She turned to see what he meant, and realized the motel room was actually a suite, with a nearly identical room on the other side of a cheap wooden door that Vincent had opened on the interior wall.

Jerry nodded and walked on through without comment, while Lana frowned at Vincent.

"Is there a door to the outside from that room?" she asked.

"No, no window either. I doubt Jerry will mind, however, since he's used to far worse. And he does have his own bathroom with a window if he wants some air."

"You should both sleep in there, then. I'll stay out here in case anyone comes snooping around."

Vincent snorted. "Yeah, I don't think so. I'm not sleeping with Jerry."

"Well, then I can—"

"And neither are you," he growled, guessing her next suggestion, even though she'd have meant it facetiously. The only thing that made sense was for both of the vamps to sleep in the bedroom with no window while she slept out here. So why was he being so difficult about it?

"I don't understand," she said, holding on to her patience with a thin thread. "You've been pissed at me all night, barely spoken a word to me, and now suddenly, you're insisting we sleep in the same bed? You don't even like—"

Without warning Vincent *moved,* and he was right in front of her, their bodies touching, his big, warm hand cupping her cheek. "I like you just fine, *querida,*" he whispered.

Heat rolled through every inch of Lana's body, that one touch igniting a vivid flashback of feeling Vincent's breath hot against her neck, the sting of his bite all too quickly swamped by a firestorm of sensation that built to an orgasm unlike any she'd ever experienced. She took a blind step backward, hitting the sharp corner of the dresser with enough pain that her head cleared. She blinked and moved sideways, putting even more space between herself and the temptation of Vincent's touch.

"It's nearly sunrise," she said brusquely, giving up her argument about the sleeping arrangements. After all, what did it matter? Once it was daylight, it would be like Vincent wasn't there anyway. "Do you want to shower?" she asked.

"Is that an invitation?"

He said it lightly, but the look in his eyes belied the teasing tone of his words.

"Vincent," she said almost desperately, but anger was beginning to seep in too. He was toying with her and she detested that.

"Fine," he said, dragging the word out and making his suffering clear. "I'll shower. Don't leave the room."

"Yes, Master."

She meant it sarcastically, but he crooked a half smile at her, then, in typical Vincent fashion, he proceeded to strip off his clothes before strolling into the small bathroom with every inch of his naked body on display. *Every* inch.

Lana sucked in a breath, holding it until the door closed and the shower came on. Thank God for Jerry. Because she was weak. If the other vampire hadn't been only a few feet away, she'd probably be in that shower with Vincent right now.

She stared at the closed bathroom door and frowned, not knowing if she was disappointed or relieved at her current predicament. One thing she knew for sure, though; she was tired. Wiped out. Not so tired that she was going to sit on that bedspread, however. Tossing the faded and threadbare covering in a corner, she sat on the bed and untied her boots, then tugged them off one at a time, followed by her socks. She eyed the carpet doubtfully, then thought about putting the dirty socks back on her sweaty feet, and said the hell with it. It felt too good to be barefoot. So she ignored the likelihood that the carpet hadn't been cleaned in the last decade or three and curled her unfettered toes in pleasure.

There was no closet, only hooks on the wall near the door. She hung her jacket on one and wished she could take off the rest of her clothes, too. They'd been traveling steadily southward and temperatures were going up, along with the humidity, and it was hot and stuffy in the room. She looked around for some sort of thermostat or fan unit, but didn't find one. Normally, she'd have opened the door to let some air in, but Vincent would probably freak if he emerged from his shower to find the door open. Not because he was naked. No, that wouldn't bother him at all, she was sure. But because they still didn't know if Camarillo's people were on their trail.

She lifted her gaze to the lone window, which Jerry had said was meant for circulation. There was a crank handle to open and close it, but looking around, she couldn't find any means of reaching that handle way the hell up near the ceiling. She started eyeing the furniture, figuring out what might serve as a ladder, then sighed. It didn't matter. The window would have to be covered anyway, since that stubborn-ass vampire insisted on sleeping out here instead of inside with Jerry.

Muttering imprecations against vampires in general and one in particular, she walked over to study the window more closely and saw the remains of a miniblind stuck at the top of the frame. It was so crusted with dirt and grease that it blended into the shadow of the ceiling in the poorly-lit room, which was why she hadn't seen it right off. It was also missing any sort of rod or rope pull, but she could release it if ... She went back to her earlier examination of the furniture. There was a tiny table and two unmatched chairs, neither of which appeared sturdy enough to hold her weight. The table, on the other hand ... she dragged it over to the wall under the window and clambered up. The table was actually a little too high, and she had to bend her head to avoid hitting the ceiling.

She examined the blinds and discovered that, while the rod was total history, the rope was still there, tangled and knotted, but in working order. Fortunately, in an act of poor planning or dumb luck, she hadn't taken her pants off yet and so still had the small knife in her pocket. Not caring about being able to raise the blind again, she simply pulled out her knife and cut the rope, which freed the slats to slither downward in an untidy shower of filthy aluminum. Lana coughed as God knew how many years of dirt and dust wafted outward. She waved a hand in front of her face and examined the now-lowered miniblind, making small adjustments to seal off as much light as possible. And as she worked, she noticed something unexpected. There was light in the sky already. Not the full-on sun beaming into her eyes kind of light, but not the barely-there gray sky kind either.

She had a moment of worry for Vincent in the shower, concerned that he'd cut it too close and been taken unaware, but then the water turned off and she could hear him moving around. She climbed down, then hurried over to her duffel and threw it on the bed. The door opened and she forced herself to continue rearranging her clothes, separating the clean from the dirty, counting her socks. Anything to avoid thinking about the fact that Vincent was standing a few feet away from her, and probably naked. She wondered if it was his habit to walk around that way, or if he only did it to torment her. Not that she *was* tormented. Not at all.

"The shower's all yours, Lana," he crooned. How did he do that? Make everything sound like a seduction. He was telling her the most ordinary of things, but with his deep, smooth voice, the simple words sent goosebumps shivering over her skin.

She fought to control her body's reaction, knowing his vampire senses could detect things she'd rather he didn't know. "Thanks," she said, without looking up. "How long 'til sunrise?" she asked curiously, thinking about the sunlight beyond the window.

"Official sunrise has passed," he said, surprising her into looking up. "Humans calculate sunrise with the first edge of the sun over the horizon. Powerful vampires—" At this he touched his chest. And, yes, he was completely naked. "—can hold out until the full orb rises," he explained.

"Can you go outside in this light?" she asked, more curious than embarrassed.

He walked over to the bed and bent to pull back the covers. Lana jerked away from it, like it was on fire, then covered her reaction by grabbing her duffel and moving it to the top of the well-used dresser. Vincent didn't answer her question. Instead, he asked, "Is it only that I'm close to you, *querida*, or is it rather hot in here?"

"It's hot," she confirmed. She heard the glide of skin on the sheets and dared to turn around again. Vincent was sitting up in bed, his back against the flimsy headboard, the white sheet pulled barely up to his hips in a stark contrast to the beautiful mocha skin he'd inherited from his Guatemalan mother. He gave a low, masculine chuckle that snapped her eyes up to meet his, and his smile was whiter than the sheets and a thousand times sexier. Unless one considered what those sheets were barely managing to cover.

She bit back a groan. "Are you going to answer my question?" she asked, managing—just—to keep her voice cool and businesslike. "If you can stay awake in this light, can you go outside?"

"I shouldn't tell you this," he said, giving her calculating look, but then he shrugged. "No, sunlight is sunlight, whether from an edge or the whole thing. It's only the sleep I can defer. Regrettably, even that time is short, so I can't seduce you as you deserve. But we do have time to make out if you'd like." His expression was perfectly innocent . . . and it didn't fool her for a moment.

Lana gave him a dark look, which turned speculative as she considered not only what he'd said, but how he'd said it. "Your English is very good, you know," she commented. "Colloquialisms like that one, *make out*, are the most difficult thing to learn."

Vincent stretched his arms over his head, then laced his fingers and leaned back, his muscles flexing enticingly. He had to know what he looked like, had to be doing that on purpose.

"My lieutenant, Michael, is American," he said, settling in. "Born and raised in California, and not that long ago. He's been mine less than twenty years. His Spanish is quite good by now, but he still prefers American entertainment—television and movies, sports, too. And between us, we always speak English. It helps keep our language skills current."

"Well, it's working."

"Michael will be gratified to know that." His eyes drooped and he gave her a sleepy smile. "My apologies, *querida*. We'll have to save the making out for later tonight."

His arms dropped to his sides and he slid down on the bed and rolled onto his stomach. And then he was gone.

"Vincent?" Lana called, just to be sure. But there was no response.

She tiptoed over to the bed, then wondered why the hell she was tiptoeing. She stood there, admiring the physical perfection of Vincent's back—the muscles and tendons and the ripple of his spine, the upper curve of his tight butt. They were right out of an anatomy textbook. Feeling like a perv for staring, Lana quickly pulled the sheet up to his waist, but no farther. It was going to get even hotter before the day was over. She resisted the strong urge to drop a good-night kiss on his shoulder, and turned away, going over to her duffel and stripping down to her skin.

When she finally stepped into the shower, she discovered that, as in most of the other places they'd stayed, the water pressure was shit. But the water was hot and plentiful, so she took her time, washing away the sweat of a day spent hiking up and down hills, and hanging around in that horrible concrete box of a prison. She even took the time to shampoo and condition her long hair.

By the time she opened the bathroom door and peeked out to be sure Vincent hadn't moved, she felt a thousand times better. Walking naked to her duffel, she considered her options. If she was sensible, she'd get fully dressed and sleep on top of the covers as she'd done at Marisol's. But it was so very hot in this room, and Vincent wouldn't know the difference as long as she got up and dressed before he woke for the night. She could set the alarm on her cell phone—which was fully charged since she and Vincent had taken turns charging their phones in the SUV on the drive here—to wake her well before sunset. And she *had* brought along a pair of silky pajama shorts and a tank top to sleep in, never thinking that she might be sharing a bed with anyone.

Still trying to convince herself, she went back into the bathroom and combed out her long hair, taking the time to dry it thoroughly and probably doubling the motel's monthly electric bill in the process. And, as it turned out, it was that which decided her. By the time her hair was dry, it was like a warm blanket against her back. And, combined with the stifling air in the room, there was no way she was going to get fully dressed, not if she wanted to sleep. And she really needed to sleep.

So, after verifying the precise time of sunset on the schedule she'd downloaded to her phone, she set the alarm, pulled on her cool shorts and tank top, and slipped under the surprisingly clean-smelling sheets.

She exhaled a long, relieved breath when her head hit the pillow, and, before she could draw the next one, she was asleep.

Chapter Twelve

VINCENT WOKE TO the sound of Lana's even breathing as she slept next to him. He opened his eyes. She was on her side, her back to him, so close that the firm swell of her butt would press against his thigh if she breathed too deeply, so close that if he moved his head the tiniest bit, he could bury his face in the clean scent of all her beautiful hair. He shifted carefully onto his side, and her hair caressed his skin like warm silk. He raised himself onto one elbow and froze at the sight of a bare shoulder, at the gleam of her skin in the low light from the cable box's LED. Pinching the sheet between two fingers, he tugged it slowly downward and sucked in a long breath. This wasn't her usual armor of T-shirt and jeans. She was wearing a pair of tiny, blue satin shorts, cut high enough to bare her entire shapely thigh. And with it, a stretchy tank top that outlined the swell of her round breasts, her nipples twin peaks of enticing color beneath the thin white fabric.

Vincent ate her up with his eyes as the copper glow of his hunger touched the sheen of her skin. Was he made of stone that she expected him to resist this? She wasn't even pretending to put distance between them. At Marisol's, she'd slept fully dressed and on top of the covers, and that had been a huge bed. This bed was barely big enough for the two of them, and yet she'd chosen to wear next to nothing and press the tempting curve of her ass right up against his side.

A flash of light caught his attention and he moved with vampire swiftness. In the blink of an eye he'd identified the source, reached across her, and disabled the sound on her cell phone before it could ring.

He looked down at the phone and smiled. So that was it. She'd set an alarm for what some data source had told her was sunset, thinking to be up and dressed before he woke. He'd told her he could remain awake past the official sunrise. She'd obviously failed to draw the corollary between sunrise and sunset and realize he would wake sooner also.

His smile broadened as he dropped the phone onto his side of the bed then lowered his head to draw in her sweet, warm scent. She was unusual, his Lana. A woman who was smart and courageous enough to sneak into the compound of a drug lord in order to rescue a vampire she barely knew, and generous enough to feed that vampire her own blood, even though she'd probably never even considered doing such a thing before. A bounty hunter by profession, she was armed to the teeth and accustomed to taking down fugitives, sometimes dangerous and much larger than she was, in the course of her business. But for all that, Lana was all woman, with satiny, sweet-smelling skin, and a whole lot of warm, silky hair that he wanted to wrap around his fist and hold on to as he pounded deep into the wet heat between her thighs.

He dipped his nose into the curve of her neck and inhaled deeply. He could smell the delicate bouquet of her blood, could hear it rushing through the veins beneath her skin. He barely touched his lips to the swell of her jugular, hearing the change in her breathing and knowing she would soon wake and slip away from him. He brushed her hair back with his cheek and had just begun to put some space between them when she gave a soft moan that shot straight to his dick. He held his breath as she lifted her hand and reached over her shoulder to cup the back of his head, caressing him, urging him to come closer. Vincent bit back a growl of possession. His tongue slipped between his teeth to taste the sweet saltiness of her neck, a taste he remembered from the previous night when he'd awakened in the human prison, a taste that had his fangs emerging hungrily, that hardened his cock even further until the tip was pushing into her silk-clad hip.

"Vincent," she whispered and rolled over to meet him, lifting her face to his kiss, her lips soft and full, her tongue hesitant as it slid into his mouth, scraping the edges of his fangs.

Vincent did growl then, soft and low, as he deepened their kiss, sucking her tongue into his mouth, tangling it with his own as he caressed her lips, moving slowly, luxuriously. Vincent loved to kiss a woman, love the glide of their soft lips against his, the taste of their mouths. There was little better than that first touch of a woman's mouth, the first kiss that told him so much about her. Was she a hesitant lover, was she passionate, insecure, confident?

Lana Arnold was both. A woman of deep passion who was afraid to give too much, afraid to surrender control. But then, he'd known that before he'd ever touched her. The kiss was just a delicious dot on the exclamation point of what he already knew about her.

And he wanted more.

He wrapped the fingers of one hand around her hip and pulled her into the curve of his body, letting her feel the hard length of his arousal, covering her with his much greater weight.

"Vincent," she whispered again, her body undulating against him, her fingers twisting in his hair.

And then her eyes flashed open and she froze.

Fuck. Vincent realized in a rush that she'd been asleep. Dreaming of him, maybe—probably—but definitely more than half asleep. And she wasn't happy to wake up in his arms.

"Vincent?" she said in a very different tone of voice, her cheeks flushing hot with embarrassment in the instant before her hand dropped away and she rolled out of bed.

"What was..." she started to ask, then, belatedly, seeming to remember what she was wearing, rushed over to the cheap dresser and bent over her duffel to dig out some clothes. "I didn't mean, I mean... I was asleep... dreaming. Not of you, but..."

Vincent relaxed against the pillows and admired the view as the tiny, satin shorts pulled up to reveal the swell of one firm cheek. He drew in the fragrance of her arousal. Yeah, sure, he'd rather have been buried in her pussy right about now, but the view was nice, and it gave him great pleasure just to know that Lana Arnold wanted him badly enough that she was dreaming about him. Which meant he'd have her before long.

Lana clutched her clothes to her chest and escaped into the bathroom, closing the door behind her.

Vincent took her cell phone and placed it back on the bedside table where she'd put it, so she wouldn't suspect anything. Then he lay back and stroked himself off, listening to Lana in the bathroom and imagining slipping up behind her and pulling those pretty, little shorts aside, sliding his cock into her wet and ready pussy, then fucking her until she screamed.

He came with a groan, and a smile on his face.

"I'M SORRY ABOUT... before. I was still asleep," Lana said, pretending to be engrossed in packing her clothes. She was too mortified to look Vincent in the face. It would have been easier if she could have claimed that he'd taken advantage of her, that she hadn't wanted him. But she knew it wasn't true. She'd been dreaming about him, about exactly what they'd been doing when she finally woke up. Dreaming of rolling over to find Vincent's powerful body crushing her into the mattress, his knee between her legs, spreading her thighs as he made love to her with his mouth. In her dream, she'd known that was just the beginning of what he'd do to her, and she'd welcomed that knowledge.

But then she'd woken up and realized it was more than a dream. Still, she'd been tempted to let it continue. But Vincent had sensed the change in her awareness almost before she did, and he'd registered her surprised reaction. And, damn it, he'd stopped. Just once, she'd have liked him to be a jerk. He'd be so much easier to resist if he was a jerk.

"There's nothing to apologize for," he assured her, zipping his bag and heading past her to the door. "You were dreaming—"

She thought he was going to let it go at that, but while he wasn't a jerk, he was still Vincent.

"—of me," he added, leaning down to whisper the words into her ear as he passed by, his breath warm, tickling as it brushed aside a few hairs that had escaped her braid.

Lana shivered. She'd never wanted anyone the way she wanted Vincent. She was a grown woman, twenty-nine years old, for God's sake. Dave Harrington might have been her first, but he sure as hell hadn't been her last. She'd had good lovers and bad, some tender, some . . . not. But she'd never experienced the kind of sheer, burning desire that she felt for Vincent.

She straightened, lifting her duffel as Jerry emerged from the adjoining room. He was wearing the same clothes he'd worn the day before, because he didn't have anything else. Lana reminded herself to ask Vincent to stop somewhere so Jerry could shop. But despite the wrinkled and dirty clothing, Jerry looked fresher and more relaxed, and he'd obviously showered.

"Good evening, Lana."

"Hey, Jerry. Did you sleep well?"

"I did, thank you."

"Sorry about the lack of air conditioning. But at least there was a bed, huh?"

"Those things don't matter. What matters is that for the first time in two years, I woke without fearing for my life."

Lana looked at him in dismay.

"Vincent did that. I woke and I knew I was safe." He gave her a smile tinged with sadness, then continued past her and out the door.

She stared after him. He was right. Vincent had done that. He'd freed Jerry from a very long life of horrible servitude. She sighed. The evidence was piling up, and it was confirming that Vincent wasn't a jerk.

Man, she was so totally screwed.

Chapter Thirteen

"SO, JERRY," VINCENT said as they drove away from the hotel, "what can you tell me about this Salvio Olivarez?"

"I think he was made vampire around the same time I was. He was a captain with the Mexican Federal Police before that."

"What's his so-called master's name, do you know?"

"Domingo Poncio, but I don't know if that's his real name."

"Probably not," Vincent commented. "Those guys generally use street names. What does he do for the cartel?"

"He tortures people, and then kills them. For information mostly. Sometimes, he eliminates rivals, although not always. As least that's what Salvio told me. But our conversations were short and rarely private. Usually only a few words exchanged when our masters were too busy with their own business to pay attention to us."

"Does Poncio have an army? Guards of his own?" Lana asked.

"My impression was that he worked alone, except for Salvio, of course. Salvio is his favorite weapon."

Vincent growled audibly.

"He must have security in place, though," Lana said, glancing at Vincent. "I can't believe we'll find him sitting in his house all alone except for one vampire."

"I agree," Vincent said, just as his cell phone rang. Popping a Bluetooth receiver into his ear, he answered. "Yo, Michael." He listened briefly, then said, "All right, we have a pickup to make first, but that should be finished by the time you get here. Call when you're on the ground." He listened some more, then nodded at whatever his lieutenant was saying. "See you soon."

He disconnected and said, "Michael's on his way with a couple of guys, but it doesn't sound like we're going to need him to deal with Poncio."

"I still don't think—" Lana objected.

"But . . ." Vincent continued, giving her a look that said he wasn't finished. "We'll scope out Poncio's place, get the lay of the land, check out his security. If Jerry's right and there's no one but Salvio, we'll go in. If we need reinforcements, we'll wait 'til Mikey gets here."

"Why not just wait for—"

"I don't like waiting."

"If I may, sir," Jerry interrupted from the back. "We may not require additional fighters for Poncio, but I believe we will for Carolyn's master."

"Carolyn?" Vincent repeated. "Carolyn who?"

"Sir, I . . ."

Lana turned in her seat to look back at Jerry, wondering at his sudden hesitation. He'd been so forthcoming up to this point, so *soldierly* in his responses to every question asked, especially if it was Vincent doing the asking. And yet suddenly, he seemed unable, or unwilling, to face either of them directly, lowering his eyes and turning to look out the window instead.

"Jerry?" she asked, her stomach tightening with a sick feeling.

"Carolyn was another vampire," he said, meeting her stare at last. "I don't know her last name. We saw each other frequently, but she rarely spoke. I think . . ." He paused and his jaw tightened in obvious discomfort as he shifted his gaze away from Lana and met Vincent's gaze in the mirror instead. "Sir, I cannot be sure—"

"Out with it," Vincent growled.

"I believe her master is using her for something other than enforcement."

Vincent's fingers gripped the steering wheel so hard that Lana worried it would crack. But all thoughts about the damned steering wheel were blown away when Vincent's rage blasted through the inside of the SUV like an explosion, swelling bigger and bigger until she thought the windows would burst.

"Sex?" Vincent ground out, his voice so deep and guttural that she could barely make out that one word.

"Yes, sir," Jerry confirmed miserably. "Her master and others."

"God damn it," Vincent snarled. "I will destroy that son of a bitch."

"Jerry?" Lana said, twisting in her seat to face him. "You said we'd need more than the three of us for Carolyn. Why?" She spoke quietly, asking the rational question in an attempt to defuse Vincent's anger, as understandable as it was. The very idea of what had happened to Carolyn made Lana want to throw up. She'd been raped over and over again while helpless to resist her master's orders. That was beyond fucking sick.

But it wouldn't help Carolyn if Vincent let his anger determine their next move.

"Jerry?" she repeated, desperate to cut through the unbearable tension that Vincent's rage was creating.

"Yes," Jerry said finally, sounding like a man waking from a nightmare. "Her master's business is like Camarillo's, which means he will have guards."

Lana glanced at Vincent who was glaring at Jerry's reflection in a way that told her his rage hadn't eased even a tiny bit.

"Vincent," she said, keeping her voice low and easy. "You said Michael is only bringing two fighters, maybe—"

"Two will be more than enough," he growled. "I could take them all on my own if I had to."

"Maybe we should wait—"

"We're not waiting," he snapped, spearing her with a glance. And what she saw in his eyes at that moment was nothing but a cold-blooded killer. This was no longer the charming, sexy Vincent who was determined to seduce every woman he met. This was the vampire who Jerry claimed could rule Mexico if he wanted. The vampire who'd reduced Fidelia's house to rubble with nothing but a thought, who'd ripped out Camarillo's throat with dark glee written all over his face.

It would have terrified her if he'd been anyone other than Vincent.

But she wasn't afraid, at least not for herself. She knew his rage wasn't directed at her, but at the men, vampire or not, who'd taken gross and vicious advantage of a helpless woman. Even more, she wasn't afraid because she knew Vincent, and she could never be afraid of him.

"Okay," she said deliberately. "So, we'll follow the original plan. We do a recon of Poncio's place. If it looks good, we'll take him out and you can do your magic on Salvio like you did with Jerry."

"Magic," Vincent repeated darkly.

"I speak as a layman, of course," she said, being intentionally obtuse. "I'm sure it's not *actually* magic, but that's what it seems like to me."

"Magic," he said again, softer this time, a smile playing around his sensuous mouth as the tension in the vehicle ratcheted down a few hundred levels. "All right. Jerry?"

"Sir?"

"Can you direct me to Poncio's estate?"

Jerry scanned the desert outside the windows, seeing, Lana was certain, nothing but the black night despite his vampire vision, because there simply wasn't anything else out there. "When we get closer, I can," he said. "There's a turnoff from this road. I'll recognize it when I see it."

"That'll do. Lana, when we get there—"

"Don't waste your breath," she said, cutting him off. "I'm not staying with the SUV."

"It's a recon. Jerry and I are better at that kind of stealth—"

"I'm perfectly capable of surveying a target without stirring up a hornet's nest," she informed him. "That's kind of my job, you know."

"You survey hornet's nests?"

"Ha, ha. Very funny," she retorted, although privately, she was thrilled and relieved that Vincent was capable of humor again.

"I'll decide when we get there," Vincent said, as if that was the final word.

"It's already decided."

"I'm hoping for bloodshed," he growled. "I'm feeling a bit peckish."

Lana's mouth tightened irritably. She couldn't match that one, and his grin told her he knew it. Jerk.

VINCENT EYED LANA speculatively as she stood at the Suburban's open cargo hatch and geared up for their pending recon of Poncio's house. She was currently concealing an assortment of knives about her person that a lesser man, or vampire, might have found alarming. Vincent thought it was sexy as hell. Just watching her was giving him a hard-on. That didn't mean he liked the idea of her going with him, though. He entertained and dismissed the notion of "persuading" her to stay here and wait for him. First, because he still hadn't figured out how to breach that weird resistance of hers to vampiric power, but even more than that, he wouldn't do it because he respected her too much to sideline her against her will. Besides, if he tried, she'd probably be pissed as hell, and that would make it much more difficult to achieve his plan to lay her out on a big bed and fuck her until she screamed.

He smiled, thinking about that eventuality. Lana happened to glance up at that moment and narrowed her gaze at him, obviously finding his expression suspect. He winked at her, purely for the sake of his own amusement, and because he knew it would make her even more suspicious.

Muttering to herself, she turned back to her weapons, jamming a knife into her boot with enough force that he winced.

"It's best if you're not bleeding *before* we begin," he reminded her.

She puffed out a dismissive breath. "Don't worry your pretty little head, vampire. I've done this a hundred times. And, FYI, there's a custom sheath built into the boot."

"Is there?" he said, intrigued. "A hundred times, you say?"

"At least."

"But how many times have you *drawn* it?"

She gave him an impatient glance as she yanked down and shut the cargo hatch. "Enough," she said, but then added, "But mostly in practice."

An unaccustomed, and uncomfortable, tightness swelled around Vincent's heart at her admission. It revealed a vulnerability in Lana that he'd always suspected was there. He glanced around, but Jerry was in front of the SUV, crouched down and surveying the hacienda in the small valley below. Vincent came up behind Lana and trapped her between his body and the closed cargo hatch. He slipped an arm around her waist, his hand resting flat against her belly as he leaned down and rested his cheek against the side of her head. She stiffened slightly, but didn't push him away, her body tense, waiting to see what he would do.

"I won't tell you not to do this, *querida*," he said quietly. "But take care. Remember, you're dealing with vampires. Jerry and I are stronger, faster, and more resilient than you. Poncio might be human, but he can still shoot a gun, and Salvio's a complete unknown. You're—" He searched for a way to say what needed to be said that wouldn't offend her, wouldn't simply make her shut down and stop listening. "—easier to damage than we are."

She tried to pull away, but he only tightened his grip. "Promise me, Lana. Don't risk yourself for me or Jerry. I need you alive."

She softened enough to ask, "Why?"

Vincent smiled slightly and tightened his arm around her, closing the small space between them until her back was pressed to his front, letting her feel his body's reaction to her. She sucked in a breath of awareness and her heartbeat kicked up a notch.

"Because I want you in my bed, *querida*, not just to sleep, but to finish what we started earlier this evening."

Her head fell back against his shoulder for just a moment, then she turned in his arms and he let her shove him away. "Don't worry about me," she said briskly. "I have every intention of staying alive, and *not* just so that you can get your rocks off, either."

Vincent snagged her arm, bending it behind her back as he pulled her close and lowered his head until they were breathing each other's air. "You just stay alive. I'll do the rest." He kissed her then, hard and demanding. But if he'd thought she'd fight him, he'd have been wrong. Her other hand came up to cup the back of his neck, fingers twisting in his hair as she yanked him in tight and kissed him back just as hard. When she released him, they were both breathing rapidly and her light brown eyes were glittering with a desire that matched his own.

"We'll both survive," she murmured. "And then we'll talk."

Vincent stroked his hand down the length of her braid and gave it a yank. "Deal. Let's go see what Jerry's discovered."

They'd parked the SUV up above the hacienda, concealing it behind a hill to avoid detection from below. Vincent led the way down to Poncio's estate, crawling the last few yards so as not to silhouette himself in the bright moonlight. He didn't know if the moon was technically full, but it was damn close to it. Lana scooted up beside him as the three of them lay staring at the buildings down below.

"It's awfully quiet for a vamp residence," Lana observed, pulling a small pair of binoculars from her pocket. She'd changed from the skintight Levis she'd been wearing, and now wore a pair of black combat pants. Vincent liked the jeans, but she filled the combats out nicely, too.

"Anyone see anything?" Vincent asked.

"I'm on night vision here, but I'm not seeing much. How about you guys?" Lana asked, not taking the binocs from her eyes.

"We're several hours past sunset," Jerry commented. "Maybe they've all gone out already."

"Or maybe they were never home to begin with. If this guy's an enforcer, he must travel."

A sudden flash of light had Lana swearing as she dropped the night vision lenses from her eyes. "Damn. What was that?"

"The outbuilding on the left," Jerry said quietly.

Vincent nodded. He'd seen the same thing. Someone had opened and closed a door, and now two figures, two humans, were making their way across the yard away from the outbuilding. They were walking directly, but not hurrying. One walked slightly in front of the other and there was an air of confidence about him. He moved as if he was sure of his place and unafraid, even though he'd be useless in a fight. The guy was overweight and out of shape, with a belly that hung over his belt. His confidence was no doubt due in large part to the presence of the heavily-armed man accompanying him. That one moved like a bodyguard, hand on the MP 5 slung around his neck, his head constantly turning left and right as he scanned the yard, then moved quickly to open and check out a gate between the buildings before his charge could walk through.

"Both human," Vincent said for Lana's benefit. She made a *hmm* sound, acknowledging the information as she put the binocs to her eyes once more.

"There must be a basement in that building on the left, sir," Jerry said, confirming what Vincent was thinking.

"I agree. You said Poncio's an enforcer. He'd need someplace to question his victims, someplace their screams wouldn't carry."

"Yes."

"Was the guy with the gut Poncio?" Lana asked from his other side.

"It was," Jerry confirmed.

Vincent nodded. He'd guessed as much. "That makes our job easier," he said.

"How do you figure that?" Lana questioned.

"The targets are split," Jerry answered for him. Vincent was reminded that this young man had done two tours in a very hot war zone, not to mention whatever nefarious activities he'd engaged in over the last two years for Camarillo.

"But we don't know how many are still in the basement," Lana protested. "Or even if there's really a basement at all."

"There's a basement," Vincent said confidently. "All that dirt muffles the life signs, makes it difficult to say with certainty how many people are down there. But the very fact that it's muffled tells me there's a basement. Either that, or the building's shielded like crazy. Although, if it is, that's even better. I'd much rather storm a building than a basement."

"We're storming a building?" Lana asked.

"Storming might be too strong a word. We'll approach quietly, take out Poncio in the house, then do a covert entry on the outbuilding. If there's a basement, which I think likely, we'll have no choice but to check it out."

"Can't we just throw a grenade down the stairs or something?"

Jerry swiveled his head to stare silently, while Vincent's regard was somewhat more amused. "You have a grenade handy, *querida?*"

Lana shrugged uncomfortably. "I have a couple of flashbangs in my duffel."

Vincent's grin broadened. "Are those legal?"

"More or less. We get ours from a UK military source. They come in handy sometimes."

"I'm intrigued by the more or less part of your response, but we can discuss that later. For now, however, I'm reluctant to use your flashbangs. If that basement is what I think it is, then Salvio is likely to be down there, maybe with prisoners. I'm concerned about the damage your grenade might do to a vampire's more finely-tuned senses. And since we're trying to liberate Salvio, I'd rather not start out by bursting his ear drums or worse."

"He'd heal," she muttered. "But what if he has a bunch of human guards down there with him? You could be walking into a hail of gunfire."

"I won't be walking at all. Trust me, I can move fast when I need to. But first things first. Jerry, when we get down there, I want you to find a position near that building's exit. If anyone other than Salvio tries to leave, you take them out."

"Yes, sir."

"Lana, you're with me. We're going to pay our fat friend Poncio a visit."

Chapter Fourteen

LANA FOLLOWED IN Vincent's wake, trying not to make as much noise as a herd of cows rushing down the hillside. Vincent and Jerry both moved like ghosts. She wouldn't have known they were there if she hadn't been with them. Even then, she was pretty sure they were holding back, going slowly in order to avoid leaving her in their dust. Not that they were stirring up any. Bastards.

She winced as yet another piece of scrub crackled under her foot, breathing a sigh of relief when they finally hit the mostly rock and dirt base of the hill. This part wasn't all that different from their climb out of Camarillo's compound, except that in this case, she didn't dare risk even the smallest light. Everything was completely dark on Poncio's estate. There were no lights along the pathway or the gate Poncio had used, and no security system had been triggered in response to his walk across the yard, or to their movements along the edges. A very dim light had come on upstairs in the sprawling two-story adobe that was the main residence, but it was little more than an outline of a shuttered window.

If not for the bright moonlight, Lana would have been nearly blind. But even with it, she barely managed to avoid tripping over Vincent. He was crouched down, waiting for her as Jerry sprinted along the edge of the property, using the uneven hillside as cover as he made his way close to the barn where they thought Salvio would be found, and maybe a prisoner or two.

Lana rested a light hand on Vincent's shoulder to let him know she was there—although, in retrospect, he probably didn't need the warning—then crouched next to him. She quickly lost sight of Jerry in the shadows, but Vincent seemed to follow his progress easily enough. Lana kept her eyes on the rest of the property, scanning from left to right.

"It's too quiet," she whispered. "Where are the animals? The coyotes?"

"They're smart enough to know there's a predator around tonight who's much tougher than they are," he murmured.

Lana frowned, then caught the flash of white that was Vincent's grin. "You mean . . . you? Huh." She'd never thought of vampires as predators, but, of course, they were. "I'm glad you're on my side, then."

"Why, Lana. I'm touched."

She scowled. "You're touched all right. So what's next?"

"Next, you and I go find *Señor* Poncio and remind him that there are creatures afoot tonight who are far more dangerous than he is, too."

"It's a big house. How will you know where he is?"

"If his heart is beating, I'll find him. But we'll have to get through the door first. I'm a vampire. I can't enter without an invitation."

"That story's true?"

"It is. And it might be why Poncio's guard is human. He protects himself from his own vampire enforcer by never inviting him inside the house."

"I'm not a vampire," she said thoughtfully.

"No, you're not, but I'm not sending you into that house alone."

"If I got inside, could I invite you in once I was there?"

"You can't sneak in and then invite me. You'd have to be invited first, and even then you'd have to get Poncio or the guard to invite your *friends*, at least indirectly."

"If I knock, the guard will probably be the one who answers."

"Probably."

"So all I need to do is get invited inside, and then finagle an invitation for my friend. No problem."

VINCENT WATCHED as Lana stood and began stripping off her gear, her jacket first, and then, with a deep sigh, her Sig, along with the shoulder holster. The jacket she folded and left on the ground, with the weapon on top of it. She touched the gun lightly and said, "Take good care of this, okay? It's my favorite."

"The gun?" he asked, amused that she had a favorite weapon.

"Yes," she said as if it was the most natural thing in the world. She then proceeded to pull her long-sleeved T-shirt out of her pants and yanked it off over her head, leaving her in nothing but a black sports bra and the stretchy white tank top that she'd slept in.

Vincent scowled. He didn't like where this was going. "Lana, what . . ." His unhappiness grew when she turned her back to him, pulled off the tank top, and began undoing the hooks on the bra's front opening.

"What the fuck?" he demanded. He hadn't been all that sold on letting her go in there alone in the first place, and this little striptease of hers wasn't making him feel any better about it.

She removed her bra, pulled the tank top back on, then turned to face him as she began working on her braid. "When it comes to women, men are easily distracted," she said absently, as she threaded her fingers through her now unbraided hair and shook her head to loosen it over her shoulders.

Vincent straightened next to her, at least partly to ease the sudden tightness of his groin at the sight of her breasts pressing against the thin shirt. They weren't large, but they were round and firm, with dusky nipples that were in plain sight beneath the nearly transparent fabric. He realized with a start that he'd just proved her point about easily-distracted men.

"Lana," he said, her display also proving *his* point. "I won't let you—"

"You're not my master, Vincent. We're partners. I don't need your permission. Besides, this is the only thing that will work. You need inside that house and I can get you there."

Vincent glowered down at her. It was much easier working with his vampires. They did what they were told.

"You'll need to stay close," she told him, crouching down to check the position of the hidden knife in her boot. Her hair fell forward in a wave of black silk, sliding along her bare arms and curling over her unfettered breasts, which did nothing for the growing pressure in his groin. "I'm going to be the ultimate helpless female," she explained, adding her bra and hair tie to the pile of gear on top of her jacket. "My friend and I have been walking for hours. Our car broke down, we're lost in the desert, and blah blah blah." She tied everything into a neat bundle with the sleeves of her jacket.

"And if it doesn't work?"

She paused in her preparations to give him an impatient look. "Well, I don't know, Vincent. Why don't you think of something? Or better yet, wish me good luck and carry my stuff so I can get dressed once we're inside." She shoved the jacket-covered bundle at him.

"You're supposed to be helpless, *querida,* not bitchy."

Her eyes widened in outrage, then narrowed. "You're trying to make me angry so I won't be scared. But I'm not scared. I've done this before. Not exactly like this because I wasn't dealing with vampires, but close enough, when I've wanted to get inside a house where I thought my skip might be hiding."

"The many layers of Lana Arnold," Vincent said thoughtfully, accepting the jacket from her. "All right. We can't see the entrance Poncio used, but there's probably a courtyard through that gate, with the door to the house on the other side."

Vincent started off across the yard, not bothering with concealment. He'd know if anyone was watching, and no one was. They approached the wide, wrought-iron gate that Poncio and the guard had used earlier. He opened it slowly, wary of making the kind of noise that would alert the guard. But it moved on near-silent hinges, admitting them to a narrow walkway surrounded by sweet-smelling plants. There were big leafy ferns, low crawling vines with tiny star-shaped flowers, and latticed stalks with big trumpet blooms that climbed both walls. It was probably a welcome respite from the hot desert sun during the day, but at night, it created a wealth of possible hiding places.

He and Lana paused at the far end of the passage, using the thick foliage for cover when they finally caught sight of the entrance to the house, along with more evidence that someone was inside. Now that they were closer, the shutter outline was bright enough to cast a dim yellow glow on the narrow courtyard, and there was an additional lamp burning behind the drawn shade in a window next to the door. As they watched, the narrow bars of light from the upstairs shutter blinked off and on as someone passed by the window and moved around the room.

"You think that's Poncio upstairs?" Lana whispered.

Vincent nodded. "Likely. The guard probably stays downstairs." He paused for a moment, concentrating. "There are no vampires inside, and only the two humans. But we don't know how many are in the basement with Salvio. They could show up at any minute."

"Then I better get started."

Vincent stopped her with a hand on her arm. "Lana, remember, you can't lie. If you get him to invite your *girl*friend inside, it won't work."

She nodded. "But I can just call you a friend, right? Even though I don't like you?"

Vincent grinned and cupped his hand over the back of her neck, tangling his fingers in her loose hair. "You like me, *querida*." He kissed her mouth, holding it longer than he should have given their time constraints, but not as long as he would have liked. "Be careful."

She licked her lips slowly, her eyes bright in the moonlight. "I will," she whispered. "Stay close, okay?"

"Count on it," he said and then stepped back, clenching his fists as he watched her move across the courtyard.

LANA DREW A DEEP breath through her nose, then tugged her tank top low on her breasts and crossed the open courtyard, stumbling slightly for effect, boots scuffing on the paving stones as if she was too exhausted to lift her feet properly. She searched her memories and called up the death of her friend Gretchen's mother last year. She filled her mind with the image of Gretchen sobbing in her husband's arms, of Gretchen's three-year-old daughter crying, tears rolling down her soft cheeks, because her mother was sad and she didn't know why. Lana had cried too, for her friend's grief and for her own. Gretchen's mom had been a warm and loving human being who'd always treated the motherless Lana as one of her own. The funeral had been the saddest day of Lana's life, even including the day her mother had flown off to California and left her behind. And now she used that memory to bring tears to her eyes for a performance that would maybe save the life of a vampire she didn't even know.

Tears swelled and spilled over as she forced herself to hyperventilate, taking fast and shallow breaths until she had to lean against the wall next to the door for support. Reaching out with one hand, she knocked on the door, using regular pressure first, then harder and more frantic until she was pounding with her fist.

The door flew open without warning and she nearly fell into the man who stood there. As soon as she saw him, she knew he wasn't Poncio, which meant they'd been right about their target being the guy in the shuttered room upstairs. The guard facing her had a 9mm holstered at his hip and a shotgun in his hand. He was backlit by the interior light which was much brighter with the door open, but she could see that his hair and eyes were dark, and he appeared to be somewhere around forty. Vincent had said the man was human, and Lana had no reason to doubt him.

"Thank God you're home," she gasped, using her worst, broken Spanish. She bent forward to rest her hands on her thighs, looking up at him with tear-filled eyes and letting the top of her tank gap slightly to give him a better view of her braless breasts. "Please, sir, we need your help. My friend and I were almost out of gas, and we turned off the main road thinking we could find a station but we must have read the map wrong or something because there was nothing there and then we tried to turn around but . . . ." Her breathless spiel ran out as she choked on her sobs, leaning weakly against the doorjamb as she struggled to catch her breath.

"Please help us. If we could just use your phone, we can call . . . Oh my God, is there even an auto club out here?" she wailed and began crying harder, daring to reach out with one hand to grip his arm. "Please . . ." She managed to squeeze the word out in between sobs, all the while watching the guard, who was so focused on her breasts that she doubted he was hearing a word she said. His gaze dropped briefly to her hips and belly, went even more briefly to her face, then right back to her breasts which were clearly outlined beneath the white tank top.

"Relax, *chica*," the guard said in accented English, his gaze growing calculated as he reached out and lifted a lock of hair from her breast and wrapped it around his finger. "I'll take care of you."

"You speak English," Lana said, her voice breaking with relieved emotion. "Oh thank God."

"Come inside," the guard said smoothly, taking her bare arm and stepping back. "Your skin is so cold, you must be freezing and thirsty too, yes?"

She started to follow him. "Water? Oh God, yes, I'd love—" She stopped abruptly and made as if to turn back, freeing her arm. "But I can't," she said, pretending to be torn between going inside and going back for her "friend."

"I can't leave my friend . . ."

"Your friend can come inside too. You can both rest for a while, and then we'll find your car and—"

"Thank you," she interrupted breathlessly. "Let me just . . ." She started to walk away, then turned back. "We'll be right back. Please, don't leave."

"Of course, not," he said. "I'll start the fire. You go and get your friend and we'll warm both of you right up." He turned away, going off supposedly to light the fire—although who knew what he was really doing, preparing a roofied drink for her most likely, and maybe one for her "friend" too. Hell, maybe he'd invite Poncio downstairs and the two of them would have a private party with the stupid Americans.

Lana turned away before she gave in to temptation and punched the bastard in the face. His intent had been so obvious that she was amazed he thought he was fooling anyone. She wanted to scrub her arm where he'd touched her. If he'd been any more blatantly predatory, he'd have been rubbing his hands together like an old-time movie villain. But then, she'd played the harebrained ninny before and it always worked. So maybe it wasn't much of a stretch for someone to believe that she was so stupid as to have gotten lost and ended up at this hacienda in the middle of fucking nowhere.

Vincent grabbed her before she'd taken three steps away from the open doorway, wrapping his arms around her and pulling her into the heat of his big body.

"Are you okay?" he murmured.

Lana shivered, grateful he was there, letting herself enjoy a moment of comfort before pushing away from his embrace. "I'm fine. It was just an act."

Vincent studied her briefly, then nodded and stripped off his jacket. "Put this on," he ordered, sliding it over her shoulders.

She wanted to argue. She had her own jacket, she didn't need his. But she really was cold and she could feel the heat from his body still warming the material.

"Thanks." She pulled it on and had to force herself not to wiggle happily. It was just as warm as she'd thought it would be, and it smelled like him, too. That shouldn't have affected her as much as it did. Hell, it shouldn't have affected her at all. But she couldn't deny the reassuring effect of his scent, and she knew he'd been right. She *did* like him, more than a little.

"Your things," Vincent said, snapping her back to the reality of their situation. This wasn't the time to be mooning like a schoolgirl.

"Thanks," she said again. Not wanting to give up the warmth of his jacket, she set the pile of her things on the ground, then bent to retrieve her Sig. Sliding it out of its holster, she worked the slide to be certain of her load, then kept it in her hand, holding it down against her thigh. "We'd better get inside before lover boy comes looking for me."

"Right. We'll take them both out. We can leave the guard alive if you're squeamish, but Poncio has to die. Just like Camarillo and for the same reasons."

"No argument from me," she said. "How do we do this?"

Vincent grinned. "That part you can leave to me."

Lana entered the house first, looking over her shoulder nervously, still worried about Vincent. But he crossed the threshold with no problem, giving her a playful wink as he did so.

"It's good to have friends," he whispered, but an instant later, he was scanning the house, his expression deadly serious.

Lana heard a thump from the direction of what looked like the kitchen. Gun in hand, she slid around the dividing wall and found lover boy slumped on the floor, a glass of water spilled next to him. She stepped closer, saw the plastic bottle of pills on the counter, and knew she'd been right. The label was in Spanish, but the drug name was the same. Flunitrazepam, the generic for Rohypnol, known on the street as a date rape drug. Nice guy. Maybe she'd let Vincent kill him. On the other hand, the best death for him might be when his cartel masters discovered that he'd failed to protect Poncio and lost the vampire, to boot.

"Lana." Vincent's voice was soft but urgent, and she hurried back to the foot of the stairs where he was waiting for her.

"Did you do that?" she asked him, jerking her head in the unconscious guard's direction.

"Child's play," Vincent said absently and put one foot on the stairs before pausing. "Poncio's up there," he told her. "No one else. Are you coming?"

She knew why he was asking, knew *what* he was *really* asking. Camarillo's death had been horrific, grotesque in its violence and gore. Poncio's would be the same. Vincent was giving her an out.

"I'm coming," she said. "We're in this together."

Vincent took her hand, squeezing it tightly before bringing it to his lips. "Thank you, *querida*."

Lana flushed with a combination of pleasure and embarrassment, not sure what she'd done to deserve his thanks. She only knew there was no way she was going to leave him alone in this. They were in this house because of a mission that *she'd* brought to him. She wasn't going to hide downstairs while he did the dirty work so that she could pretend it never happened.

Besides, there was that whole liking thing. She wasn't going to send him off into danger with a kiss and leave it at that. Not as long as she could fight by his side.

"Are you going to do to him what you did to Camarillo?" she whispered as they climbed the stairs.

"That would be rather boring, wouldn't it? Do I strike you as an unimaginative kind of man?" he asked, waggling his eyebrows suggestively.

Lana rolled her eyes, but only half-heartedly. He was cute. Granted, he was devastatingly handsome, but also cute in a clever sort of way. But then it occurred to her that he was about to use that cleverness to improvise a particularly bloody way of killing someone, and it didn't seem quite as charming anymore.

Vincent turned left at the top of the stairs, seeming to know exactly where to find Poncio. A week ago, that would have surprised her, but she'd learned a lot about vampires in that time. He was probably following the sound of Poncio's heartbeat, or something equally impossible.

They followed the hallway to a room at the far end, away from the kitchen and on the backside of the house where it would face the desert. Vincent gave her a questioning look, and she nodded to say she was ready. He opened the door without warning and stepped inside, standing in the open doorway a second longer than he had to. Lana knew he'd done it on purpose, making sure it was safe before exposing her to whatever waited inside.

When Vincent did move out of the way, however, she discovered that what waited inside was just an overweight, middle-aged man in his underwear who was currently snorting cocaine. He straightened, staring in shock as they entered the room, a porcelain snort straw in one hand, his nostrils still bearing the telltale trace of white powder.

Lana's first thought was that Vincent was going to be disappointed, because if Poncio was flying high on coke, he might not be as susceptible to pain. But then it occurred to her that it might actually be worse for him. Not the pain, but the mind games that Vincent could use against him instead. And then she wondered what the hell had happened to her that she could even approach the subject as though it was nothing but a problem to solve.

"¿Y tú, quién chingados eres?" Poncio demanded, his eyes glazed and blinking stupidly. *Who the fuck are you?* Belatedly, he seemed to recognize his danger and made a grab for the 9mm Glock sitting on the bureau next to the mirror which still bore three neat lines of coke. But Vincent was there before Poncio came anywhere near the gun, fisting his hand in the man's thick hair and bending him backward until he squealed in pain.

"My name is Vincent, and you have something that belongs to me."

"*SOY VICENTE, Y TU tienes algo que me pertenece,*" Vincent growled, drawing in the scent of the human's fear, more intoxicating than any drug the humans could conjure up.

"*¿Qué?*" Poncio asked. His voice was a plaintive whine, and Vincent marveled that such a weakling could gain so much power in the human world.

"Salvio," Vincent replied to the man's question, and then he grinned, letting his fangs emerge from his gums with a slow glide, watching the terror build in Poncio's gaze. He tightened his grip on the man's hair and dragged him to the huge bed. Poncio was whimpering all the way, pleading, explaining, insisting that Salvio had been a gift from *el gran jefe, el gran vampiro.*

That if Vincent would only call Enrique, he would see . . .

His begging was cut off abruptly when Vincent lifted him by his hair and threw him onto the bed. Poncio screamed like a woman, and immediately tried to crawl away. Vincent stripped the covers away, grabbing the flat sheet—black satin, how original—and tearing it into four strips.

Poncio had shoved himself up against the headboard, trying to put distance between himself and Vincent, and was now scrambling for the far side, trying to escape. He was gibbering in fear and making very little sense. If he'd had a working cell left in his brain, he'd have skipped the flight to the headboard and simply rolled off the side in the first place and made a run for the door. He had a much better chance against Lana than he did Vincent, which was to say, no chance at all. Vincent was certain Lana could have stopped the terrified man's escape, too. She was a bounty hunter; she had to know how to take a man down. If nothing else, she'd probably have shot him. She hadn't said a word about Camarillo's death, hadn't blinked an eye when Vincent had made it clear that he had the same fate planned for Poncio. No, Lana wouldn't have let him out the door.

But Poncio didn't know that, which made him a fool for not taking the chance.

Not that it mattered. Vincent was on him before he'd managed to put both feet on the floor, grabbing his ankle and dragging him back across the bed, kicking and squealing. He managed to score a decent kick with his free foot as Vincent secured the other ankle to the bedpost, and Vincent cursed silently, more irritated than hurt. He was pissed enough about it, though, that he glanced up and drew on his power to deliver a directed blow that snapped the man's tibia like a twig. The fucker wouldn't be doing any more kicking. Poncio screamed, and Vincent smirked.

He snagged the broken leg mercilessly and tied it to the other bedpost, barely registering the man's agonized shrieking. His only thought was that it was a good thing he had the sheet to use for bindings, because it was a big fucking bed and Poncio wasn't that big of a guy. There was good distance between the bedposts and the man's various limbs. Not that it would matter much longer.

"You want me to gag him with something?" Lana asked, and Vincent turned to her with a pleased grin. As a vampire, it was in his nature to be what humans would consider heartless, even cruel. He didn't see it that way. He simply did what needed to be done without letting useless emotion clutter the situation. But few humans would view it the same way he did. It delighted him that Lana understood. It already made his dick hard just being around her, waking up next to her. Add this into the mix, and no more excuses. They were going to fuck . . . soon.

But first . . .

"Nah, let him scream," Vincent said, turning back to his task. "There's no one to hear it, and he won't be screaming much longer. I don't want to keep Jerry waiting."

"I have money," Poncio begged, using English now, barely intelligible through his sobs.

"What a coincidence," Vincent said dryly. "So do I."

"Please, what do you want from me?"

"Your pain, mostly, but you can answer a question for me first."

"*Si, si,* anything," he choked out.

"I know you've been using Salvio as an enforcer, so don't deny it. I want to know who gave him to you."

"*Señor* Enrique. Ask him. He'll tell you it is okay what I do."

"Oh, I'll ask him. But it's not okay. It was never okay." And with that, Vincent jammed both fists into the man's chest, one on each side, breaking several ribs and driving them into his lungs, shredding both organs, before stepping back and watching as Poncio struggled to breathe, to *scream*. The human's eyes grew comically wide, his mouth gaping open like that of a fish, horror filling his gaze as he realized there was no air.

Lana came up next to Vincent, her hand moving to his lower back, warning him she was there. As if he wasn't exquisitely aware of her presence, as if he hadn't known the moment she'd started across the room toward him.

Her fingers clenched in Vincent's shirt as Poncio fought for oxygen, his lips turning a blue that eventually spread to his entire face, a red-tinged blue that bordered on purple as he strained against the inevitable.

"How long will it take?" she asked softly, and Vincent knew she wasn't as blasé as she liked to pretend.

"I can end it now," he told her. "We should rejoin Jerry anyway."

Lana didn't say anything at first, and he figured she was torn between wanting it over with and not wanting to appear weak. But then she said, "We can't waste too much time here. We still need to rendezvous with Michael and get to Carolyn."

Carolyn. Vincent cursed himself. Lana was right. There was no time to waste. He stabbed a spear of power into Poncio's chest and incinerated his heart, ending the man's useless life once and for all.

Vincent took Lana's arm as he turned, momentarily startled by the fresh sight of her braless chest beneath the white tank and covered by his jacket. Shit.

"You should get dressed before we head over to the barn."

"I'm okay if you don't want to—"

"You'll get dressed, Lana. It will only take a moment, and it's cold," he added, though it sounded lame even to his own ears. The truth was, he didn't want Jerry or Salvio or anyone else seeing her like that.

"Yes, sir, master, sir," she said, but she sounded more amused than anything else. Vincent suspected she knew the real reason he wanted her covered.

They didn't linger in the house. Poncio had already given them what they wanted. Vincent went ahead of her down the stairs, mostly so he could grab her bundle of clothing and bring it back inside. The guard in the kitchen was out cold and would stay that way for several hours still. So, there was no reason for her to change out in the open . . . where anyone might see her.

Lana removed his jacket, then disappeared into the sitting room opposite the kitchen to get dressed. It took only a few minutes, but when she returned, he saw that her bra was back in place, as well as her long-sleeved T-shirt, and that her shoulder harness was once more secured as she pulled her own jacket on over it.

"So what's the plan?" she asked, handing him back his jacket, and then working to re-braid her hair.

"I can't be sure, but it's very possible that Salvio felt Poncio's death. Had Poncio been a vampire master, Salvio would definitely know. But if—" Vincent froze as a sudden strong thread of alarm jolted his senses. It wasn't his own perception, which meant . . . Jerry. There was no other vampire around who belonged to him.

"Let's go," he said urgently. "Something's happened."

He would have waited for Lana, but she slapped his shoulder and said, "Go. I'll catch up."

Vincent did a quick survey to be sure there was no danger lurking in the shadows, then took off with a burst of vampiric speed that had him out of the courtyard and in sight of the barn in a moment's time.

Jerry was no longer concealed in the shadows, but had moved to the center of the yard. He was staring at the barn where Vincent could see the outline of a bright light around the closed door.

"Jerry?" he asked.

"Sir," Jerry said, acknowledging him. "Lana?" he asked.

"Right here," Lana said before Vincent could answer. She came up behind them, not even slightly short of breath from her run.

"I heard shots, sir. Automatic weapons on full, and screaming. Lots of screaming," Jerry said. "Not one person, but many."

Vincent frowned, contemplating the possibilities. But then the barn door opened and he didn't have to wonder anymore. A single person was silhouetted in the doorway, a vampire, not a human. Salvio?

Jerry started forward and the unknown vampire did the same, stumbling to his knees when the two were less than ten feet apart. He'd been shot. His chest was a bloody mess, and his left arm appeared broken at best, ravaged by gunfire at worst.

"Jerry?" the new vampire said, his voice weak with blood loss.

"It's all right, Salvio," Jerry assured him, rushing forward to kneel at his side. He spoke English, which told Vincent that Salvio at least understood that language. "My human master is dead," Jerry continued, "As is yours."

Salvio nodded weakly. "I felt him die. It was my chance." He tried to brace himself using his injured arm and gasped. His voice, when he continued, was tight with pain. "I killed my guards to get away. The other prisoner, the one I was questioning, he died in the crossfire."

Jerry put a hand on Salvio's shoulder in a gesture of support, then gave a sideways nod of his head to indicate Vincent, who still stood just behind him. "This is—" he started to say.

But Vincent spoke up, not waiting for an introduction. There was a protocol among vampires, and it didn't include waiting for lesser vampires to make introductions. "Salvio," he said. "I am Vincent." He bared his power for a heartbeat, long enough to let Salvio know who and what it was he now faced.

"My lord," Salvio whispered, his head bowed, shoulders slumped in resignation.

Vincent felt a moment's pity for the vampire. Salvio assumed he'd gone from the proverbial frying pan into the fire. From one cruel master to another even worse, with barely time to breathe in the fresh air of freedom in between.

"It's all right, Salvio," Jerry was saying. He rested a gentle hand on his friend's shoulder in reassurance. "Lord Vincent is not like our human masters. You'll see for yourself. There is a whole new world for us, my friend."

"Salvio," Vincent repeated, demanding attention as he stopped before the kneeling vampire. "Your human master is dead. I killed him. If he were vampire, that would make you mine. But your situation, like Jerry's, is not that simple. Enrique enslaved you to a human, which goes against every tenet of vampire society. But he is still your Sire, and for now, you belong to him. So, I'm offering you a choice. You can return to Enrique, who may very well hand you over to another human, if he doesn't execute you on the spot for knowing too much. Or . . . you can pledge your loyalty to me. But know this, Salvio, I do not tolerate disloyalty in my people. Betrayal will be punished swiftly and permanently."

"Sir, may I?" Jerry asked, looking up at Vincent.

Vincent frowned. He didn't want Salvio persuaded against his will. On the other hand, given his experience with Enrique, the vampire had no reason to trust anything Vincent said. He nodded for Jerry to go ahead.

"Salvio, you know me. Our situations were the same, and I'm telling you, you can trust Lord Vincent."

Salvio looked up at last. He was smaller than Jerry, with dark hair and eyes, and the characteristic features of Mexican Indian descent.

"How do I do this?" he asked, and Vincent realized that although his appearance was Mexican, he'd spent enough time in or around the U.S. that he both understood and spoke American English.

"Your last name is Olivarez, is that right, Salvio?" Vincent asked as he stripped off his jacket once more and handed it to Lana. She took it, and then without a word, handed over the same small knife he'd used before. He grinned as she moved slightly away from him. Far enough that she would be out of his way if Salvio made a hostile move, but close enough that she could see what was happening. It might have been curiosity on her part, or a desire to be within reach if he needed her. But whichever it was, it gave him a strange, warm feeling that she didn't shy away from what he was. Just as she hadn't been horrified by what he'd done to Poncio, she wasn't turned off by the bloody aspect of the ritual he was about to engage in with Salvio.

"Yes, Master," Salvio answered. "My last name is Olivarez. My family is from Los Cabos."

Vincent gave him a pitying look. "Not anymore, Salvio. Your family is with me and mine."

Tears filled Salvio's eyes, but he nodded. "I know."

Vincent touched the young vampire's bent head briefly. "It will get better, *mijo*." He remembered what it was like to leave his family behind without so much as a letter to say good-bye. It was how it had to be, but that didn't make it any easier.

With these thoughts running in his head, he sliced his arm open with Lana's knife. It hurt like a motherfucker, but he kept his expression carefully blank. It wouldn't do to let the newbies know that even a powerful vampire could feel pain.

He lowered his arm and blood surged from the wound, running down to pool in his cupped hand. He held his bloody hand out to the kneeling vampire and spoke the formal words.

"Do you come to me of your own free will and desire, Salvio?"

Salvio's dark eyes were slightly puzzled as he looked up at Vincent, but then his nostrils flared as he caught the rich scent of Vincent's blood, and the puzzlement turned to raw hunger.

"I do, Master," he growled.

"And is this what you truly desire?" Vincent demanded.

"Yes, Master. Please." They weren't the formal words, but they would do.

Vincent offered his cupped hand and said, "Then drink, Salvio Olivarez, and be mine."

LANA WATCHED THE ritual that apparently bound Salvio to Vincent in some vampish way. She didn't pretend to understand the ties, but she couldn't deny they were there. She'd seen the transition in Jerry. Not only in his newfound devotion to Vincent, but the lightening of his entire persona, as if he'd been carrying some huge weight for the two years he'd been enslaved to Camarillo and was now free of it. Even though he wasn't actually free. Or was he? It was all very confusing and she made a note to herself to ask Vincent about it the next time they were alone.

And that thought made her shiver in anticipation. If she was smart, she'd make a point of never being alone with Vincent again. But (a) she wasn't that smart, and (b) she didn't *want* to be that smart. What she wanted was one night with Vincent's naked body all to herself. She'd barely tasted what he could do when they'd woken together earlier, or rather, when she'd awoken in his arms. All they'd done was kiss, but she could still feel the heat of her desire for him like a banked fire in her belly that was biding its time. And when that time came, she knew it would burn white-hot. She saw it every time Vincent looked at her, saw the hunger in his gaze, the promise of what was to come.

A tiny breeze passed through the yard, bringing with it the copper smell of blood. Lana blinked away visions of a naked Vincent and focused on the bloody scene in front of her. This new vampire, Salvio, had clearly been through hell and survived. His arm looked like it was about to fall off, and his shirt was clinging to his chest and stiff with blood. He was probably lucky to be alive since Jerry had said he'd heard automatic weapons fire. Leighton had told Lana that anything that destroyed a vampire's heart would kill him, she figured being ripped in half by bullets would do the trick.

Salvio shuddered as he drank Vincent's blood, and Lana had a momentary flashback of how good it had felt when Vincent had taken blood from her. She wondered if tasting his blood was the same thrill, or if that was only for vampires.

After a few minutes, Vincent rested his free hand on Salvio's head and pulled away from the young vampire's questing mouth. Salvio gave a sigh of more than satisfaction—it was satiation, bliss. On the other hand, when Lana glanced at Vincent's face, she caught a flash of exhaustion as he stared down at his ravaged arm.

"Let me," she said instantly, drawing him away from the other two vampires. Jerry was a good guy, and she had no reason to think Salvio wasn't the same, but they looked to Vincent for everything, and right now, he needed someone to take care of him, instead of the other way around.

"Come on," she said, pulling him across the yard to a primitive wooden bench that sat next to an old-fashioned hitching post that had probably never seen a horse. "Sit," she said.

Vincent smiled as she ordered him about, but he did what she asked without comment, which told her how tired he was. When was the last time he'd had blood? He'd fed Jerry and now Salvio, but he'd been drained by that bitch Fidelia Reyes only two days ago and he'd only fed from Lana that once.

"Are you okay?" she asked in a low murmur that was meant for his ears alone. Taking her knife from him, she wiped it on her pants leg, and slipped it back into her pocket. She'd clean it properly later.

"I will be," Vincent assured her.

"Let me clean that. I have my big kit in the SUV, but . . ." She pulled out the small first-aid kit that she carried with her no matter where she went. Fortunately, she'd thought to restock it after using it on Vincent the other night.

She turned Vincent's arm into the light of the nearly full moon so she could see the damage better. Her mouth tightened at what she found. It was the same arm that he'd fed Jerry from, the arm that had healed remarkably fast, but still bore the fading scars of Jerry's feeding. Or rather, it had before Vincent had cut it open again to feed Salvio.

"This has to stop," she muttered, and Vincent laughed.

"This never stops, *querida*. It's what we are."

"Isn't there some other way?"

"Sadly, no. We are creatures of blood."

Lana sighed. "I don't suppose you'd let me take you back to the kitchen to clean this up."

"We don't have time."

"That's what I thought." Lana started opening packages of gauze. She didn't have many. It was a travel kit, after all. But then, her main job here was to clean up the blood since Vincent's super-vampire system would heal itself without any help from her. She used the regular gauze first, finishing with the antiseptic wipes. By the time she was done, the wound had stopped bleeding. It still looked angry and raw, but the blood was down to a few seeping spots closest to his wrist where he'd dug in the knife before ripping upward to his elbow.

Lana forced away the gruesome image, then stared down at the small pile of bloodied bandages at her feet.

"Do we need to burn these or something?"

"You mean because my blood's on them?"

"Well, yeah."

Vincent gave her a crooked smile. "We're not witches, Lana. No one's going to cast a spell on me." Without warning, he leaned in so close that his beard tickled the skin below her ear, his breath a brush of warmth when he whispered, "Except you."

Desire surged, and suddenly her clothes were too hot, too tight. She grabbed the pile of bandages, squishing them in her fists along with the paper wrappers as she stood. "I can't just leave this. It's not . . . sanitary."

She heard herself talking and knew she sounded like a prissy idiot, but Vincent . . . unnerved her. He made her feel things she'd never felt for another man, things that threatened to make her forget all of her training, her experience, her common sense.

"I'll just . . ." She gestured with her joined hands. "I have a lighter."

"As you wish," Vincent said with a knowing smile. "I'll rest here, shall I?"

Lana was pretty sure he was making fun of her, that he didn't need to rest. But that was all right. As long as he stayed where he was and she went far enough away from him that she could think.

She found a spot away from the dried brush in the area. No need to start a wildfire just to soothe her rampant hormones. She made a neat pile of the bandages, then flicked her lighter beneath a single branch of scrub that she'd placed at the bottom of the pile. It flared quickly, the paper wrappers fueling the fire until the bandages themselves caught and began to burn.

By the time her mini bonfire was reduced to ash, Vincent had crossed the yard and was looming over her impatiently.

"Let's go." He started to add something, but then reached for his cell phone. "Michael," he said, and Lana realized the phone must have been on vibrate for their sneak attack on Poncio. She had a moment of embarrassment because she hadn't done the same. Then again, she didn't do that much sneaking around in her business as a bounty hunter. Sure, she frequently pretended to be someone she wasn't and just as frequently lied her ass off, and there were hours of sitting in her SUV on surveillance, but she didn't creep around in the dark much.

"We'll be there within the hour," Vincent said after listening for a moment. "I'll fill you in then."

He disconnected, then turned his phone's ringer back on and slipped it into his pocket. "Michael's at the airport. We'll leave Salvio on the plane when we get there. He's not up for any more fighting tonight."

"Should you leave him alone like that?"

"He won't be alone. Michael brought a couple of vamp soldiers, plus daylight guards. One of the vamps and all the daylight guards will stay behind." He hesitated, then added, "You should, too. This next guy won't be as easy as fat Poncio. We'll have to fight our way in."

Lana didn't dignify his suggestion with an answer. She simply gave him a go-fuck-yourself look and walked over to where Jerry and Salvio were waiting. She didn't bother updating them, because their bat ears would have picked up the entire conversation. She was beginning to appreciate how difficult it was to keep anything private with vampires around. She'd have to remember that for future reference.

"How are you feeling, Salvio?" she asked. It was a human response to his injuries; she knew that. But she was human, wasn't she? How else could she behave?

"Better," he said, seeming almost unable to look at her. "Much better. Thank you, miss."

Lana sighed. It had already been a long night and it wasn't even half over. "Call me Lana," she told him, then turned and headed off to the hill she'd have to climb in order to get back to the SUV. It occurred to her she was doing an awful lot of hiking and climbing on this job. If nothing else, she was probably losing weight, which wasn't always the case. All of that sitting and waiting for a fugitive to show often meant snacks and caffeine.

Vincent caught up with her before she'd gone halfway up the hill. "Are you all right?" he asked.

"Fine."

"Every male alive knows that when a woman says *fine*, it usually means the opposite. Tell me what's wrong."

"I'm going after Carolyn with you."

"I know."

"You might be glad I'm there before the end."

"I'm glad now."

"No, you're not. You'd like to tuck me away in a corner somewhere until you're ready to go to bed every morning, then pull me out, drive me a little crazy with your pointless flirting, then put me back in the corner."

They reached the top of the hill and Lana stomped her feet a little to get the dirt and tangled bits of brush off her boots. She started down the short incline toward the SUV, but Vincent snagged her arm, pulling her to a stop.

"I drive you crazy?" he asked, his voice deep and slow and sexy.

Lana looked up at him, not surprised that the crazy comment was the one he'd latched on to. She glanced down the hill, where Jerry and Salvio were just starting to climb, and said softly, "You know you do, Vincent. That's why you do it. You like to play."

"I like to do other things, too, *querida*."

"Big talk," she said. Then, wondering what game *she* was playing and if she'd suddenly lost her mind, she pulled her arm out of Vincent's grip and continued down to where the SUV waited.

She heard the locks pop open as she rounded the vehicle to the cargo hatch and glanced back to nod her thanks to Vincent who was still standing at the top of the hill, watching her.

Let him watch. She had things to do. Opening the cargo hatch, she pulled over her duffel and emptied her pockets, keeping the Sig and her knives. She made a mental note to resupply her first-aid kit yet again, then closed the hatch and opened the back passenger door.

"Sit up front," Vincent ordered. "I'm driving. Jerry and Salvio will sit in the back."

Lana opened her mouth to protest, but in the end, she simply shrugged and slid into the front seat instead.

VINCENT GLANCED over at Lana as they made their way back to the main highway. It was a bumpy ride, but she hung on to the bar above the door and bounced along with the rest of them. She hadn't said a word since they'd returned to the Suburban, and he couldn't figure out if she was pissed or disappointed. This was hardly typical for him. He was quite good with women, good at pleasing them, and at figuring out what they wanted from him. He'd been told by many women of his acquaintance that he *listened* to them. But then, most of his relationships with women were of short duration and involved blood and sex. Even his relationship with Marisol, whom he'd known for more than a decade, was based on sex. They'd been lovers who discovered a shared love of classical guitar. But sex and blood were still at the heart of it. Usually, when he visited, he gave her a little taste of his blood. Just enough to prolong her youth and, more importantly to Marisol, her looks. It wouldn't keep her young forever, wouldn't make her immortal or tie her life to Vincent's, but she'd always look younger than her years. He didn't doubt that there was real affection there, but it wasn't exactly a friendship.

Maybe it wasn't possible for a man to be friends with a woman. Of course, he didn't want to be *friends* with Lana. She thought he was playing with her. And maybe he was, a little. He liked to tease, liked to flirt. But if she thought that was all he was about, she had a hard lesson coming.

He smirked to himself at the thought of exactly how *hard* that lesson would be.

"Master?" Jerry called from the backseat.

"Yeah, Jerry."

"Do you still plan to deal with Carolyn this evening?"

"Absolutely. That's why we're meeting my lieutenant, Michael, at the airport. He's brought some more fighters, as well as daylight guards just in case we need them. Do either of you know the name of Carolyn's boss?" He couldn't bring himself to refer to the human who'd enslaved her—with Enrique's help—as her *master*.

"He's not her boss," Salvio mumbled. "He's her master."

"No, he's not," Vincent said sharply. "Your first lesson, Salvio. No human can master a vampire. The three of you were betrayed by Enrique when he enslaved you to humans, but as your Sire, he was also your master."

"It doesn't matter what you call it," Salvio retorted, his voice stronger and angrier. "I was a dog and Poncio held the leash."

"And now he's dead," Vincent said mildly. The dynamics of vampire society demanded that Salvio know his place in the power structure right up front. Anything else would get him killed very quickly, either by someone—like Michael—who took offense on Vincent's behalf, or by Vincent himself if he got angry enough. So, he made sure that his next words bore the lash of his power—not enough to harm, but enough to make certain Salvio understood. "But understand that I am not that worm Poncio, not even close. I do not enslave those sworn to me. They, and you, have a choice in how you live your life. If you want to sell books, go to school, be a farmer—although that last might be difficult at night—you are free to do so. If you want to be a fighter, you will join the ranks of my guards and fight only for me. But you will respect me and you will honor the bond between us. If you fail, or if you betray me, the punishment will be far worse than anything Poncio could come up with."

Salvio was silent for a long time, then he said, "Forgive me, Master."

Vincent rolled his eyes. The Fates save him from baby vampires. It was bad enough that he had Lana sending out mixed signals, now he had to contend with Salvio who didn't know the difference between a human who treated him like a slave and a true vampire master. And speaking of Lana, he caught her watching him and gave her look that said *what the hell do you want from me?*

And she gave him a silent look right back, one that replied *look who's talking.*

Vincent wanted to growl, but instead, he unclenched his jaw enough to remind the two newbies in the backseat of his previous question. "Carolyn's boss's name?"

"Albert Serrana," Salvio said, sounding somewhat sulky. "He has an estate northwest of Pénjamo, perhaps eighty kilometers—fifty miles—and, yes, many more guards than my . . . than Poncio had."

"Why is that?" Lana asked, probably because even her human senses were picking up on the tension in the vehicle. Maybe she hoped a woman's touch would make it easier to extract the information. Maybe she had a point.

"My . . . that is Poncio—"

Vincent went back to gritting his teeth, wondering what he'd been thinking. It would have been so much easier to let someone else school the new vamps in the realities and protocols of life as a vampire.

"—was a specialist, someone the others called on to extract information through torture, which is something he enjoyed. The torture often lasted long after the information had been given over," he added with no emotion. "But he needed little in the way of security. Serrana, on the other hand, is like Jerry's *Señor* Camarillo, directly involved in the harvest and transport of product, which requires many armed guards."

"How many?" Lana asked before Vincent could get to it.

"It depends on where they are in the distribution cycle, but I've seen him with as many as thirty men. Of course, that might have been a display for my . . . for Poncio's benefit."

"Will Michael have enough—" Lana started to ask.

"I told you, Michael and I alone would be enough," Vincent interrupted, knowing he was being rude, but tired of all the second-guessing going on in his vehicle. He was far more accustomed to his word being taken as law and no one questioning whatever strategy he came up with.

Lana raised her eyebrows and returned to staring out the window.

Great. How far away was that fucking airport anyway?

Chapter Fifteen

VINCENT DIDN'T think he'd ever seen a sweeter sight than the international airport in Silao. It was still some distance from Pénjamo, but that was okay, because it was north of the city, which meant tonight he'd arrived there sooner. And that was all for the good. Besides, the only other airport in the area couldn't handle the Gulfstream 450 that was Vincent's only private jet. He had a couple of small prop-jets, but he rarely flew in those himself. He seldom traveled alone and so needed the larger aircraft for his various guards and staff.

He punched up Michael's number as soon as the airport came into view.

"Sire."

"Yo, Mikey. I'm here." He managed to stop himself from adding a "thank God" to that statement, figuring his passengers might be offended. Not that he cared about Jerry or Salvio, but he had plans for Lana that didn't include her being pissed off at him.

"Shall I send up a flare, my lord?" Michael asked.

"I don't want to get arrested, asshole. Just tell me where to go."

Michael laughed, and Vincent took a moment to be glad he was back with vampires who understood what it meant to *be* a vampire. He knew it wasn't the baby vamps' fault that they didn't have a clue, but that didn't make them any easier to deal with.

"Go past the main terminal. You'll see some construction, then general aviation. It's not a huge airport, but we've got a private hangar all to ourselves. I'll be waiting outside."

Vincent made the designated turn, but he didn't need the directions by then. He could feel the draw of his child's blood. His connection to Michael was stronger than any other, stronger than the tie to his own Sire, Enrique, much stronger than what he had with vampires like Jerry who were sworn to him as master, but were not vampires of his own making.

He passed the main terminal and the early-phase construction site of what the signs said would eventually be a cargo terminal. And then finally he spotted the single hangar building that was set aside for private jets. It was divided into three bays, which was far from ideal, at least for Vincent's purposes. He much preferred a stand-alone hangar, especially if any of his people ended up spending the day here. He hoped Michael had brought along human pilots, too, just in case the decision was made to fly back in the morning instead.

Michael was standing outside, waiting for them. He waved, directing Vincent to drive right into the hangar alongside the jet.

Vincent parked where Michael indicated, switched off the ignition, and opened his door.

Michael was waiting right outside. "Sire!" he said, the formal address contradicting the big grin on his face.

"Mikey!" Vincent was equally happy to see his lieutenant. Vincent was well-liked in Hermosillo, and he knew that several of the vampires there would stand beside him in a fight . . . as long as the enemy wasn't Enrique. But the only vampire he could trust completely to have his back was Michael, and he'd missed having that strength behind him. Vincent pulled him into a hug which ended with the two of them pounding each other on the back to assert their manliness.

"I'm glad you're here," he said quietly, letting a bit of the seriousness of their situation seep into the pleasure of seeing each other.

"I'm glad to be here. No disrespect, Sire, but I'm looking at *that* guy—" He nodded at Salvio who had climbed out of the backseat and was just now coming into sight around the SUV. "—and I'm thinking I should have been here earlier."

"I had Lana—" Vincent grinned at the speculative look Michael gave him, and finished, saying, "—but that's Salvio, and his damage happened before I got there."

"Lana?"

"She's tougher than she looks. She also saved my life."

Michael did a double take. "Saved your life?" he repeated carefully. "Is there something you want to share with me, *jefe*?"

"A thing or two. Who'd you bring with you?"

"Four daylight guards, including two pilots, just in case."

Vincent nodded. He should have known Mike would come prepared. After all, he'd had the best teacher—Vincent himself.

"Two vamp fighters, Ortega and Zárate," Michael continued, naming two of those who'd been among the vampires brawling at the club on the night Lana had shown up in Vincent's office. "I let it be known I needed fighters for some action down South. I didn't say what for, figuring it's not that unusual for you to be called in to hand out a little discipline. And since we haven't exactly advertised your absence, it lets the curious figure that's where you've been. Anyway, Ortega and Zárate were feeling guilty over breaking up the bar. I think they were looking for a way back into your good graces."

"Assuming they were ever there," Vincent muttered.

"I didn't tell them that part," Michael said, grinning. "But they're good fighters."

"Obviously. All right. Here's what we have going on . . ." He walked Michael out of the hangar, using the noise of the airport for cover as he filled his lieutenant in on Enrique's latest sins, turning people against their will and then forcing them into slavery for human masters.

"God damn it, Vincent!" Michael swore, shocked into using his Sire's first name, which he rarely did. "That's low even for Enrique. Have you ever heard of that happening before?"

Vincent shook his head. "Never. But I know the Council would condemn it, which is why Enrique's been so secretive."

"Fucker."

"It gets worse. You've seen Salvio. He was wounded after Lana and I killed the human holding his leash—"

"He defended the human?" Michael asked, frowning.

"No. But when the human died and the binding Enrique had put on him was gone, he got some of his own back. He killed all of his human guards. They were armed and didn't go down lightly, but it apparently was worth it to him to be free. He was a Captain in the Mexican Federal Police. And Enrique made him a slave."

"Fuck! That is the worst—"

"Not even close, Mikey. Jerry's human kept him in a concrete box in the middle of a courtyard during the day. He barely fed him, and if Jerry didn't behave as expected, they left the shutters open. He slept curled up in a corner like a dog."

"He told you this?"

"I saw it. That's when Lana saved my life. I have a feeling Enrique had warned Jerry's boss about me. So when Jerry happened to see us drive into town, he was compelled to warn the humans. Unfortunately, they figured that if Jerry was a handy slave, someone like me would be even handier."

"Fuck me! They didn't?"

"They did. Took me down in a bar, I'm ashamed to say. Used a beautiful woman to get to me. Sliced my neck—"

"God damn it, Sire. I should have been—"

"Lana was there. She saw what was happening and was smart enough to fade into the woodwork. Jerry must not have known she was with me, because he didn't warn them about her. She grabbed the bitch who cut me, found out where I was, then waited until daylight."

He faced back into the hangar, watching as Lana stood in the open cargo hatch of the SUV, checking her weapons and probably restocking her handy first-aid kit. He smiled as she pulled the knife from her pocket, the one he'd used to slice his wrist for Salvio, and started wiping it with a cleaning cloth.

"She snuck into the compound, Mike. You know what those places are like—they're armed camps. But she came over the wall and spent the day in that hot, concrete box with me, putting herself between me and the door, just in case."

"If you bled out, then—"

"She did that, too. She'd never given blood before, but she offered me her vein."

Lana looked up and saw him watching. She tilted her head curiously, then shook it and went back to what she was doing with a bemused smile.

"Well, fuck," Michael said. "You don't need me, after all."

Vincent turned and clapped Michael on the shoulder. "If I didn't need you, you wouldn't be here. So far, it's been as much about sneaking around as killing people who need it. But tonight, I'm going to need power and strength, and that's you."

"We're going after another of Enrique's pet humans?"

"Oh, yes. And if you thought Enrique deserved to die for the other two, this one will clinch the deal."

"Christ. Do I wanna know?"

"Probably not, but you need to. Because this one's taking us to Mexico City, my friend. Enrique has finally crossed the line."

LANA KEPT HER GAZE low and watched through her eyelashes as Vincent briefed his lieutenant. She could almost mark the points in the conversation by Michael's growing anger, knew the moment Vincent told him about Carolyn and why they were rescuing her tonight. She couldn't hear what Michael said, but he cursed loud and long, and had to walk several paces away and back again before facing Vincent. She could see him listening closely, every inch of his muscular body tight with anger.

He was a good-looking guy, big and blond, and, like Vincent, all muscle. Under other circumstances, she might have found him attractive—other circumstances being if she hadn't met Vincent, who she was quite certain had already ruined her for all other men. At least for the foreseeable future. She'd get over him just like she had everyone else, but he might take a while longer.

Vincent was speaking to Michael intently, one hand on his shoulder, while Michael nodded every once in a while. Vincent was clearly giving his lieutenant orders for tonight's mission. She wondered what his plans for her were. She'd made it clear she wouldn't be left behind, but that didn't mean he wouldn't try.

Vincent slapped Michael's shoulder with a final word and the two of them broke apart. Michael headed directly for the plane where all sorts of activities were going on. Salvio had disappeared inside the jet almost as soon as they arrived. Jerry had gone inside with him, but had reemerged very soon thereafter. Lana assumed Salvio was getting whatever passed for medical treatment for a vampire. Even with Vincent's blood, he'd been pretty shot up. He'd improved quite a bit over the last couple of hours, but he still hadn't been moving all that well.

Michael didn't board the plane, but headed instead for a pair of vampires who looked like fighters. They were both huge, bigger than either Michael or Vincent, and looked like they belonged in a particularly vicious cage match on cable TV. As Michael started talking to them, they seemed to swell even further, hands fisting, fangs emerging . . .

"Do you fancy my lieutenant, *querida?*"

She spun around to find Vincent standing right behind her. While the question had been phrased lightly, there was nothing light about the look he was giving her.

She smiled. He was jealous. Cool. But she wasn't stupid enough to bait the monster. She shook her head. "He's not my type," she told him. "I was reading his body language earlier, when you were briefing him. I know you told him about Carolyn."

He bent his head and nuzzled her cheek, his beard feeling like velvet against her skin. "Not your type?" he repeated, almost predictably ignoring everything else she'd said. "What is your type?"

She rubbed her cheek against his, then pulled back and met his dark gaze. "You," she said honestly.

His eyes flared with copper-colored heat, and his arm came around her waist, pulling her flush against his body. "Remember that later," he said, then slid his mouth against hers in a gentle kiss, before releasing her. "And stay safe tonight."

She nodded. "I will. You, too."

He grinned and said, "Always." Then he stepped back and added, "We roll in five minutes."

THEY HAD ALL piled into the one SUV. Vincent hadn't wanted to stir up attention by leasing a second vehicle, and the Suburban was large enough to hold them all, albeit not with the comfort they were used to. Five vampires, none of them small, and Lana made for a tight fit. Vincent had relinquished the wheel reluctantly, but only because there was no way he was letting Lana sit in the back surrounded by males, and it made no sense for her to take up the front passenger seat when she was the smallest person among them. So, Vincent sat in back with Lana and Zárate, while Michael drove with Ortega in the passenger seat, and Jerry squeezed into the third seat all by himself.

Lana now sat between Vincent and Zárate, although Vincent had made sure there was plenty of air between her and the big vampire fighter. She'd accepted the new seating arrangement without a word, compliantly tucking herself in tight against Vincent's side after he'd put his arm around her shoulders to make room for Zárate.

She didn't say a word, but Vincent could feel the tension in her body where it was pressed up against his. She didn't seem worried, though, so much as . . . focused, preparing herself mentally for the battle to come. Vincent had briefed everyone on what to expect, making it clear that the night's work would probably include a level of violence greater than what they'd faced already that evening, with either Camarillo or Poncio.

Vincent wanted to say something to her, to offer encouragement, a joke, or even a lascivious comment about what they'd do after the battle, but with a vehicle full of vampires, there was no such thing as a private word. So he dropped his arm from where it lay over the back of the seat behind her and caressed her shoulder. She shifted her gaze from the road ahead and looked up to give him a small smile. Its warmth reached her eyes before she turned away again, and Vincent counted that victory enough for now.

The estate of Albert Serrana, the *narco* Enrique had given Carolyn to, was in the low hills, down a curved and poorly-maintained lane. The twisting nature of the road served them well, since no one at the main gate could see when they broke the first perimeter of security and took out the forward checkpoint while still a good hundred yards away. There had been four guards total, with one of them going for his radio the moment their vehicle came into sight. Vincent had dropped them all before the lone guard's finger hit the "send" button. They were now sleeping peacefully inside their guard shack, where they'd remain until morning . . . or until Vincent decided it was wiser to eliminate them permanently.

Once past that checkpoint, they'd proceeded on foot, going over the hills rather than taking the road around them. Before long, they had a bird's-eye view of Serrana's compound from a nearby hilltop. In terms of layout, it was much like Poncio's, but the similarities ended there. Serrana's security was much greater and more obvious, even at night. But he'd counted too much on the single road in as a tripwire security measure. The humans below had no way of knowing that invaders now stood looking down on them, plotting their destruction. Because Vincent wouldn't settle for anything less. As with the others, Serrana needed to be executed, not only for his crimes against Carolyn, but as an example to anyone who thought to use a vampire in this way ever again.

"Busy place," Michael commented, standing next to Vincent.

"Ants on an anthill," Vincent sneered. "Particularly vicious ants, but ants nonetheless."

"Army ants," Lana said quietly. "Don't they cannibalize their own?"

They watched in silence a moment longer, then Michael asked, "Are we going to kill them all?"

Vincent considered the question. "No," he decided suddenly. "We're going to create a new legend tonight, a cautionary tale for those who think to cross us in the future."

He looked up and saw his own savagery reflected in Michael's grin . . . and in Lana's carefully blank expression.

"Vincent?" she said, and at first he thought she was afraid of him. That bothered him more than it should have. But then her lips curved upward in a smile that matched his, and she asked, "Did you ever see the movie Silence of the Lambs?"

It took Vincent a moment, but then he laughed, throwing his head back in delight. He knew exactly what she had in mind, and it definitely worked for him. He glanced over and found Michael chuckling in understanding even as he stared at Lana with an expression that combined puzzlement with respect.

"Okay, *jefe*," he said, turning to look at Vincent. "How do we do this?"

"Quick and quiet."

"The guys are going to be disappointed. I think they were looking forward to some old-fashioned mayhem."

"There will be mayhem enough for all of us over the next few days. But not tonight. Tonight, I need one guard awake and functioning. The others are going to take a long nap."

LANA PATTED HER various pockets, making sure she had everything, unhappy that everything didn't include her Sig. It was only temporary, since she'd once again stripped off her jacket in order to flash some skin, but it still didn't make her happy.

"I'm getting a little tired of being your flesh puppet," she muttered to Vincent, who was standing next to her, waiting.

"Flesh puppet?" he asked, clearly amused.

"What else do you call this?" she demanded, indicating her cleavage-baring tank top, although she'd left her bra on this time.

"*Querida*, you don't want to know what I call that. At least, not in present company."

Lana's face heated, but she admitted to herself that the blush was as much pleasure as embarrassment.

"I want that gun back the minute we're inside," she informed Michael.

"Yes, ma'am," he said, fighting a grin of his own.

Lana glared at him, not particularly thrilled to be the source of entertainment for a bunch of vampires.

Sensing her mood, Vincent bent down and said quietly, "Thank you for doing this, Lana."

Lana narrowed her eyes at him, but he seemed sincere, so she shrugged. "It's all for a good cause. And don't forget you promised I could be there when you take this asshole down."

"Definitely," Vincent said, abruptly serious. "Carolyn doesn't know any of us. I can calm her quickly enough, but initially, she's likely to be more reassured by a female presence."

In the face of that sobering reminder of why they were doing this, Lana forgot her own discomfort. What was showing a little skin compared to what the female vampire had been through? Nothing.

"I'm ready," she said, tugging her tank top down and tucking it more tightly into her pants. She couldn't help noticing Vincent's unhappy expression as she did so. Well, too bad. This was his idea, after all.

"Let's go," he said gruffly.

They'd come down from their hilltop perch and now started around the final curve of narrow road that would take them to the front gate of the compound.

The plan was for Lana and Vincent to approach on foot. At first glance, they would come across as a couple of hikers, tourists who'd gotten lost in the foothills.

Lana smiled broadly as they approached. "Hi. I mean, *buenos días*," she called, in her worst Spanish. "*Por favor, estamos perdidos,*" she continued. Then flapping her hands in front of her as if flustered, she added, "I'm sorry, my Spanish is . . . bad. Can you help us? I think we're lost."

The guards' gaze kept shifting between her and Vincent, who was clearly the greater threat. He hadn't said a word, but then, he wasn't supposed to. His job was to work his vampire mojo, which as she understood it, was pretty much a silent endeavor. She hoped he did it soon, though, because, that old cliché about being undressed with a guy's eyes? Yeah, that's how she felt, and it was getting more and more uncomfortable with every minute. The guards were fingering their guns—HK MP5s, every criminal's weapon of choice these days—and looking increasingly nervous, torn between staring at her boobs and sizing up Vincent.

Lana was just about to shoot Vincent a what-the-hell look, when both guards slumped to the ground, their weapons falling with a tinny clatter. She stared at them for a moment in surprise, then turned to ask Vincent a question. Only, she found herself breathless at the sight of him. He was always an arresting sight, beautiful and fit, with a charisma that surrounded him like a sparkling cloud. But she'd never seen him like this.

He stood perfectly still, barely breathing, the copper glow of his eyes so bright that it was like twin spotlights shining in the darkness. She felt that same electrostatic sizzle over her skin that she'd felt before, but this was stronger, almost painful in its intensity, a tightening shroud rather than a silken touch. But despite that, she stared up at him unafraid, knowing in her heart that even as he focused on the enemy behind the gates, he was protecting her.

The soft scuff of movement behind them warned her that Michael and the others had arrived, but she didn't turn to look. Her attention was all on Vincent who was blazing with his power, fearsome in the intensity of his focus. With no warning, he blinked, and slowly turned his head to look at her. He smiled.

"Do you trust me, *querida*?"

Lana didn't even have to think about her answer. "Yes."

His smile warmed. "Michael," he said without looking away from her.

"Here you go, beautiful," Michael said to her in a teasing voice. He held out her jacket and weapon, which she donned quickly, not knowing exactly how much time they had or whether Vincent's spell would hold.

"Let's go," Vincent said, once she was ready. He held out his hand, and she took it automatically, giving the two unconscious guards a puzzled look.

"Aren't you going to tie them up or something?"

"Not necessary," Vincent replied dismissively. "They'll be out until morning." Then he pushed open the gate and Lana got the surprise of her life. Beyond the gate was the main building, and in front of that a dirt courtyard . . . that was littered with bodies.

"Are they—?"

"Unconscious, just like the others," he said.

Lana was having trouble breathing. She knew vampires were powerful, and that Vincent was ranked among the strongest. But this . . . it was one thing to take down a couple of guards, but there were twenty or more men in the yard, and those were only the ones she could see. Many of them were clustered around a big truck, as if they'd been in the process of loading it and had simply dropped where they stood. And there had to be others she couldn't see, in the main building, in the big garage. But no one had come to investigate the sudden collapse of their fellows, and no one challenged Vincent and the others as they strode into the compound.

Vincent paused, which meant Lana did, too, since he was still holding her hand.

He went perfectly still again. Lana tensed and started to pull her hand away, but Vincent tightened his grip. "A moment only," he murmured.

When he moved again, it was to pull her against his side as he headed past a pair of wide-open wrought-iron gates and straight for the big double doors into the main house.

"There's only one other vampire on the premises, and I'm assuming it's Carolyn," he told Michael, speaking over Lana's head to where his lieutenant walked on her opposite side. "I've put her and everyone else down for now. Let's get inside and find someone who can tell us where to find the lord of the manor. Then we'll go wake him up."

Michael nodded, stepping ahead of Vincent, his posture alert, his gaze moving constantly. Lana heard, more than saw, the others close in at their backs, forming a circle of protection as they approached the front door, stepping around the unconscious bodies littering the broad porch.

But while the other vampires were tense and ready to fight, Vincent seemed more relaxed than ever. Holding Lana's hand, he strolled up to the wide-open entryway as if the two of them were here on a house-hunting mission, inspecting a piece of real estate.

"That one," Vincent said suddenly, pointing to a middle-aged woman lying just short of the front doors. Like the others, she looked as though she'd passed out in mid-step. She wore a simple, black blouse and skirt and sensible shoes, and was surrounded by a pile of sheets and towels which had been folded before they'd been dropped.

Michael went to his knees next to the woman and touched her shoulder lightly. She stirred, then woke with a gasp, her expression one of fear at finding a strange *gringo* kneeling over her. Michael offered his hand to the woman and helped her to her feet. *"¿Como se llama, señora?" What's your name?*

"Dolores," she said, her face pale as she took in the bodies surrounding her.

Michael smiled, looking like a nice all-American young man with no ulterior motives.

"Dolores," he repeated. *"Que bonito nombre." Lovely name.*

Dolores stared up at him silently, her fingers gripping the crucifix around her neck. Michael continued, his Spanish fluid and easy. "Do you know where Albert Serrana is right now?" he asked her.

The woman nodded.

"And do you know the vampire he keeps with him? The woman?"

Dolores's expression dimmed. "The pretty one," she said. "So sad."

"You mean it's sad that she's here?"

"No, *señor. She* is sad. All the time. So pretty, but so sad."

Vincent's hold on Lana's hand tightened almost painfully and she squeezed back, partly to keep him from breaking her hand, but also to let him know that she shared his anger.

"Where is he?" Vincent growled, and Dolores's eyes shot to him in alarm.

"Tranquilo, Dolores," Michael said soothingly. *Take it easy.* "We're here for the pretty one. She belongs with us. Can you show us where she is now?"

"Si," Dolores said firmly and gestured toward the stairs inside the front door. "Come inside." Michael smiled and indicated she should lead the way.

Dolores went through the doors and up the stairs with Michael following. Vincent went next with Lana beside him, but she loosened her hand from his. She did it gently, squeezing his hand tight before letting go, but she had no intention of walking into a potentially hostile situation with her right hand filled with something other than her gun. Vincent glanced over as she drew her Sig and nodded his understanding. Carrying the weapon down along her thigh, she following Michael and Dolores up the stairs and along the mezzanine, then down another hallway that ended in a single oversized door of dark, banded wood.

Dolores stopped in front of the door. "Shall I knock, *señor*?" she asked, looking to Michael for direction.

"No, thank you, Dolores," he said gently, then caught her before she fell. Lifting her easily, he kicked open the door to what turned out to be a small sitting room and laid her on an orange velvet couch. Leaving her there, he returned to the hallway and closed the door behind him.

"Sire?" he asked, turning to Vincent.

"Carolyn's in there," Vincent said, looking at the dark wooden door, his expression one of revulsion. "But only one human. I'm guessing that's Serrana, since your new girlfriend seemed eager to please."

"What can I say, my lord? The ladies love me."

"Especially the ones old enough to be your mother," Vincent responded drily. "Open the door."

Michael tried the knob. It resisted his effort for all of a second until he applied a little of that handy vampire strength and broke through the lock with childish ease. He entered first and stopped, blocking the doorway. Lana frowned at the maneuver—it wasn't smart to frame yourself like that, giving whoever was waiting inside a clear shot. But then she remembered that everyone inside was unconscious.

He moved finally, walking inside as Lana followed, stepping in ahead of Vincent. The yellow flicker of a fire cast shadows over the dimly-lit room, making it far too warm and stuffy for her taste. It was a bedroom, naturally. Where else would a rapist keep his captive? There was a king-sized bed with an ornate headboard and two matching bedside tables. Lamps on either side lit the room brightly, their pounded copper bases gleaming.

Lana ventured further into the room, feeling the others enter and spread out behind her. She found the master of the estate slumped between the bed and the shuttered windows. He was completely naked, and her first thought was that he should have left off the lights. But then she heard the deep murmur of Vincent's voice and turned to see him wrapping a blanket around a naked young woman. Lana immediately swung back around to Serrana and kicked him in the balls. She only hoped he could feel it. But then, she had confidence that whatever Vincent had planned for the bastard would be much worse.

"Lana," Vincent said, his voice low and urgent.

She forgot all about Serrana and hurried over, dropping to her knees next to him. The woman, presumably Carolyn, was awake and cowering away from Vincent, clutching the blanket around her. Lana's heart clenched with sorrow for the woman and hatred for the man, the pig who had done this to her.

"Carolyn," she said softly, pushing in front of Vincent, placing herself between him and Carolyn so that she was the only one the abused young woman would see. And, yeah, she knew this was a vampire, with strength enough to throw a man across the room, but right now, she was simply a woman, just as vulnerable and damaged as any human female would have been in these circumstances.

Carolyn's downcast eyes came up and met hers, filling with tears. "You have to run," she whispered. "Get away while you can."

Lana blinked in confusion, before realizing that Carolyn thought Serrana, or maybe Vincent, had somehow taken Lana prisoner and meant to torment her as well. Because Carolyn had no reason to believe that vampires were any better than the humans she lived with.

"No, Carolyn," Lana said gently, tears stinging her own eyes as she pulled the blanket more securely over the vampire's shoulders. Her instinct was to hug her, to hold her close and tell her everything would be okay. But the first move had to be Carolyn's. She'd been touched in too many ways and by too many people against her will. She needed to know she was in control again.

"We're here to get you out of this place. This is Vincent," Lana said, jerking her head in his direction. "You can trust him. He and these others have come here to free you."

Carolyn stared, first at Lana, and then raising her gaze, she took in the other vampires filling the room, making it seem small with their size and bristling anger. She flinched slightly, but Lana spoke quickly, saying, "They're not angry at you. They're angry at him." She nodded toward Serrana, letting her hatred fill her words, wanting Carolyn to hear it and know where she stood.

Carolyn lowered her gaze to Lana again, and then she suddenly burst into tears, gripping the blanket around her and letting her head fall against Lana's shoulder. Lana wrapped her arms around the young vampire, cautiously at first, but then tighter as Carolyn's body began to shudder with the force of her tears, her sobs raw and heartbreaking.

Vincent swore viciously beneath his breath. He shot to his feet and Lana was peripherally aware of his footsteps as he pounded across the tile floor. She turned enough to see him grab the unconscious Serrana and throw him onto the bed, then his fingers dug into the man's throat and he growled, "Wake up, you sick bastard."

Lana couldn't see the human's face, but she heard his terrified shout when he woke to find himself being choked to death—not to mention surrounded by—a group of hulking and angry vampires, every one of them staring at him with fangs fully distended and eyes glowing.

171

"How shall I kill you?" Vincent crooned. "I could rip out your heart, but that would be too fast. I could break every bone in your body and slice your veins. Let you bleed out slowly, feel your life dripping away as you lay helpless to stop it." Serrana cried out suddenly, and Lana twisted further to see Vincent toying with him, flicking his fingers at the major veins in the man's neck, moving down to do the same to his shoulder and on to his chest, except that now, Lana could hear the muted sound of bones breaking with every flick of Vincent's fingers.

Serrana screamed and Carolyn's head shot up, her eyes taking on a pale glow of their own as she stared at her former tormentor.

"Mine," she whispered hoarsely.

Lana's first thought was that Carolyn was identifying with her captor somehow and was ready to defend him. But then she registered the rage and hatred in the young woman's voice. It slid over Lana's skin like a living thing before wending its way across the room to the screaming Serrana.

"Mine," Carolyn repeated more strongly as she rose to her feet, clutching the blanket around her. Lana stood with her, turning to face Vincent, who was lifting Serrana off the bed, still gripping him by his throat, holding him high as he curled his other hand into a claw aimed at the rapist's pitiful sex organs.

"Vincent," Lana said sharply.

He swiveled his head in her direction, pissed at having his fun interrupted. Until his gaze shifted over her shoulder and he saw Carolyn standing there, her own eyes lit with enough power to give them a soft, blue glow.

Vincent smiled slowly, and it was a terrifying thing to see. Serrana saw it, and he whimpered in horror, but Lana's only thought was that he'd have been far better off with Vincent than he was going to be with Carolyn.

Vincent opened his fingers and let the human fall to the bed. Serrana immediately tried to scramble away, but Vincent stopped him with a negligent glance, holding him like a bug pinned to a board.

"He's all yours, Carolyn," Vincent said, stepping away from the bed with a grand gesture in Serrana's direction. "Do take your time."

Lana heard a low rumble of sound behind her. She turned to see Carolyn in full vamp mode, fangs gleaming as they pressed into her lower lip, eyes glowing as she let the blanket fall and stalked across the room, her nakedness forgotten. All of the males stepped back, giving her plenty of room, allowing her this moment to take her revenge.

Serrana's gaze had been following Vincent as he moved away, but then he caught sight of Carolyn. His eyes widened in terrified realization and he squealed in fear, thrashing about aimlessly, held in place by Vincent's power.

Carolyn stopped in front of him, then raised her gaze to Vincent. "If you would, my lord," she said, her voice low and raspy, though whether it was from disuse or screaming, Lana didn't know.

Vincent held her gaze for a moment, as if judging whether she could handle the human, but then he tipped his head slightly in acquiescence and took a step back. Lana felt a brief frisson of power, and then Serrana jumped as he was abruptly freed from his restraints. He immediately tried to roll off the bed and make a break for it—as foolish an idea as that was—but it didn't matter. Carolyn's hand shot out faster than Lana could follow, grabbing the man's balls and crushing them in her fist, her fingers tightening until Lana could see the white bone of her knuckles. Serrana shrieked, the sound gaining pitch as Carolyn's grip tightened, until with a final hard yank, she tore them off completely. Ignoring Serrana's anguished screams, Carolyn held the bloody pieces of flesh in her hand, eyeing them curiously and long enough that Lana began to wonder if she'd finally lost it. But then, it was as if she was coming out of a trance. Her eyes blinked and her entire body shuddered hard, once. She shifted her gaze from the shredded testicles to the sobbing Serrana and back again, then bared all of her teeth in a vicious grimace, gripped Serrana by the hair, and shoved the bloody bits down his throat.

She turned to Vincent and, speaking in a soft, slow drawl that betrayed her Southern origins, said, "I would be obliged, my lord, if you would keep this vermin alive while I play with him."

"Consider it done," Vincent said, as if keeping a man alive to be tortured was something he did every day.

Carolyn smiled for the first time since they'd found her. And Serrana screamed.

Chapter Sixteen

LANA STARED UP at what was left of Albert Serrana and had to swallow hard to contain the nausea roiling her stomach. She couldn't complain about the gruesome tableau since the whole Silence of the Lambs thing had been her idea, but she hadn't considered the reality... or the stench. It would be even worse when Serrana's people woke sometime after dawn to discover their boss's body on display. Most of them would be missing a pint or two of their own blood, too. Vincent had permitted all of his people to dine at will on the unconscious guards, instructing them to leave the neck wounds bleeding. He wanted there to be no doubt as to who it was that had visited them in the night. Serrana's grisly display was intended as a warning, after all. A warning not to fuck with vampires unless you were willing to pay the price.

But Lana and the others would be long gone by then. Which was one thing to be thankful for, she supposed, that she wouldn't be around for sunrise. The flies would come then.

She shuddered and turned away, only to run smack into Vincent.

"So what do you think?" he asked, gazing up at the tall iron gates in front of the main door. They'd been propped open earlier, but now they'd been shut in order to better display their new decoration.

Lana forced herself to look once more. Ortega and Zárate had bound Serrana's bloody and ravaged body to the gate, using some heavy baling wire they'd found in the truck. They'd taken pride in their work, binding his legs and arms outstretched, even wiring his head back so that his sightless, and eyeless, gaze seemed to be surveying the yard.

When she didn't say anything, Vincent put his arms around her, hugging her back to his chest. "Carolyn needed this," he whispered, both an apology and an explanation.

"I know. And the bastard deserved every bit of it."

"So does Enrique," he growled against her ear.

Lana twisted in his arms to look up at him. "But Enrique's far more dangerous. Don't—"

Vincent placed two fingers over her lips. "I've no desire to die young... Well, young-looking anyway," he amended with a lopsided grin. "Come on, sunrise isn't far off and we have to get Michael and the others back to the airport."

"What about Carolyn?" she asked. The female vampire had all but collapsed in emotional and physical exhaustion after she'd finished dealing with her rapist. Lana had found some clothes in an adjacent bedroom for her. They were men's sweats, but they were clean and easy to make fit on the smaller woman. Vincent had then spoken to Carolyn, his words soft and for her ears alone, before he'd slit his wrist and let her drink. She hadn't drunk as much as Jerry or Salvio had, but apparently it was enough. Vincent had caressed her face once and then caught her as she fell into a deep sleep, holding her for a moment before transferring her to Michael who'd carried her to the SUV waiting in the yard. Ortega had retrieved the vehicle before he'd helped Zárate display Serrana.

Carolyn was there now, in the cargo compartment, still sleeping under the compulsion that Vincent had laid on her, one that he'd assured Lana would last until she woke in Hermosillo the next night.

"We have a couple of female vamps in Hermosillo," Vincent told Lana. "Also a few human women who are mated to vampires. They'll provide whatever care Carolyn needs. But she's a vampire, Lana, and she's mine now. She can draw on me for help and whatever strength she needs to recover. It won't be easy, but it won't be as painful as it would be for a human either."

Lana nodded. He'd told her all of this before, but she still felt responsible somehow.

"You can see her when this is all over," he reminded her gently.

"I know."

"You ready to get out of here, then?"

She drew a deep breath. "Definitely."

The others were already piling into the SUV, which was even more crowded now. Jerry was riding in the cargo area with Carolyn, first because he knew her somewhat, but mostly because he was the most slender of the vampires present, and Vincent still refused to permit Lana to ride anywhere but next to him.

Lana nearly dozed off as they raced for the airport. Vincent and Michael had agreed en route that the jet would depart as soon as everyone was aboard. The human pilots would be at the helm since most of the flight would take place after sunrise, but apparently once in Hermosillo, they'd "daylight"—that was what Vincent had called it—at the airport itself. Lana's only thought was that she hoped the human guards were trustworthy, but then Vincent had pointed out that the same guards protected the Hermosillo compound every day. And that they were very well compensated. There was also some sort of vampire taboo against attacking your enemy in daylight, because no one wanted to start that particular snowball rolling.

The other reason for their hurry to reach the airport was that Lana and

Vincent would not be returning to Hermosillo with the others. They were continuing the search for Xuan Ignacio, which meant they needed enough time to drive to a hotel and get checked in before daybreak. The sensible thing to do would have been to stay in Silao, which was the city nearest the airport, but naturally, Vincent had other plans. He'd insisted on choosing their hotel, reminding Lana rather snidely about the charming accommodations with the broken miniblinds that she'd arranged the last time he'd left it up to her.

That wasn't altogether fair since there was a world of difference between finding accommodations in the middle of nowhere and in a real city. But she'd held her peace for two reasons. One, Vincent was a pain in the ass when he didn't get his way; but, two, he was used to the best of everything, and after the last couple of nights in motels that probably rented rooms by the hour, Lana was more than ready for whatever luxury he could find.

Vincent had tapped away on his cell phone, grunted once or twice, then apparently made a reservation, though he wouldn't share the details. Lana was too tired to care, however. She just wanted to see the others safely on their way and then find her own way into a hot shower as soon as possible.

Michael turned into the airport, speeding past the main terminal and the construction site, and zipping into the private hangar. They'd called ahead, so the hangar door was open, and the jet already prepped and waiting for them. Ortega and Zárate waited until Vincent exited the SUV, then gave him a respectful nod and disappeared up the stairs into the Gulfstream. Jerry popped the cargo hatch and was reaching inside to pick up Carolyn when Vincent stopped him.

"I never had the chance to ask you, Jerry," he said, drawing the other vampire's attention. "How did you know who I was? I mean, obviously I'm a vampire, but you knew me specifically. How? I've never met you."

Jerry responded with the same sincerity and respect he always showed Vincent. "Lord Enrique. We were in Mexico City for a meeting, and you walked in as we were leaving. We were across the room, but Enrique made a point of stopping Camarillo and telling him to avoid you, because you were very powerful. I don't think he knew I was listening, or maybe he didn't care. But I think Camarillo decided right then that he wanted you for his own, because Enrique feared you."

Vincent seemed to think for a moment. "I remember that meeting. He'd created a problem with some vampires in Cabo and wanted me to clean up his mess. I was only in Mexico City that one night." He looked up and found Lana's gaze upon him, and she knew he was thinking the same thing she was, how a chance meeting had changed so many lives. If he'd arrived a few minutes later that night, if Camarillo had never received Enrique's warning, Jerry and the others would still be enslaved, and Vincent might not now be set on destroying Enrique sooner rather than later.

Vincent clapped Jerry on the shoulder. "You'd better get Carolyn onto the plane. They'll be leaving soon."

Jerry gave a little bow, then easily lifted the sleeping Carolyn and carried her up the stairs. Finally, only Michael was left, but he clearly didn't want to leave at all.

"You've made enemies with all of this. If Enrique hasn't already heard of it, he will soon. And he won't want word of what he's done getting out, not even to his own vamps. And especially not to the other lords. I don't like you being out here alone."

"I'm not alone. I have Lana."

"No disrespect intended," Michael said, giving her an apologetic glance, "but Ms. Arnold isn't . . ." He let out a long breath, clearly searching for a word that wouldn't offend her.

"You mean she isn't a vampire," Vincent supplied, seeming more bemused than anything else.

"Exactly."

"We'll be fine, Michael. I think we both know Enrique has more pressing matters on his plate right now. We have a few days before he can realistically act, and that's all we'll need. We'll finish this mission of Raphael's and see what comes next."

Michael gave him a somber look. "Mexico City is next."

Vincent nodded. "The only question is the timing. And I have a strong suspicion that what Xuan Ignacio has to tell us will bear on that decision."

Michael didn't look happy, but he nodded his agreement. "Remember your promise, Sire."

"Yeah, yeah, no Mexico City without you. You're like a nagging child."

Michael laughed, then glanced back at the jet as the engines increased in pitch. "That's the pilot telling me to get my ass on board. Take care, *jefe*. And keep me informed."

Vincent pulled Michael in for a hug, then pushed him toward the stairs. "Go, before we humiliate ourselves by weeping in front of Lana."

Michael grinned and loped up the stairs, taking them three at a time. Lana envied his energy. The way she was feeling, she'd have been clinging to the handrail and dragging herself up one step at a time.

Vincent pulled her away from the jet as someone retracted the stairs and swung the hatch closed. By the time the plane was taxiing slowly from the hangar, the two of them were already in the SUV. And before it turned onto the runway, they were speeding back through the airport, heading for the main highway.

Lana checked her seatbelt, then settled into the front passenger seat with a relieved sigh, feeling oddly at home, as if she was back in her seat, and she could relax now that the SUV was restored to its proper order. And that meant it was once again just she and Vincent racing through the night.

"How far to the hotel?" she asked, stifling a yawn.

"Fifty miles give or take."

She stared at him in disbelief. "Fifty miles? Wasn't there anything closer?"

"Of course there was, but not the kind of place I wanted. You'll be glad once we get there."

"I'll be dead once we get there. I'm tired and I'm hungry. I need to eat, you know. Real food." She was beginning to sound like a whiny child, but she didn't care. She was starving and she wanted a shower.

"Close your eyes, *querida*. I'll wake you before we arrive," he said calmly, as if he hadn't heard a word she'd said. Or that it didn't matter. Probably the latter, since he was so used to calling the shots.

Lana could have argued, but it would have been only for argument's sake, because the stubborn ass wasn't going to change his mind. He'd just smile and do whatever he wanted anyway. She leaned against the door and closed her eyes, not really believing she'd sleep, but not in the mood to argue, either.

The last thing she heard was Vincent speaking to someone on the phone, arranging in rapid-fire Spanish for a meal to be waiting when they arrived.

Lana woke with a start when Vincent stroked her cheek with the back of his fingers. She stared around with the dazed perceptions of someone who'd fallen asleep in one place and awakened somewhere else. Somewhere she'd never been before.

She looked over and found Vincent watching her. "You ready?" he asked.

She blinked in confusion, then studied the busy city around them. It could have been almost any big city, anywhere in the world. Anywhere in the Spanish-speaking world, anyway. Ducking her head, she looked out Vincent's window at the hotel. She had no idea where they were, but discovered she didn't really care. As long as there was a bed and a shower, and at least a candy bar in the minibar, she'd survive.

"Ready," she told him. She went to open her door, but found an eager young man had beaten her to it.

"*Bienvenida, señora,*" he said with an eager politeness that fit the elegant façade of the hotel before them.

Vincent was waiting for her on the other side of the SUV. He held out his hand and she took it, bemused at how completely natural it felt. Only a few days ago . . . she was sure if she counted back, she could figure out exactly how long they'd been traveling together, but it didn't really matter. What mattered was how completely things had changed. They'd gone from being distrustful strangers to reluctant partners, and now? Now, they held hands as they walked into the elegant hotel Vincent had chosen, looking for all the world like a real couple.

A doorman pulled open the heavy glass door precisely as they arrived, echoing the valet's welcoming sentiments, seeming not to notice that the new guests were dusty and dirty and that their clothes bore some rather mysterious stains that one didn't want to examine too closely. Lana ran a self-conscious hand over her hair, knowing even as she did it that there was nothing she could do to repair the wreckage before they reached the reception desk.

Vincent, of course, strolled into the sweet, cool air of the lobby like he owned the place, as confident in his filthy and blood-encrusted clothing as he'd have been in a tailored tuxedo. Lana caught one well-toned female patron giving Vincent a bold and admiring gaze as she headed out for an early morning jog. Or at least her clothes made it look like she wanted everyone to believe that's where she was going. Lana wasn't convinced any serious jogger would wear that much makeup. But then she wasn't feeling particularly charitable on the subject. She glared at the female barracuda and tightened her grip on Vincent's hand, pulling herself closer to his side.

He glanced down and gave her a knowing wink. Lana rolled her eyes, but the damage was done. He knew what she'd done and why.

There was a short line at the reception desk, but Vincent didn't stop. Instead, he walked right up to the other end of the counter where a serious-looking man stood, concentrating on something on the screen in front of him. He glanced up when Vincent arrived, and his eyes went wide.

"*Señor Kuxim, bienvenido,*" he said, seeming pleased as punch that Vincent had deigned to drop in at the last moment.

"Felipe," Vincent greeted him, continuing in English, "Is our suite ready?"

"But, of course. I shall inform the kitchen of your arrival." Felipe switched languages smoothly as he pulled an already-prepared folio and keys out of a drawer and handed them over. "Your usual."

"Efficient as always. Thank you."

"My pleasure." And Felipe beamed so brightly in saying it that Lana believed him.

They had the elevator to themselves, which was good, because in the confined space Lana could smell herself and it wasn't pleasant. The perfect Vincent wasn't exactly an ad for men's cologne, either, which she actually found rather reassuring.

He slid his key card into the slot reserved for certain floors and the elevator sped upward without stopping. The hallway stretched out to either side when the doors opened. It was perfectly silent, partly, Lana was certain because of the early hour, but the thick carpet and wallpapered walls were designed to absorb sound, and the rooms were probably well-insulated.

There'd be no banging headboards in this hotel.

Their room, or suite according to Felipe, was almost all the way down at the end, and Lana was sure that if she'd had the energy to turn around, she'd have found little deposits of dirt and mud from where her feet were dragging along the rich carpet.

Vincent inserted the key and pushed open the heavy door, entering ahead of her and checking out the room before walking back and pulling her all the way inside. Then he closed and locked the door.

Lana was more than tired, but that didn't stop her from admiring the room. It was spacious and elegant, with subdued lighting, a big flat screen TV, and huge fucking bed that looked like heaven.

"I need a shower," she said.

"Go ahead," Vincent told her. "The luggage should be here by the time you're finished."

She considered waiting. After all, Vincent probably wanted a shower as badly as she did, but since he offered, she decided to be selfish and take it.

The hotel bathroom was all gleaming pink marble and golden faucets, and it was bigger than her bedroom back home. Through a door on the left was a dressing area with enough closet space to house her entire wardrobe and still look empty. A basket of organic bath supplies sat on the counter, so, rather than wait for her duffel bag, she plucked out the bottles of shampoo and conditioner, along with an unscented soap and placed them all in the shower. Turning on the hot water, she let it run to steam up the room. There was a rainfall shower head, but she left that one off. Tonight, or rather this morning, she wanted a hard, pounding massage. Besides, she *needed* to wash her hair. The images of what Carolyn had done to Albert Serrana kept running through her head, like a video on replay. But it wasn't the brutality of it that bothered her, because the bastard deserved everything he got. No, what made Lana shudder was the conviction that bits and pieces of him were still clinging to her hair and skin and clothes.

In minutes, she'd left her boots and clothing in a pile on the floor and was standing under the pounding water, letting the heat soak into sore muscles. The door opened and she recognized Vincent despite the fogged-up shower glass. There was no mistaking his height and breadth, or the graceful way he moved. She thought at first that he meant to join her and wasn't sure how she felt about that. She had no doubts left that they'd be having sex sooner rather than later, but at the same time, she didn't know if she wanted her first time with him to be in the shower. Especially not when the water was still running pink with the blood she was trying to wash out of her hair. Ick.

Vincent must have had similar doubts, because he turned around and left the room. Or maybe it was simply too close to sunrise. That thought had her hurrying to finish up. It wouldn't be fair if she got to shower and he didn't.

She rinsed the conditioner from her hair and stepped into the relatively cooler air of the bathroom, wrapping a big fluffy towel around her hair. She'd noticed terry bathrobes in the closet, so rather than taking time to towel dry, she pulled on one of the robes and walked out in the main room.

The first thing she noticed was the scent of food. Delicious, spicy food. Her stomach growled loudly enough that Vincent noticed. But then what *didn't* he notice? He looked up and nodded at the room service cart that had shown up while she showered.

"As you requested," he said.

Lana lifted the metal cover on the main dish and her stomach growled even more loudly. She didn't know exactly the proper name for this meal, but she called it *carne asada*. There was a separate covered container with freshly-made flour tortillas, and she nearly swooned.

Vincent's laugh made her glance up at him. "Just looking at you eyeing that food is making me hard, *querida*."

Lana blushed. "Sorry."

"Oh, don't be sorry. You'll be looking at me like that very soon." Her whole body heated as he continued. "Unfortunately, sunrise is near and I need a shower."

"I'm sorry I took so long."

Vincent walked over and cupped her face in his hand. "Don't be sorry. I like you sweet and clean." He kissed her lips softly, just a quick brush of his mouth. "Eat your dinner, Lana."

She waited until she heard the water go on, then sat down and tried not to groan with pleasure as she ate her first real meal in days. One thing about hanging with vamps, they tended to forget that humans needed food. The meals she'd managed to find over the last few days had all been grabbed on the run, and even she got tired of candy bars and chips.

Lana had finished eating and was pushing the cart over to the hallway door to put it outside, when she heard the bathroom door open.

"Don't open that door," Vincent said from behind her.

She turned to find him standing there completely naked, of course. Vincent had only two settings, naked or fully clothed. He was drying himself with a big towel, but didn't even pretend to be trying to cover himself. She told herself to focus on his face, but it was difficult. Vincent clothed was gorgeous. Vincent naked was the kind of beauty you usually saw only in museums.

He caught her admiring look and gave her a wicked grin, teeth flashing white against his dark skin and even darker beard.

Lana sighed. "Should I call someone to retrieve the cart?" she asked him, trying to ease the sexual tension in the room. Or maybe she was the only who felt it, because he seemed relaxed enough.

"I'll take it out," he said and started across the room toward her.

"You don't have any clothes on," she said primly. "I'll take it."

"There's no one out there to see," he commented and grabbed hold of the cart.

"Then there's no reason that I can't do it."

Vincent rolled his eyes, then grabbed the handle and pulled the door open, standing there in all his naked glory holding the door for her. "Are you going to be this stubborn when we fuck?"

Lana's face heated as she pushed the cart past him. But she rallied, giving as good as she got. "Who says we're going to fuck?"

She took more time than she needed to situate the cart against the hallway wall, stalling for time. Vincent hung the *No Molestar* sign on the doorknob, waited until she was back inside, then closed and locked the door and crowded her against the wall with his big body. His big, *naked* body.

"Your body tells me we're going to fuck," he murmured, his fingers making quick work of the knot on her robe. He pushed the plush fabric away, his hand gliding over the bare skin of her belly to rest on her hip. "And you know it, too. I see it on your face every time you look at me." He lowered his mouth to hers and kissed her. Not a teasing touch of his mouth, not a fast, hard smack, but a lingering, luscious kiss that had her rising up on her toes to meet him, her lips opening in welcome, her tongue caressing his, warm and sensuous, tasting of heat and spice and maleness. His hand dropped to her butt and pulled her against him, letting her feel the length of his arousal.

She arched against him and he groaned. "Damn it."

Lana pulled back and stared up at him, her brain so fogged with desire that it was a moment before she understood the problem. Sunrise.

"Oh, God, Vincent, I'm sor—"

"Stop apologizing, damn it." His eyes closed suddenly and he seemed to slump where he stood. When he opened his eyes, it was slowly, as if the lids were too heavy. "I have to get to bed, *querida.* There's no time."

Lana didn't hesitate. Putting her shoulder under his arm, she walked with him to the big bed, tossing the decorative pillows to the floor and pulling back the covers just in time for Vincent to fall onto the mattress.

"Tonight, Lana," he whispered. Then he rolled onto his belly and he was out. Lana stroked her fingers over his back, feeling the firm bands of muscle beneath smooth golden skin, tracing along the length of his spine all the way down to his very fine ass. She was tempted to touch that, too. To squeeze the firm round muscles. But she didn't. That was a little too pervy for her.

She sighed and pulled the sheet and blanket up to his waist. A jaw-cracking yawn reminded her that she'd been up all night, too. Hurrying back to the bathroom, she brushed her teeth and more or less dried her hair. It would take too long to dry it all the way, and she was too tired. Doffing the robe, she shuffled into the big closet. A tired smile crossed her face at the sight of the two dusty duffels sitting in the middle of the elegant dressing room. She dug through hers and found another tank top and the blue, satin shorts. She eyed the skimpy outfit doubtfully, then shook her head. It was pointless to pretend any longer. She'd been sleeping in the same bed with Vincent for days. If they'd arrived at the hotel even an hour earlier, he'd probably be buried inside her by now. She yanked the tank top over her head and stepped into the short shorts, thinking she probably should have saved time and gone to bed in the buff. But she wasn't quite *that* certain of him yet. Maybe when he woke at sunset, he'd have changed his mind. Or maybe something would come up. Something other than the impressive erection she'd felt against her belly earlier.

A shiver of desire rippled over her skin as she turned off the bathroom light and made her way to the bed. It was what they called a California King, which meant she could easily have crawled in and never touched Vincent at all. But instead, she found herself moving all the way over to his side, pulling the covers over both of them and curling up next to him. And as her eyes closed, she dreamed about what it would be like to make love to a vampire.

VINCENT WOKE TO the warm press of woman against his side and the brush of silken hair over his skin.

He turned and scooped Lana against him, tucking her under his body, letting her feel the weight and heat of him as he nudged his knee between her thighs. Her arms circled his neck even before she was fully awake, her eyelids fluttering, her mouth opening to his with a sweet, hungry moan as she pulled his head down for a kiss.

Vincent swallowed the delectable little noises she was making as she arched against him, her tongue sliding into his mouth, sweeping over his swollen gums, tormenting him as he struggled to keep his fangs in check. He could still remember the dark honey taste of her blood, feel its slow glide down his throat when he'd taken her vein in that hot box of a prison. She'd offered herself to him then to save his life, but tonight, she would know the true carnal pleasure of his bite, would cry deliciously as heat and desire sped throughout her body, as her pussy squeezed around his cock until she screamed his name.

"Vincent," she whispered and her eyes opened. "I was dreaming about you."

"And what did you dream, *querida?*"

She undulated beneath him, the satin from her tiny shorts caressing his swollen cock as her breasts pushed against his chest, her nipples poking against the stretchy fabric of her shirt.

"This," she said and met his gaze in bold demand.

Vincent's smile was slow and confident. "I can do that," he murmured, then stripped away her shorts, tearing them down to her thighs and leaving them there, trapping her legs together.

He stroked her body, skimming her breasts through her shirt, flattening his fingers over her belly and caressing along her hip to her thigh. Lana arched against his hand, her knees turning the satin shorts into binders as she tried to open her legs to his touch.

"Vincent," she murmured fitfully, half pleading and half demanding that he free her. She twisted her fingers in his hair and tugged hard, punishing him. But he only smiled and slipped his hand between her thighs, dipping one finger into the creamy center of her sex. Lana moaned, straining against the binding satin as she thrust against his hand. She was so wet, so fucking hot. He added a second finger, plunging deep inside her, feeling the shiver of her inner walls as he began to fuck her, pressing the heel of his hand against her clit, rubbing back and forth as he thrust his fingers in and out, watching her thrash beneath him. He groaned at the sight of her breasts straining against her top, her nipples round and plump and enticing. Bending his head, he closed his mouth over her nipple through the fabric and sucked hard, until she cried out, until the fingers she had twisted in his hair were holding him against her breast, until her shirt was soaked and he could see the rosy outline of her areola. He closed his teeth over the swollen cone of her nipple and she cried out, her pussy clenching around his fingers as she came apart for him, her cries muffled as she bit her lip trying to be quiet.

Fuck that.

Vincent lifted his head to admire the dark rose circles of her nipples, swollen now into puffy points from his suckling. She was still breathing hard from her orgasm, her breasts moving up and down enticingly. His gaze traveled upward, lingering at the line of her engorged jugular, drawn to the drop of blood where her teeth had sunk into her lip as she bit back her screams.

Catching her gaze, he slowly removed his fingers from inside her, dragging them over her still-sensitive clit. His eyelids drooped heavily when she cried out, when her hips lifted against his fingers almost without volition, as if her body knew better than she did what it wanted, what it needed. Her gaze upon him was frantic, almost fearful, but she wasn't afraid. Not of him, anyway. There was no scent of fear, only of arousal and desperation. She wasn't afraid of what he would do, only of what he would make her feel.

He trailed his fingers, wet with her juices, over her bare belly, then raised them deliberately to his mouth, licking away the creamy taste of her, watching her pupils flare with desire.

"Delicious, *querida.*"

She blushed with embarrassment even as her pulse rocketed. Vincent lowered his head and touched her bloody mouth with his tongue, savoring that small sip of her blood as it mingled with the taste of her pussy already in his mouth. And then he kissed her, letting her taste herself as his tongue twisted with hers, making love to her with his kiss until she bucked beneath him, trying to kick her shorts off, wanting to spread her legs around him.

But he wasn't ready for that yet.

She moaned in protest when he broke off their kiss, but he wanted to hear her scream his name the next time she came. There would be no more muffled cries, no more biting back her passion. He licked his way along her jaw to the delicate shell of her ear, felt her skin shiver as he teased his tongue inside, tracing the outline, biting the lobe, then kissing away the tiny pain. Her heart jumped against his chest when his mouth touched the swell of her vein, when his tongue followed the line of it from behind her ear, down along the curve of her neck. He could hear the rush of blood over the thump of her heartbeat, could smell the richness of it, could taste it on his tongue. He knew just what she would taste like, how her blood would slide like rich molasses down his throat and fuel his desire.

His gums split as his fangs emerged, a growl rumbling in his throat. It had been days since he'd last fed, days since Lana had given him her blood to strengthen him for the battle to come. If she'd been one of his regular lovers, his fangs would already be buried in her neck while he fucked her as hard as he could. But Lana was more than that, and she wasn't accustomed to having a vampire lover. Not yet.

So he kept kissing and licking. Following her vein down to her chest, nibbling his way along the tender arch of her clavicle, baring her shoulder, and kissing the upper swell of her breast. Driven by the hunger in his veins, the frustration of her blood so close, he gripped the thin material of her top and ripped it apart, baring her breasts. Lana gasped, her heart pounding so loud it was all he could hear. He licked every inch of her silky skin, sucking almost her entire breast into his mouth, his tongue rasping over her nipple until it too was engorged with blood, pulsing in time with her heartbeat, begging for his bite. He closed his teeth over the swollen flesh, hard enough to leave his mark, but not to draw blood. Lana moaned softly, breathy little pleas murmured in time with the thrust of her hips against him.

Vincent gave her nipple a final rasping lick, then switched his mouth to her other breast and gave it the same attention. She cried out in frustration, her short nails scraping against his scalp, her entire body undulating beneath him.

"Vincent," she breathed.

He lifted his head, meeting her gaze, her normally sparkling eyes hazy with need. "What do you want, Lana?" he asked, his own lust so great that he was unable to do much more than growl the words.

"You," she whispered. "I want you."

Vincent bared his teeth in a wolf's grin. "You have me."

He ripped away the satin shorts, spreading her legs wide as he cupped her ass in his hands and put his mouth to her pussy. Lana protested. She wanted his cock, not his mouth. But he wasn't finished with her yet. She struggled to catch her breath, almost sobbing as he gave a long lick between her folds and over her clit, as his lips closed over that delicate pearl. He shut his eyes then, fighting against the urge to bite. There was no place more succulent on a woman's body, no blood more luscious. She would scream if he bit her there. She would scream his name as she came so hard that she'd pass out. But he needed to fuck her first.

He snarled a curse. Enough.

"Spread your legs," he demanded, pushing his hips between her thighs when she didn't move fast enough, bending her knees to her chest until she was bare and open to him. And then he fucked her. Grasping his cock in his fist, he placed it against the creamy heat of her sex and slammed deep into her body, gliding in easily with the wetness of her arousal, driven by the scent of her need, the clench of her sheath around him. She moaned as her body adjusted to him, her inner muscles trembling as they stretched to accommodate his size. But she didn't wait. Instead, she lifted herself urgently to his thrusts, gripping his ass as their hips pounded against each other, skin slapping in their urgency, teeth and lips clashing as their mouths met in sudden, frantic need.

Vincent's fangs scraped across her tongue, her teeth smashed into his lips, and their blood flowed and mingled. Lana cried out as his blood sparked along her nerves and her muscles tightened beneath him, her body shuddering as she was thrown almost instantly into another orgasm. Vincent fought against the overwhelming desire to taste her further, to sink his fangs into her neck, her thigh, her sex. He didn't care. But instead, he fucked her, pounding his cock into her tight body, feeling her shiver all around him, her sheath rippling along his length, caressing him with a thousand fingers, squeezing and releasing, demanding that he surrender, that he fill her with heat of his own. Until finally, it was too much. His climax was a burning weight as his balls tightened until his release roared down his cock and boiled forth, filling her as she screamed his name.

LANA STROKED HER hands over Vincent's shoulders and back, feeling the strength, the breadth of him. She was still trembling from her multiple orgasms. She wasn't even sure how many. She'd never had to count before. Most of her lovers had barely managed the one. But not Vincent.

She'd known he would be like this. That he'd make love to every part of a woman's body, that he'd leave her limp, her pussy shivering, still clenching with mini orgasms as his cock flexed deep inside her. That he'd leave her hungering for more.

He kissed the side of her neck, his tongue slipping out to taste her sweaty skin. Lana trembled in anticipation of his bite, tilting her head to one side and baring her neck to him in brazen invitation. She remembered what it felt like, the searing heat, the fire running through her veins and along her nerves. It had been beyond sensuous in the hot confines of the prison. She'd dreamed every day since then of what it would be like to have him bite her while he made love to her, while he was buried deep inside of her, his erection hard and thick, the power of his body pressing down on her as he thrust over and over.

Lana shuddered just thinking about it, and Vincent raised himself up on his elbows, lifting his weight off of her so he could see her face.

"Everything okay?"

She nodded, her throat too tight to speak as she searched his copper-flecked eyes, her fingers combing through the waves of his black hair, when abruptly she frowned. Why didn't he bite her?

Without warning, he levered himself off the bed and walked over to the small refrigerator. Lana felt abruptly naked, her tank top in tatters, her shorts . . . somewhere. She got up and headed for the bathroom, not certain what she'd do there, only knowing she couldn't lie on the bed like a rejected lover, one whose blood obviously wasn't desirable unless he was trapped with no options.

Vincent caught her hand as she walked past him. "Lana?" he said, scowling as he tugged her to a stop. "What's wrong?"

"Wrong? Why would anything be wrong?" she snapped, refusing to look at him. She tried to pull away, but his grip on her hand strengthened and he tugged her against his chest, his powerful arms coming around to hold her there.

"Tell me," he demanded.

Lana gritted her teeth, refusing to give him the satisfaction.

"I can make you tell," he murmured.

"But you won't," she replied smugly.

His arms tightened around her. "Don't be so sure," he growled. "A moment ago, you were screaming my name while your pussy squeezed my cock so hard I thought I'd lose it. What happened between now and then?"

"It's not what happened," she said, fighting uselessly against his hold. "It's what d—" She shut her mouth before she made an even bigger fool of herself.

"What didn't?" he guessed, too clever for his own good. "What didn't happen, Lana?" he asked, sounding genuinely puzzled.

She pushed back enough to bite his arm, but he only laughed.

"You think biting will make me release you? I'm a vampire, *querida*. Biting only turns me on." She could feel the truth of his words in the hard length of his shaft pressing against her belly.

"Well, at least one of us is using her teeth," she snapped. And almost immediately, she wished she could take the words back as Vincent grew very still, his arms suddenly like iron bands.

"You want me to bite you?"

"Don't put yourself out," she snapped. "I'm not some pity—"

She never finished her sentence as Vincent fisted his fingers in her hair, yanked her head to one side, and sank his fangs into her vein. Lana's entire body convulsed as she went from trembling in surprise to full-body orgasm in the space of a heartbeat. She cried out, gasping for air, her heart racing so hard that it was pounding on her lungs, stealing her breath. Vincent's strong arms enclosed her, one around her neck, her jaw cupped in his hand as he held her still for his bite, his other around her waist, crushing her against his body, her feet barely touching the floor as she shuddered in wanton hunger.

Lana reached up and caressed the back of his head, threading her fingers through his long hair as she struggled not to pass out from the sheer, overwhelming pleasure suffusing every inch of her body.

"Vincent," she whispered, clutching his shoulders, her nails digging into the thick muscles.

With a snarl, Vincent lifted his head, his fangs gleaming red with her blood. His muscles flexed as he swung her around and threw her face first onto the bed. Kneeling behind her, he gripped her hips in both hands and lifted her ass into the air. There was no finesse, no seduction. His thick fingers reached between her thighs and found her wet and ready for him, and then his cock was slamming into her, his hips slapping her ass as he went balls-deep with a single stroke.

Lana buried her head in her arms and hung on, her nerves still thrumming with arousal from his bite as he fucked her wildly, his growls punctuating every thrust, until he gripped her hair once more, and pulled her onto her knees. With her back pressed against his chest, he buried his fingers in her pussy and his fangs in her neck and they both came so hard she thought the room would break apart around them.

Lana cried Vincent's name, over and over again, the euphoric in his bite shrieking along her nerves while his release filled her with heat until finally she couldn't stand anymore and she screamed wordlessly.

The next thing she knew, Vincent's tongue was wet and warm on her neck, and some vague memory told her he was sealing the puncture wounds. They were lying down, stretched out on the bed, her back still to Vincent's front, but he was caressing her now, soothing her as she came down from the dual euphoria of having his bite and his cock. It was every bit as devastating as she'd dreamed it would be, and she didn't think she'd ever be able to move again.

"Did I hurt you?" Vincent inquired quietly, and she heard the genuine concern in his voice. The worry.

She shook her head silently, reaching back to caress his jaw. "It was beautiful," she whispered. "You're beautiful."

Vincent kissed the side of her neck. "That's *my* line," he murmured, smiling against her skin. "Besides, I'm supposed to be devastatingly handsome, not beautiful."

Lana smiled. "Vain, too."

"Oh, absolutely."

She laughed. "Do we have to move now? Because I'm not sure I can."

"We can do whatever you want, but I've no objection to spending the night inside you."

Lana shivered. She knew he meant it. "I'll need food."

"I can do that."

"All night it is, then," she breathed and turned into his kiss.

Chapter Seventeen

LANA WOKE BEFORE sunset the next night. She knew this because Vincent was still out and because a quick check of the sunset app on her cell phone confirmed she had several minutes before the sun went down. She slipped out of bed long enough to use the facilities and grab her laptop, then settled back in and logged on to the hotel's Internet to check her mail while she waited. Her in-box had the usual junk, plus five new messages from Dave Harrington and one from her dad. She opened her dad's and found nothing new. He still talked about Dave like he was the second coming and instructed her to meet up with Dave to finish whatever this assignment was that she'd taken on without telling anyone. He didn't ask how it was going, didn't ask if she needed help. Hell, the guys took on private jobs all the time, and he never complained. In fact, he thought it was a good thing—it kept them happy and flush when business was slow. But he obviously didn't think the same way when it came to her. This attitude was why she hadn't told him about the job for Raphael in the first place. She'd known what his reaction would be.

She read on, wondering just how deeply he'd snooped into her business. It seemed he knew the job had a vampire element, but not much else. That meant Dave Harrington had probably tracked her as far as Hermosillo, but hadn't managed to squeeze any info out of Vincent's people. Given what she now knew about the vampire hierarchy, that didn't surprise her, especially since the only vampire who actually knew what was happening was Michael. Dave could still find her if he was determined, but it would take a long time, maybe even long enough that the job would be over.

And she considered, for the first time, that when the job was over, she and Vincent would go back to their separate lives. The idea that she might never see him again . . . hurt. It was an actual, physical pain in her heart. She pressed a hand to her chest and tried to tell herself it was something else, all the spicy food, maybe. But that didn't explain the tears stinging the back of her eyes.

The sheets rustled as Vincent stirred awake behind her. Pasting on a smile, she looked over her shoulder to see him watching her.

"You can read my e-mails, too, if you promise to do it naked," he purred.

She laughed, relieved that he hadn't noticed her mood. "I was waiting for you. I need a shower."

"Shower sex. Even better than naked e-mail."

"Who said anything about sex?"

He didn't say a word, simply threw back the covers and stood in all his naked beauty, his erection jutting hard and thick and proud. Lana didn't realize she was staring until he walked over and lifted her chin, forcing her to look at his face.

"Hellooo? My face is up here," he said in a singsong parody of the time-honored female objection.

Lana laughed again, feeling it this time, as she rose to wrap her arms around his neck. "Shower sex sounds good," she murmured, nuzzling his skin. She took Vincent's hand as she stood and headed for the bathroom, pausing only long enough to close her laptop without opening any of Dave Harrington's e-mails.

VINCENT LIFTED LANA against the tiled wall and slammed his cock into her, driven by the need to possess her as much as by anger that she made him want her that much. They'd spent the entire previous night in bed, mostly with him inside her, with only brief pauses for rest and food, in Lana's case anyway. He didn't need any food but her blood, and he didn't need much rest either.

And still, he'd woken this evening hard as a rock and reaching for her. Maybe if he fucked her enough, he'd get his fill. Maybe this hunger driving him to claim her, to make sure no other man so much as looked at her, would finally be sated, and he could go back to his life. Back to fucking whatever woman caught his fancy. Except he didn't want to fuck any woman but this one.

He snarled his anger, grabbing her thigh and wrapping it higher around his waist, crushing his mouth against hers. Lana echoed his snarl, digging her fingers into his hair so hard it hurt, which only fueled his desire for her. He tasted blood as her lip split from the ferocity of his kiss, then more blood as she bit him back, her laugh low and sultry. His cock grew impossibly harder at the sound and her sex, hot and tight, pulsed around him. He pulled back and met her gaze, her eyes as full of wild abandon as his own must be. Christ, they would fuck each other to death at this rate.

And what a way to go.

He let his fangs emerge, relishing the pain as they split his gums, the widening of Lana's pupils as she eyed their sharp, gleaming lengths. And then, with her eyes never leaving his, she grinned and tilted her head, baring the elegant length of her neck.

Fuck. Me, he thought and snapped his head forward, his fangs slicing into the dewy heat of her skin, piercing a vein so swollen with blood that it burst like a ripe fruit, flooding his mouth, rolling down his throat. So much blood, and so delectable, that he had to close his eyes against the ecstasy lest Lana see it and know the power she had over him. This was more than blood. This was the blood of the woman who could be his mate if he allowed it to go that far.

Lana's scream had his eyes flashing open. He pulled his head back, wanting to watch as she climaxed around him, as she lost control, caught in the same trap that he was, her body shuddering in the throes of an orgasm that Vincent had given her, that she was helpless to resist.

"Vincent," she whispered his name, so soft and sweet, so full of emotion. So vulnerable.

Fool that he was, his heart swelled. Bending his head, he licked the puncture wounds from his bite, sealing them shut and stopping the flow of blood. Then he nibbled his way to her mouth, taking her in a different sort of kiss, one full of desire and longing. And as he did, he slid his cock in and out slowly, feeling her body convulsing around him, her nipples scraping his chest, her heart racing as the orgasm rolled over and through her. And when she was nearly done, when he felt the contractions of her belly begin to slow, the caress of her sheath start to lose its frenzy, he cupped her ass, holding her wide open, and he fucked her in earnest, slamming his cock as deep as he could go, grinding against her clit with every thrust.

Lana's eyes flashed open in shock as a fresh climax seized hold of her, as her pussy rippled around his cock once more. Her arms tightened convulsively over his shoulders and she cried out helplessly. Vincent felt his own body respond, his orgasm rising up like the heat of a volcano, roaring through every muscle, searing every nerve until his release poured forth, claiming his woman with his cock as certainly as he'd done with his fangs.

LANA HUNG IN Vincent's grip, so overheated between the hot shower and the even hotter vampire between her thighs that she thought she'd melt away. Either that or explode. She wasn't sure which. She wasn't sure she cared, because it was worth it. Vincent was worth it. Maybe that made her an idiot, because he wasn't just a vampire, he was a man. And men like Vincent didn't tie themselves down to one woman. She had to remember that. Had to remember that whatever they had was fleeting. That it could be hot and incredible, but in the end it was just fun. Something glorious to remember when she was old and gray.

She stroked her hand over the back of Vincent's head. His forehead rested against the tile behind her, and his breath was hot and loud in her ear. A cramp reminded her that her legs were still wrapped around his hips and she grimaced, not sure she had any strength left to move them . . . or to stand on her own two feet if she did.

"I think I need a shower," she murmured, aware of her sweaty skin, of the wetness between her thighs, both his and hers.

Vincent chuckled and lifted his head, his eyes flecked with copper when they met hers. "Can you move?"

"Maybe. If you help."

He squeezed her butt cheek, then trailed his fingers down into her wetness and along her thigh.

"Stop that," she scolded weakly. "We'll be here all night."

"Is that a bad thing?"

"I don't know about you, vampire, but I'll wrinkle like a prune. And that's not attractive in a lover."

He slapped her ass, then stepped back, easing her legs to the floor and holding on to her until she was more or less steady. But this was Vincent, which meant he couldn't let it go at that.

Reaching behind her, he pumped a good handful of shower gel and began washing her, sliding his strong hands all over her body, washing between her thighs and over her ass. Feeling more relaxed than she'd ever felt, Lana closed her eyes and enjoyed the massage.

"Rinse."

She blinked her eyes open to find Vincent gazing down at her in bemusement.

"Rinse, *querida*. You're all soapy."

"Right," she said, as if she hadn't been half asleep. Vincent backed away so she could get under the spray, but then grabbed the handheld sprayer and danced it over her body, pretending to be helpful by aiming it between her legs.

"Give me that," she snapped, taking it away and aiming it at his face briefly before finishing her own rinse. It was fortunate, she thought, that she'd washed her hair before they'd had sex. Because if she had to stand this close to a naked Vincent much longer, there was only one way it could go. And then she'd be a prune for sure.

Handing him the sprayer, she rose up on tiptoes to kiss his mouth, then slapped his ass on her way out of the shower enclosure. Instantly feeling about ten degrees cooler, she pulled on one of the fluffy robes, then grabbed a towel and a comb, and walked through the dressing area and out into the bedroom.

Wrapping the robe more closely around her body, she tied it loosely shut, then stood in front of the mirror and began combing out her wet hair. Someone knocked on the room door and she frowned, checking the time. Maybe Vincent had ordered room service for her breakfast . . . or dinner . . . or whatever you called it when you slept all day and woke up at night. Or maybe it was the maid, since they'd missed the regularly scheduled cleaning.

She crossed to the door and checked the peephole, covering it with her hand first, just in case someone was standing out there with a gun. She'd seen that in a movie once. The movie itself hadn't made much of an impression, but the scene had.

Pulling away her fingers—which were still whole and free of bullet wounds—she put her eye to the peephole and found something much worse.

Dave Harrington. What the fuck was he doing here?

She snapped the locks and ripped open the door.

"What the fuck, Dave?"

"You ask me that?" he demanded, shoving his way into the room. "I've been leaving messages, e-mailing . . . your dad's worried sick. No one knows what you're working on, or why you're down here in the middle of cartel country . . . and on your own, for fuck's sake."

"Get out," she said, stepping in front of him, trying to stop him from going any farther into the room before disaster struck. "What I do isn't any of your business or my dad's. Now get out."

"Not until you tell me why you're here. What are you working on?" He took several steps into the room, forcing her to move aside, a big man by any standard, strong and fit . . . and Vincent would tear him apart.

"Not here," Lana said firmly. "I need to get dressed. Why don't I meet you in the coffee shop?"

Unfortunately, Dave might be clueless, but he wasn't stupid. He turned in a circle, taking in the tousled bed, staring at the closed bathroom door. She knew the moment he heard the water running in the shower. His entire body stiffened, and he spun around, his eyes wide with disbelief.

"You're fucking somebody? You ran out on your dad, on me, to have a fuckfest in Mexico?"

But Lana wasn't looking at Dave anymore. The bathroom door opened and she met Vincent's gaze.

"You didn't tell me we had a guest, *querida.*"

VINCENT HAD JUST stepped out of the shower, feeling terrific, when he'd heard a man yelling at Lana in the next room. He'd grabbed his sweats, pulled them up his wet legs, and opened the bathroom door to find a human male shouting something about a Mexican fuckfest.

Vincent looked over the human's bulky shoulder and met Lana's worried gaze.

"You didn't tell me we had a guest, *querida.*"

The human spun around, one hand going to the big pistol at his hip as he glared at Vincent, his gaze raking him from head to toe with unmasked hatred. Vincent didn't have to dip into even the man's most shallow thoughts to know what he was thinking. There might as well have been a light bulb blinking over his head. He saw a mostly naked Vincent, his hair and skin still wet from the shower, and he saw Lana, all shiny clean, wrapped in the enveloping robe, her long hair still dripping water.

The human cast a stunned look at Lana, then Vincent. And his expression changed, becoming more calculated, noting Vincent's size and strength, the way he stood, balanced and ready to fight. And even more, his complete lack of concern over the human's sudden appearance.

This was Dave Harrington, Vincent assumed, based on Lana's description of both the man and his disposition. He was an inch or two shorter than Vincent, but bulky with muscle, and probably used to intimidating people with his size alone.

Only Vincent wasn't intimidated, and Dave Harrington knew it.

"You were saying?" Vincent asked mildly, hoping the fool would persist in insulting Lana, thus giving Vincent a reason to pound the asshole into the ground.

"Who the fuck are you?" Harrington demanded.

Lana stepped around him and took up a position next to Vincent, a significant move that was not lost on Harrington if his gaping glance at Lana was any indication.

"I believe that's my question," Vincent answered, "since this is my . . . that is, *our* room that you've so rudely barged into."

Harrington looked to Lana, clearly expecting her to do something. Introduce him, maybe? Declare her undying love?

But then Lana's robe shifted, and Harrington got a look at her neck where Vincent had so recently bitten her. There wasn't much in the way of a mark, but it was enough, given what the man obviously already knew, that he drew the right conclusion.

But then he made the wrong move.

"You're fucking a vampire?" Harrington demanded and reached for Lana, though whether to push the robe aside for a better look or to grab her, Vincent didn't know. And he didn't care.

Moving faster than the human could follow, he snagged the man's wrist before his hand could touch Lana, then stepped into his space, stopping a hair's-breadth from the human's chest.

"Don't touch her," Vincent snarled. "And you will keep a civil tongue in your head, or I'll rip it out and shove it down your throat."

"Vincent," Lana said quietly.

He waited just long enough for the human to realize he was helpless against Vincent's greater strength, then let go, shoving the man a step backward away from Lana.

Draping a blatantly possessive arm around Lana's shoulders, he touched his head to hers in a way that shouted intimacy and asked, "Who is this clown?" Even though he already knew.

Harrington glared daggers at him. "I'm her fiancé, asshole. Who're you?"

Lana snorted in disgust, but tellingly made no attempt to dislodge Vincent's arm. "You are *not* my fiancé, Dave. We have *never been* engaged."

"As for who I am," Vincent interjected. "I'm the one fu—"

Lana turned her head slowly and stared, as if daring him to finish that sentence.

Vincent grinned and finished, saying, "—following Lana around the country. Keeping her safe . . . among other things."

"Vincent," Lana chided softly, turning to touch his jaw with her fingers, fighting a smile that she probably didn't want him to see. She turned back to Harrington.

"I'm sorry you came all this way for nothing, Dave. But this isn't your business, or my father's. I appreciate your concern, but as you can see, I'm perfectly safe. Now, I'll ask you to leave."

Harrington, who was either clueless or had a major case of denial, stared at Lana in disbelief. "You're choosing a vampire over us?"

"There is no us," Lana shouted, having finally reached her limit with the asshole. "Will you please get that through your head! We dated! A long time ago! Get over it!"

"Lana—"

"No. Damn it!" Calm Lana had disappeared for good. "Go home," she snarled just as viciously as any vampire could. "And tell my father to stop butting into my business. I'm on vacation. Now, leave me the fuck alone!"

Harrington finally seemed to clue in. "Fine," he snapped. "It's your funeral." He stormed over and yanked the door open, pausing for one last volley. "Or maybe your dad's, since this will break his fucking heart."

Lana rolled her eyes at that last bit of drama, but didn't say anything until the door slammed shut on his useless ass.

"As if," she muttered. "Sean Arnold will outlive us all just to prove he can."

Vincent slipped an arm around her waist and tugged her back against his chest, leaning over to rub his cheek against hers. "You okay?"

She nodded.

"He still wants you, you know."

"He wants my father's business."

"Maybe. But he wants you, too."

"Too bad for him, then."

"Do you want him?"

She turned to give him the kind of look a person gives someone who's particularly clueless. "No, Vincent," she explained patiently. "If I wanted Dave Harrington, I'd have been fucking *him* in the shower ten minutes ago instead of you. Happy now?"

Vincent grinned, then leaned down and closed his teeth over her full lower lip before licking away the hurt. "I apologize."

"Hmph. I don't need you to protect me, you know."

"I know that. But *I* need to."

She smiled reluctantly. "Vanity, thy name is man, or male, anyway."

"Naturally," Vincent agreed.

"Yes, well, now that the entertainment portion of our evening is concluded, we need to start looking for Xuan Ignacio. He's the reason we're here, after all."

"I thought we were here so you could take shameless advantage of me."

"That's true. But I thought maybe I'd give you a break. You know, some time to recover your strength."

Vincent lowered his head to give her a mischievous look. "Is that a challenge?"

She shook her head with a smile. "I'm not that foolish. But we really do have to find Xuan."

"All right," he conceded. "We should change hotels anyway. If Harrington found us, others can, too."

"He's probably been tracking my cell phone. This is the first time we've stayed in one place long enough for him to catch up with us."

"Another good reason to move. Let's pack up and get out of here. We'll get you some food and I'll make some calls. Xuan's not the only vampire in Pénjamo. It's time I reminded the locals of who's in charge."

"You mean Enrique?" Lana asked, feigning innocence.

Vincent growled and grabbed her by the lapels, yanking her face up to his and laying a hard, fast kiss against her sweet mouth. "Me, *querida*, and don't you forget it."

"Pfftt. As if." With that dismissal, she slammed a kiss of her own against his lips, then disengaged his fingers from her robe and walked back into the bathroom, leaving him to wonder how it was that he could be falling for a woman who didn't seem to need him at all.

Chapter Eighteen

WHILE LANA ATE dinner in the restaurant, Vincent sipped a glass of wine, for appearances' sake, and made phone calls, beginning with Michael.

"Sire," his lieutenant answered.

"Mikey, what have you got for me?"

"First off, the ducklings are doing well. Jerry just needed a few good feedings, and he's already walking patrol with one of the regulars. Salvio's a bit harder to connect with. He doesn't seem as blood-deprived as Jerry—"

"He killed a bunch of guards just before we found him. I'm guessing he fed."

"That explains it. He seems a little uneasy, but he's starting patrol tonight. I thought to keep the two of them together, but Salvio seemed reluctant."

"Problem?"

"I don't think so. We'll see how he adjusts, but for now, he's working security at the club, backing up the door. I've got Ortega keeping an eye on him since he knows the history."

"Good idea. And Carolyn?" he asked, covering his mouth and speaking so softly that Lana wouldn't hear.

"I haven't seen her since we got back, but I'm getting nightly reports. Physically, she's fully recovered, of course. As for the other, it might be a while before she's comfortable being around males of any species, but she's okay with the other women. She's strong."

"She'd have to be to survive that and stay sane."

"Speaking of insanity, *jefe*, I got word from my source inside Enrique's HQ today, and it's not good. He says Alexandra's dead."

"Fuck. Enrique killed her?"

"Not Enrique. A visitor from France. The same one who masterminded the assassination attempt on Raphael in Acuña. Word is that he's still in Mexico City, hiding out in Enrique's villa."

"Why is he still there? You'd think he'd be running for home, especially since he was stupid enough to kill Raphael's sister."

"No one seems to know. Raphael must already know she's dead, right?"

"Count on it. Damn, this situation just gets more and more complicated. Fuck. All right, one thing at a time. Did you find anything to help me with Xuan Ignacio? I'd like to find the guy and get this over with."

"The bloom is off the rose already?"

"Hell, no. What I'd like is to spend a few quality weeks with this particular rose at the house in Cabo. No visitors, no politics."

"Huh."

Vincent frowned at the phone. "Huh, what?"

"Oh, uh, nothing. Just checking my notes. And, yes, I do have some help for you. Celio—you remember him, the older vamp who claimed to have seen Xuan—"

"Yeah, yeah."

"Well, wanting to please your magnificent self, he devoted himself to thinking back over the years and came up with a name for you. It's another vamp like him. Old, but not strong. Still living in Pénjamo." Michael paused. "Do you ever think about how many guys there must be like that, living out in the world? Really old vamps hanging out in small villages, getting by on a sip from a lovely young thing—girl or boy—"

As Michael went on being clever, Vincent was caught up in the sight of Lana taking a drink of her Coke. Her lips, full and wet with some pink stuff she'd put on them upstairs, wrapped around the thick straw as she sucked . . . He placed his hand over hers on the table, curling their fingers together. Lana looked up and met his eyes with a soft smile.

And all Vincent could think about was getting her naked and beneath him as soon as possible.

"—no power, but not worried about it, because there are vamps like you maintaining order in the land," Michael finished.

"You know, Mikey," Vincent said, his gaze never leaving Lana. "I can't say I ever thought about it. But you know what I *can* say?"

"I'm guessing it's that you don't give a fuck about it either."

"Smart man. I knew there was a reason I kept you around. Now tell me what Celio has to say that will help me find Xuan."

"His friend knows Xuan's current whereabouts, and he's willing to meet with you."

"Excellent. Text me the info."

"As we speak."

"I'll call you later," Vincent said and disconnected. Then he turned to Lana. "We have a meeting with a guy who knows where to find Xuan."

"That was quick. Who is he?"

"An old friend of Celio's who still lives in the area."

"How soon?"

"I need to call him and set it up, but not here. I'll call from the road."

Lana disengaged her hand and immediately started gathering her things, getting ready to leave. She took a final sip of her drink, wiped her mouth, checked the bill, and put some money on the table . . . but the only thing Vincent was thinking about was how much he missed the warmth of her fingers in his.

He blinked and gave himself a mental slap on the head. What the fuck? He was a love-'em-and-leave-'em-happy guy. He wasn't some lovesick teenage girl.

"You ready?" he asked. When Lana glanced over at him in surprise, he realized his voice might have been a bit hard.

"Everything okay?" she asked.

"Yeah, sorry. It just feels like we're finally doing what we started out to do in the first place."

"Too many side trips," she observed.

"Exactly."

"So let's go see a man about a thing."

Vincent chuckled and dropped an arm around her shoulders as they walked out of the restaurant. "You've been reading too many cop stories."

"Are there any other kind?"

"Good point."

"YOU'RE SURE THIS is current?" Vincent asked. He was speaking to Celio's old friend, using the in-dash speaker function as they drove to Pénjamo.

"Unless you've scared him away. He know you're coming?"

Lana thought the other vampire's voice sounded old, like human old, and she wondered what he looked like. Was it possible that some humans got turned when they were close to the end of their lives? And if so, what happened then? Did the vampire virus or whatever start repairing them so they would eventually look young again? Or were they stuck being old forever? Surely, at least their health improved. They wouldn't have to endure immortality with arthritis or brittle bones, would they?

"You should have a care whom you're speaking to, old man," Vincent growled.

"What're you gonna do, chase me down and kill me because I don't kiss your ass?"

Lana's eyes went wide.

"If you fuck this up, I just might," Vincent snapped, then slammed his fist against the on-screen disconnect button.

Of course, the screen wasn't designed for smashing fists, so they could still hear the old vampire on the other end muttering about fucking vampire lords who think their shit don't stink, just because they got the best of the genetic lottery before Lana touched the screen with her finger and disconnected the call.

"Ignore him," she said calmly. "He's an unhappy old man. All we care about is whether his information is good. Do you think it is?"

"Probably," Vincent admitted grudgingly, obviously still pissed. "I don't know anything about him except what Celio told me, but there's no reason for him to lie. There's nothing for him in this either way."

"He sounded old."

"Yeah, so? We knew he was old. Celio told us."

"But he sounded like an old human, with a quavering voice and stuff. Do vamps eventually age like that?"

Vincent seemed to think about it. "Some do. It's as if their brains can't sustain them anymore, even the strong ones. The last Lord of the Northeast was like that. To look at him, you'd have thought he was no more than thirty. But his mind was shot to hell."

"What happened?"

"His lieutenant took him out."

"Kind of a mercy killing?"

Vincent bared his teeth. "I don't think Rajmund had much mercy on his mind at the time. The quickest way for a vamp to get dead is to threaten another powerful vampire's mate."

Lana absorbed that bit of information, then asked, "So where are we going, then?"

"South of the city, in the foothills. The guy says it won't show up on GPS, but he's been there once or twice. He's texting me some natural markers that will get us there."

"How far do you think it is?"

"Sixty, seventy miles. It'll take us two hours or so. Why, are you in a hurry?"

"I'm curious. Aren't you?"

"Yeah, I guess I am. It's unusual enough that Raphael sent a private message to one of Enrique's vampires. But when he made it personal, sending you to me specifically, making it clear that he wants me there for the delivery, there's obviously something up. How did he know I wouldn't go right to Enrique with it? Hell, how'd he know I wouldn't take you and the message *both* to Enrique?"

"Why didn't you?" Lana asked, ignoring the chill that shivered along her spine at the very idea. She hadn't thought about that possibility. If she had, she'd probably have sent the money back and told Cyn and Raphael to find another messenger.

Vincent reached out and took her hand, the same way he had in the restaurant. It made her heart flutter and her stomach kind of queasy. She wanted to trust her heart, but she had a feeling her stomach had the right idea.

"I couldn't pass up the chance to go on a private road trip with you, could I?"

Lana scoffed noisily.

"You underestimate yourself, *querida*. But I admit I was intrigued by the mystery of Raphael's request. That you were the messenger was a beautiful bonus."

He squeezed her fingers and Lana got that queasy feeling in her stomach again.

"Well . . . two more hours and you'll know everything, won't you?"

"*We'll* know," he amended. "You're a part of this, too."

Lana wanted to believe that, wanted to believe there was a *we* in their future. The problem was, she couldn't see a future that included her and Vincent together.

IT WAS A GOOD thing the old vampire had sent that list of natural markers, Vincent thought to himself. It was also a damn good thing that his vehicle was both four-wheel drive and had an armored undercarriage, or they'd have bottomed out and been hung up on some rock a long time ago. The so-called road they were following was barely a dirt track. If it hadn't had two barely visible, parallel lines of dirt amidst the scrub, he'd have assumed it was nothing but an animal trail and ignored it. But it was obvious that *someone* was using it on an infrequent but regular basis, and every single one of the old vamp's markers was showing up where he'd said they would. So they kept going.

"Xuan Ignacio must really want to be left alone," Lana commented.

That was the most she'd said in the past few hours. Other than a word or two pointing out upcoming turns, she'd been unusually quiet. Not that she was normally a chatterbox, but there was *emotion* beneath her silence this time. A human wouldn't have sensed it, but he did. His vamp powers were good for more than just tripping along his victim's memories. He had the full complement of vampire telepathic abilities all amped up by the power that made him a potential vampire lord. And his vamp senses were telling him that Lana was *thinking*. In his experience, when a woman started *thinking*, he needed to start worrying.

"Almost there," she told him, checking the text on his cell phone. "One more turn."

"You ready for this?"

She glanced at him, then back at the road. "I should be asking you that. You're the—Wow, look at that organ cactus! It's huge."

Vincent eyed the giant cactus that was looming in the headlights like a space alien, then he looked over at Lana.

She noticed his amused expression and blushed hotly. "Sorry. I've just never seen one that big. That's your turn by the way. The house shouldn't be far now."

Vincent had to slow almost to a stop to make the sharp left-hand turn, and even then that stupid cactus that Lana admired so much scraped along the side of his SUV, making his teeth grind in irritation. Michael laughed at him about it all the time, but Vincent liked his vehicles to look *good*. And that didn't include fucking cacti scratches all down the driver's side.

"Smoke," Lana said suddenly. "I thought I saw smoke in the headlights."

Vincent nodded. He smelled it. "When we get there, you stay behind me, *querida*, until we know what's what. This is a vampire we're dealing with. One who's wily enough to have survived a very long time."

He brought the SUV to a halt twenty or so feet from the front door, and sat for a moment, sending a tendril of his power out, sliding it through the cracks of the stone block house in front of him, wanting to learn as much as he could before knocking on the front door.

"There's one vampire inside," he informed Lana softly. "No one else."

"Does he know you're here?" she asked, whispering, as if the vampire could hear them from inside the house.

"He knows someone's here. But I've been masking my signature. Not to brag or anything, but I'm a major power. I didn't want him to freak out."

"Not to brag or anything," she repeated dryly.

Vincent shrugged. "It is what it is. Whoever's inside that house isn't in my league. Still, there's something . . ." He tilted his head, curious. He didn't know if the vampire inside was Xuan Ignacio, but whoever it was, there was something oddly familiar about the *feel* of him, as if the vamp was someone Vincent *should* know.

"What is it?" Lana asked.

Vincent frowned, shaking his head. "A taste of . . . something. A connection. It might simply be that we were both sired by Enrique, but I've never . . . Never mind. I'll know more once I touch him. You ready? You've got the envelope?"

"Right here," she said.

Vincent noted the steadiness of her voice and hands as she opened her door, and he felt oddly proud of her courage. He shook away such fanciful thoughts and flicked the headlights down to parking lights only. There was enough of a moon that he didn't need them, but Lana would. He opened his own door and slid out of the SUV, walking around to meet her. He didn't take her hand, although he wanted to. But, like her, he understood the necessity of keeping one's hands free in potentially-hostile situations.

Not that he was sensing any hostility from the vampire inside. If anything, there was . . .

The door swung back, and a vampire stood framed in the opening, orange light dancing behind him from the glow of a fireplace.

"Vincent," the vampire said in a voice full of emotion. "I knew you would find me someday."

Chapter Nineteen

VINCENT FELT LANA'S eyes upon him as he stared at the vampire who was called Xuan Ignacio. He was short of stature, with black hair and the broad, flat features that spoke of indigenous roots, Central American or Mexican. Vincent was certain he didn't know this vampire, but he also felt sure that he *should* know him. It was just one more question on a journey that was already full of them. Too many questions. It was time for some fucking answers.

Without warning, Vincent shed the mask he'd donned for Xuan's comfort and loosed the full measure of his power. It roared through his blood, thrumming along every nerve, flexing muscles, expanding his lungs almost to bursting, and lighting the copper glow of his eyes. They hit the figure of Xuan Ignacio like a spotlight, burning twice as hot as the flames at his back inside the cabin.

Vincent waited for the vamp to react, but Xuan only smiled, almost proudly, as if he'd expected his visitor to be exactly who and what he was. The vampire then addressed Lana, starting forward with an outstretched hand and, speaking in accented English. "Forgive me, I didn't introduce myself. My name is—"

He didn't get any further than that. Vincent stepped in front of Lana, shielding her from Xuan's approach even though he knew she wouldn't thank him for it. Her anger pulsed at his back, but it was far better to have her angry and alive, than dead. Or worse.

"Who are you?" Vincent demanded.

The vampire pulled his hand back and looked up at Vincent. "My name is Xuan Ignacio. But you already know that, Vincent Kuxim."

"How do you know me?"

"Everyone knows Enrique's powerful lieutenant," Xuan said mildly. "But what brings you to my door?"

Lana shoved Vincent aside, and not gently. But he noted that she wisely maintained her distance from Xuan even as she addressed him. "I'm Lana Arnold," she said. "We're here because a client of mine asked that I deliver this to you."

She held out the envelope with Raphael's message in it, but Xuan didn't take it right away.

"Who is your client?" he asked cautiously.

Lana would have answered, but Vincent beat her to it. He wanted to see the vamp's reaction. "Raphael."

Xuan's eyes closed, and he nodded to himself, as if accepting something he'd known would happen, but at the same time had dreaded . . . or feared. He held out his hand.

"May I?" he asked.

Lana glanced at Vincent, then took a necessary step forward and handed over Raphael's message.

The vampire held the envelope in his hands, turning it over and around, studying his name written in Raphael's flowing script.

"Do you know what the message says?" he asked Lana, but his attention was on Vincent.

"No," Lana answered for both of them.

Xuan nodded. "You should come inside. I suspect I have a story to tell."

LANA WAITED TO see what Vincent would do. She hadn't liked it when he'd stepped between her and Xuan, as if she was incapable of protecting herself. But she suspected Vincent knew that and had done it anyway. So, okay, she wasn't stupid enough to let her pride get her killed, and Vincent understood this situation far better than she did. But *he'd* been surprised too, maybe even a little shaken, by Xuan's appearance. Still, there had to be more to it. Vincent had been uneasy even before they got here.

Did that mean that Xuan was more powerful than Vincent expected? Did he have some talent that could reach out and touch someone . . . and not in a good way? Was that what Vincent had been feeling as they'd drawn closer?

She couldn't ask Vincent any of these questions without giving away her ignorance, and maybe Vincent's too, so she waited to see what he'd do.

Vincent studied Xuan for a moment, and, while she couldn't *see* anything, she was pretty sure there was some sort of vampire dick-measuring going on, with Vincent demonstrating to Xuan just how much power he could bring to the table.

Xuan didn't seem prepared to fight, though. He simply bowed a little from the waist and stepped back from his door, as if to invite them inside.

"We'll talk," Vincent agreed, then reached out and put his arm in front of Lana, curving his big hand over her hip, pulling her slightly behind him. "But don't touch her."

Xuan straightened and tilted his head in a smiling acceptance. "Of course not. Will you join me for coffee? I confess a lingering fondness for it, despite our . . . dietary requirements."

Vincent waited until Xuan's back was turned to pull her against his side and murmur, "You can be mad at me later, but *please* follow my lead in this.

Don't let him touch you."

"I'm not an idiot."

"I know that," he said, tightening his grip into a hug and placing a soft kiss against her temple.

Lana's heart wiggled happily and she told it to behave. This was just Vincent being Vincent. He was a naturally protective alpha male. Nothing more.

She followed Vincent into the small house as Xuan went around the room, turning on lights. She suspected that was for her benefit, just as she knew Vincent had left the Suburban's parking lights on for the same reason. Which reminded her . . .

"The SUV lights?" she said to Vincent.

He gave her a puzzled look, then leaned back and glared at the SUV. The lights blinked out almost instantly.

"Handy trick," she muttered.

"Don't be a hater," he muttered right back at her.

"Please, sit," Xuan said, gesturing at a short couch and single chair that sat in front of the fireplace.

The room was small enough that the furniture took up half of the available space. The other half was a minimal kitchen, with a sink and refrigerator built into a set of cabinets. There was a basic wooden table with two chairs and against the other wall sat an old-fashioned chifforobe that looked like it had seen some years. Judging by the closed doors at the other end of the house, she suspected there was a bedroom and bathroom. She frowned, thinking he must have a septic tank system and a generator, too. Xuan might live like a hermit, but he'd embraced the conveniences of modern technology.

Lana sat on the couch, leaving room for Vincent on the side closest to the lone chair where presumably Xuan would sit. "You must have a generator," she commented to Xuan as he handed her a cup of coffee in a thick ceramic mug.

Xuan nodded. "I need the refrigerator for blood, of course. I'm alone most of the time and books are my only company. I don't need much light, especially since I bought an e-reader on one of my trips into the city for generator fuel. Whenever I go down for fuel now, I fill up my reader. It's a wonderful invention."

"I agree," Lana said, giving the old vamp a genuine smile. He seemed like a nice guy, gentle and . . . a little lonely. She almost felt sorry for him. Almost. Life and the business she was in had made her cynical enough to consider the possibility that it was all a ploy.

"You don't look the way he described you," she said thoughtfully.

"Someone described me?"

Vincent had been prowling the room, but now he joined Lana on the couch, slinging an arm behind her in a blatantly possessive move. Lana wanted to roll her eyes, but she managed not to.

"More than one, actually," Vincent picked up the conversation. "They said you were a demon, that you had white hair, a white face, and your eyes were red."

Xuan laughed gently. "Well. My eyes are still red, but that's not unusual among vampires, as you well know. The white . . . when I first came to Pénjamo, I lived much closer to town. I wanted to be left alone, but the peasants were curious. Fortunately, they were also primitive. I covered myself and my clothes in white wash and wandered the El Cero San Miguel for a few nights. With my eyes going vamp red, I'm sure it was quite frightening. The locals already believed the hill was haunted. I simply added to the legend. They left me alone after that. Eventually, I moved out here and everyone forgot me." He glanced up at Vincent. "Or nearly everyone. Raphael has a long memory."

Vincent was silent for a moment, then abruptly said, "Enough. Open the envelope."

Xuan settled himself in the chair. He had the envelope in one hand and a cup of coffee in the other. Placing the cup on a side table, he held the envelope in both hands, then turned it over and slid a finger under the sealed flap. It opened easily. He reached in and removed Raphael's note.

Lana wanted to snatch it out of his fingers and read it. Raphael had wanted Vincent here. Why? The answer was in that note.

She leaned forward impatiently, silently urging Xuan to go faster. Vincent's arm slid lower on her back and tightened, as if he was worried she was going to leap on the other vampire and rip the note out of his hands. She could feel the tension in Vincent's arm and knew he was as anxious as she was.

Xuan's mouth tightened briefly as he read, then he looked up and met Vincent's gaze, his own eyes bright with tears.

What the hell was that about?

Xuan handed the note to Lana. She resisted the urge to grab it, taking it slowly from his hand, then turning so that Vincent could read with her.

It was one line, written in the same script as Xuan's name on the envelope. And it said . . .

It's time to tell the story.

Chapter Twenty

Texas, 1876

XUAN IGNACIO STOOD in the darkness, shielding his eyes against the bright flames of the campfire. It was a big fire, much bigger than the two young men needed. Surrounded by the pitch black of a desert night, it probably made them feel safe. Unfortunately, it did the opposite.

"The fools might as well paint targets on their backs," Enrique commented disdainfully. But then, Enrique didn't understand that the fire brought the young humans comfort as well as light. Enrique had embraced his new vampire existence without a backward look, shedding his humanity like an unwanted shirt.

"We could take them now," Xuan said. "They don't need to go through the rest of it." He wasn't happy with Enrique's plan, he never had been. But Enrique was powerful, a vampire destined to lead others while Xuan . . . Xuan mostly wanted to be left alone. But Enrique wouldn't let him. He'd grown weary of wandering the countryside and terrorizing peasants. He wanted to carve out a territory of his own and settle down. He needed soldiers to do that, so he'd set the two of them on a campaign to create loyal followers. It was simple, really. They'd located a pack of thieves and murderers and then followed them around, "saving" their victims from certain death.

But not until they were on the very precipice of that death first.

The first angry shouts broke the deceptive serenity of the night as the outlaws attacked the two young men, firing wildly, their shots missing more than they hit. The two travelers reached for their own weapons, but far too slowly. They'd been foolish, naïve, to think that there were no dangers in the darkness. Foolish not to recognize that their fine horses and gear would attract the worst of those who roamed the desert looking to rob the unwary.

The taller human reached his revolver first and managed to get off a few good shots, killing one of the thieves and mildly wounding another. But it wasn't nearly enough. It was only minutes before both young men were on the ground, mortally wounded, their lives bleeding into the dirt. The thieves kicked their limp bodies aside and took what they wanted. They didn't bother to kill the young men, assuming the desert would do that for them. And they certainly had no interest in easing their suffering.

Xuan glanced over and caught the gleam of Enrique's grin in the moonlight, his fangs fully distended as he watched the mayhem.

"I'll take the farther one," Enrique told him. "The other's yours."

Xuan concealed his surprise. Enrique rarely asked Xuan to sire any of the new vampires. He wanted their loyalty to be uncompromising and only to him. But Xuan didn't argue. He never argued. He didn't have the strength to refuse Enrique whatever he wanted. It had always been that way, even though Xuan was much older than Enrique. They were children of the same Sire, a vampire who had no interest in building an empire or even a small kingdom. There was no rhyme or reason to the humans he chose, and he didn't care what happened once they were turned. When Enrique had come across Xuan Ignacio in his wanderings, he'd latched on, telling Xuan they had a better chance of surviving together than they did alone. The truth was that Enrique didn't like to be alone. He'd always needed an audience, and now he'd decided he needed an army. Xuan had gone along, because that's what he did.

Until now.

Xuan had decided he was almost done with Enrique's plan. Enrique now had plenty of vampires to help build and defend his territory. He no longer needed Xuan. And Xuan had no stomach for the bloodshed that Enrique seemed to revel in.

Turning his attention back to their current hunt, Xuan followed Enrique to the campsite and knelt next to the half-dead human Enrique had chosen for him. The young man was mortally wounded. Xuan took some consolation in that. Without his intervention, the human would surely die this night.

He bent his head to the dying man's neck and drank deeply. The human's blood was thick and rich. He was, or had been, strong and healthy, his obvious wealth granting him a life of ease and good nutrition. And Xuan relished the taste of his blood, relished the knowledge that he could drink his fill. What vampire wouldn't take pleasure in drinking so deeply? More often than not, he was forced to school himself to moderation, whether by Enrique's dictate or simple survival. He and Enrique both usually took only what they needed to live, leaving their victims alive so as to avoid drawing attention to themselves.

But not anymore. Enrique meant to rule, and moderation was a thing of the past.

When the human was on the very edge of death, when his brown skin was pale and his heart beat so weakly that even a vampire's enhanced hearing could barely hear it, Xuan sliced open his own wrist and held it above the young man's mouth, letting the first drops slide onto the human's tongue and down his throat. And then he waited.

He'd seen Enrique do this enough times. He knew it wouldn't take long. It never did. And sure enough, the human suddenly swallowed, his tongue working at the unexpected sustenance of Xuan's blood. A moment later, the man's chest swelled with the first full breath he'd drawn since Xuan had started, and then a second breath as his heart gained strength, as it began pounding in his chest like a drum.

Wincing in anticipation, Xuan lowered his wrist to the man's mouth, closing his eyes against the mingled pain and pleasure as the human closed his lips over Xuan's ravaged wrist, as his still-blunt teeth tore into Xuan's flesh, digging in to hold him in place as the human drank . . . and drank.

Xuan swayed in a sort of euphoria. He'd never felt this way before, almost as if his own power had been doubled by the taste of the human's blood. He almost asked Enrique about it, but something made him remain silent. He'd never noticed Enrique reacting this way to the creation of a new vampire, and he didn't know what it meant. Perhaps it was just him, a weakness that made him vulnerable. And it was always better not to reveal any frailty when Enrique was involved.

"It's nearly dawn."

Xuan's eyes flashed open at the sound of Enrique's harsh voice. He gently disengaged the human's teeth from his wrist, brushing dark hair away from the young man's forehead. He was handsome; both of the brothers were. But it was more than that. There was a hint in their features of the old race, the Mayans, descendants of the same empire that had birthed him and his forefathers as far back as he could count.

Xuan would have liked to keep this one for himself, to be his younger brother, the one he never had. But Enrique would never permit it. He swallowed a sigh and said, "Mine's ready to travel."

"Yours?" Enrique scoffed. "There is no yours. They're both mine. Now, come on, help me get them into the cave."

They carried the two new vampires into the cooler darkness of a nearby cave. It was the reason they'd chosen this particular location, that particular band of thieves. The exchange of blood was exhausting not only for the new vampires, but for the old as well.

They made it back to the safety of the cave before dawn and with time to spare. The two humans were big men, but Xuan and Enrique had the strength of their Vampire blood to help them. Xuan made the two brothers as comfortable as possible under the primitive conditions, then settled into his own bedroll. Tomorrow night would be a new challenge. Introducing two young vampires to their new lives and their new lord.

XUAN WOKE THE next night to the hated sound of Enrique's voice. This would be their last night together. He'd fulfilled whatever obligation he had toward the other vampire, but more importantly, he had no desire to be a foot soldier under Enrique's rule. He knew the kind of lord Enrique would be. He sometimes felt guilty over his role in creating an army to make it possible.

"They're not doing well," Enrique informed him, with the strained patience of someone who'd had to repeat himself. "It's cold in here. Help me get them back to the fire."

Xuan hefted the nearest vamp onto his shoulder and trudged back to the campsite. Without warning, the fire flared, courtesy of Enrique's power. Xuan was used to it by now and didn't react other than to lay his burden down close to the warmth, taking a moment to straighten the new vampire's limbs, making him more comfortable.

Enrique laid his burden down also, but instead of making the unconscious vampire comfortable, he pulled a knife and nicked the newly-turned vampire's neck, sliding a finger through the trickle of blood it produced. He brought the finger to his mouth and sucked, tasting.

"Weak," he pronounced. "And we can't stay here another night."

Without warning, he slashed out with his knife, slicing the big artery in the vampire's throat. Then switching the grip on his knife, he stabbed him in the heart as blood spurted from his neck in a gruesome fountain of red.

Xuan stared, not quite believing what he was seeing. This was a new level of brutality, even for Enrique. The young vampire needed only another's night's rest to thrive. They could have given him that. But it hadn't been the boy's slow recovery that influenced Enrique's decision, it was the strength of his blood. Enrique wanted strong warriors, and this young vampire had apparently not suited.

Xuan placed a protective hand on the chest of the vampire at his side, even knowing that he couldn't win against Enrique.

"This one's strong. He'll wake soon."

"He's mine," Enrique reminded him.

"Of course," Xuan agreed. "They're all yours. I'll go get our things from the cave."

Enrique didn't say anything. Instead, he simply hunkered down next to the sleeping vampire and waited for him to wake to the first night of his new life. The younger the vampire, the later he woke after sunset, but it wouldn't be long now. And Enrique liked to be sure his was the first face the youngsters saw upon waking.

Xuan stood and stared at the avarice in Enrique's expression as he studied his newest soldier and, next to him, the greasy pile of dust that only yesterday had been a healthy young human.

At that moment, Xuan made a decision. He walked back to the cave and gathered their gear, packing what he could into their saddlebags. And then, taking his own small pack in hand, he left the safety of the cave and the dubious companionship of Enrique, and he walked into the night.

Pénjamo, Guanahuato, Mexico, present day

XUAN FINISHED speaking, but still sat there, staring into the flames as he had during the telling of his tale. Lana started to ask a question, but Vincent spoke first.

"How do you know Raphael?" he asked. It was a natural enough question, but there was nothing natural about the way he asked it. Vincent's voice was low and raw, each word precisely bitten off, as if he was suppressing some violent emotion. Even more telling were his eyes, which had taken on a copper glow that put the flames in the small fireplace to shame.

Lana studied him in concern, but he wasn't looking at her. Vincent's attention was fixed on Xuan, but Xuan wasn't looking back. He was studying the fire intently, as if it held the secrets of the fucking universe.

"I met Raphael not long after I left Enrique, here in Mexico," Xuan said finally, still refusing to look at Vincent. "Raphael never said why he was here, but looking back, I think he was trying to decide how far south he wanted to expand his territory. Enrique likes to pretend that Mexico has always been his, but it's only his because Raphael didn't want it."

"Get to the point," Vincent growled.

Lana turned her head sharply to stare at him. She'd been right. He was furious. Of course, he had a right to be, since he'd just discovered Enrique had been lying to him all this time about how his brother had died, and who had killed him. But there was more to it than that. Some deeper dimension to what Xuan had revealed, something she didn't understand, maybe something she *couldn't* understand. Something tied up with being a vampire.

But she understood this much. The key to it all was Raphael's insistence that Vincent confront Xuan directly. Why would he do that? Why send them all the way down here just so Xuan could tell Vincent that it was Enrique who'd killed his brother? Why not simply tell Vincent that himself? A five-minute phone call would have done it. There was something more, some reason why Raphael wanted Vincent to meet Xuan Ignacio in person, something that was pushing Vincent right to the edge of violence.

"Raphael asked me about Enrique," Xuan continued. "He was trying to understand what kind of man Enrique was, what kind of lord he'd be. So, I told Raphael that story, and I told him about you."

Xuan risked a short glance in Vincent's direction, but whatever he saw there didn't encourage his gaze to linger. He quickly lowered his eyes again. "Raphael could have killed me then. He was certainly angry enough to do it after hearing what we'd done, because I was as guilty as Enrique. But he agreed to let me live on one condition—that if you ever showed up at my door, I would tell you the truth."

Vincent jolted to his feet, fairly vibrating with anger. He stretched out his hand in Lana's direction but he never took his eyes off Xuan Ignacio, as if he didn't trust him.

Lana stood and slipped her fingers into Vincent's. His grip tightened immediately, and he tugged her away from Xuan, putting himself between them.

"You have five days," Vincent snarled, "to get out of Mexico. I don't care where you go. But if you're still here after five days, I'll kill you."

Finally, Xuan looked up. "Do you think you can take him?" he asked, his gaze suddenly sharp and penetrating.

Vincent's reaction was immediate . . . and terrifying. He seemed to swell with rage, to grow even taller than he was, muscles straining beneath his T-shirt and at the seams of his black denims. Energy abruptly filled the small house, making the wooden beams creak overhead, sending the few pieces of furniture skating for the walls, dousing the candles and setting the flames in the fireplace to dancing wildly.

"*¿Dudas de mi, viejo?*" he growled, his voice deep and threatening, the words spoken in a Spanish so guttural that she could barely make out their meaning. *Do you doubt me, old man?*

Xuan had shrunk lower by the second until Lana almost felt sorry for him, cowering on the floor as if certain that terrible death was imminent.

"*No,*" he whispered. "*No, yo le creo.*" *No. No, I believe you.*

"*Cinco días,*" Vincent repeated, as the overwhelming sense of danger abruptly drained from the room. "*¿Comprendes?*" *Five days. Do you understand?*

Xuan nodded without looking up. "*Comprendo.*" *I understand.*

Vincent spun around and, shoving Lana ahead of him, strode out of the small house, not speaking again until they were in the SUV.

"Put on your seatbelt," he ordered as he slammed the SUV into gear and did a spinning 180° turn, spewing dirt and dust as he sped out of the yard and back onto the narrow road.

"Tell me what just happened," she said, clicking the belt into place.

Vincent's jaw was clenched so tightly that she could see the muscles bunching even with only the dash lights to see by.

"Vincent, if you don't tell me what's going on, I'm going to jump out of this vehicle and go back and have Xuan tell me."

He shot her an angry glare. "Even you aren't stupid enough to jump from a moving vehicle."

She figured he was furious enough to say stupid things himself, so she ignored *his* stupid comment . . . for now. Instead, she said sweetly, "The vehicle won't be moving when you make the turn around that big organ cactus."

"Don't push me on this, Lana," he said in a hard voice.

"Don't shut me out, Vincent," she retorted just as hard.

He slammed his hand against the steering wheel with such force that she heard it groan.

"Enrique murdered my brother," he spat.

"I got that. Now, tell me the rest."

"That's not enough for you?"

Lana didn't fall for it. He was trying to shame her into letting it drop, but she wasn't going to do that. She was part of this pilgrimage, too, and she needed to know the whole story.

"Tell me the rest, Vincent."

His jaw clenched again and she thought he wasn't going to answer. But then he said, "He was careful in how he told the story."

She frowned. What the fuck did that mean? "You mean Xuan Ignacio."

"Yes."

"And …?"

He took so long in responding that she thought they'd have to do the whole song and dance all over again. But then he took her hand, threading their fingers together and resting their joined hands on his thigh, his thumb stroking back and forth as if he needed comfort.

"Vincent?" she said, growing alarmed. Was it really that awful?

"Xuan was careful in how he told the story," Vincent said again, "because Enrique isn't my Sire. Xuan Ignacio is."

Chapter Twenty-One

LANA BLINKED IN surprise. That was it? That was the big secret? Clearly, she was missing something.

"How do you know Xuan's your Sire instead of Enrique?" she asked, trying to figure out why it was such a big deal.

Vincent scoffed. "Because I heard what Xuan said, how he described that night. And I was there, damn it! But mostly because . . . the moment we drove into that yard, the moment I saw Xuan . . . I felt something, and I *knew*."

"But you didn't get angry until—"

"Until I found out they'd murdered my brother because he was *inconvenient!*" Vincent interrupted. "Instead of giving him one more night to recover, they killed him. *They* did that. Not the bandits, but Enrique and Xuan, my *Sire*."

He said the word *sire* like it was something dirty, something disgusting.

"But why does it matter who your Sire is?" she asked carefully.

"Why does it matter?" he repeated, turning to stare at her in disbelief.

"I'm not a vampire, Vincent," she reminded him sharply.

He let out a long breath. "The one connection that is sacrosanct in vampire society is the relationship with your Sire. No matter what else happens in your life as a vampire, that connection is always there." He snorted a harsh laugh. "Why do you think Raphael sent us after Xuan? Manipulative bastard. He knew that if I found out what really happened, that Xuan was my Sire and that Enrique murdered my brother . . . Raphael knew I'd kill Enrique. And Raphael wants Enrique dead."

"So, it's not about Xuan being your Sire. It's about who killed your brother."

Vincent seemed to deflate suddenly, all of his anger disappearing in an instant. "The betrayal . . . it's both. That Xuan walked away, that Enrique . . . I've been a loyal lieutenant for more than a century to the vampire who murdered my brother."

Lana squeezed his hand. "But you've always hated him. Even when you were loyal. Maybe a part of you knew without really knowing."

Vincent smiled bitterly. "Every powerful vampire reaches a point when he no longer *needs* his Sire to survive, when his own power is enough to sustain him. But even then, the ties of affection can remain, making the idea of killing the one vampire who gave you this life unthinkable. I say this only because I've seen it in others. For my part, I always knew I'd challenge Enrique someday, and it never bothered me to know that I'd gain power literally over his dead body.

"But now that I know the truth, now that I know what he did, his death will taste even sweeter. I'll rip his beating heart from his chest and watch his life fade into dust. And then I'll seize his territory and everyone in it. Everything he ever cared about, everyone he ever loved—if a black heart such as his is capable of such a thing—will be mine."

Lana's eyes went wide, her lips flattening into a narrow line. "Okaaay," she said eventually, figuring it was best not to challenge Vincent when he was plotting mayhem.

Vincent squeezed her hand, as if trying to reassure her that *her* heart was safe from the whole 'getting ripped out of the chest' treatment.

"Can I ask you a question?" she asked carefully.

He gave her an almost amused glance. "Of course."

"Why are you driving like the hounds of hell are on our heels?"

He gave a bark of laughter that had no joy in it. "Because if I had to spend one more minute in that bastard's presence, I'd have ripped him to bloody pieces. And I didn't think you'd understand."

Lana's chest filled with warmth. That was almost sweet. And then she choked at the thought. It was *sweet* that her vampire lover didn't want to rip a person to bloody shreds in her presence? Clearly, she'd fallen down the rabbit hole without noticing.

She drew a deep breath through her nose. "Well. Good. So, are we driving to Mexico City, then?"

Vincent almost smiled as he squeezed her hand tightly. "Michael will bring the plane and we'll fly. But not tonight, *querida*. Tonight, we're going to find a hotel, and I'm going to show you what it means to have a vampire lord in your bed."

FIGURING THERE WAS at least a small chance that Xuan Ignacio would ring up his old buddy Enrique and fill him in on current events, Vincent decided he and Lana had to get as far away from Pénjamo as they could before sunrise. They ended up in Guadalajara, which was only a hundred miles, but it was big enough, with over one million residents, to afford them some anonymity, not to mention lots of hotels and a major airport.

Vincent selected a hotel at random—not his usual *modus operandi*, but probably safer under the circumstances. Anyone who knew him well—and Enrique did—would know his preference for high-end lodging, which meant staying in a cookie-cutter businessman's hotel near the airport was probably the most secure place for tonight.

The check-in went smoothly. They used Lana's ID and credit card to at least slow Enrique down if he came looking, and they were the only ones riding up in the elevator. Most of the lobby traffic consisted of businessmen going in the other direction, off to catch an early morning flight. Neither of them spoke in the elevator or on the long walk down the bland hallway to their room. Lana inserted the key card, but Vincent pushed in ahead of her, ignoring her exasperated sigh. She was going to have to get used to his protective nature, because there was nothing he could do about it. Well, he supposed he could have changed if he'd wanted to, but he really didn't want to.

He grinned as Lana came in behind him and threw her bag on the bed. At least he'd let her carry her own duffel. That was enlightened of him, wasn't it?

"What are you grinning at?" she grumbled.

He dropped his own duffel to the floor and grabbed her. "You," he told her. "You make me smile."

"Right," she dismissed, pushing away from him. "I need a shower before it's too late. You up for that?"

Vincent quirked an eyebrow at her words, and Lana tsked at the obvious path his thoughts had taken, but she didn't manage to hold on to her stern expression for long. She was already smiling when she dropped to the bed and started unlacing her boots.

"Big plans, vampire?" she teased, pulling off first one boot, then the other.

Vincent tugged his T-shirt off over his head and sat down to work on his own boots. "Big vampire, *querida*," he riposted.

Lana's only response was to stand and remove her T-shirt and pants, leaving her in nothing but her bra and panties, both of which were simple, black cotton, not lacy, not sheer. Not particularly sexy. But then she stripped them away and, with a coy look over her shoulder, headed for the shower, her naked ass swaying as she pulled the tie off the end of her braid and threaded her fingers through her long hair until it fell like black silk over her bare back.

"Son of a bitch," Vincent muttered. He made fast work of the rest of his clothes, catching Lana as she pulled back the shower curtain and stepped into the tub. He *hated* tub showers. There was never enough room for a proper shower. But tonight, he especially hated it, because there wasn't enough room to fuck Lana the way he wanted to.

"I hate these showers," he said as he pushed in behind her, leaving the shower curtain half open, not caring about the water splashing onto the floor.

"You're spoiled," she said, reaching for the tiny, paper-wrapped bar of soap.

Vincent took it from her and ripped off the paper. "I hate bar soap, too."

Lana laughed. "You're awfully grumpy. You want me to step outside so you can be alone?"

Vincent grabbed her around the waist. "Not if you value your life."

She turned in his embrace, her naked breasts pressed against his chest, her head tilted back to look up at him. "You'd never hurt me."

Vincent lowered his head until their lips were almost touching. "You're right. But that doesn't mean you can get away with anything you want. I have my ways, you know."

"Do you?" She stretched up on her toes, closing the small distance between them as her arms twined around his neck and her mouth touched his. She kissed him tentatively at first, her lips opening slowly, her tongue gliding along the crease between his lips, asking for entry. Vincent slid his hand lower on her back, holding her in place, while his other hand twisted in her long hair, tugging her head back as he took control of the kiss, feeling the heat of her mouth, the delicate dance of her tongue as she explored his gums . . . her gasp of surprise when his fangs responded so quickly that he nicked her tongue, filling their joined mouths with blood.

Vincent swallowed, closing his eyes against the jolt of lust. His cock, already aroused by her naked body, grew even harder at the taste of her blood, pressing against her belly, her skin satiny wet and slick, just like her sex would be.

He growled and lowered his hand to cup her ass, lifting her higher. Lana's arms tightened around his neck as she curled her leg around his thigh, trying to fit her pussy to his cock. She made a small frustrated noise, no more than a needy little moan, but it sent him over the edge. Spinning her around, he grabbed the soap and lathered it between his hands as he reached around to caress her breasts, pinching her nipples into hardness until she laid her head back against his shoulder with a pleasured sigh, covering his hands with hers as he stroked down over her belly, as his fingers dipped between her thighs.

She gasped as his fingers slipped deeper, as he began pumping her with long, slow thrusts, while his thumb toyed with her clit, rubbing circles around it, grazing over the tight bundle of nerves without quite touching it. Lana wiggled against him, trying to maneuver his hand where she wanted it, to force his teasing fingers into giving her what she needed. But he held her in place, his other hand still cupping her breast, pinching one nipple, then the other, his mouth at her neck, kissing and sucking, tasting the damp saltiness of her skin, reveling in the scent of her blood so close.

Lana slid her hand between their bodies and wrapped her fingers around his cock where it was nestled against the firm cheeks of her pretty butt. She stroked him once, twice, then released him, only to reach back and grab his ass, holding on as she rubbed herself against him, squeezing his cock against the tempting curve of her backside. Too tempting.

Vincent cupped her breast a final time, pinching her nipple until it was bright pink and swollen, and then he slid his soap-covered hand between their bodies, stroking down into the cleft of her ass, finding her opening and dipping inside. It was as slick as her pussy. And then, as Lana's nails dug into his thighs, as her cries filled his ears and her pussy squeezed his fingers, as she came so hard that she bucked in his grip, he slid his cock into the hot, tight channel of her ass with a groan of pleasure. This was perfection, her pussy pulsing around his fingers, his cock buried in the velvet heat of her ass, her helpless cries in his ears as multiple orgasms rocketed through her body.

Vincent forced himself to move, to pull his cock out of the warm caress of her body, but only long enough to plunge it back in as he began fucking her pussy with his fingers, sliding his cock in and out of her ass . . . and piercing her vein with his fangs as he bit into her neck, drawing on the rich fullness of her blood.

Lana screamed, her already-overwhelmed senses shaken anew by the euphoric in his bite. She convulsed in his arms, every muscle in her body tightening, squeezing down on his fingers, his cock, even his fangs as she snaked an arm around his neck and cupped the back of his head, holding him inside her.

Vincent groaned deep in his chest, the searing heat of his own orgasm building hotter and hotter, until it poured forth, filling Lana with his fiery release, contracting his own muscles until he thought he, too, would scream with the delicious pain of it. Until finally, he lifted his head, Lana's blood dripping from his fangs, and her name on his lips.

LANA MADE SURE the *No Molestar* sign was out, then she closed the door and checked the locks, settling the swing bar securely into place. She was both more tired and more relaxed than she could ever remember feeling. Multiple orgasms would apparently do that to a person, which was something she hadn't known before meeting Vincent. She didn't know if his incredible sexual prowess was a vampire thing or a Vincent thing, and she didn't care. She only knew what she felt when he made love to her, and pretty much all the rest of the time, too.

Vincent was on the phone when she walked over to the bed, his dark eyes lifting to meet hers. He was talking to Michael, but he pulled the covers back and patted the mattress next to him in invitation. Was there a woman alive who could resist that? Lana smiled at the exaggerated look of seduction he was giving her. Because, really, a naked Vincent was all the temptation she needed.

Before joining him, she checked the load on her Sig and left it within easy reach on the side table. Vincent didn't think Enrique knew where they were, not yet anyway, but she wasn't taking any chances. If someone came through that door, she was going to assume they were up to no good and react accordingly.

Just for good measure, she tucked a knife under her pillow before sliding beneath the cool sheets.

Vincent disconnected and tossed the cell phone on his side table. He pulled her into the curve of his hard, muscular, and unbelievably gorgeous body.

"Michael says hi."

"What else does he say?" she asked, turning to face him and rubbing an appreciative hand over the firm planes of his chest.

"He'll get the plane in the air as soon as he can after sunset tomorrow. Jerry and the others asked to come with him. They want revenge."

Lana frowned. "Carolyn, too? Is that wise?"

Vincent shrugged. "She has the right to be in on the kill. I left it up to Mikey, but he tells me she can handle it."

"You say they want revenge, but you need to be the one who kills Enrique in order to take over his territory, right?"

"That's right. But I'll need people at my back, vampires I can trust and draw on for strength if I need it. I know I can take Enrique, but I don't fool myself by thinking it will be easy. He's powerful and he's ruthless. And he also knows I'm coming. He'll be ready for me."

Lana frowned. "This is dangerous," she said slowly. Her eyes widened and she stared at him in stunned realization. "He could kill you!"

Vincent hugged her tightly, wrapping both arms around her. "I won't die, *querida*. I'm stronger than Enrique."

"But you said he'll be ready, and he won't play fair. How do you know—?"

"Lana." He claimed her mouth in a slow, luscious kiss that left her nerves tingling all the way down to her toes. "I'm not going to lose," he whispered against her lips. "I know Enrique. And I know his tricks. I can do this."

Lana nodded wordlessly, but she was more terrified than she'd ever been. She'd faced down desperate fugitives and murderous drug dealers, but nothing had ever scared her as much as the idea of Vincent confronting Enrique. What if he died? What would she do then?

She closed her eyes against the awful image of Vincent's bloody body lying on the floor while his killer crowed in victory. She pushed that image as deep into her mind as it could go, not wanting Vincent to catch even a hint of it. The last thing he needed going into the fight of his life was her fears for him.

"So, Mexico City tomorrow night then?" she asked, even though she already knew the answer.

"Mexico City," he confirmed. Then he put a finger under her chin, forcing her to look at him. "I don't suppose I could convince you to go somewhere safe, somewhere—"

"Not a chance," she interrupted.

Vincent sighed. "This isn't a game, Lana," he said, more serious than she'd ever seen him.

"I'm aware of—"

"I know you're smart and capable, and I've seen your courage, but this . . . this will be like nothing you've ever witnessed. Enrique will do anything, *anything*, to win this. You saw what he did to Carolyn. He'll do even worse to you, because you're human; you'll mean nothing to him. But you matter to me, and he'll use you if he can."

"Are you trying to scare me? You think I'll run home if—"

"You *should* be scared. But the only thing I care about is that you live. If I thought you'd run home, I'd do whatever it took to make that happen. But I know you won't go."

"Damn straight."

Vincent gave her a crooked smile. "Why not?"

Lana turned away, making a show of plumping her pillow, shoving it behind her as she sat up. "Because I care about you," she said, intentionally not looking at him, not wanting him to see the truth in her eyes.

"You care about me."

She swallowed and nodded. "We're partners. We've been in this together from the beginning. I need to see it through."

"Partners."

Why did he keep repeating everything she said?

Vincent tilted his head, studying her. "Is that what you—?"

Lana pushed the covers down, suddenly hot all over. She needed him to stop talking. "What time is it?"

She went to roll out of the bed, but Vincent snagged her with an arm around her waist, pulling her back and sliding a knee between her thighs where Lana knew he'd find her wet and ready all over again.

"The time is too late," he murmured, nuzzling her neck. "But feel free to use my body for your pleasure after I'm asleep, *partner*."

Lana slapped his chest. "I can't believe you said that. I would never—"

Vincent hummed wordlessly, and she could feel his lips smiling against her skin.

He lifted his head. "Kiss me, *querida*. It's almost time."

Lana gave in to what she wanted, stretching up to touch her mouth to his, feeling the soft brush of his beard on her skin. "Sweet dreams," she whispered.

"Will you be in them?" he mumbled, and then like a child sliding into his favorite position, Vincent rolled over onto his belly and was gone.

Lana stroked her fingers gently over the smooth expanse of his back, and then over to his arm where she outlined the Mayan god of his tattoo. Placing her lips on the sun god's smiling face, she offered a silent prayer to the ancient deity, asking him to protect the child of his worshippers, hoping as she did that the fickle god was listening.

Chapter Twenty-Two

MICHAEL WAS WAITING when Lana and Vincent arrived at Guadalajara's international airport the next day. Vincent steered the somewhat scratched and battered SUV into the private hangar, then waited until the big doors had closed behind him before stepping out to greet his lieutenant.

Lana stood on the running board, watching over the top of the SUV as the two men, two vampires, embraced. Vincent had told her the link between a vampire and his Sire was the closest bond two vamps could have. She hadn't known what that meant until this moment, when she saw Michael's reaction to Vincent, the instant comprehension on his face of what Vincent had been through, all of the emotional turmoil and the anger. There was genuine love between them, something she knew Vincent would never experience with his own Sire. Certainly not from Enrique who had usurped Xuan's rightful place, and not from Xuan Ignacio either. He'd abdicated that role without a care for what it would mean to Vincent.

Vincent and Michael broke apart, thumping each other's backs hard enough to break bone in a human, as the rest of the team gradually appeared from behind the private jet. Jerry and Salvio were there, along with Zárate and Ortega who'd been with them when they'd rescued Carolyn. Her heart constricted with unaccustomed tenderness when she saw that the two big, vamp fighters had Carolyn between them. They weren't being obvious about it, but it was plain, to her anyway, that they were keeping an eagle eye out for anyone who might mean Carolyn harm.

Lana considered her sudden and irritating tendency toward squishy emotion. If this was what falling in love did to a person, it was no surprise she'd never done it before.

Even as she had that thought, Vincent smiled at her over his shoulder and she couldn't stop herself from smiling back. More squishy emotion. He held out a hand in her direction, and she forced herself to stroll over to him slowly.

"Lana," Michael said, greeting her. "My Sire tells me you're joining us in Mexico City. What's your weapon status? Do you need ammo, any additional guns? I understand you like knives?"

Lana blinked in surprise. She'd half-expected Vincent's lieutenant to try to talk him out of letting her come along, maybe even try to dissuade her directly.

"I'm good on weapons," she told him slowly. "But I could use some 9mm ammo, whatever has the most stopping power. Vampires are a little harder to kill."

Michael nodded. "You'll have to talk to Cynthia Leighton when this is over, or maybe Lucas's mate, what's her name?" he asked, directing the comment at Vincent before supplying his own answer. "Kathryn Hunter. I always thought that was a particularly suitable name for an FBI agent," he added with a smile.

"Or a vampire lord's mate," Vincent agreed, grinning.

Michael nodded amiably, then turned back to Lana and the topic at hand. "Unfortunately, we don't have either of those experts here tonight, so for now—"

"For now, we'll try to avoid gunfights," Vincent interjected. "My challenge is for Enrique, no one else."

"But you know he's not sitting around, waiting politely for you to show up. He'll try to stop you before you get there," Michael commented.

"That's why we're going to move fast. We'll fly to Mexico City tonight, set up in the condo, and talk to friends. Tomorrow night, we go directly to Enrique's HQ. Once I'm in the villa, he'll be hard-pressed to do anything but accept the challenge. If he sets his guards on me then, it will make him look weak. He can't afford that."

Michael didn't look happy, but he nodded. "I hate this, but you're right."

"Have faith, Mikey," Vincent said, grabbing the younger vamp's shoulder. "I can take him."

"I know. And you know I'll be at your back when you do."

Michael shifted his gaze to something over Vincent's shoulder just as a deep voice said, "We would also like to be there for you, my lord."

Lana turned with Vincent and saw Ortega and Zárate going down on their knees. "We would swear our fealty if you'll have us," Ortega said.

Vincent's hand tightened briefly around Lana's hip before he released her to shrug off his jacket and toss it onto the hood of the SUV. Rolling up the sleeve on his T-shirt, he went to lift his wrist to his fangs, but Lana got there first, handing him the wickedly sharp Spyderco knife from her pocket.

Vincent's dark eyes warmed with emotion. "Thank you, *querida.*"

"Hey, *mi navaja es su navaja.*" My knife is your knife.

Vincent flashed her a quick grin before his expression shifted and he regarded the two vampires kneeling before him.

"Richard Ortega," he said, addressing the vampire who'd spoken, "Do you come to me of your own free will and desire?"

Ortega met Vincent's gaze directly and said, "I do, my lord."

"And is this what you truly desire?" Vincent asked solemnly.

"It is my truest desire," Ortega responded, his eyes still locked with Vincent's.

Vincent nodded, then popped Lana's black, steel blade open and cut his arm vertically from wrist to forearm. Blood welled immediately, dripping down his arm and coating his hand and fingers.

"Then drink, Richard Ortega, and be mine," he said and held his wrist out to Ortega, whose eyes closed in something close to ecstasy as he inhaled the coppery fragrance of Vincent's blood. He seemed to hold his breath for a moment, as if trapping the scent within his sinuses, savoring the rich aroma. Then his eyes flashed open, gleaming redly in the dim light, and he put his mouth to Vincent's wrist and drank.

Lana had seen the process before, with Jerry and the others, but that had been different somehow. It had been in the midst of a crisis, a battlefield commitment rather than this slow, ritualized ceremony. Even having seen it before, she'd had to bite down on her reaction to Vincent slicing up his own arm that way. Especially when the blood started to flow. She knew how sharp her knife was, how deep it would have cut. But Vincent hadn't even winced. Another vampire thing, she guessed. Never show pain. Or maybe he'd simply done it so often that the nerves were destroyed. She made a note to ask him later, when the troops weren't around to hear his answer. There were appearances to be maintained, after all.

She stood by patiently while Ortega finished drinking, and then while Vincent went through the same ritual with Zárate. After that, things moved along swiftly. The SUV was emptied out—Vincent assured her someone would be back for the vehicle later—and everyone piled onto the jet.

The flight to Mexico City was short, just over an hour. Vincent and Michael spent much of that time discussing logistics. Vincent already had allies in Mexico City, vampires who were prepared to swear to him as soon as he landed. Apparently, the more vamps Vincent had behind him when he confronted Enrique, the stronger he'd be, since he could draw power from his supporters as he fought. Some sort of metaphysical vampire magic. Ugh. She groaned inwardly. She didn't believe in magic, or at least she never had before she met Vincent. But she had to admit that a lot of what went on with vamps couldn't be explained any other way. At least not by her.

The minute they landed in Mexico City, Vincent's supporters made themselves known. Five long, black SUVs with the requisite tinted windows were waiting in a private hangar, with a number of vamps lined up in front of them, almost like soldiers standing at attention. And, like soldiers, they were all carrying guns—HK MP5s, with a sidearm thrown in here and there.

Those were the first vampires she'd seen carrying guns. Obviously, something had changed.

Lana disembarked with Vincent, but went to grab her duffel from the pile of luggage, while he crossed directly to his line of supporters and made a point of greeting each of them personally. Lana stood back and watched, half-expecting a mass blood ritual to cement the relationship between Vincent and this new group. She was thankful to see that wouldn't be the case. At least for now. Maybe they'd do a group bloodletting later, she thought with an inward grimace.

Despite the greeting committee, the vamps didn't linger at the airport. Vincent's pilots shut down the jet and, surprisingly, joined the rest of the vamps in piling into the SUVs and speeding off into the night. Lana felt a little like she was in a movie, with the security types all talking into what she guessed were Bluetooth devices, while she and Vincent were hustled into the middle seat of one of the SUVs. A vamp she didn't know took the wheel, and Michael sat up front in the passenger seat.

Lana didn't know Mexico City. Most of the fugitives she pursued stuck closer to the U.S. border. So she had no idea which district or suburb of the city they ended up in when the convoy finally pulled to a stop.

She peered out the window curiously while Vincent's new security people spilled out of the other vehicles and ran around checking things out. They were in front of a four-story residence complex, presumably the condo Vincent had referred to earlier. The building was on a large lot, which permitted a substantial setback from its neighbors. Gardens and trees filled the space, and a curved walkway led to a glass front door. Each of the four levels had a balcony along the side facing the street, and on every balcony were pots and flower boxes overflowing with color under discreetly-placed accent lighting. It was pretty, although it sure didn't look much like the stereotypical vampire lair. On the other hand, one could easily miss the equally discreet security cameras at every turn. Just as one could mistake for decoration the heavy metal shutters over each door and window, shutters she had no doubt descended daily at sunrise, sealing the vampires in and the humans out.

Vincent's vamps surrounded them as they exited the SUV, and Vincent held her hand as they were escorted directly into the building. She saw the entrance to an underground parking garage to one side and wondered why they hadn't entered that way—it would seem to offer more coverage, and hence more security. But then she saw a whole new greeting committee waiting for them in the lobby, and she understood. One didn't make a grand entrance via the garage door.

Once inside, Vincent was drawn away to greet his supporters, which left Lana with plenty of time to look around. She was surprised to see that the lobby looked like it belonged in an office building rather than a condo. She also noted that no one seemed to be around except vampires. Where were the other tenants? What did they think about having a vampire setting up headquarters in their building, about his security taking over the way they did?

"I own the building," Vincent said in her ear. She spun around, happier than she should have been to find him next to her. It was a little disconcerting to be the only human in the crowd. "The penthouse is mine alone," he continued, "but there are eight other units all occupied by my people." He held her arm as they entered the elevator, pulling her against his side while Michael and two other vamps she'd never met piled in after them forming a solid wall of muscle in front of the door.

"Eight units?" she repeated. "Four to a floor?"

Vincent nodded. "There aren't any units on the ground floor, but there's a pool and a complete gym, as well as the building's offices."

"Do you come here often?" she asked. She'd gotten the impression that he avoided Mexico City, and yet here was this very expensive building and a whole bunch of vampires who seemed to have been just waiting for his arrival.

"It was necessary from time to time. I have duties as Enrique's lieutenant."

"There's more to it than that, though," she commented.

Vincent hugged her close and put his lips to her ear. "There is, but not here."

Lana nodded. One didn't discuss plans for a coup while standing in the elevator, no matter who owned the building.

The penthouse floor turned out to be half residence and half strategy center. To the right, as they exited the elevator, were a couple of nice office desks, fitted with phones and computers. Beyond that was an open seating area complete with a big wall-mounted flat screen TV that was muted and tuned to—what else?—CNN. A pair of open doors off the seating area revealed a big, empty conference room, with a wooden table and leather chairs in front of a wall of windows.

Everything was supersized. Big spaces, big furniture, big screen TV. But what struck Lana more than anything else was the utter lack of noise. It was as if they'd entered an acoustic chamber where no sound penetrated from the outside, while everyone inside was afraid to disturb the silence. Except there was nobody here. She figured that would change once the gang from downstairs made their way up. But for now, it was almost eerie—an empty space waiting to be filled.

Vincent pulled her attention away from the office area, taking her hand and leading her to the left, their footsteps making no sound on the deep pile carpet as they made their way to a second set of double doors. Like those guarding the conference room, they were nearly floor to ceiling, around ten feet tall, and lacquered a uniform black with no embellishment other than the burnished steel hardware. The difference was that these doors were secured by a digital keypad which sat to the right of the doors and included a biometric lock with a scanner. Vincent entered an eight digit code, pressed his thumb on the scanner, and the doors popped open.

"We'll scan you into the system tonight," Vincent commented. "No one but the two of us and Michael will have access to this suite."

Lana nodded, secretly relieved. With the sudden appearance of so many strange vampires whose only job seemed to be keeping Vincent safe, she'd been a little concerned. She knew some people lived with a constant security presence and eventually forgot the guards were there, but she'd never wanted to be one of them. She liked her privacy too much.

Once they entered Vincent's condo, however, all worries about privacy and too many guards fled her thoughts, replaced by a single certainty . . . she didn't belong here.

The room was breathtaking—high ceilings and an entire wall of glass with a view that felt like it went on forever. She knew there were many days in Mexico City where the air quality was crap and the haze closed in, but tonight, with clear skies and the waning half-moon high in the sky, the lights of the city lit up the valley floor in a way that told her they were on a rising edge of the basin.

This was expensive real estate. Really expensive. And Vincent owned the entire damn building. Even if he hadn't been handsome and charming, he was rich enough to get any woman he wanted. So what was he doing with her? Maybe when he'd tried to persuade her to stay behind earlier, he'd actually wanted her to stay behind, rather than being concerned for her safety.

She sighed and wandered into the bedroom, which, like everything else in this penthouse, was built on a huge scale. The furnishings were dark and masculine, the wooden furniture heavy and deeply stained. The bed was enormous and clearly custom-made. Granted, Vincent was a big man. But even he didn't need all that space, unless he was hosting orgies. Which, for all she knew, was exactly what he did.

Lana pushed on into the extravagant bathroom, but instead of being soothed or even delighted by the beautiful fixtures and the shower big enough for six, everything she saw only raised the volume on the whispering voice inside her head, the one repeating over and over again that she didn't belong here.

"Lana?"

She spun around to find Vincent leaning against the doorframe, studying her with a concerned look. She wondered how long he'd been there and what he'd seen on her face in the meantime. He might not be able to read her mind, but he could read her body language well enough.

"This is lovely," she said, meaning it. She didn't tell him that she felt like a total intruder. That she was almost afraid to touch anything for fear of leaving her grubby fingerprints behind.

He glanced around as if seeing it for the first time. "It's nice. I haven't stayed here that much."

"Why have it then?"

"Because I knew this day would come, and appearances matter, especially to vampires. If I'm to unseat Enrique, I need to look like a vampire lord."

She smiled weakly. "I'd say you succeeded."

He walked over and rubbed his hands up and down her arms. "You okay? You seem—"

"Tired," she supplied, sparing him the search for a suitable adjective. "And hungry. There must be a kitchen here somewhere, yes?"

Vincent frowned, clearly not buying her excuse, but willing to let her get away with it for now. "There's a kitchen," he said, "but probably no food. Maybe some blood, since they knew I was coming, but that doesn't do you any good," he said with a forced chuckle.

Lana nodded. "That's all right. I'm sure there's a grocery store nearby. And you must have meetings to go to."

His scowl deepened, but he nodded.

"Right. So, I'll go to the store, then make myself some dinner and maybe take a swim. We can meet here later."

Vincent studied her a moment too long. "You're going to be here when I get back, right?"

Lana fought back the blush that would have given her away, because she'd actually considered going straight to the airport and catching a flight home. Mexico City had a big airport; she was sure there were plenty of flights going her way.

But just as she'd considered it, she'd rejected it. Vincent deserved better than that, because regardless of what other feelings she might harbor for him, they were partners. And partners didn't desert each other on the eve of battle.

"Of course I'll be here," she assured him, as if any other suggestion was absurd. "You think I'm going to leave without trying out that shower?"

Vincent gave her a slow smile, and he seemed to relax. But there was nothing relaxed about the hard brand of possession in his kiss, nor the deep warning in his voice when he slid his lips up to her ear and said, "I'll hold you to that, *querida.*"

Lana kissed him back, letting him think it was anticipation that caused the tremble of emotion that rippled over her frame. But it was the unmistakable threat in his words that made her shiver, that told her he'd find her no matter how far she ran.

VINCENT DIDN'T WANT to leave Lana. There was something going on in her lovely head, something he couldn't quite figure out. He would in time, but time was in short supply this evening. He had people to meet with, vampires who'd risked everything to show up here tonight. There would be no going back after this. Plotting to assassinate one's lord wasn't something a vampire did lightly, or in secret.

Enrique would know he was in town, and why. Vincent could take tonight to shore up his support, to reassure his loyal vampires that he had what it took to defeat Enrique and become the new Lord of Mexico. And even more importantly, that, as their lord, he would be a better ruler. Enrique had many allies but few friends. His centuries-long rule had been based purely on strength and the certain knowledge that disloyalty would be met with brutal death.

Vincent wasn't naïve enough to think he could rule benevolently. He was about to become a vampire lord, not a priest. Most vampires lived quiet lives and wanted only to be left alone. But those few who didn't, the ones who would form Vincent's court and warrior cadre, they needed to know that force would be met with force, disloyalty with death.

But they also needed to know that loyalty would be rewarded, and that the wealth of the territory would be shared among those who created it, not hoarded and doled out to anyone who kissed his ass, as Enrique had done.

Unfortunately, all of that had to be conveyed tonight. He wanted to stay with Lana, make love to her in that giant bed until she didn't have the strength left to even think about leaving him. But he had a duty, a responsibility to the vampires who'd already put their lives on the line simply by agreeing to meet him.

He had to put his faith in Lana's word and his feelings in the kiss that they shared, although he couldn't stop himself from whispering a warning in her delicate ear. *"I'll hold you to that, querida."*

She could run, but she couldn't hide. Not from him. She shivered and he knew she'd caught the underlying message of his words.

He strode through the living room of the suite, turning to face her when they reached the front doors. "You'll have a guard with you wherever you go."

She grimaced. "I don't need that. I don't like strangers—"

"I know, and I'm sorry. But it's necessary."

"What if I wait until daytime?" she argued. "All the bad guys will be asleep, right?"

Vincent's heart twinged at the suggestion that she wouldn't be sleeping with him, but he didn't let it show. After all, she was human and needed sunshine. He should probably get used to the idea, since that wouldn't change.

"Daytime is no guarantee of safety," he told her, sliding his hand down her arm and linking their fingers together. "Enrique has human guards, just like I do. If you'd rather, I can assign one of them to you instead of a vamp. That way, it won't matter what time it is."

Lana tilted her head back and forth unhappily, but eventually nodded her agreement. "Okay. I guess that works. When do I meet him?"

"I'll have someone sent up now. I'll wait until he gets here."

"That's not necessary. I promised you—"

"I'll wait," Vincent insisted, not quite trusting her intentions. "Besides, you need to be scanned into the security system before you leave, and you'll need the code." The buzzer on the door sounded, and he said, "That'll be Michael."

"I thought you said he had access."

"He does. But as long as we're here together, he won't use it. Come on, let's get your print in the system, so you can go shopping. You'll feel better once you've had some real food."

Lana stepped away when he opened the door, her fingers slipping away from his. Vincent told himself that she only backed off because he needed to open the door for Michael, but that didn't explain why it felt like she was pulling away a lot more than her hand.

Chapter Twenty-Three

VINCENT SHOVED open the vehicle door as soon as Ortega brought the SUV to a rolling stop in front of his building. Only one night, and he was already tired of the security protocols that surrounded his comings and goings. One of the things he'd miss after he killed Enrique and became Lord of Mexico was the freedom to move around unencumbered by all of this ceremony. As he'd told Lana, he understood the need for it. At least half of it was only for appearances, but the other half dealt with real security issues. He could defend himself, but a territorial lord was a big fucking target, and it would serve no one if he spent all of his energy fighting off every David who thought to take down Goliath.

Still, it grated on him. He'd had to leave the condo building earlier. His supporters were rallying around, but not everyone could, or should, come to him. It made better sense for him to go to some of them, rather than have them all show up here. Especially since Enrique almost certainly had someone watching. Better to leave the old lord guessing as to which of the vampires in his court would support him in the final challenge tomorrow.

But that wasn't what was bothering Vincent, wasn't what had made him rush back to the condo tonight. What had been nagging from the corners of his mind all night long was his last conversation with Lana. Everything had happened so quickly, he was sure she was feeling overwhelmed, maybe even threatened as the only human in a building full of vampires. After all, in the space of a few hours, they'd gone from taking a road trip, with the two of them driving from motel to motel across Mexico, to having an entire entourage and a Mexico City penthouse at their disposal. Even he was feeling claustrophobic. How much worse must it be for her?

Which explained his rush to get back upstairs. He'd gotten reports from the human guard assigned to her, so he knew she'd run her errands and returned already. And now Vincent wanted to catch her before sunrise, to make sure she understood how important she was to him, that together they'd handle whatever problem arose with these new arrangements, just as they had when it had been only the two of them. All of those other vampires, the security types, his supporters and hangers-on, they were peripheral. It was Lana who mattered.

He'd gone no more than five feet from the SUV, outpacing the security team in his hurry, when in his peripheral vision, he saw a man rushing toward him. A human, big and vaguely familiar.

Vincent turned, trying to get a better look through the wall of flesh his security people formed around him, while some of the others grabbed the human and began to ungently hustle him away.

"She doesn't belong to you," the human shouted.

Vincent stared, then pushed through his bodyguards to get his first good look at the human. Harrington. Dan, no, *Dave* Harrington. Lana's former boyfriend or fiancé, depending on whom you believed. Vincent went with Lana's version. But either way, he wanted to know what the man was doing here.

"Let go of him," he ordered and watched as the human immediately stormed closer, seemingly too stupid to understand his own danger.

Harrington stopped just out of arm's reach. He looked exhausted and truly distressed. Vincent almost felt sorry for the man. He'd told Lana that Harrington still wanted her, and now he knew he'd been right. Harrington didn't understand that he'd blown it all those years ago, didn't believe he'd really lost her for good. What a fool.

"She's not for you, vampire. She belongs with her own," the human said, his eyes filled with hatred.

"And *her own* . . . that would be you?" Vincent asked coldly.

"You're damn right. Lana's mine. She's always been mine."

"I don't believe *Lana* sees it that way."

"Because you've screwed with her head. I won't let you have her."

"Lana goes where she chooses. You're a fool if you don't see that." Vincent glanced around, seeking a familiar face, someone he could trust. "Ortega, Zárate," he said, falling back on his own people from Hermosillo. "Escort Mr. Harrington to the airport. See that he catches his flight home."

The two hulking vampires stepped up to either side of Harrington. They didn't touch him, but they didn't need to. The threat was clear. Harrington was a big man, but the vamps were bigger. And they were *vampires*.

"This isn't the end. You can't make her happy."

Vincent's gut clenched as he signaled Ortega and Zárate to get on with it. Not because he gave a damn about Dave Harrington or his hollow threats, but because the human's dire warnings echoed his own fears. And Vincent hadn't been afraid of anything in a very long time.

Spinning on his heel, he strode into the building and went directly into the elevator his security was holding for him. It was only three floors up to the penthouse, but it seemed to take forever.

"She won't thank you for that," Michael muttered next to him.

Vincent shot a silent glare at his lieutenant, but he didn't say anything because he knew what Michael said was true. When Lana found out about Harrington, about how Vincent had shuffled him off to the airport, she wouldn't be pleased. She didn't like him fighting her battles. And she especially wouldn't like him taking action without even checking with her.

"Is Lana in the building?" he snapped instead, not directing the question at anyone in particular.

"Yes, my lord," someone said. "In the residence."

Good, Vincent thought. That's where he needed her. They'd close the door and be alone again, and then they could talk.

The elevator doors opened and his step faltered at the level of activity that greeted him, and the noise that went with it. When he'd left, things had still been gearing up. Now, it seemed as if half of the vampires in Mexico City were hanging around outside his front door. He didn't have time for this. He started out of the elevator, intending to go directly to his condo, but a familiar voice stopped him.

"Vincent."

It was a voice that was as familiar at his own, but one he hadn't heard in a long time. He turned with a smile that conveyed all of the warmth and joy he felt at seeing her again.

"Camille," he said, taking the final step to meet her, his hand cupping her elegant jaw. "When did you get here?"

"To Mexico City? Or to your headquarters?"

"Both."

Her laugh was a delicate chime. More men than he could count had made fools of themselves just to hear that sound. He and Camille were siblings of a sort. Both children of Enrique—or so he'd thought at the time—they'd "grown up" together, having been turned around the same time.

"I arrived just this evening," she told him. "Enrique had me shoved away on the coast. He always resented our closeness, and I'm sure he knows my allegiance is more to you than him. He won't like it that I'm here, but I couldn't miss the big finale. And, besides, I brought some friends." She indicated the conference room with a slight shift of her eyes.

Vincent stroked the back of his fingers over the velvety softness of her cheek. "Thank you, *bella*. It's good to see you," he murmured. He was about to say more when a small noise drew his attention down the hall to his left. He turned and saw Lana standing in the open doorway of the condo, staring at him. She was dressed in sweats and carrying a towel, as if on her way downstairs to the gym.

She looked beautiful and strong, and he abruptly regretted his pride-driven confrontation with Harrington. He opened his mouth to call to her, but with a single unreadable look, she strode down the hall until she was close enough to touch.

Except she ducked his hand when he reached for her, holding her own out to Camille and taking a step closer.

"Camille," Vincent said, stinging at Lana's rejection. "This is Lana Arnold. Lana and I are—"

"Partners," Lana interjected. "Vincent helped me with a job assignment I just finished."

Vincent saw Camille's eyes dancing with laughter, but he didn't find anything funny. He turned his scowl on Lana and was about to make some excuse to Camille while he dragged Lana back to the penthouse and figured out what the *fuck* was going on, but before he could say anything, Lana was speaking again.

"Well, I'll leave the two of you to your . . . consultations," she said, backing away. "Nice to meet you, Camille. Vincent," she said with a brisk nod, then she was gone before he had the chance to say anything, ducking into the stairwell with her human bodyguard in tow.

Vincent took a step to go after her, but Michael appeared at his side and said softly, "Sire, Camille brought Tulio."

"I'm sorry, Vincent," Camille said softly, her gaze filled with understanding for his plight. "But Tulio *is* waiting in the conference room," she reminded him.

Vincent swore softly. Amado Tulio was a powerful master from Baja who hated Enrique, but would never be powerful enough to take him on himself. He was willing to support Vincent's bid, but only if he could be convinced that they would win. Tulio wanted Enrique gone, but he wasn't willing to risk his own neck to get it. If there'd been more time, Vincent would have said to hell with Tulio and gone after Lana. But there wasn't any time at all. He needed to know *tonight* where Tulio would stand tomorrow.

"Make sure she doesn't leave the building," he growled at Michael, and then turned with a smile for Camille and headed for the conference room.

LANA HUGGED THE folded bath sheet like a security blanket as she ran down the stairs to the first floor. She'd been on her way to the pool even before seeing Vincent with his girlfriend, hoping to relieve some of the stress she'd been feeling ever since they boarded the plane for Mexico City.

That idea was blown all to hell now. She'd have to swim until she was exhausted to erase the image of Vincent and *Camille*, staring at each other with that *look* on their faces. All that picture needed was fairy dust twinkling around their heads, it was so fucking sweet.

The irony was that Lana had been happy to see him. She'd heard his voice even before the doors opened, and her heart had done the proverbial jump for joy. She'd known in that moment that, while she might not belong here, this was where she wanted to be. With Vincent.

Her first thought when Vincent had emerged from the elevator was that he looked tired. But then the woman—Camille—had said his name, and his exhaustion had seemed to drain away.

Camille was lovely, of course. Petite and delicate, with a tiny waist and overflowing breasts, her lush lips painted red, her black hair falling in graceful waves down her back. She'd laughed at something Vincent said and heads had turned at the sound. Vincent's smile had grown wider and he'd brushed the back of his fingers over the woman's elegant cheek, murmuring something for her ears only.

Lana had felt the touch of those fingers like a punch to her gut. She hadn't meant to make a sound, but she must have, because Vincent's head had turned, and in that first unguarded moment, she'd seen the guilt in his eyes. And suddenly, the whispering voice in the back of her brain, the one she'd convinced herself was wrong because she'd wanted so much to stay with Vincent, had become a warning shriek, reinforcing what she'd known all along. She truly didn't belong here.

Lana had forced herself to walk down that hallway, to hold out her hand and be polite. But when Vincent had tried to touch her, when he'd given her that hurt look as she'd avoided his hand, she'd known she had to get away before she started screaming.

She'd mumbled something polite, then, taking advantage of the distraction provided when Michael whispered something in Vincent's ear, she'd ducked into the stairwell and been gone, the heavy door slamming behind her.

And now she was racing down the stairs, expecting at every turn to hear him following, to hear his voice calling her name, but he never did. She had to decide what to do, where to go from here. Her best bet would be to wait until sunrise, go back to the penthouse, pack her things, and leave. She no longer believed Vincent would try to stop her from going. Now that his vampire girlfriend was here, he'd probably be relieved to discover she was gone, that she'd made it so easy for him.

She kept moving, her feet keeping pace with her thoughts which were running too fast and making no sense.

Before she knew it, the bodyguard was opening the door to the first floor, reminding her that he was still with her. She'd forgotten all about him for a moment. His name was Jeff Garcia and he'd been with Vincent for almost four years. What would Jeff do if she headed for the airport? Would he try to stop her? Go with her? Once she left Mexico, she wouldn't need a bodyguard anymore. She wasn't even sure she needed one now.

Lana paused for a moment, one hand covering her closed eyes. She needed to think about what she was doing. She was letting emotion carry her instead of reason, running scared. *Running* being the operative word. She needed to stop and *think*. She became aware of the smell of chlorine, the muted echo of water against tile. Opening her eyes, she realized that the stairwell opened directly into the pool area. Through a wall of windows to her right was the main part of the gym, with the usual equipment and a few hardy souls getting in a workout before sunrise. She assumed they were all vampires, but it was possible some of them were human guards like Jeff.

No one was using the pool.

She'd come down here to swim, and that's what she was going to do. Without even thinking about it, she threw her towel on a chaise and stripped off her sweatshirt. She sat down to step out of the pants, not because she had to, but because she didn't want Jeff to see that she had her little Spyderco knife tucked into the little inside pocket on the sweatpants. The pocket had been designed to carry keys and maybe a cell phone, but Lana had always thought a knife was more useful. And bodyguard or no, she wasn't going anywhere without some kind of weapon. She folded the pants carefully, then stood up to survey the pool. She was wearing a simple black one-piece suit that she'd bought from a shop right next to the grocery store where she'd gone earlier. She tugged it down over her ass somewhat self-consciously. She was in good shape, but the suit was cut a little higher than what she normally wore.

She tugged on the cheap bathing cap she'd bought with the suit, then with a nod to Jeff, who had taken up a position at the door they'd just come through, Lana stepped up to the edge and dove in. Swimming was like meditation for her. After the first few strokes, she didn't have to think about it anymore, didn't hear the nagging voice in the back of her mind, didn't see the affection on Vincent's face, the softness of his words when he'd touched the woman, Camille, upstairs. She simply moved through the water, falling into the familiar rhythm of a forward crawl ... stroke, breathe, stroke, breathe, hit the wall, turn, glide, and start all over again. She swam until her muscles began to burn, and then she swam some more, until her strokes were no longer smooth, her turns no longer graceful.

When she hit the wall on her next lap, she stopped, hanging onto the side of the pool, breathing in the chlorine smell of the water as the exhaustion started to creep in. She might not be a vampire, but she'd been living like one for the last week, which meant she'd been up all night and her body needed sleep.

And, at some point during her swim, her brain had reached a decision, or maybe it was her heart. As easy and uncomplicated as it would be, she didn't have it in her to creep away without saying good-bye to Vincent, without any explanation at all. Maybe they were only partners, after all, but even a partner deserved the respect of a decent farewell.

Lana sighed, knowing what she was going to do, what she had to do.

"What time is it?" she asked Jeff, who was standing exactly where he'd been when she started swimming.

He gave her a crooked smile and said, "Nearly sunrise. The vamps have deserted the gym."

Lana pulled herself out of the water. It took more effort than it should have and it occurred to her that she might have done a few laps more than her body could handle. At least she wouldn't have to worry about her mind keeping her awake today. The only thought in her head right now was sleep.

She pushed to her feet with an effort and wrapped herself in the big towel, jerking off the uncomfortable bathing cap and tossing it in the trash. She thought about hitting the elevator without getting dressed, but there were a whole lot of people she didn't know between her and her bed, so she dragged her sweats back on, not caring that her suit was still wet.

"Let's go," she told Jeff, pressing the towel around the wet braid of her hair.

Jeff was talking to someone on the Bluetooth bud in his ear. Lana waited patiently, leaning against the wall, because she worried if she sat down, she'd simply fall over, asleep, and not get up again.

Jeff touched the bud in his ear, disconnecting the call. "The elevators are locked upstairs," he said, shaking his head in sympathy. "Some big vampire honcho getting ready to depart. You up for the stairs?"

Lana looked from him to the stairwell door, thinking, *Hell, no.* But what she said was, "Sure."

He gave a sympathetic chuckle as Lana opened the door to the stairs.

"Lana," Jeff said urgently and she remembered he was supposed to go first. But then a movement in the stairwell drew her attention, and she stared in shock at the person standing there.

"What are you doing here?" she asked as she heard Jeff curse, and then the jagged sound of a Taser filled the concrete stairwell.

Vincent

Chapter Twenty-Four

VINCENT PACED AS the shutters deployed over the windows. Where the hell was Lana? He'd called her cell phone, but there'd been no answer. So he'd tried Jeff Garcia and got no answer there either. GPS on both phones told him they were in the building, but he couldn't discover anything more specific than that, and now sunrise was about to take away his ability to go looking for them. He could still ask his daytime security people to find them, but he wasn't exactly in a hurry to announce to everyone that his lover was avoiding him. His phone rang. It was Michael with a final check-in. His lieutenant was young as vampires went, which meant he'd crash into daylight sleep well before Vincent did.

"Mike," he answered tersely.

"Building's locked down. No one in or out until sunset. How'd it go with Tulio?"

"He's onboard for now. But he's hedging his bet. He'll be at Enrique's when we get there, but won't visibly side with us."

"So he doesn't want to be seen with us until he knows who's going to win."

"Better that we find out now what kind of weasel he is. I'll know not to depend on him in the future."

"Lana?"

"Still in the gym as far as I know."

Silence greeted this statement, and then, "She didn't leave the building."

"I know. Sleep well, Michael." Vincent hung up without waiting for a response. Michael might be the closest thing he had to a friend, but he wasn't about to discuss his love life with him. Not when it came to Lana, anyway. She wasn't some pretty thing picked up in a bar and quickly forgotten. She mattered to him, but it was obvious that he hadn't convinced *her* of that fact.

So where the fuck was she? Hiding out until he was asleep for the day? He wouldn't have thought that was her style. In fact, he *knew* it wasn't her style. But then, she hadn't quite been herself ever since they'd arrived in Mexico City, and she'd seen the way he lived here, seen all the vampires courting him, heard them calling him *lord*. He hadn't missed her reaction to the penthouse either. She'd walked through it like a museum instead of a home. Maybe because he'd never lived here. It was just the place he stayed when politics didn't give him a choice. He'd bet if Lana had seen his place in Hermosillo, she'd have been completely at ease.

He simply hadn't had enough time with her before all of this descended upon him. He hadn't planned on confronting Enrique so soon. His hand had been forced on several fronts. First, by what Enrique had done to Jerry and Salvio, and especially Carolyn. How could he let that stand unchallenged? And then there was Raphael, making sure Vincent ran into Xuan Ignacio, so the old vampire could drop his little bomb of truth. Vincent might have been ready to challenge Enrique after Carolyn, but it was learning of his brother's murder at Enrique's hand that had sealed the deal. Just as Raphael had known it would.

If only Vincent could have had one more day with Lana, one more day with just the two of them, to prepare her for all of this, to let what he felt for her sink in and take hold.

So where the fuck was she? He reached for his cell phone, intending to call her one last time, but he staggered suddenly, nearly falling as sunrise asserted its inexorable control over him. Footsteps dragging, he barely managed to reach the bedroom before falling face first onto the big empty bed.

Vincent

Chapter Twenty-Five

VINCENT'S PHONE WAS ringing when he stepped out of the shower. He picked it up from the tiled counter where he'd left it, hoping that Lana would call. She hadn't come back to the penthouse during the day, not even to get her things, and the concern he'd felt upon waking this evening to find her gone had cemented into something much worse as the night deepened. Michael had assured Vincent that he'd personally checked every video feed and seen no sign of either Lana or Jeff Garcia, who'd been guarding her. But video feeds could be hacked, and their cell phones, which had been registering inside the building before dawn, were now not registering at all. They'd either been turned off and the batteries removed, or they'd been destroyed.

There was no reason for Lana to do something like that, and he knew, sure as hell, that Garcia *wouldn't* do it. Not willingly. Jeff Garcia was loyal to Vincent. Michael swore it, and Vincent believed it. Which meant that whatever had happened to Lana had probably happened to Garcia first.

Vincent laughed with no humor at all as he realized that his fondest hope at this point was that Dave Harrington had her. That he'd somehow managed to sneak out of the airport and back into the city in order to drag Lana back to the so-called safety of her familial bosom. That would explain the absence of a cell signal. Harrington would know how to avoid detection, and how to get her out of the country with no one the wiser. And if Lana was confused, or pissed, enough about her relationship with Vincent, she might not even fight it. But even as he had that thought, he rejected it. No matter how pissed Lana was, Vincent didn't believe she'd leave without saying good-bye. Even if that good-bye was only telling him to fuck off.

The phone rang again and Vincent checked the caller ID, swearing when he saw the name of yet another of his vampire supporters. From almost the moment the sun had dropped below the horizon, they'd been calling him, as nervous as cats in a roomful of cactuses. He hadn't answered any of them, letting Michael soothe their nerves, offer reassurances. He shouldn't be expected to hold hands on the precipice of the most dangerous battle of his life. At least that's what Michael was telling them. They didn't need to know the truth of it. That he was afraid something terrible had happened to his lover and was fighting a battle with himself over whether to march into Enrique's lair and offer a challenge, or to say *fuck it all* and go looking for Lana instead.

Unfortunately, he was beginning to fear that those two things were the same. That it was Enrique who'd gotten hold of Lana, and that he intended to use her against him.

The phone rang again, and Vincent nearly threw it against the wall before he saw Michael's name come up.

"What?" he snarled.

"Sire," Michael said formally, falling back on protocol in the face of Vincent's anger. "Forgive me, but . . . I need to know what to tell your security team."

Vincent looked away and his gaze fell on Lana's black, zippered vanity case. She didn't wear much in the way of makeup, wasn't a high maintenance woman who fussed with creams and lotions. Her one vanity, if she had one, was her hair. She had travel bottles of expensive shampoo and conditioner, and a variety of hair ties and bands to secure her braid. But the one thing she used the most was her brush. He'd noticed it because it was unusual, not one of the typical plastic kind found in a local big box store. Lana had told him that she'd had it for years, that it was designed for long hair like hers and had cost her a fortune, but it was worth it. And when he'd watched her brush her braid out every night, watched the long, slow strokes through the black fall of her hair, he'd had to agree with her. Just watching her made him want to throw her on the bed and fuck her 'til she screamed. He'd buy her a hundred of those brushes if that's what she wanted.

So why, if she'd decided to leave him, would she not at least have gathered up her brush and hair ties to take with her?

"We're going to Enrique's," Vincent told Michael. Because he was convinced that's where he'd find Lana. And if Enrique had hurt her . . . well, the vampire lord was already going to die tonight, but Vincent would make sure his suffering was so excruciating that he'd beg for death before it was over.

NO ONE CHALLENGED Vincent when he arrived at Enrique's headquarters on the outskirts of the city. It was a huge estate, acquired long before the city reached its current limits. Vincent arrived with only a small entourage—three SUVs, filled mostly with his security people, but every one of them had taken his blood. Everyone was sworn to him personally and would back him in a fight if he needed it. And that was in addition to his less obvious supporters, like Tulio, who would already be with Enrique.

The gate guards took one look at him and rolled the heavy wood and iron gates open. Not even Enrique would expect his guards to bar the gates to Vincent. The Mexican lord would suck them dry if he needed their strength to defeat Vincent's challenge, but he wouldn't expect them to stand against Vincent on their own.

No one was in the courtyard when Vincent climbed out of the SUV and headed inside. His security team formed a circle around him as they moved through the deserted corridors, boots striking the tiles, echoing in the empty spaces. Michael walked at his side, Ortega and Zárate at his back, along with Jerry, Salvio, and Carolyn. Vincent figured they had as much at stake in this battle as he did. They deserved to be here. Everyone else, supporters and detractors alike, had either vacated the estate to avoid being caught up in the conflict, or they were waiting with Enrique behind the big double doors where Vincent was headed.

Vincent didn't need anyone to tell him where Enrique would be waiting for him. It would be the room where Enrique held court, the place Vincent had always thought of as the throne room. It was huge and mostly empty, with no furniture and no place for anyone but Enrique to sit, because, after all, subjects didn't sit in the presence of their king, did they? The ceiling overhead was vaulted, with a small glass dome at the center. The glass had once been clear so that Enrique could gaze out at the stars—or maybe so the stars could shine on Enrique—but it had become too much of an effort to stop the pigeons from shitting on it, or to clean it up when they inevitably did. So, Enrique had compromised, installing a stained glass nightscape instead. Even back then, when Vincent had known very little about such extravagances, he'd still understood that the glass inserts had to have cost a small fortune. Now, it was just one more reminder of Enrique's selfishness, that he'd devote so much to decorate this one room at a time when most of his own people had been sleeping unguarded in holes dug beneath their homes.

Vincent pushed open the doors without a word and strode forward until he hit the middle of the room, not willing to stand like a petitioner in front of the vampire lord he was about to kill.

Michael and the others spread out behind him, making their allegiance clear. Their support would cost them their lives if he failed tonight. And that certain knowledge forced Vincent to put aside the last shred of doubt he had over whether he could defeat Enrique, the final reservations as to whether he really wanted this job. He pushed back his worries over Lana's safety, too.

Too many lives rested on his success tonight. He couldn't afford to fail, and so he wouldn't.

"Vincent. What a surprise," Enrique sneered, hatred in every syllable.

"Let's not pretend, Enrique," Vincent responded. "You're no more surprised to see me here than I am to find you surrounded by your gaggle of worthless sycophants."

The vampires in question shuffled in affront, but not one of them had the balls to challenge Vincent's assessment. He dismissed them with a glance.

"I see you've acquired a gaggle of your own," Enrique observed, then raised his voice. "Jerry, Salvio, oh, and especially you, darling Carolyn, on your knees," he commanded, putting enough power into it that several of the vampires in the clique behind him dropped to the floor in submission.

But none of the three vampires Enrique had named moved a muscle.

Enrique's face distorted with anger. "I am your master and your lord, and you will obey me," he snarled.

Vincent again felt the power in Enrique's command and drew on his own power to shield the vampires standing behind him.

"They are no longer yours, Enrique," he called, diverting the vampire lord's ire. "You never had their love, and you lost their loyalty the day you enslaved them to human masters."

A mutter of shock ran through the room as this piece of history was absorbed.

"So you've made them your slaves instead," Enrique said dismissively. "How is that any better than what I can offer?"

"Not slaves. They've given me their loyalty in return for my protection. *That* is the ages-old bargain between vampire and master, between a vampire lord and every vampire living in his territory. It is a responsibility, not a right."

"Oh, listen to you," Enrique scoffed. "Such lofty words from the bastard son of a whore." He meant the barb as an insult, something to enrage Vincent into acting foolishly. But Vincent only shook his head, mocking the weakness of his opponent's verbal volley.

"Your words mean nothing, Enrique. I know who I am, who my parents were." He paused, seeing Xuan Ignacio enter the room to one side. "I also know who my brother was," Vincent continued. "And I know how he died."

Enrique saw Xuan, too, and his eyes went wide in surprise, an uncontrolled reaction that was there and gone so quickly that Vincent wouldn't have noticed if he hadn't been looking for it. But it was the final confirmation he needed that Xuan had been telling him the truth. The same truth that Raphael had known would set Vincent on this path.

"I see you've met my old friend Xuan Ignacio," Enrique said smoothly. "Has he been rewriting history again?"

"Don't bother, Enrique," Vincent said. "Blood speaks to blood."

"Perhaps, but it changes nothing. You speak so eloquently of loyalty, what of yours to your rightful lord?"

"A vampire lord owns only what he can hold. It has always been thus."

Enrique's response was a smile so smug that it sent a chill worming into the tiniest and most distant of Vincent's bones.

"I thought you might feel that way," the vampire lord said and gestured at the small door behind his throne.

The door was pulled back, but Vincent didn't need to look to know what he'd see. He'd scented her blood the moment the door cracked open. This was where Lana had gone, where she and her guard had disappeared to. She hadn't gone into hiding, hadn't run from him and everything he represented. Somehow, one of Enrique's spies had succeeded in kidnapping her, sneaking her out of the building, despite all of Vincent's security.

But the how of it could be dealt with later. The why of it was now and very clear. Enrique thought to bargain with Vincent, to exchange Lana's safety for Vincent's surrender.

It might have worked if Vincent hadn't known Enrique as well as he did. But he did know him, knew the duplicity, the depravity the vampire lord was capable of. Even if Vincent fell on his knees in this moment and pledged eternal fealty to Enrique, the old lord would not let Lana live. He would slit her throat in front of Vincent and let her blood paint the floor simply to prove that he could, to punish Vincent for even thinking of defying him.

Enrique had thought to weaken Vincent by producing Lana like this, but he'd only hardened Vincent's resolve instead.

Lana's gaze found Vincent as she was dragged into the room. She was wearing nothing but a bathing suit and sweatpants, not even shoes, despite the chill in the room, and her hair was a tangled mess. Her arms were gripped to either side by vampires who each outweighed her by fifty pounds, as if she was such a threat that two of them were needed to contain her. Vincent wanted to smile at the stupidity of that, and to show Lana that there was nothing to worry about. But there was. As long as Enrique remained alive, she was in danger.

Enrique signaled when the vampires drew closer, and they released Lana with a shove that would have thrown her to the floor if Enrique hadn't caught her first, wrapping a casual arm around her neck, his thin fingers caressing her throat.

"Your taste in women has improved, Vincent. This one had spirit . . . before I fucked it out of her."

"He's lying," Lana rasped as loudly as she could with Enrique's hand gripping her throat. "He tried, but he couldn't get it up."

Enrique snarled furiously, curled his free hand into a fist, and plowed it into her stomach. She dropped to the floor and curled over her knees, clutching her stomach and retching. Enrique reached down and casually twisted her long hair around his fist, yanking her head up so that Vincent could see the tears streaming down her face, the blood flecking her lips.

"Too much spirit is not attractive in a female," Enrique said fastidiously.

Vincent ground his teeth against a rage so powerful that it felt like he had a wild animal trapped within his body, raking long claws over his ribs and against the walls of his chest, demanding to be released, howling for revenge against the monster who had *dared* to harm his woman. Vincent's fists curled into claws in an unconscious mimicry of the creature as he stared at Lana, her face crumpled in pain, tears streaming from beneath lowered lids as she gasped for breath.

But then her eyes suddenly flicked open, and her gaze, when it met his, was direct with intent beneath the pain. Vincent saw her determination, but didn't know what she wanted, what she intended to do. He stared at her, wishing she wasn't so resistant to his telepathy, wishing she could tell him somehow . . . He caught the slight movement of her right hand, saw the flash of fear in her eyes as he followed the move, lest he give it away. And in that instant, Vincent knew what she planned, and it was so dangerous that the beast inside him that was his rage against Enrique began to howl and thrash in its effort to break free.

But Vincent held on, and he waited. He would not buy Enrique's death at the cost of Lana's. He needed her free of Enrique's grip before he attacked.

"Vincent," she gasped, and he stared at her sharply, alarmed at the weakness in her voice. "Salvio," she whispered. "It was Salvio."

Salvio broke from behind Vincent, seeming intent on reaching Enrique's side, as if he actually believed the vampire lord could protect him. But it was too little and far too late. The moment Vincent heard Salvio's name, he reached out with his power and froze the lesser vampire in place.

"Sire," Salvio breathed, his pleading gaze on Enrique who sat on his makeshift throne, watching the tableau unfold with a gleeful expression.

"Why?" Vincent demanded. "I gave you your freedom."

Salvio turned a vicious look on Vincent. "But you never asked me if I wanted it," he snapped. "Maybe I liked my life as a nightmare in the shadows. I had power, I was *feared.* And what did *you* give me instead? The life of a lowly soldier."

Vincent stared at him. "Then why not walk away? You could have gone back to Enrique. I wouldn't have stopped you."

"Because my Sire had a better use for me within your circle, close to your woman," he added, with a smug smile.

Vincent's rage redoubled. "I told you when you swore to me," he said, his voice low and harsh with anger. "I do not tolerate betrayal."

He didn't lift so much as a hand in Salvio's direction, didn't waste the energy on unnecessary theatrics. A thin thread of power slashed the air between him and Salvio, becoming a hot poker that slammed into the traitor's heart, ripping into the muscle, heating the flesh.

Salvio fell to his knees, hands tearing at his chest, keening in anguish as he turned to stare in disbelief at Enrique who did nothing but lean forward on his chair, eyes burning with hunger, lapping up the fear and pain radiating off of Salvio like sweat from his pores.

Vincent bared his teeth. "Look at your Sire now," he snarled at Salvio. "Do you still think he'll save you?"

And with that, he increased the power burning in Salvio's chest until the traitor screamed in agony, until the fire incinerated his heart in an instant. Until Salvio was no more.

Vincent shook his hand, as if sloughing off the residue of Salvio's death, and then he turned to face Enrique once again.

"He was loyal to you," he said loudly, mostly for the benefit of the many vampires crowded into the big room. "He gave you what you wanted, he betrayed his oath to me. And still, you made no effort to save him."

"He was of no more use to me."

"And so you killed him."

"Oh, no, that was you, Vincent. Champion that you are."

Vincent barely heard Enrique's sneering reply. His attention was focused instead on Carolyn who'd remained staunchly at his back in the face of Enrique's cruel taunt. She was a low-burning fire of anger and determination behind him and he reached out with his mind, finding her easily, her bond to him still strong and shining brightly.

"Carolyn, when I go after Enrique, you grab Lana and protect her. Do you understand?"

"I will protect her with my life," she responded immediately.

Vincent hoped it didn't come to that, but he didn't insult Carolyn by telling her so. The young vampire's confidence, her sense of self-worth, was too recently restored. So, he sent his gratitude down the link, then turned and waited for Lana to make the first move in this dance.

As if she understood that he was ready, that he might not like it, but he accepted her plan, Lana gave him a bloody smile that defied her predicament and conveyed so much love for him that it broke his heart.

And then in a single practiced move, she slipped the little knife out of her pocket, popped it open, then twisted around and stabbed Enrique in the thigh.

Several things happened at once.

Enrique roared in mingled fury and pain, and threw Lana across the room.

And Vincent . . . attacked.

Most battles among powerful vampires were fought at arm's length or better, battles of power and mental strength, with weapons made of energy and magic. But that wasn't enough for Vincent, not today and not for Enrique. He needed to rend the old lord's flesh, to feel his blood spurt hot and wasted as he tore out his throat.

Vincent crossed the room in an eyeblink and grabbed Enrique by the throat, his hand so big that it nearly circled the smaller vampire's neck entirely. But he wasn't such a fool that he thought physical strength alone would be enough. Even as he choked the breath from his former master, he snapped a shield of power into place around himself, sealing it a split second before Enrique lashed out with his own considerable might. Enrique was an asshole and a traitor to his own people, but he was also a damn powerful vampire lord who'd ruled Mexico for nearly 200 years. And while Vincent had a handful of loyal vampires at his back, Enrique had the full resources of a lord. He could draw on every single one of the souls who looked to him for protection, thousands of vampires whose hearts beat by Enrique's will alone. And Vincent knew the bastard would drain the territory dry before he'd surrender.

Gathering every ounce of his own strength, relying on every hour of experience he'd acquired, every technique he'd learned over his long life, Vincent delved into Enrique's mind. Using the unique ability that was his alone, he forced the vampire lord back into his youth, back to when he'd first come to Mexico, and then back farther still, to his childhood on the streets of southern Spain.

Because just as Enrique knew Vincent's history, so did Vincent know Enrique's. It was his talent, after all, to know the secrets that every vampire hid from the world.

And Enrique's secret was one that he'd guarded desperately, not only from Vincent but from himself. Because although Enrique had taunted Vincent as being the bastard son of a whore, it was Enrique himself who'd been born on the streets, the child of a teenaged prostitute who'd sold her son for the price of a good meal. He'd been the lowest servant in a wealthy household, everyone's dogsbody, kicked and abused, forced to see the rewards of tremendous wealth every day, but existing in abject hardship and degradation. It wasn't until he was older and slaving long hours loading cargo for his owner that he'd caught the eye of a vampire on the hunt for new followers—young, strong men who could serve him in the vampire wars so common in that time. The vampire had turned Enrique, and Enrique's first act upon waking as a vampire was to hunt down his human master and rip out his throat.

But it wasn't the murder of his former owner that haunted Enrique. It was the years he'd spent at the mercy of others, tortured, starved, too young and weak to defend himself. It was a horrible childhood and one that would have gained him sympathy and even understanding, if he hadn't become a monster himself.

If he hadn't threatened the life of the woman Vincent loved.

So the battle was joined. Vincent was familiar with Enrique's power, familiar with how he used it to punish and intimidate. While Vincent's talent was a thing of subtlety and intricate manipulation, Enrique's strength was a blunt instrument, a cudgel wielded by a bully, quite literally. He would try to physically destroy Vincent, to crush organs and shatter bones. Vincent could have cudgeled him back, but only at the expense of his efforts to destroy Enrique's mind. Instead, he hardened his shield, determined to survive the battering long enough to permit his own unusual talent to work on Enrique's mind, to dig into his memories and savage without pity until there was no intellect left to drive the vampire lord's tremendous power, until he was trapped in a circle of his own thoughts, his own childhood nightmare.

Vincent tore through Enrique's memories like tissue paper, digging recklessly, shunting aside any memories that didn't help him, anything that gave Enrique pleasure or satisfaction, obliterating them in his wake. He didn't care about the destruction he left behind. Enrique would no longer need a functioning mind when Vincent was through with him. He'd be nothing but a pile of dust.

But Enrique wasn't defeated yet. Vincent felt the wave of power slice through him a moment before he was slammed to the floor with such force that the parquet cracked beneath his weight. Flesh split and muscles screamed and still he held on, burying Enrique in the horror of his past, forcing him to relive every humiliation, every instant of childhood terror, until Vincent was certain the tide was about to turn.

But again, Enrique rallied, pummeling Vincent with a series of blows that were like boulders flying through the air, smashing into him with such speed and force that one of Vincent's arms broke under the assault. He howled in agony, but he held on, forcing himself to ignore the pain, to forget the grinding of his bones as he gripped Enrique in a headlock, hindering his assault while Vincent continued to plow through his mind, leaving a trail of ruin and torment.

The two of them had long ago rolled to the floor, Vincent crushing the smaller lord beneath his greater bulk while Enrique shouted his fury, punctuating his attacks with enraged screams. But even as Enrique continued to fight, as his defiant shouts shook the glass dome overhead, every vampire in the room sensed the moment when the momentum shifted, when their lord's defiance turned hollow. The mood among the watching vampires shifted in that instant, as they realized—many for the first time—that Enrique could very well die in the next few minutes.

Fear became a monster lurking in the dark depths of the huge room, fear that Enrique would die, that they all would die with him, fear that in victory, Vincent would execute Enrique's followers; and there were many of those. And that fear sucked the power out of Enrique even as he fought for his life, as he reached out to his vampires, willing to drain them dry to save himself, only to find them shrieking in terror, siphoning his strength instead in their desperate need for reassurance and safety.

Without warning, something . . . changed, an indefinable something, a sudden deprivation of air, a bubble of static electricity exploding outward, clinging to the skin of every vampire present and cutting off Enrique's enraged roar mid-howl. The whimpers of a small boy emerged to replace the snarls of the powerful lord. And Vincent knew immediately what had happened. He grabbed hold of the memory he'd found and spun it ruthlessly, forcing the grown man to confront the horrors of the child, to relive it over and over again, the terror, the helplessness, the hunger and thirst.

Until finally the blows that had been driven by the force of a vampire lord's might became nothing but the fists of an ordinary man.

Vincent straightened with a roar of victory, a roar flavored with agony as he clenched his broken hand and slammed it into Enrique's chest. In an act of sheer willpower, he squeezed the life out of the vampire lord's heart, destroying the organ and finally, *finally* ending the long life of Enrique Fernandez del Solar, Lord of Mexico.

Vincent knelt in the blood and dust of Enrique's destruction with only one goal—to get to Lana. The image of Enrique's savagery when he'd thrown her across the room was stuck in the forefront of Vincent's mind, playing in a loop eerily similar to the one he'd used to torture Enrique to his death. He forced himself to turn, ignoring the pain, blinking against the blood filling his eyes as he searched for Lana, when suddenly he was struck by a blow from nowhere, a blow more powerful than anything Enrique had delivered. Shoved backward until he was bent nearly flat, he would have collapsed if Michael hadn't caught him, if he hadn't felt the power of his vampires surrounding him, if they hadn't protected him as the mantle of lordship crashed into him. Thousands of vampires all cried out at once, clinging to him, demanding life and protection, pleading for comfort as the order they'd known for centuries under Enrique now disintegrated and coalesced around a new center, a new Lord of Mexico. Vincent.

Vincent rocked back, ass on his heels, eyes closed, head held in bloody, broken hands. He groaned, amazed that there was any new pain left to feel, that there was a single inch of him that could hurt more than it already did. Enrique had spoken once of the burden of leadership, complaining about the whining and the demands, about the constant barrage of need, until he felt like he was never alone in his own head. Vincent had dismissed it, thinking it was simply one more sign of Enrique's hateful personality. But now he understood. And he wondered why he couldn't have left well enough alone, couldn't have let some other vampire kill Enrique and take on this burden of responsibility and leadership.

But even as he thought it, he knew it wouldn't have worked. Maybe when he'd still been human, he would have willingly accepted a secondary role in life, accepted the inherent limitations of his bastard birth and followed someone else's lead. But from the moment he'd been made Vampire, something had been born inside him, something that had goaded him into action and made him claw his way to the top, seizing power from vampire after vampire until it culminated in this moment in time.

Vincent was Lord of Mexico. It was what he had been reborn to become.

He reached out to the thousands of vampires who were now his to protect. Shielding them from his pain, he sent them a message of reassurance first, a soothing balm of care. But he followed it with a taste of his power, a demand that they cease whining like toddlers and go back to their lives. They were safe, and they should now *shut the fuck up*.

Silence descended and Vincent had only one thought. Where was Lana?

He opened eyes bleary with sweat and blood and scanned the huge room. The scent of her blood struck a hammer blow—it was too strong, there was too much blood—and he knew real fear for the first time in decades. He tried to stand, but his legs wouldn't hold him, so he crawled. She lay where Enrique had thrown her, limp and unmoving, still hidden behind Carolyn who crouched protectively, fangs gleaming, glaring daggers at anyone who drew too close. Her head snapped around and she hissed a warning at Vincent's approach, before her gaze cleared and she blushed in recognition.

"My lord," she whispered, cringing back as if expecting punishment.

"Thank you, Carolyn." He managed to say it softly, without growling, though all he wanted to do was shove her aside to get to Lana.

Seeming to understand, Carolyn scooted away, clearing his approach.

Vincent did growl then. When he saw what Enrique had done to Lana, he wished he could bring the bastard back, wished he could keep him alive for weeks, toying with his memories, making him relive every torment, every humiliation over and over again.

Lana's soft moan snapped him out of his fantasies of torture. He crawled closer and stroked the back of his fingers over her cheek.

"Lana," he said quietly.

Her eyes fluttered opened and her lips curved into a bare smile. "Vincent," she whispered, her voice so weak and so laced with pain that he wanted to howl.

Scooping her into his lap, he ignored her cries of pain and wrapped his arms around her. Then leaning back against the wall, he ripped open his wrist with his fangs and held it to her mouth. "Drink, *querida*."

She turned her head away at first, eyes closed, her face scrunched in protest.

"I need you strong, Lana," he murmured, knowing it would persuade her. "The fight isn't over yet, and I need you with me."

She sighed, a long, exhausted exhale, then rolled her head back and parted her lips. Vincent placed his bleeding wrist over her mouth, then closed his eyes and rested his head against hers as she began to suck. Every draw of her mouth, every touch of her tongue felt as if it was his cock in her mouth instead of his wrist. He fought back a groan, keenly aware of the many eyes watching his every move.

"Michael," he said finally.

"Sire?"

Vincent opened his eyes to look at his lieutenant. "Find secure quarters for my people and bring in our own daylight guards." Even as he said it, he realized that every vampire in the room was now included in *his people*. But that would take some getting used to, and Michael would know what he meant.

Vincent looked down to see Lana's eyes open and looking up at him. She drew her mouth away from his wrist with a lingering stroke of her tongue and said, "Jeff Garcia." Her voice was weak but urgent. "He's injured, but he's alive. In the room where they held me."

"Michael," Vincent said, never looking away from her.

"I heard, Sire."

Lana closed her eyes and breathed, as if gathering her strength, then her eyes opened again. "Did we win?"

Vincent grinned. "We did. Thanks to you and your knife."

Lana smiled and tried to laugh, but she only managed a breathless cough. "I feel like I could sleep for a month," she breathed.

"We'll both sleep," he said, holding her to his heart. "There's just one more thing you need to know."

She looked up at him in question and he bent his head low, speaking for her ears only. "I'm not your fucking *partner*."

Epilogue

Malibu, California

RAPHAEL GLANCED over when the dedicated phone line rang, noting the caller's number on the display. He exchanged a knowing look with Cyn, who understood as well as he did who was likely to be calling on that line and from that number.

"Vincent," he said, picking up the phone and greeting North America's newest vampire lord. He didn't even try to conceal the smug satisfaction he felt at Enrique's death, nor did he need this phone call to let him know the old lord was dead. He, along with every other vampire lord on the continent, had felt Enrique's demise the moment it happened.

"Raphael," Vincent responded, using no title or honorific. Intentionally, Raphael knew, a way of establishing that the two of them were equals now, both lords, both members of the Council.

"Congratulations," Raphael said. "Enrique will not be missed."

"Not by anyone I know," Vincent agreed.

"And Xuan Ignacio?"

"Alive last I saw him. Although he if wants to stay that way, he'll find himself a new lord sooner rather than later."

"Very generous," Raphael said, and meant it. If he'd been Vincent, he'd have executed Xuan on the spot.

"Lana pled his case. She was eloquent."

"Ah." Raphael understood exactly what Vincent meant. One's lover, or mate, could be very persuasive if one cared enough about her. And apparently Vincent did. Interesting.

"Speaking of such things," Vincent said, "I have a gift for you."

"A gift," Raphael repeated, letting his doubt flavor the words. He and Vincent did not exchange *gifts*. They were not friends. His role in Vincent's nascent rise to the Council had been purely out of self-interest.

"A rather unique gift," Vincent continued. "Parisian in origin, I believe. Difficult to transport, but Lana and I would welcome you and your mate to Mexico City if you're interested in taking a look."

Raphael was silent for several minutes as he considered what Vincent was saying—and what he wasn't.

"We'll be there tomorrow night," he said finally. "My people will contact yours with the details."

"Excellent. I'm quite confident you'll find your visit . . . fulfilling."

Mexico City, Mexico

Cyn strolled into the building on Raphael's arm. Raphael was as devastating as always in one of his elegant suits, while Cyn had chosen a dark gray silk sheath. It was sleeveless, in deference to the muggy heat of a Mexican spring, form-fitting and simple, except for the plunging neckline in back, which bared skin down to her waist. Raphael loved that dress, which was why she'd worn it. Meetings among powerful vampires reminded her of those Mafia movies where a guy's success was judged by how his woman dressed. Except, of course, in those movies the women had no taste at all, whereas Cyn had an excellent sense of style . . . if she did say so herself.

She hugged Raphael's arm closer as they left the muggy nighttime air behind and entered the building. Jared and Juro followed, while the rest of Raphael's security took up positions outside. To all outward appearances, this was nothing but a friendly visit from one lord to another, a welcome-to-the-club sort of meet-and-greet for the new Lord Vincent.

But no one was fooled. The tension level soared the minute Raphael stepped foot into the foyer of what used to be Enrique's Mexico City villa. Cyn glanced around. It was an ancient dinosaur of a house, dark and dusty. She preferred a more modern style, more air, more sunlight . . . or at least moonlight.

"How old is this place?" she asked Raphael, fighting to keep her distaste from showing.

"Nearly as old as Enrique . . . before he died, of course."

"You are *so* proud of yourself for that one," she chided softly.

Raphael paused as a pair of doors opened directly in front of them. Jared started to move around, to take up a protective position, but Raphael stopped him with a low signal.

"It's Vincent," he assured his lieutenant.

The doors opened fully and Vincent emerged. Cyn had only seen him once before, and that was from a distance. He was big, tall and broad-shouldered, wearing a dark jacket and slacks, but with a black silk shirt and no tie. He had longish black hair and a rather elegant and neatly-trimmed beard and mustache. Combined, the hair and beard gave him a rakish handsomeness, although he didn't need the enhancements. He was a very good-looking guy. Nothing compared to Raphael, of course, but good-looking nonetheless. And he'd definitely perfected that master-of-the-universe attitude that Cyn associated with all of the powerful vampires. It was more than arrogance, it was a confidence that when he walked into any room, anywhere, he'd be the toughest badass in the place.

Except in this case, that wasn't quite true. Vincent was certainly *one* of the toughest badasses in the world, but in this room, he was outclassed by Raphael. And he knew it.

That was part of the reason for the soaring level of tension she was sensing. The other part came from the simple fact that two powerful vampire lords were meeting in a confined space. Vampire lords didn't play well together.

Which was another reason that this meeting was a little unusual. In the normal course of things, it wouldn't be one lord, but the entire Council who would meet to welcome to the new lord to the club. And they would in this case, too. Just not until after Raphael took home the *gift* that Vincent was holding for him.

Vincent stepped forward, looking relaxed, belying the tension in the room. "Raphael, welcome to Mexico."

Raphael kept several feet between them. "Vincent," he said, nodding an acknowledgement. "I don't believe you've met my mate, Cynthia Leighton."

"Ms. Leighton, a pleasure," Vincent said smoothly, giving her a smile that she was sure had charmed the pants right off of women all over Mexico.

"Call me Cyn," she said dryly. She might have offered her hand if Raphael hadn't been there, but then she might not have. Cyn tended not to trust vampires she didn't know. And for all that Raphael had played a crucial, behind-the-scenes role in Vincent's rise to power, neither he nor Cyn really knew Vincent.

"Cyn," Vincent amended, then turned slightly and put out his hand, as if reaching for something . . . or some*one*, Cyn saw, as a tallish woman took Vincent's outstretched hand and stepped up next to him.

"Lana, this is Raphael," Vincent said. "And I believe you've spoken to his mate, Cynthia Leighton."

Lana either didn't feel or didn't care about the stress in the room. She came right up to Cyn and offered her hand, saying, "Cynthia, it's so good to finally meet you in person."

Cyn met her halfway. "Call me Cyn, and likewise."

Lana Arnold was lovely and not at all what most people would have expected from a bounty hunter. She was dressed much more simply than Cyn, in black slacks and a red silk blouse that did wonderful things for her coloring, with a pair of stylish, but simple black pumps.

Someone who didn't know the two of them might think Cyn and Lana Arnold had nothing in common, but Cyn knew better. Cyn dressed the way she did, looked the way she did, because she enjoyed it. But her looks didn't define her any more than Lana's did. Lana Arnold was going to be a terrific addition to the Mates Club, although that conversation would probably have to wait for the next full Council meeting. Or maybe a nice long Skype chat. Tonight's visit wasn't going to last long enough for social niceties. Vincent had told Raphael he had a *gift* for him. And Raphael had told Cyn that the so-called gift was almost certainly the vampire who'd killed Raphael's sister, Alexandra. And very likely the one who'd orchestrated the assassination attempt on Raphael, too.

That being the case, Raphael wouldn't want to question the vampire under Vincent's roof. The plan was to accept delivery of the gift, take him back to California, and question him there. After which, he would die a painful death at Raphael's hand.

Cyn agreed that the foreign vampire needed to be interrogated and executed. They needed to learn as much as they could about the plot to take out Raphael and the larger strategy behind the Europeans' planned invasion of North America. And, of course, having tried and failed to kill Raphael, the vamp had to die. But as for Alexandra's death . . . to Cyn's mind, that bitch had earned her fate. Although Raphael didn't see it that way.

"Come inside," Vincent said, returning to the business at hand. He glanced around the wide open foyer. "We'll have more privacy."

Vincent led the way into a well-appointed room with oversized wood and leather furniture and a huge stone fireplace, cold now that the weather was warmer. Vincent's lieutenant, a tall blond surfer-boy type whom Vincent had introduced as Michael, was there along with a hulking male vamp named Ortega, who looked like he should be guarding the velvet rope at a nightclub.

Ortega and Juro stationed themselves on either side of the closed doors, Ortega giving Juro a challenging eyeball which Juro ignored the way one would a misbehaving puppy. He was kind about it, but he left no doubt who would win if Ortega was naïve enough to throw down a challenge.

Cyn smiled, then slid her hand down Raphael's arm and laced her fingers with his. Let Vincent think what he would, let him think she was nervous and needed the reassurance of Raphael's touch. The reality was that Raphael was riding a fine line of rage. He wanted the vampire who'd killed his sister. It was necessary to play this little game of diplomacy to get him, but Raphael's patience was not unlimited. Cyn's touch drew him back from the edge, and, since touching Raphael wasn't exactly a hardship, she was happy to be of service.

Jared stood to Raphael's left, while Michael stayed close to Vincent and Lana. Everyone was here. Everyone in their place. Raphael's black gaze lifted to Vincent, his expression completely blank.

"Thank you for coming so quickly," Vincent said.

Raphael tilted his head in acknowledgement. "You're eager to be rid of him." He said it as a fact, not a question.

Vincent grinned, breaking the almost painful politeness they'd all been maintaining. "He's a pain in the ass. If I hadn't known you'd want him, I'd have killed him two minutes after meeting him."

"I appreciate the courtesy," Raphael said wryly.

Vincent shrugged. "I figured I owed you, for Xuan Ignacio, if nothing else. And I don't like owing people."

"There was no debt incurred," Raphael replied smoothly. "Enrique was a fool who thought he could remain apart from the coming conflict. His ignorance endangered us all."

"Consider it a gift then, against future good will."

Cyn bit back a sigh. These guys took twelve words to say what anyone else could have managed in two. She caught Lana's eye and saw the other woman covering her mouth, fighting a laugh.

Vincent's gaze slid down to his lover? Mate? Cyn didn't know, but there was more than simple affection between them, that was for sure.

"He's in the next room," Vincent admitted *finally*. "Perhaps the ladies should wait—" Lana's dismissive snort cut off whatever he'd been about to say.

Cyn laughed out loud and leaned into Raphael's side, holding his hand in both of hers. "I wanna see, too," she said cheerfully.

Lana didn't even try to cover her laugh this time.

Vincent's eyes met Raphael's. "I'm new to this," he said. "Is it worth it?"

Raphael turned his gaze on Cyn and gave her a slow smile. "Oh, yes." Cyn rested her head briefly on his shoulder, straightening when Vincent shook his head in surrender.

"All right," he said. "Let's all go, then."

RAPHAEL HAD BEEN aware of the other vampire's presence from the moment they entered the building. Standing there trading polite words with Vincent had taken all of his restraint. He was here for one reason only, and that was to pick up Alexandra's killer.

Vincent finally had enough of the polite chitchat, or maybe it was the women's scorn that motivated him to get things underway. Normally, Raphael would have objected to being the object of Cyn's amusement, especially given the circumstances. But in this case, he had to agree with her. He wanted to get the fuck on with it.

Vincent led the way to a single, unassuming door, and entered an eight digit code on the keypad. The door buzzed, then slid smoothly open to reveal a bare room with a holding cell on the far wall.

Raphael loosened his fingers from Cyn's and stepped closer to the cell and its lone occupant. The vampire glared back, eyes gleaming faintly, his mouth twisted into a sneer.

"I tire of this, Vincent. Release me now and my mistress—"

"Silence," Raphael said quietly.

The prisoner's eyes went wide, fear replacing the scorn as his gaze settled on Raphael and he seemed to recognize him for the first time. Raphael could feel him trying to speak, fighting against the compulsion Raphael had set on him. Amused by the other vampire's efforts, and curious as to what defense he would offer, Raphael eased the restriction, but did it in such a way that the prisoner would think he'd succeeded in breaking it on his own.

Triumph flashed in the captive's eyes as he sucked in a breath. "The great Raphael," he derided. "I'm not impressed."

Raphael bared his teeth in a predator's grin and promised, "You will be."

End

To be continued . . .

War is breaking out!

The North American vampire lords have all united behind Raphael.
But who, exactly, will they be up against?
Find out in *Deception* by D.B. Reynolds
Available in March 2015
(Excerpt)

Deception
by D.B. Reynolds

JURO SHOWED UP in Raphael's office just a few minutes after they were settled, with Raphael in his big chair behind the desk, and Cyn pacing around the room restlessly. She couldn't help it, couldn't stand still. This was too big; it was what they'd all been waiting for. The doors opened, and she stared as Juro strode in, with Jared only a few steps behind him.

Cyn stopped pacing and glanced at the envelope in Juro's hand. Knowing it was from a powerful vampire, maybe more than one, she half-expected it to morph into something else. A shrieking, flying lizard maybe, one that would spit poison to blind them while it tore Raphael's heart out. Vamps were magic, after all. What was a little morphing between enemies?

She was letting her imagination, and her fear, run away with her. But she couldn't seem to stop it. Ever since Mexico, she'd had this lingering sense of doom, as if, despite all of their precautions, some insidious enemy was about to slip inside the barriers they'd erected and destroy everything that mattered to her. And the only thing, the only person, who mattered to her that much was Raphael. She'd never survive it if something happened to him. She wouldn't want to.

Her fears were an ache in her chest as she walked over to stand protectively next to him, inching over until her leg touched his. Seeming to sense her unease, Raphael ran his fingers along the back of her thigh before scooting closer to his desk and reaching for the envelope which Juro had placed there.

"Wait!" Cyn said, stopping him, "How do we know there isn't something inside, something other than a letter, or in addition to the letter?"

Juro gave her an understanding look. "You're familiar with our security protocols, Cynthia," he said patiently. "It arrived via Federal Express, and the package was carefully examined before it was opened. When the separate letter envelope was discovered inside, it, too, was tested for all manner of threats, both physical and biological."

"What about magic?" she asked, feeling her cheeks flush with embarrassment.

"If it was magic," Raphael told her, his deep voice easy and unhurried, "I would know."

Cyn let out the breath she'd been holding. "Okay," she said reluctantly. What she wanted to do was toss the damn envelope in the industrial incinerator downstairs where they disposed of empty blood bags and, Cyn suspected, the occasional body. But she knew Raphael would never go along with that.

He gave her thigh another light caress, then reached for the letter once more.

It was a heavy linen envelope. The kind one rarely saw anymore, especially in this day of electronic communication. Raphael's name was written on the front with lots of extra pen strokes and curlicues—the sort of writing one found on wedding invitations and little else. The flap didn't have adhesive, but was closed with a wax seal.

"Pretentious fuckers, aren't they?" she muttered.

"They're very old," Raphael replied.

"So are you, but I don't see you sending people letters written in blood and secured with a fucking royal seal."

"The seal isn't royal, only personal."

"Raphael."

He smiled without taking his gaze off the letter. "Are you ready, my Cyn?"

"No, but go ahead."

Raphael slipped a finger beneath the flap and broke the wax seal, then turned the envelope upside down and let the letter fall to his desk. Cyn watched as Raphael used an elegant opener in the shape of a sword to flatten the letter to his desk.

She could see the writing. The reddish brown "ink" bled slightly into the heavy linen paper with every character, and she couldn't help but think that was appropriate, since it wasn't ink at all, according to the vampires, but blood. She wondered if they watered it down to make it easier to work with or if the vampire writing the letter simply ordered a minion to open a vein so he could use him as a living ink pot. She frowned at her own gruesome imaginings, then leaned forward to get a closer look at the text.

"French," she said.

"It is," Raphael confirmed. "Can you read it?"

"I spent two years in a French boarding school."

"But did you learn anything?" he murmured teasingly.

"Enough to know that's written by someone a lot older than I am."

Raphael nodded. "The text is somewhat archaic."

"What does it say?"

"They want to meet." Raphael's gaze lifted to meet Juro's, holding for a moment before dropping to the letter once more. "To discuss terms."

"Terms of what?" Cyn scoffed.

"They want us to accept their troublemakers, younger vamps who want more than the European lords are willing to give up," Jared suggested. "But I bet they didn't phrase it that way."

Cyn glanced at him, then back at Raphael who said, "The letter simply requests a meeting to discuss a reasonable accommodation, in order to avoid a war that none of us wants."

"That's it? Where's this meeting supposed to take place?"

Raphael seemed to be reading further, and then he said thoughtfully, "Hawaii."

Cyn stiffened in surprise. "I didn't know there were any vampires in Hawaii."

"A few, less than ten that we know of," Juro said slowly, as if he, too, was surprised by the request.

"But . . . who's their lord, then?" Cyn asked, confused.

"Strictly speaking, the islands are mine," Raphael responded. He leaned back a little, his fingers steepled thoughtfully under his chin. "But the distance is great, and their true master is a vampire named Rhys Patterson. Most vampires don't like islands. But Patterson wanted his own territory and knew he wasn't strong enough to hold one, especially not against me. So, he requested permission to journey to Hawaii and set up a colony of his own. He sailed to Oahu with a diplomatic delegation from the U.S. just before the turn of the century."

Raphael had lowered his hands and was tapping one finger on the arm of his chair, a gesture of stress from a guy who rarely showed any outward signs, no matter how bad it got. Cyn wanted to comfort him, to sit on his lap and put her arms around him, but that wouldn't do. So, instead, she moved closer under the guise of bending over the desk and studying the vampire missive. Raphael immediately made room for her, pushing back a little and curling his arm around the back of her thighs, his touch comforting them both.

"He made vamps after he got there?" she asked.

"As Juro says, only a few," Raphael told her. "He's master enough to create his own children, but not strong enough to control too many. He's never sired a vampire more powerful than he is, at least none that he's permitted to live beyond the first night."

Cyn blinked at the casual, and brutal, revelation of the comment. "Does he come to the Council meetings?" she asked.

"He's not a member of the Council. He thrives in Hawaii by my goodwill. But I've never bothered with him. I did visit once, after air travel became feasible—I had my fill of sea travel on the journey here from Europe. It was an uneventful visit, but that was some years ago . . . ." He looked up at Juro, silently asking if he remembered exactly the date.

"1968?" Juro suggested.

Raphael considered it, then nodded. "1968."

"And you haven't been back there since?" Cyn asked.

He shrugged. "No, but we talk on the phone a few times a year."

"Where do they suggest meeting, my lord?" Jared asked, returning to the matter at hand. It was a practical question and one Cyn wished she'd thought of. It galled her to admit it, especially since it was Jared who'd pulled them back on track, but she was too emotionally involved in this situation and wasn't thinking straight.

Raphael didn't even glance at the letter. "Kauai, which is where Patterson lives."

"Are all of his people on one island?"

Raphael nodded. "As far as I know. He originally set up on Oahu, but he didn't think far enough ahead. He hadn't bought enough territory to ensure privacy for him and his children, and the island got too crowded. By the time I visited in '68, he'd already relocated to Kauai and secured a big enough parcel of land to ensure he wouldn't have to move again."

"May I see the letter, Sire?" Jared asked.

Raphael handed it to him.

"You read French?" Cyn asked, concealing her surprise. She knew that Jared had been brought to this country as a slave, although, now that she thought about it, she wasn't exactly sure which country he'd been brought from. France had been very active in the slave trade, more active than the U.S., if truth be told. She'd have to ask Raphael later, because God knew she wasn't going to ask Jared about it.

Jared glanced up at her question and gave a single nod. "They're asking to meet on Kauai," he repeated, reading the letter. "But there's no mention of Patterson. You think he's still alive?"

Raphael shrugged. "He's sworn to me, but he's not my child. I'm not certain I'd feel his death at this distance."

Jared looked up with an unhappy expression. "You're going to go." He said it as a statement, as if Raphael's decision was a foregone conclusion.

Raphael nodded. "There is no other way . . ."

Acknowledgments

Thank you to my editor and ImaJinn guru, Brenda Chin, and to Debra Dixon, Danielle Childers, and everyone at BelleBooks for all they do.

Huge thanks to Carlos Looney and Danielle La Paglia for their extensive help with Spanish translations in this book. I quite literally couldn't have done it without them. Rebel love is a wonderful thing. Any mistakes, however, are solely my fault, not theirs. Thanks also to the wonderful and talented artists at Warvox.com for letting me use Vincent's beautiful tattoo.

As always, I want to thank Michelle Muto and Steve McHugh, friends and talented writers, who give me so much encouragement and provide invaluable feedback on everything I write. You really need to check out their books on Amazon and elsewhere. They're both terrific.

Thank you to my darling husband and my family for their love and support, with special thanks to Michael Mineo who requested (aka demanded) to be a vampire in this book. He's lucky I love him, which means he's not only a good vampire, but one who will live on for a long time. Hope you like your alter ego, Mikey!

And finally, writing is a solitary endeavor. That's just the way it works. I sit for long hours, all alone, typing away in the middle of the night—just me, my laptop, and Buffy on the TV. But I'm never lonely, because I can reach out night or day to my many friends and readers around the globe, and someone is always awake. I love you guys! You keep me company, you keep me sane.

Please visit me at dbreynolds.com for the latest information on my books and more.

About the Author

D. B. Reynolds arrived in sunny Southern California at an early age, having made the trek across the country from the Midwest in a station wagon with her parents, her many siblings and the family dog. And while she has many (okay, some) fond memories of Midwestern farm life, she quickly discovered that L.A. was her kind of town and grew up happily sunning on the beaches of the South Bay.

D. B. holds graduate degrees in international relations and history from UCLA (go Bruins!) and was headed for a career in academia, but in a moment of clarity, she left behind the politics of the hallowed halls for the better-paying politics of Hollywood, where she worked as a sound editor for several years, receiving two Emmy nominations, an MPSE Golden Reel, and multiple MPSE nominations for her work in television sound.

Book One of her Vampires in America series, RAPHAEL, launched her career as a writer in 2009, while JABRIL, Vampires in America Book Two, was awarded the *Romantic Times* Reviewers Choice Award for Best Paranormal Romance (Small Press) in 2010. ADEN, Vampires in America Book Seven, was her first release under the new ImaJinn imprint at BelleBooks.

D. B. currently lives in a flammable canyon near the Malibu coast with her husband of many years, and when she's not writing her own books, she can usually be found reading someone else's. You can visit D. B. at her website, dbreynolds.com, for information on her latest books, contests and giveaways.

Made in the USA
Middletown, DE
14 January 2015